GODS & MONSTERS

GODS & GHOSTS BOOK 4

CINDY D. WITHERSPOON

T.H. MORRIS

PROLOGUE
EVA MCRAYNE

JANUARY 18TH

I AM SET to be released tomorrow. Thank all the gods that I am able to walk out of this horrible jail in less than twenty-four hours, though I know the screams of my counterparts will haunt me for years to come.

Yes, screams. My cellmate, Ellie, calls them the screams of the damned. I suppose that's what we all are. Damned. Damned by the Curaie. Damned by the Networkers and the guards who hold us here.

I'm not supposed to be writing. I stole a pencil from the woman who searched me after dinner. She won't miss it. Not like she missed the napkins I had stolen to get my thoughts on paper.

I am going to be free. The thought alone is enough to make me burst into tears. I haven't had contact with anyone from outside these walls in six months. I've barely had contact with anyone inside of these walls. I step in often and am thrown in a tiny hole called Solitary. It's meant to deter me from interfering, but how can someone stand by and watch as people are being abused? Sexually assaulted?

I couldn't live with myself if I did that. I'd never know another moment of peace. So I step in. I learned pretty quick that the guards had been told not to lash out against me. I knew it was because of my Olympian connections. I used that to my advantage, though it didn't stop them from throwing me into the one place no one here wanted to go. The one place where they forgot about you until they needed the space for someone else.

I relished in the silence Solitary provided. I used that time to talk out loud to Jonah instead of whispering my words as I had to do when others were around. I know he can't hear me. I know, too, that he may have moved on with his life. He'd never leave the estate, but six months is a long time. Perhaps, he still has his arrangements. Perhaps, he has found someone else.

No, I don't believe that. Jonah and I were too close. We are too close. I don't know how I am going to see him again. Once I am released tomorrow, I will have to leave the United States. Hera isn't strong enough to follow outside the country. I am still deciding whether or not I should go to France or Australia. My heart is leaning towards France.

I am still beholden to Hera, and I know she will come to me. I should have taken her poison the night Jonah came into my room. I couldn't do it. Not after I saw the sadness in his eyes and heard the sorrow in his words. So, I tossed the wine away.

I won't have the luxury to do that again. I promised my life to Hera in exchange for Jonah's freedom. She will give me a few days before she sends someone after me. The only reason I haven't been killed yet is because not even she could get past the barriers that held me here.

Tomorrow. I will think about it tomorrow, when I am no longer held in these horrid walls. Tomorrow, I can go anywhere in the world. Anywhere but home. … Anywhere but where she could find me.

ONE

EVA MCRAYNE

MARSEILLE WAS PERFECT. The little town nestled on the Mediterranean coast was exactly what I had been looking for. The centuries-old house I had bought three weeks ago was exactly what I needed. Two bedrooms, one bath. It was small, but cozy. I never wanted to leave it. I breathed in the salt air as I watched the ocean smooth out against the sands beneath my balcony. The past three mornings, I'd taken my coffee out here. This morning, though, my routine had changed. I was going to meet Jonah at a cafe in town. It was within walking distance from the house, so I needed to head out a little early.

I smoothed out the skirt I was wearing before I grabbed my keys. I had twenty minutes. Plenty of time.

As I walked, I considered how much had changed in the month since I had been released from the ethereal prison I'd been thrown in. I'd gone into hiding, though I knew it wouldn't last forever. I'd squared things away at work so that I could be away for two years when I had been sentenced. Researching locations had been the cover used in the press release.

Granted, I hadn't expected to live long enough to go to jail, much less have time to enjoy what was left of my life after I was released.

I knew meeting with Jonah was a risk. If Hera were smart, she'd have people tailing him. So, when I finally broke down and called him, I had given him the address to the local cafe. I didn't want her henchmen to find out where my house was.

I waved to the florist who was opening her shop when I crossed the cobblestone streets. The old woman beamed at me, but I barely saw her. I wondered how Jonah would be when I saw him again. Would he still be with Lola? Had he moved onto someone else? Someone more serious?

I should have called him the second Ulysses dropped me off at the Parisian airport, but I couldn't bring myself to pull him into my mess. As much as I had missed him, I knew that I was doing the right thing by distancing myself from my life. I was protecting him. Protecting myself from having to say goodbye when the time came.

So, I traveled the country that had romanced me after my first trip to its shores. I spent my days talking to people throughout the small towns I had traveled to by train from Paris. Learning their stories, their histories, their ghosts. I began to construct the confidence that Eva the *character* was known for, but Eva the *woman* never really had.

I spotted Jonah sitting at a bistro table in front of the cafe and my heart flipped. He looked good. His shoulders seemed larger. His face was even more angular than before. What had he been doing the past seven months? I shook my head to chase that flutter away. Jonah had always had that effect on me. I supposed he always would, no matter how long we were separated.

"Don't you look like a sight for sore eyes?" I teased as I approached him. "Welcome to Marseille, Blueberry."

Jonah glanced up from his phone and he took a moment to look me over. Maybe it was because I'd changed my appearance, thanks to a spell Ulysses had taught me in Paris. The golden hair had been shifted to a dark auburn. The golden eyes I was famous for had been transformed to blue.

"Eva?" Jonah grinned so big, I was afraid he was going to hurt himself as he stood to pull me into his embrace. "What have you done to yourself, Superstar?"

"I'm not Eva here," I whispered in his ear. "Please, don't call me that outside."

Jonah pulled back and I could see the questions swirling in his mind, but he didn't ask them. Instead, he pulled out my chair and I thanked him for the gesture.

"I'm loving the red hair," he began as he sat back down. "It suits you."

"It's alright." I gestured to the waiter standing by the door. "It's necessary right now."

"You have me at a loss here, Superstar." He sat back as the waiter approached. Once our orders had been taken, Jonah continued. "I was wondering how you disappeared without the paparazzi all over you. The new persona must be how you did it. How's your life these days?"

"Wonderful." I leaned forward on the table. It was true. The peace and quiet I had gotten on this trip would last a lifetime. I was sure of it. "I took the train from Paris to the coast. Stayed in the smallest villages along the way. I got to Marseille three weeks ago."

"And you stayed?"

"I'm thinking about making it my permanent residence," I admitted with caution. Jonah didn't know that I wasn't sure how long "permanent" was going to be for me. "I bought a house on the beach. It's tiny, but perfect. When I'm not on the road, I can stay here."

Jonah reached across the table and linked our fingers together. He studied them before he spoke again.

"I missed you, Superstar."

"I missed you, too." I swallowed the emotion those words brought out of me. "So much."

"What should I call you now?" A small smile played at his lips. "Since you're changing everything about yourself."

"Lea Renaud," I answered automatically. I was proud of myself. I didn't grimace. I wasn't a fan of the name. Or the hair. But it was necessary. "It's ... temporary."

"Lea? I like it. Should I start calling you that all the time?"

"No. Eva in private. Lea is the name I use to hide in public." I made a face. "It's awful, but I had to do it. Otherwise, the press would catch onto me through the real estate records."

"Lea's not that bad."

"Yeah, but it's not me. It feels strange not to see myself in the mirror, you know?" I sat back as the waiter returned with our coffee. When he left, I continued. "Although, all this hiding has given me a peace I never expected to find."

"What do you mean?"

I twirled a strand of red hair around my finger and considered my response. I didn't want to bring up my time in jail. I didn't want Jonah to know I was on the run. When I had the correct phrasing, I responded. "I've come to peace with being alone. With solitude. With not having anyone around me because there's no one to please other than myself. Helps me find out who I really am. Does that make sense?"

"Makes perfect sense," Jonah said. "Back to Lea, though. I imagine playing a character when you're trying to find yourself is a little counterproductive. Did it piss you off having to wear another mask?"

"No." I stirred sugar into my coffee and Jonah smiled. "What?"

"Some things never change."

I stuck out my tongue at him. "At any rate, no, the mask didn't piss me off. It made me realize some things. Who knows? Maybe I'll keep it."

"Why?"

"Because Eva is hunted. Hated by those close to her. Heart-broken time and time again. She's the one with the history of betrayal and abuse, after all. Maybe as Lea, I can at last find people who actually want to be around me." I gave him a small smile. "Maybe this change is the death of Eva outside of *Grave Messages*."

"Don't say that." Jonah took my hand again. I wondered why. "I understand why you feel that way, but that's not right. Sure, there are those who hate you, but that is more of a reflection of them than you. They resent the fact that they can't ride your glory. Whatever. And fuck Lawson for what he did. *You* are the beautiful one. *You* are the golden one. You've saved people who don't even know you have.

Just be yourself. You've got more character in your index finger than they have in their entire bodies."

I didn't know what to say to that. I didn't have the heart to tell him that Eva was as good as dead if I slipped up. Instead, I pulled my hand free and took another sip of coffee. "Right now, I don't know what's going to happen in the future. I have another year and change before I have to go back. Plenty of time to figure it out."

Jonah started to say my name, but I cut him off before he could.

"Enough about me. Tell me what you've been doing the past seven months."

"Training," Jonah gave a slim smile. "Hermes hooked me up … Thor - the god? He runs a survivalist course in Siberia. I spent six months there."

"That explains why you look like you're about to pop the seams of that shirt."

Jonah chuckled and I could have sworn he blushed. "Anyway, it was good for me. Let me work out a lot of anger and resentment. Reena is there now. She joined up about two months after I did."

"Yeah? I can see you doing that. I bet you were having the time of your life, living in the woods."

"I don't know about the time of my life, but it was fun."

"Well, as for Reena, she's going to come back even more badass than ever."

"You'll see her next time you come to the estate." Jonah watched the pedestrians who walked the sidewalks beside us. "You going to come home soon?"

I'll probably never get to come home again.

I didn't say that out loud. Jonah was already suspicious. He was right to be. So I played the one card I knew he couldn't resist. "I don't think so. I am working on my own mental health, Blueberry. If I go home, I'm afraid all the bad memories will come back and disrupt my progress. But tell everyone that I miss them."

"Maybe they can come here?"

"No. No offense to anyone, but I want to keep this place to myself. It's too precious to share."

Jonah raised his eyebrows at that as I continued.

"I can't wait to hear the stories though. I'm sure Re put every man there to shame."

"She did," Jonah laughed. "She came back with me and bragged about it with no shame."

I laughed, too. It felt so strange to do such a simple action.

"Had any dates now that you're free?"

I nearly choked on my coffee at Jonah's question. It had taken me completely by surprise. "Um." I began to play with a napkin on the table. I threw my hair over my shoulder, then nodded. "I've been on a few dates with a man I met on the train to Marseille."

"Really?" Jonah's eyebrows shot up. "Is it serious?"

"I haven't slept with him, if that's what you mean." I studied the corner of the napkin I was picking at with my nails. "But it's nice to be romanced, you know? Not be a footnote in someone else's life."

"Did you go as Eva? Or Lea?"

"Lea. I always go as Lea now." I cleared my throat. "How's Lola these days?"

"Don't know."

"What?"

"I don't know." Jonah went back to focusing on his coffee. "I haven't talked to her since she moved to London."

Oh. I was about to say I was sorry, but never got the chance.

"Lea?"

We both looked up and I smiled out of habit. Pierre Bernard was absolutely dashing. Tall, thick blonde hair, perfect aristocratic face. His family was descended from the court of Louis IV, so he had money to burn. He would have been a perfect match for me except … I didn't feel anything for him.

"Pierre, what a lovely surprise!" I gave him a kiss on each cheek in greeting. "Please, meet a dear friend of mine from the States. Jonah, Pierre."

"The pleasure is all mine." Pierre kept his arm around my waist as he shook Jonah's hand. "Are you familiar with France?"

"Not as much as I'd like to be." Jonah's smile was tight when he returned the man's handshake. "Tell me, how do you know … Lea?"

"We met on the train into town." Pierre gave me another dazzling smile before he turned back to Jonah. "She was most curious about the area."

"I'll bet."

"Shall I call you later? We have much to discuss about the gala next week."

"Sure." I smiled again when Pierre kissed the back of my hand. "Sounds like fun."

Pierre bowed, then waved goodbye to Jonah before he disappeared into the crowd. Jonah watched Pierre leave with a dark look until I playfully slapped his hand.

"Stop it. He's nice."

"Uh-huh. I find it funny that he just happened to be passing by this cafe at this particular moment."

"It's not uncommon," I explained. "Marseille is very small. You'll run into the same people over and over again."

"What's this gala?"

"It's for one of his wineries in Milan. Still have to find something to wear though."

"You should wear a gold dress," Jonah suggested and I looked up. Was he really giving me fashion advice for a date? "Goes well with the auburn hair. Or something black."

"Black? It's formal, but not a funeral."

"May as well be. You're going to be bored out of your mind."

"I'll have you know that I considered the gold dress I wore to the Emmys the other year," I admitted. "But it would be too recognizable. I think I'll find something similar to that style though. Maybe Apollo can send me one in green."

"Green?"

"Yeah. Something to go with this awful hair color."

"So, is he ethereal, immortal, or tenth?"

"Tenth." I tucked a strand of hair behind my ear as I tried to figure out how to change the subject. "He's nice. Good company."

"Hmm." Jonah beckoned to the waiter for a refill. "How long before you tell him the truth?"

"What truth?"

"About who you really are." Jonah studied me with a veiled

expression. I hated it when he did that. "You can't keep the facade up forever."

"I haven't decided yet. Maybe I'll never tell him. Maybe he'll just wine me, dine me, screw me, and never be the wiser."

"Screw you, huh?" Jonah snorted. "Sounds like a plan, Superstar. You've been on the internet getting tips or something?"

"Nope. No need."

"What does that mean?"

"I've fooled around." I shrugged. "Nothing farther than third base, but I'm trying to learn."

"Third?"

"Yeah."

"With *him*?" Jonah stared at me in shock. "Seriously?"

"Yes, seriously. It wasn't anything more than ... than third."

"You said you didn't sleep with him."

"I didn't. We had our date, went back to his place, fooled around, and I left." I frowned a little. "I was expecting more fireworks, but I guess I have to work up to that."

TWO
JONAH ROWE

JONAH COULDN'T COMPREHEND what he was hearing. Eva was actually dating another man? No, that couldn't be right. She needed him, not some damn stranger. The image of Eva being with someone else just seemed wrong. He wiped his mouth with a napkin as he tried to wrap his mind around what she was saying.

"What?" She raised an eyebrow at him. "What's wrong with Pierre?"

He's not me.

Jonah didn't know if he wanted to hear anymore, but he had to ask his next question. "Are you going to see him again?"

"I plan on it." She mused aloud. "He's a bit of a charmer. He's trying to sweep me off my feet."

I bet he fucking is Jonah thought to himself.

Eva continued. "But for me? It was just bleh. There weren't any sparks, you know? Nothing like ..."

She stopped and Jonah knew exactly what she was about to say. She was thinking about that night in the garage. Good. Eva cleared her throat.

"Anyway, we'll see what happens after the gala. Maybe he'll be successful."

Jonah didn't want there to be a next time for Pierre. He wondered briefly if anyone would actually miss the Frenchman if he ended up in the ocean before that happened.

"Want to go see the house?"

"What?" Jonah blinked back the thoughts of drowning the asshole. "Sorry. Thinking."

"Um, I asked if you wanted to see the house." Eva gave him a quizzical look. "You can't tell anyone where it is though. I want to keep it completely private."

"Sure."

Eva threw down some money on the table before they started walking through the streets. She began to tell him about the routes she took when she ran in the mornings, then showed him the path that led down to the beach. That was good. Got his mind off other things.

Eva stopped in front of a slender stone house that butted up against the sands. She pulled out a keyring and Jonah swore he saw her use a skeleton key on the lock.

"This is it." She opened the door and stepped aside so that he could enter. "This is home."

Jonah had been expecting a mansion, not the tiny house that extended up towards the sky. But the decor was bright. The walls were painted a soft gray that made it seem bigger than it was.

"It was built around 1793," Eva explained while she slipped off her jacket to hang it up by the door. "People were smaller back then, but I absolutely adore it."

Jonah turned to see that the shirt she had been wearing was backless. The collar and a thin ribbon were the only thing keeping it closed. The sight of her skin made him realize something else. The Frenchman had seen her naked. He'd touched his Eva in ways that not even Jonah had done. His fists balled up before he realized it.

"The kitchen is in here." She beckoned him to follow her before she headed onto another room. "It's not good to drink the tap water, but I have bottled water and a bottle of merlot in the fridge. What would you like?"

"Um, just water, thanks," Jonah said, really needing to loosen his fists. Damn Frenchman. Getting perks he couldn't possibly know what to do with. Lucky bastard. "What about this house called to you?"

"The view upstairs." She passed him a water and took one for herself. "Come on and I'll show you."

Eva went up the winding staircase and Jonah followed. He took the time to admire her tight little skirt as they ascended.

"How many bedrooms are here, Superstar?" he asked once they reached the top. He had to focus on the house. Not the woman who owned it.

"Two bedrooms, one bath." Eva opened the door right next to the stairwell. "This one is mine."

Jonah stepped into the space decorated in blues and greens. The bed wasn't huge. A queen at best. But just like every one of Eva's houses, it was kept in meticulous order.

"This is what drew me to the house." She opened a door and Jonah whistled as he followed her out to the balcony.

As far as he could see, the Mediterranean and all its glory spread out before him. Boats dotted the horizon, white against blue. "Eva, this is magnificent!"

"I know. This is where I spend most of my time nowadays." She stood next to him and stared outward. "I haven't shared this with anyone else … I won't share this with anyone else. Just you, Jonah."

"Why me?"

"Because you're as sacred to me as this space." She glanced up at him. "It only seems right that you're here."

That touched Jonah's heart. It almost made him forget the French guy. Almost. "I see what you mean. Life makes the most sense when I'm around you."

"It makes the most sense around you, too." Eva pulled out a chair. "Sit down. Stay awhile. I'll go grab an ashtray."

"Why do we need an ashtray?"

"So we can smoke." She laughed. "I know you have your case with you. And the laws here are very lenient on pot."

Jonah lowered onto a chair and watched the ocean. Eva didn't seem all that serious about the French guy, but she had felt comfortable enough around him to get naked.

She returned and placed the ashtray between them, and sat in the second chair to sip her water.

"So did he recognize your mark of the gods?" Jonah asked as he pulled out his case. "That would have told him who you are."

"Who? Pierre?" Eva opened her water with a twist of her wrist. "No. For one, the lights were out, so he couldn't see me. And I learned a glamor spell at Apollo's temple in Normandy so that I could hide it."

"Is it hidden now?"

"Of course, it is. I'm not Eva here. I can't have any of the same identifiers. So, no mark of the gods. No gold. Nothing."

"Huh." Jonah pulled off the joint. "It seems when you're Lea, Eva disappears. Lea's actions don't actually apply to Eva. Would you say that's right?"

"I'm still the same person." She took the joint when he passed it to her. "I still have the same mind. But Lea is the woman that isn't weighed down. If I create a disconnect, it's in the personas themselves."

"So," Jonah watched as she pulled on the joint. She passed it back so he could take a hit. "What would Lea want to do right now?"

Eva raised an eyebrow at him, and he raised both of his as he blew out smoke.

"What are you implying?"

Jonah had a split second to make his decision. It took less than that. He sat the joint in the ashtray, then leaned over it before he caught Eva in a kiss that made her groan in surprise.

The second Jonah made contact with her, he knew that what he had felt in the garage hadn't been because of Ares' possession. When they parted, Eva swallowed. She still had her eyes closed as she tried to catch her breath.

"Are you kissing me? Or Lea?" she whispered as she opened her eyes. "I need to know which one you actually want."

"There is no question." Jonah leaned against the table to hide the fact that she made him weak in the knees. "I want *you*. It's always been you."

Eva pushed back and Jonah stood as well. She came around the table, then grabbed him by the back of the neck to pull him into another heart-stopping kiss.

Jonah barely registered the fact that they had made it into her bedroom. He was too busy losing himself in the woman he had dreamed about for years—the only woman who had been stubborn enough to stay by his side no matter how many mistakes he made.

Jonah wove his fingers through Eva's hair and pulled her head back. "You're mine, Eva. Say it."

"Always yours." She swallowed. "And you're mine. Say it."

"Always yours," he responded. There was no question. There never was. "Always."

———

The two of them alternated between sex and sleep throughout the afternoon. It was during one of those nap periods that Eva's phone rang. She shifted off Jonah's chest and checked the screen before she answered it.

"Hello?"

Jonah watched her through half-open eyes as she slipped on a robe. She tied the belt before she headed towards the balcony.

"Pierre, I can't attend the gala with you."

At that, Jonah sat up. Eva stepped outside, but left the door open. He put his pants back on as he listened to her side of the conversation.

"No, I really can't. I can't see you anymore."

Another round of silence. Jonah headed towards the door. If this guy gave Eva grief, he'd be in the ground as fast as Jonah could manage it.

"No. I'm in a relationship now. That wasn't the case a few days ago. I hope you understand." She was leaning one hip against the balcony as she watched the sunset over the ocean. "Yes. Jonah. The man you met today. Uh-huh. Thank you. Goodbye, Pierre."

She hung up the phone and Jonah crossed the small balcony to stand next to her.

"Sorry, I was hoping that didn't wake you. I take it you heard my side of the conversation?"

"Was he trying to coax you into giving him a chance?"

"He reminded me that he has an extensive portfolio and five vineyards," Eva replied. "He also told me his net worth. I tripled it in a year, but I didn't have the heart to tell him."

"You should have. Would've put him in his damn place." Jonah studied her. "What did you thank him for?"

"He wished us the best." She sat her phone down on the bistro table. "Said he thought something was up when he saw us together."

Jonah sat in one of the metal chairs and pulled Eva onto his lap. He stroked her back before he spoke. "You were really going to sleep with him?"

"I was. Just trying to work up the nerve to do it." Eva trailed her fingers over Jonah's chest. "I'm glad things worked out the way they did."

"Me, too. He would have ended up in the bottom of the ocean."

"What?"

"What?"

"Jonah!" She laughed at his innocent expression. "He was nice."

"*Was* nice? That means you aren't going to see him again?"

"As friends, maybe. But nothing more than that. It seems wrong after what we just did."

"Maybe he should end up in the ocean."

"Stop it." She shifted against his lap. "You're being silly."

"No, I'm not!" Jonah gave Eva a look of innocence. "It's just the principle now."

"Principle, huh?"

"Yeah." Jonah ran his fingers along Eva's shoulder. "I want us to be together, Eva. Not as friends. Actually together. A couple."

"I want that, too. I've wanted that from the moment I first saw you, to be honest."

Jonah took the opportunity to kiss her. A way to seal the promise they had just made to each other.

When she broke away, she whispered against his mouth. "So, what do I call you? Boyfriend? Partner?"

"Boyfriend works. Partner sounds too much like a business deal."

"Hmm, then I'm going to scream to the world that Jonah Rowe is my boyfriend. Good thing we're on the balcony."

She made a move to get up and laughed when Jonah tightened his arm around her waist. He buried his nose into the side of her neck to breathe her in.

Eva was home. She was his. Every bit of her.

"How long before you have to leave?" She rested her cheek against his head as she ran her fingers through his hair. "Were you supposed to go back to Rome tonight?"

"I'm not expected back till Friday," Jonah replied. "I'm here with you. "

"Really?"

He looked up to see the excitement on her face. He'd expected to stay until the end of the week. But now, he didn't know if he was going to be able to leave her side when the time came. "Yeah. Really."

"I can show you the town and the beaches. And in the mornings, we can go take walks through the fresh market to get you something to eat. And—"

Jonah smiled, truly amused by her excitement. "You really love this place, don't you?"

"I really do. I love it even more now."

"Me, too." Jonah looked at the ocean. The night had darkened the waves. He could hear them, but barely see them. "This is my first time in France."

"When you can stay longer, we'll take the train ride through the country to let you see more of it. Get you all cultured."

Jonah nipped her nose and she laughed again. He allowed the question plaguing his mind to slip out. "You sure you want to turn down someone like Pierre for me?"

Eva pulled back a little with a frown. "What does that mean?"

"You know. Someone who has more money than—"

"Jonah, I don't want money. I want you. I don't want his stupid portfolio. I want to hear you say that I'm yours and when the time's right, that you love me. I don't give a damn about what he has. I *do* give a damn about how you make me feel."

"Good." Jonah met her eyes. Even though the color had been changed, he could still see the fire behind them. "Because the time is now. I love you, Eva. More than anything."

"I love you, too. More than anything." Eva tightened her grip around his neck when he closed his eyes. "I do. I'd give up my life just to see you smile. You have to know that."

Jonah let her words wash over him. Eva loved him. He knew it was true. He'd known it for a while, but he'd been so damned determined to be free. To show everyone that he had complete control. That Vera hadn't made a fool of him. Then, Persephone happened, and Eva had been taken away. Jonah's prospective had changed after that. A lot.

"I do, baby," Jonah responded after a few minutes. "I am the same. I've known I loved you for a while."

"Have you?" Eva leaned back into him again. "How?"

"Nana used to have this gift, Superstar. She would wake up the second my feet hit the floor. It never failed. I'd try to sneak out of my room, only to find her standing in the hallway. She explained it to me once. Said that anytime someone she truly loved started moving, she did too. I was sure her gift had died with her, even though she swore I would know it someday. She would tell me, 'You'll see, J.J. One of these days, somebody special is gonna come along. And you'll wake up too.' Turns out, she was right."

Jonah traced her spine with his knuckles. She didn't say a word to interrupt him. He had a feeling she wanted to hear every bit of this story.

"It's how I knew I had fallen for you, Superstar. All the way back to that morning you were going to take Hestia's Oath. You had woken up before me to go for a run. I didn't know it until you told me what time you woke up. Scared the hell out of me, but it started happening every time we slept in the same house together. The second you move, I get this overwhelming need to get up and I can't go back to sleep until I know you're ok."

"That's why you were up so early that morning." She stroked the back of his neck. "And why you are always awake whenever I am. I thought it was because I disturbed you when I got out of bed."

"No, nothing like that." Jonah cleared his throat. "But when you were gone, things got worse for me."

"Worse? What does that mean?"

"Eva, I was a wreck without you," he admitted. "I was. That's why I had to leave. I swear, the reason the Networkers wouldn't tell us where you were was because they knew I'd break into that damn jail and get you out."

"Jonah." She rested her forehead against his. "That's the sweetest thing I've ever heard."

"I would have."

"No, not just the jail. About your gift. I am just amazed by the sweetness of it."

"It's the truth," Jonah told Eva. "It's been true since almost minute one."

Eva just held him. She buried her head into his shoulder, and he held her against him. Jonah knew then that he had made the right decision. This felt right. It felt real. Not some flash in the pan arrangement that would be here today, gone tomorrow.

Seeing Eva taken away had made him realize how much time he had wasted. Isolating himself in Siberia had given him a clarity he never would have expected. He'd known within the first week at Thor's training camp that he would come back and tell Eva how he felt.

"You should eat," Eva interrupted his thoughts when she pulled back. "I have bread and cheese in the kitchen. But if you want anything more substantial than that, we have to go back into town."

"No, not at all," Jonah responded. "I'll make toast and have cheese with it."

"Let me fix it. It's not that kind of bread. Or cheese."

Eva got up and led him back downstairs. The one thing Jonah noticed more than anything was how quiet the house was. Aside from the occasional foghorn out at sea or the waves behind them, there was nothing.

"This would be the perfect meditation space," he commented as Eva pulled out a container from the fridge. "It really is quiet."

"That's one reason why I want to be here. There's no noise. No one clamoring at me to do something. No radio, no television to distract me. It's heaven."

"No television?" Jonah looked horrified. Was she serious? "How do you watch *Marvel* then?"

"I only watch *Marvel* with you." She began to cut slices of thick bread and sat it next to the cheese on a plate. "That's our thing. And when you weren't here, there was no point in watching it."

"Want to binge tonight?" Jonah suggested. "I got my laptop."

Eva sipped her coffee. "Can't we just go back to bed?"

Jonah grinned. "I like that idea, too."

She pushed the plate towards him.

"So, serious question—"

"You weren't serious about going back to bed?"

"I was," Eva chuckled. "But how should we do this, handsome? Because I want to be with you, but I feel like I need to stay here awhile longer. I'm still trying to get my head on straight and I'm just not up to facing the people I used to know just yet."

"Then you stay here as long as you need," Jonah advised. "I'll keep coming back to you. My job is remote, so it's not an issue."

"You don't mind?"

"Evie, it's not that big of a deal." Jonah sat the plate down and took the napkin she handed him. "Hell, if you let me, I'll stay with you indefinitely."

"I want you to stay." She leaned against the counter. "Do you have a passport?"

"Why would I need a passport?"

"Because I figured we could check out other countries, too. Switzerland. Austria. The possibilities are endless for us."

Jonah nodded, turning the thought over in his head. It was a damn great plan. "I do have a passport, actually," he answered. "Needed it for Puerto Rico and the Bahamas."

"Then I think we need to start planning where we want to go."

She wrapped her arms around his waist. "I like this plan best. I'll get to be selfish and have you all to myself for a while."

"I think the both of us have reserved the right to be selfish," Jonah said. "Lord knows we've sacrificed plenty time and again. We've earned some shore leave."

"Hmm, I like the sound of that."

"Shore leave?"

"Uh-huh. But I think I'm going to have to break down and do some shopping tomorrow. Get you a television. Have Wi-Fi installed. I want you to be comfortable here."

"You don't have Wi-Fi?" Jonah's eyebrows shot up. "Evie, you couldn't live without it before!"

"I can now." She shrugged. "There's a cafe in town where I go to check my emails, so I've kept in touch with work a few days a week. But other than that, I don't need it."

Jonah smiled. Eva would go to hell and back for a loved one. She'd pump their blood with her own heart and in so doing, she'd completely deny herself. "Baby, don't do that."

"Don't?"

"Don't." He rubbed her back. "You came here for peace, solitude, and sanctity. I'm not going to disrupt that by letting you buy a television and get Wi-Fi. You have a great setup, and I can tell by looking at you that it's served you well. I can't, in good conscience, alter that. We're good."

"Are you sure?"

"I am." He kissed the top of her head. "And I think we should get those train tickets tomorrow. No plan. No map. Let's just see where we end up."

"That sounds wonderful." She squeezed his fingers. "Want to go back to bed? Or check out the paperback library I've amassed upstairs?"

"I didn't see that in your bedroom."

"To be fair, you didn't really see that much of it." She laughed. "But no. That's what I turned the second bedroom into. A library of sorts."

"You know I adore *all* things books," Jonah grinned. "Show me!"

21

Eva led him back upstairs, flipping off the lamps as she went through the room. Once they were upstairs, she opened the second door and reached over to switch on the lamp.

Jonah stared at the small room. Every wall was covered with bookshelves. Against the far wall, a desk faced out against the window with a single pad and pen in the center.

It was by far the most perfect writing spot he could have imagined. He resisted the urge to go to the desk as ideas began to fill his mind.

"I haven't filled the shelves yet," Eva admitted. "Not even a quarter. But someday, this room will be a library of sorts."

Jonah took Eva by the hand. "Can this be my writing haven when I come visit? It's damn perfect!"

"Jonah, this can be your writing haven whenever you want." She tilted her head to the side. "Bring your books from home. Whatever you want to make this your space."

"I don't want to take it away from you."

"You're not. I don't work here, and I always read on the balcony. So, if you love this space, it's yours."

Jonah felt like his body was on fire. Flames of inspiration. Desire. Creativity. The fierce love and joy of being with Eva finally. They were on fire within him. "Thank you *so* much, baby."

"Don't thank me, just use the space. I told you I wanted you to be happy here."

Jonah wrapped her up in a hug and just held her. There were no words for the emotions he felt. None.

THREE

JONAH ROWE

THE NEXT DAY began a lazy routine which the two of them fell into with ease over the next five days. Slow, sleepy sex before dawn, a run along the beach, then Jonah did his Gotch Bible workout while Eva got ready for the day. By eight, they were out the door. Breakfast was at the small cafe where they had met up the day before, followed by a walk through the farmer's market to get the ingredients for their meals to make later. Once they were back at the house, Jonah went into the second bedroom and began to write.

He couldn't explain the magic behind it. He didn't want to even try. The story he was telling began to unfold in the notebook that Eva had set out with such ease; he barely looked up when Eva brought him a cup of tea nearly two hours later.

But Jonah knew he had to pace himself. So, when Eva came up and told him that lunch was ready, he would finish his line and came down with her. Afterwards, the two of them walked through the shops to get Jonah more notebooks. Pens. He was going to need them.

Nights were by far the best part of the experience. After dinner, Eva would curl up at the bistro table on the balcony with her book while Jonah went to his writing space and wrote. It didn't matter where he stopped when he got up to use the bathroom or check on Eva outside. The words just kept coming. Bedtime happened at nine when the two of them would come back together for sex that shook the pictures on the wall before they passed out, wrapped in each other.

By the time Friday came, Jonah didn't want to ever leave. He was the happiest he'd ever been. But as he and Eva sat at the table outside the cafe, he remembered something.

"We never got those train tickets, Superstar."

"I know." She peeled off a piece of her croissant and popped it in her mouth. "I thought we'd just play the train trip by ear."

"Yeah? Why?"

"Because this week has been so magnificent. I could spend the rest of my existence living like this with you and never change it."

Jonah sighed with contentment as he looked over the cobblestone streets. "Baby, me too."

"Are you missing television and streaming?"

"Eh, it's fine," Jonah replied. "I've got my phone if I have an itch for a show, but mostly, I'm good. Remember, I had *no* tech at all in Siberia."

"Ah, yes." Eva sipped her coffee. "This may seem like a dumb question, but I'm legit curious ... are all couples like us?"

Jonah chuckled to himself as he lifted up the danish he had ordered. "I don't know. I'm not in another couple. Just this one."

Eva picked off another piece of her croissant and threw it at him. He laughed.

"I think what we have is pretty special," he conceded before he got serious. "I'm going to the estate for about three hours, then coming right back. I want to pack my suitcase. Grab some books."

"You're coming right back?" Eva's expression brightened. "I thought you would at least stay home for the night to see everybody."

"I'm coming right back," Jonah promised. "Best believe it. I won't stay away from you for long, because I won't be able to anyway."

"Charmer."

"Besides, I have to finish Chapter Five tonight." He laughed as another piece of croissant bounced off his shirt. "Are you just going to throw pieces of that at me?"

"Nope. I haven't gotten to the chocolate part yet. I'm working my way to it."

"I couldn't help but notice that you're eating more," Jonah commented. It was true. Whereas before Eva would take two bites from an entire plate, now she could eat half before she called it quits. "Any particular reason why?"

"Two, actually. The first is that you work up my appetite." She sucked a bit of chocolate off her thumb. "And two, I'm happy."

Jonah grinned. "Then I'm happy to have aided you in that."

"You have no idea how much you've helped me."

"You've helped me, too."

"I have?" Eva sat the croissant down and wiped her hands on a napkin. "How?"

"You tame the beast, baby."

"What beast? You're the most civilized man I've ever met."

"You wouldn't say that if you'd seen me in Siberia."

"Not to sound like a broken record, but why do you say that? Were you that wild?"

Jonah lowered his mug. "The training was Berserker style. There were actually psychics and readers in our group, who could divine past lives. I found out that I actually was a fierce warrior in many of my past lives. It plays a part in the super aggression I have in this life, in addition to all the bullying and shit. Thor taught us to tap into that, mine it, and whatever is excessive, purge it. It was survival and strength building in the most primal of states. So yeah, I was wild. We all were. But damn it was fun."

"I bet you had the time of your life," She chuckled, then sipped from her mug. "I can see you now with a wild beard and scraggly hair. I bet you were hot as hell."

Jonah laughed. "My beard and hair had grown out extensively. But I had to remedy that as soon as I was back to civilization."

"I like you like this." She reached over to scratch his beard. "This is how I know you."

"Speaking of appearances, any idea when you're going to go back to being the golden girl?"

Unless Jonah was very much mistaken, a brief bit of fear flashed in Eva's eyes. He sat up, on the defensive. "What's wrong?"

"I don't want to talk about it right now." Eva went back to her croissant. She started to pick it up, then placed it back down. "I'm just ... I'm not ready to be Eva again. Not yet."

Jonah wondered what was going on with Eva, but then he remembered, and chastised himself. It was obvious. Eva was still processing being in that stupid detention center. He couldn't imagine what she encountered there and wasn't about to try to. The fear came from ... fear. To be Eva again meant facing that reality that, yes, she'd paid for Joey's mistake, and yes, she'd gone through hell to do so.

How could he have asked her such a dumb question? "Baby, it's okay," he promised. "You be Lea as long as you need. It wasn't a criticism or throwing shade, I swear. Mere curiosity."

"It's fine." Eva smiled a little. "But back to you. You never did tell me what beast I tame."

"Sure, I did. The savage in me. The one that wants to find that French guy and beat his ass for thinking he could touch you."

"Jonah!" She laughed as if he were joking. "In all fairness, I didn't realize we were about to become an item. I gave him permission."

"Which is why he isn't fish food right now."

"Fine. Then I'm going to admit I wanted to break every bone in Lola's hands."

That was a surprise. Jonah raised his eyebrows and Eva scoffed. She swallowed another bit of the crescent-shaped pastry before she spoke. "What? Don't give me that look. I did. I didn't want her touching you."

"Seriously?" Jonah laughed in disbelief. "But she was nothing but nice to you! Unlike ... others."

Vera Haliday's name didn't need to be spoken. Eva skirted past it herself.

"Yeah, she was nice," Eva conceded, "but she had the man that I loved. I'll hate her forever on that fact alone."

"You're so cute when you're jealous."

"How is that being jealous?" Eva pointed towards Jonah with the croissant. "You were the one giving Pierre the death glares."

"Didn't like him. He wasn't your type."

"My type?" she repeated. "Is that because my type is *you*?"

"Damn straight." Jonah finished his danish. He wiped his hands on a napkin, then changed the subject. "I'll leave right after lunch. What do you have planned this afternoon?"

"Might as well come back here and get some work done. We can meet back at the house around six if you want, handsome."

"Six it is, my love," Jonah said. "I'll come, bag and backpack in tow."

"You know, we're in France," she teased. "I'm sure they have plenty of new backpacks. Even ones that are better than your old raggedy thing."

"My backpack is *not* ragged," Jonah insisted. "It's full of character and battle scars."

"Uh-huh." She finished her coffee and pushed her plate away. "Battle scars are a little different than fatality wounds."

"That was harsh, baby."

"Remind me again, how many patches does it have now?" She gasped and her eyes widened. "It needs a Marseille patch!"

"I thought you were giving me hell." Jonah laughed. "Why are you so excited now?"

"'Cause if you insist on using the poor thing, it should at least have patches that mean something to you on it."

"My bag is a Boss," Jonah scoffed. "It would give your Prada a run for its money."

Eva released a mock gasp. "That is heresy!"

"That is *fact*," Jonah teased. "I promise you that my patched stuff is badass. It will last eternally while your Prada will have long since been done. My bag is a survivor."

"Then I'm getting a patch for it today … while you're at the estate."

"I have to approve it." He narrowed his eyes at her. "No patches with trash bags on them."

"Do they make those?"

"If they did, I certainly wouldn't tell you."

"That's not fair!" She grabbed her napkin, then wiped chocolate from her fingers. "Fine. I'll pick out a very nice patch. A big one that will outlast your bag."

Jonah pretended to scowl as the waiter came to clear the table. Once he was gone, she leaned over to kiss him quickly.

"Let's go take a walk through the market. I can get the stuff for dinner, though I have a feeling Terrence is going to try to stuff you full of his food."

"I don't think you're wrong." He pulled out his wallet and took care of the check. "Let's go. The sooner I go, the sooner I can get back home."

Eva wove their fingers together when they stepped onto the side-walk. "You consider this home?"

"Anywhere with you is home, Evie." He kissed the back of her hand. "So, yeah, I do."

"I think you're trying to make me melt."

"Is it working?"

"Yes," she laughed. "Yes, it is."

Jonah chuckled to himself as they turned down the street lined with vendors, selling everything from apples to rugs. He spotted a familiar face in the crowd, then kissed the side of Eva's head when Pierre Bernard turned towards them. The Frenchman's expression was one of ice as he approached.

"*Bonjour*, Lea and ... what was your name again, American? I can't seem to recall it."

Jonah was instantly in alpha mode. American? "How about you tell me *your* name, Frenchie? I don't recall yours, either."

"Pierre—"

"As nice as it is to see you again," Eva cut him off. "We really must be going."

Unless Jonah was very much mistaken, Pierre was sizing him up. "You got a problem, Frenchie?"

"None." Pierre gave him a cold smile. "Have a nice day, American. Lea."

He pushed past them and bumped Jonah's shoulder in the process.

Eva held his hand tightly when he started to turn around. "Not here. Please."

"I'll be damned if some baguette-eating bitch-boy will disrespect you or me like that."

"He ain't worth it, handsome."

Jonah gave one last look over his shoulder before he let Eva pull him to the side. "What?"

"You said I tamed the beast."

"You do tame it. That's why I'm standing here right now and not pounding his smug face into the pavement."

Eva stroked his beard with both hands. "I'm sorry that we ran into him, but let's just spend what time we have together before you leave in peace, ok?"

Jonah glanced over at Pierre the Pussyfoot once more before he kissed Eva's forehead as reassurance. "Absolutely. Of course."

FOUR

JONAH ROWE

JONAH LEFT Marseille right at noon and appeared in the foyer of the estate less than two seconds later. He wanted to make this quick, but he headed to the kitchen to see Terrence, Spader, and Liz Manville gathered around the table.

"Hey, guys."

"Jonah!" Liz hopped up to hug him. "Oh my god, how are you? How was France?"

"It was damn wonderful," Jonah answered. "I've made some friends with shop owners who love that I'm a gentleman ... and, oh, yeah." He loved hooking them in. "Do *not* go blast this on social media or spread it like wildfire just yet. Eva and I are a couple now."

The room went silent before Liz squealed. Terrence hopped up to pat Jonah on the back as Spader spoke over the chatter.

"About damn time."

"How is Evie?" Liz pulled him over to the nearest chair. "We thought she would come back to Rome."

"Not right now," Jonah shook his head. "Not for several months. France has been perfect for her ... mentally detoxing from Joey's bullshit and the detention center. She's gonna hang there for a little while longer. I'll be with her."

"Wait, you're not going to stay?" Terrence started before Liz cut him off.

"You're living in France? How romantic!"

"Uh-huh." Spader studied him over a bowl of cereal. "I was gonna say you were just in time. Minako should be here any minute."

Jonah frowned. "Why does that make me just in time?"

"She said she needed to talk to you because of your Olympian connections," Terrence explained. "We told her you'd be back today."

"Okay, great." Jonah grabbed a slice of buttered toast from a platter near Terrence. "She's got me curious, I must admit."

"Minks didn't know if you would even see her." Terrence pushed another piece of bread Jonah's way. "She's with the Curiae now. An investigator."

Jonah took a deep breath and absent-mindedly tapped his finger on the table. He was never fond of the Curaie to begin with, but after they'd jailed Eva and left Joey scot-free, they and a bunch of their staff were on his shit list, namely Marlon Hardy. He was unaware that Minako Saito, a close friend of the family, was now a member of the Curaie. But in the end, he just sighed.

"Not everyone in the Curaie is a crock of shit," he said. "Katarina, Patience, Elijah, Stephanie ... there are just as many great people as there are pricks. Minako is good. I'm choosing the whole 'don't hate the player, hate the game' approach."

"I appreciate that mindset, Jonah."

An Asian woman stepped over the threshold and it took a minute for Jonah to recognize her. Minako Seito was dressed in a mixture of ripped leather and velvet. Her long black hair had been dyed purple and shaved on one side and Jonah stopped counting her face piercings after five.

"Minks?" he grinned as she approached him. "What have you done with yourself? You look like a total badass."

"Because I am?" She laughed and hugged him back. "It is good to see you, Jonah, though I am sorry it is under these circumstances."

"Sit down." Jonah pulled the closest chair out for her. "Let's talk. What's going on?"

Minako seated herself next to Spader and sighed. "Guys, we have a potential storm brewing. There is an Eleventh assassin murdering Olympians."

"Excuse me?" Terrence stared at her with as much shock as everyone else. "A what?"

"An assassin." Minako pulled a folder from her briefcase and sat it on the table. "We know next to nothing about him, other than his aura is white and he goes by the name Ange De La Mort. We got wind of him when the Council sent ambassadors to the Curaie, reporting that several high-ranking Olympians were found murdered."

"How do they know ethereality is involved?" Jonah reached over Minako's shoulder to flip open the folder. "Could be anyone."

"No, it can't. The victims all had enhanced lifelines. The only thing that could have ended their physical life is a god or ethereality."

Jonah looked over the file. It was scant. The information wouldn't cover a gum wrapper. "You know nothing of him, but you must have gleaned something from crimes? How he kills or something?"

"What little we have discovered is that he is a white aura. He changes his methods often but prefers to garrote his victims with a wire. Security footage retrieved from the last crime scene showed us that it is a man and he left a calling card."

"A calling card?"

"Indeed." She flipped through the file until they saw a copy of a business card. The words Ange De La Mort were stamped on it in thick black letters.

"This is how we know his name."

"Ange De La Mort," Liz said. "It means Death Angel, roughly translated. Do you know if it's always been Olympians? Or is this reputation new?"

"The calling card is unusual." Minako focused on Liz. She pulled out a list of towns and cities with a series of numbers beside them. "And the fact that he is taking out Olympians told us that this isn't his first time."

"So, what's this?"

"A list of all the homicide cases reported to tenth police and the Networkers where a calling card with this moniker was left behind."

Jonah whistled and read over the list. "How many cases is this?"

"One hundred and fifty-two over the past ten years."

"One hundred and fifty-two?" Jonah nearly choked. "How exactly was the Curaie expecting to end this guy? Old age?"

"He's *good*, Jonah," Minako reiterated. "Scary good. Ten years he's been active, and the only thing they've ever gotten was an aura. I assumed the guy had a cover with a day job, but ... it's got to be more. This takes resources. Income. Access to everything. And we don't know a damn thing, except if he keeps killing Olympians, it's going to strain relations that are already held by fibers."

"What does that mean?" Liz's eyes widened in alarm. "I thought we were on good terms with the Olympians."

"The binds between the Olympian Council and the Curaie have always been frayed, Liz," Minako explained. "The Olympians don't understand us, and we think they are a bunch of pompous assholes too obsessed with perfection. But things have improved over the past few years. Mainly, because of you guys."

"Us?"

"Indeed, Spader." Minako tapped her pen against the table. "Your assistance into Olympian affairs caused the Council to approach the Curaie and request a parley of sorts."

"That's good though." Spader sat back. "Wait. It was good until the Curaie threw Evie into a hole."

Minako nodded in time with her pen. "Exactly right. Zeus himself approached the Curaie once McRayne was sentenced. The Curaie refused to even see him. The only reason war was not declared in that instant was because McRayne went before the Council herself and convinced her patriarchs that war would last a hell of a lot longer than a six-month jail sentence. Thankfully, they listened to reason."

Jonah felt his lip curl. Those fucking Curaie pricks. And they called the Olympians the pompous assholes? "You know, those moth-erfuckers are gonna get us all killed if they keep thinking their way is the only one. They refused to see the King of Olympus? That's some bold shit. I'm surprised Zeus didn't waylay the Median with lightning bolts."

"Jonah, you only know half the story. There is fear on both sides," Minako told him. "The word in Spectral Law is that the Curaie didn't see Zeus because they were afraid he might bully them into submission, and they'd look weak in the eyes of us ethereals. Meanwhile, our sources say those in Olympus—some on thrones, some not—are *very* leery about war with a power they don't understand, let alone a power that can harm immortality."

"Minako, I'm sorry, but you're lying," Reena said suddenly. "Ethereal humans can kill immortals? I've *never* heard that. Not once. And your blood pressure spiked when you mentioned it. So, what's up?"

Minako swallowed. Jonah straightened. What fresh hell was this?

"Ange De La Mort's garrote … it … it kills Olympians as easily as a Tenth. I don't know what material it's made of, but we were told to keep it quiet. If things got volatile out of Olympus, other Elevenths could possibly try to find similar weapons, just for self-defense. See the mess this is?"

"What do you want from us, Minako?" Jonah leaned back in his chair. "Because if you are looking for Curaie cheerleaders, you're in the wrong estate. Those fuckers punished an innocent woman simply because they could."

"Jonah, if there is war, you would be expected to fight for us. You realize that?" Minako turned towards him. "Every single one of us will be required to fight for the Curaie and our survival. It doesn't matter what connections you have to the Olympians."

"Oh, so once again, we're expected to be blindly obedient, for no other reason than the Curaie says so?" Jonah nearly spat on the floor but remembered Minako was a friend. He showed restraint. In that regard, anyway. "Minako, I repeat, they imprisoned an innocent woman just to make a point. The *true* guilty one, Joey Lawson? They didn't even bat an eye. The only single, solitary reason he's had this rough patch is because I went to Hermes and asked of him to give Lawson bad luck."

"Seriously?" Liz piped up. "That was because of you?"

"Damn straight," Jonah answered. "Yeah, I'm a white guy obviously, but I'll be damned if white privilege allows someone to get off completely. Hermes made an oath that Joseph would get less respect than the *Sharknado* series until Eva returns to *Grave Messages* and not a second sooner."

He returned his attention to Minako. "Minako, you're family now, and I love you. I am sincerely glad to have had a hand in you being able to break away from the stifling environment Gamaliel Kaine made at Sanctum Arcist, and blossom into your true self. But if the Curaie thinks they can bully us into their cause simply because they sit on high, pass. *Hard* pass."

"Jonah, your words are passionate. Honorable. But do you truly believe you have a choice?"

"I got free will, Minks. That's enough."

"No. I want you to realize something. War would mean that the Olympians are our enemy. Every Eleventh who has been trained to fight will have to fight. If they don't, their access to their homes, to spiritual endowments, the Astralimes will be stripped away. If you are lucky, you will be banished to the Plane until your physical life ends."

"And if I'm not lucky?"

"Then they will neuter you." She held up a hand. "Not make you a eunuch but neuter your ethereality to the point of non-existence. You will barely be able to expose your aura at all—a glimmer at best. For an Eleventh Presenter to be unable to express their aura can slowly drive them insane. And they will ensure that you can never end your own life … by putting you in a detention center so they can watch you go crazy."

Jonah was instantly furious, but he said simply, "That will never happen."

Minako blinked. "I'm sorry?"

"You heard me." Jonah's voice was cold. "These spirits think they can pull people into their war by bullying them into doing it. No way in hell will I ever fight as a result of tension *they* created. We've been aiding Olympus all this time, slowly improving relations, and then we're put right back at square one by locking Eva up. Now a killer is making things radioactive, and we're supposed to just forget every fuckup the Curaie is responsible for and drop to our knees and grovel for their cause? *Fuck* that. If that is their plan, fuck *them*. I'll *never* be neutered. I'd love to see them try, but they'll never do it. If they delude themselves into thinking they can, and try to go for it, they will fail. I'll go Dark Blue before I let that happen."

The entire room stared at Jonah in stunned silence. He was neither awkward nor put off. It was the truth.

"You don't mean that, Jonah," Liz said.

"I do," Jonah responded. "If the Curaie comes for me simply for not bowing down, they'll have the fight of their lives."

"Jonah, no," Minako implored, looking terrified. "Please don't talk like that!"

"Then, please, don't come in here bullying me, Minako," Jonah said quietly. "That's a sure shot way of getting on my hell side. I don't tolerate bullying from anyone, not even the Curaie."

"Stop." Reena stood up; she'd paled when Jonah mentioned Dark Blue, but her voice was steady. "Everybody, just stop. This has gone to a place that I do *not* like, and don't care to continue. Minks, we need to be objective here. War has not broken out yet. What measures can be taken to prevent it from going that far? What if Ange De La Mort were stopped? Are there any leads on him, however thin?"

"Ok." Minks shifted in her chair and focused on Reena. "There's not much on the killer, that's true. We are focusing on the victims."

"Ok. What do they have in common?"

"Obviously, there's the Olympian angle." Minako pulled out another folder and placed it in the center of the table. "The first victims were nymphs who worked in the various homes of Olympian officials. All were garroted around the properties. We're pretty sure he was testing the security measures."

"You said 'first'. That means he moved upwards."

"Indeed. He began to target ambassadors. Keepers. At least two treasurers were found beheaded."

"Treasurers?"

"Yes. Again, we believe he is testing security around higher level officials, but in the process, he is further harming our reputation with the Olympians."

"Look, I don't know much about the Olympian hierarchy, but the Council themselves are gods." Jonah leaned forward. "If he is trying to go up the ranks, he won't be able to reach the top. You can't kill a god."

"No, but he can get as close to them as possible." Minako studied Jonah. "Which is where I need your help. I need to know exactly who is one step below the Council. Then, I need to know who is below that. If we can trail the potential victims, we may be able to stop this."

"You're asking the wrong person, Minks." Spader gestured to Jonah. "Let me borrow your phone."

"Why?" Jonah took it out and passed it to him. "Who are you calling?"

"Evie. She's the Olympian politician. She can tell us."

Spader pressed a button on Jonah's phone.

Two rings later, Eva answered. "Hey, handsome. That was fast."

"Handsome?" Spader grinned wide. "I am that."

"Ugh, Spader! What are you doing with Jonah's phone?"

"If you hadn't blocked me, I'd have called you from mine."

"If you hadn't sent me a damn dick pic, I wouldn't have blocked you."

Jonah glared at Spader. He did *what*? So did everyone else, except Terrence, who looked resigned to the fact that Spader would always cross lines. Spader noticed Jonah's glare and hastily returned to the call.

"Let the past stay in the past, Goldie," he said. "I was ... intrigued by the hierarchy of Olympus. Call it a random whim. I know they nymphs, stewards, pleasure girls and guys, and minor demigods are that low tier. Then the ambassadors, Keepers-in-Training, and the treasurers. Who is next on the totem pole, up to the gods themselves?"

"So, that's random." Eva sighed. "Alright. Think about the structure as a family tree. You have Zeus at the very top. Beneath that, the Council members. They are followed by beings such as the Fates, the Erinyes, Oracles, and monsters who are all gods in their own right. Well, all but me. I'm only half."

"You are in the third tier then?"

"Unfortunately. That's why I always get called up to do the shit the Council doesn't want to do."

"Ok." Spader tapped his fingers thoughtfully against the table. "After that?"

"Security. That's the Agema, the Keepers, the Greens."

"The Greens?"

"Our spies and assassins."

"Then?"

"The ambassadors and statesmen. After that, the pleasure people and the staff. At the very bottom is everyone else."

Spader nodded. "Thank you, Goldie. That was informative. I appreciate it."

"Why did you need to know something so damn random?"

"I was curious," Spader answered. "Hey, you never know, this might be a question on a game show one day."

"Yeah, ok. Give Jonah his phone back."

"You gonna unblock me?"

"No chance in hell, Spades."

"Miss McRayne?" Minako cleared her throat. "Pardon the interruption, but my name is Minako, and I am a friend of the Grannison-Morris estate. I am also an investigator with the Curaie. I was wondering if I could—"

"You are *with* the Curaie?"

"Yes."

"Then I have nothing to say to you. Goodbye." Eva disconnected and the line went silent.

After a minute, Spader shrugged. "Honestly, Minks, you should have expected that."

Minako sighed. "I know. It's just ... we're not all the same."

"Feelings are still raw there, Minks," Jonah said, his tone warmer now that Reena had removed the tension from the conversation.

"Eva is dealing with a lot of turmoil due to their bullshit decision to scapegoat her and leave Joey free."

Minako leaned in. "Jonah, he didn't get off completely."

"What are you talking about?"

She leaned in. "Patience was furious that the Curaie took the approach they did. It's actually strained his friendship with Marlon, who supported their call. They haven't spoken since Eva got jailed. But Patience called in a favor. In addition to whatever you had Hermes do, Patience got Joseph Lawson's credit trashed and his accounts frozen. He got evicted from his loft and is now in a motel in East Los Angeles."

"Ok, but Lawson's still free. Yeah, his life got trashed, but he was still able to live it. Eva didn't have that luxury."

"We're not your enemy, Jonah. One day, both you and Eva will have to let what happened go."

"You're not my enemy, no. But Eva may see things completely different than I do. Even then, she still went to bat for us to prevent the damn war from happening, before she went to that damn jail. God knows what all she saw in there. I don't blame her for not wanting to talk to you, or anyone associated with the Curaie, Minako. And I sure as hell don't see her ever letting that go."

Minako sighed again. "I guess I can understand that. Jonah, I'm sorry. I was clumsy with my words. The threats were not threats; they were things I did not want to see happen to you. But Reena is right. War has not broken out yet. We should be proactive, not reactive."

Jonah nodded, albeit stiffly. "Apology accepted. It's not *your* fault they make questionable choices at times."

Minako looked slightly relieved that Jonah didn't hate her. "Would you really go Dark Blue willingly?"

"If the Curaie came at Eva or me with a tyrannical stance? Without question," Jonah answered. "Of course, I don't want to, but you can't be in a snake pit acting like a mouse."

"Jonah!"

"What? If you think I'm playing, Reena, I'm not. For one, if the

Curaie comes after us, there'll be hell to pay. And two, if they try to force me to choose between them or Eva? Eva wins, hands down."

"Wait." Reena looked at Spader. "Eva said she's in the third tier, right?"

"Yeah, so?"

"Everyone else in her tier and up are all gods. They can't be killed, but she can. So the highest target for this assassin would be Eva."

Jonah froze. That hadn't occurred to him. Truth be told, when Eva was talking about the hierarchy, he was more occupied with hearing Spader sent Eva a dick pic. He looked at Minako. "Any chatter that Eva might be a target?"

"Um, no. Not that I've heard."

"What was that 'um' for?"

"Eva has been labeled as a criminal to the Curaie. We aren't allowed to say her name unless she is suspected of committing a crime. If she's a target, we wouldn't be allowed to speak on it."

"An unmentionable." Terrence shook his head. "Minako, surely you know how stupid *that* is?"

"I know, Terrence," Minako muttered. "I didn't invent it personally."

"He ain't gettin' to Eva.," Jonah picked up another piece of bread. "Who else is on the list?"

"Jonah, this guy is good. You saw his numbers! Surely we could get her put in a safe house—"

"You can't even say her name outside the fact she's a criminal, but you are offering her a safe house?"

"Ok, let me try this again." Minako took a moment to collect her thoughts. "If McRayne loses her physical life to this man—"

"She won't."

"How can you be so sure, if you are refusing our assistance?"

"For one, Eva's no slouch. She can fight damn near anybody. And two, he'll have to get through me. I'm no slouch either."

"I am not convinced that's enough. I'm just not."

Jonah shrugged. "That's totally fine, Minks. Trust me, you're not the first person to doubt me, and you won't be the last. But I ain't losing in this. Anyone who tries to come at me or Eva will lose, and they'll lose big."

"I'm trying to help—"

"Then help. Have you talked to anyone with the Council? Have you warned them?"

"No, not yet. I wanted to get the information from you first."

Jonah took his phone back and scrolled through his contacts. Three rings later, Apollo answered.

"Jonah. What can I do for you?"

"Listen, a friend of mine is here and talking about some assassin killing Olympians. We might have some information for you to pass onto the Council."

"A friend with that information must be with the Curaie. What do you know?"

"Dude's moving up through the hierarchy. You need to get extra security assigned to members of rank, Apollo. Hell, get them off the earth plane for a while or something. You take away this guy's victims, and there won't be anyone left to kill. No reason to start a war. My suggestion? Start sending agents to help find this guy."

"The Curaie has forbade us from any interference in ethereal matters. The fact that I am speaking to you now about this is a personal matter."

"What does that mean?"

"If the Curaie continues to insult and sanction us, we will have no choice but to respond."

Jonah looked over at his friends at the table. Minako looked fearful. As well she should. "Apollo, sir, I look at it like this. Sure, the Curaie has been jerks about this; I'm sure they have their own motives. But the fact of the matter is this assassin is murdering Olympians. Surely, no one in their right mind would expect you guys to sit idly by while people in your ranks get picked off? This is an ethereal matter as far as it's an ethereal doing the killing. But his murders have crossed into your zone. That makes this fair game, so *fuck* the Curaie's strictures."

Minako took a sharp intake of breath, but Reena raised a finger to her lips to silence her. Apollo responded; his voice neutral. "What do you propose?"

Jonah let his brain run back to this table conversation and replied accordingly. "Lord Apollo, we've discussed that Olympus has its bad apples, but that doesn't take away from the great and good amongst you. The ethereal world is no different. I say reach out to those of us who will listen to reason. Starting with Jonathan. There is a man amongst the Networkers who doesn't follow the hardline named Halloran Patience. I know he's not alone. Send your emissaries to them."

Apollo went silent. Jonah waited, not sure if the god was considering his words.

Finally, Apollo spoke. "I will speak to Jonathan. Perhaps, we can gather enough allies from your ranks to form a meeting. Will you attend, son?"

"I'm honored, but if this asshole is going after high-ranking Olympians, then I'd prefer to stay close to Eva, just in case he is stupid enough to try something."

"You have been in contact with her then?"

"Yes. I spent the week with her in—"

"Do not disclose her location! While I am sure you are surrounded by your friends, we must use discretion. These are very ... dangerous times."

"Would Olympus really go to war with us, Apollo?"

"If pushed hard enough? Yes."

Jonah thought about the god's response. He didn't give a damn about the Curaie. And the only reason he gave a damn about Olympus was because of Eva. As long as the two of them were safe —along with his family—he couldn't give two damns about a war.

"Are you in contact with Eva, Apollo?"

"Yes. Sporadically. I check on her now and again."

"Then let her know how the meeting goes. I'm heading back that way soon."

"Very well, son. I shall be in touch, now that you and my daughter are together."

"What? But—"

"We will talk soon, son," Apollo said, a ghost of a laugh in his voice. "Be well."

The call ended. Jonah lowered the phone, eyes on Minako.

"You came for help, Minks, there it is," he said. "That's me, trying to be diplomatic. Now it's your turn to reach out to anyone in your department and anyone you know who's not up the Spirit Guides' asses. We've seen what stubbornness achieves; now let's see what intelligence achieves."

Minako's lips parted before she nodded. "I'll speak to whomever I need to, Jonah. Thank you."

Minako collected the files and put them away. She stood and the others watched her.

"You heading out?"

"Yes. I want to get started."

"I'm heading out, too." Jonah pushed his chair back. "Stay safe, Minks."

"You, too, Jonah."

Minako vanished and Terrence scoffed. "Already? Come on, man. Have dinner with us. There's no telling when we'll see you again."

Jonah thought on it and seated himself. "You're right. I'm good with that."

Terrence beamed and went to ingredients for ... something. Whatever it was, it'd be good. It was Terrence, after all. Liz leaned into Jonah, inspecting him with those sharp jade eyes of hers.

"Are you going to tell Eva any of this?"

Jonah didn't answer immediately. He took two sips from his bottled water before he did. "I will if necessary. She's recovering now. I don't want to put something like that on her unless I absolutely have to."

"Ok. When will we get to talk to her again?"

"I don't know," Jonah shook his head. "I really don't. She is off from *Grave* for another year, I think."

"Plenty of time for the two of you to get domesticated." Spader grinned. "If you haven't already."

"Work in progress, man," Jonah said. "But I love that idea. Love it hugely."

The group looked at each other, then to Jonah. He stared right back. "What?"

"Um, J, it's only been a week, right?"

"Yeah … like I said, work in progress."

"And you're already in love with the idea of domestic life? Are you ok?" Spader leaned back in his chair. "Cause the Jonah pre-*Fargo* training would have run out of the room screaming at that idea."

Jonah eyed Spader. "Now I'm a new Jonah. The Jonah that'll snap your neck for sending my girlfriend a damn dick pic."

"Dude, that was a long, long time ago."

"Uh-huh. How long?"

"Back when she was gonna do Hestia's oath. Thought she should know what she was missing out on. Lucky for you it worked, right?"

Jonah narrowed his eyes. "I'm bread now for you to butter? Nice try, dude."

"Tying my damnedest to get out of this, J. You could give me the benefit of the doubt. And think of what could happen. You might sprain your wrist or something."

"You know, Spader? You're absolutely right," Jonah mused aloud, allowing his fingers to spark. "Maybe I should fry you. Make your fluids evaporate in your body. A *lot* less risk involved, wouldn't you say?"

"Um, no? How about we skip murder and go straight back to friends?" Spader swallowed. "We can just chalk this up as a bonding experience."

Jonah thought on it, then reached across and smacked Spader across the back of the head.

"Ow!" Spader protested.

Jonah smiled. "*Now*, we're good."

"Dammit." Spader rubbed the back of his head. "Well, at least you didn't fry me."

"Send Eva another dick pic and I will."

"Yeah, fine. Lesson learned," he grumbled as Reena shook her head. "What?"

"Are you two done? Because we have more important things to talk about."

"Like what?"

"Like this assassin. Maybe we can track him down ourselves."

"You think we can?" Terrence asked dubiously. "You think we can succeed where the Curaie has failed?"

"They've proven themselves as failures about a dozen times by this point," Liz muttered. "It's just par for the course nowadays."

"Where would we even start?"

"Dunno, Terrence." Jonah shook his head. "Besides, I gotta get back to France in a few hours. Eva's expecting me back tonight."

"She'll understand if you stay," Terrence pointed out from his spot by the stove. "Evie knows you're with us."

"True," Jonah said, "but I'm eager to get back to her. You guys can send me correspondence though."

"What exactly have y'all been doing over there?" Liz piped up. "Besides the obvious."

"The obvious?"

"Uh-huh," she grinned and rested her chin on her hand. "You're way too relaxed for it to be anything else."

Jonah laughed. "Well, we have a bit of a routine. Workouts, walks through town, I write at night while she reads. It's peaceful. Very therapeutic."

"I told you. Domesticated."

"Back up. You're writing?" Reena's eyes widened. "Jonah, it's been ages since you've written anything! That's amazing!"

"Yup," Jonah grinned. "I'm working on a book I've had writer's block on for a couple years. Finished two short stories as well. "

"J, what happened? How?" Reena laughed as she leaned forward. "Like, is it the French air or what?"

"I don't know, Re. I don't. Just rolling with it."

"I know what it is."

"Yeah? What's that, Terrence?"

"Eva's good for you. About time you listened to us about her."

Jonah laughed.

Liz grinned happily. "It's the Eva Effect," she said. "You're already hopelessly devoted."

"Damn right," Spader said. "You're willing to flick off the Curaie. Not that I blame you. 'Cause Eva, boy ..."

"Spader," Jonah said quietly, "you need to be as quiet as humanly possible. "

"Right. Sorry, man."

"Thank you," Jonah said both to Spader and then to Terrence when he handed him a bowl of chicken stew. "Anyway, we're happy. Life's peaceful over there. Hell, Eva is talking about making the place her permanent residence."

"Jonah, no!" Liz cried. She dropped her spoon as she spoke. "You guys belong in Rome! If Eva stays overseas, you will too, and we'll never see either of you."

"Lizzie, you act as if ethereal travel isn't a thing," Jonah laughed. "I just want Eva to be alright, you know? Her current spot is good for her. And it's not set in stone. She's just talking about it. One thing at a time. It's all about her healing. That's the priority."

"Just as long as you know that." Liz pouted. "And you come home *often*."

"That depends on what's going on, but I will try."

Jonah began to eat as the rest chattered around him. Terrence bumped his arm. "I don't like this, brother," he said when he began to eat. "Us separated with a threat out there. You need back up, you call."

"Always, bro," Jonah responded. "You know I'll reach out; why would I not? Unlike the Curaie, we *know* who our friends and enemies are. "

"I don't know what to think about all this. I don't." Terrence took a bite of stew and swallowed. "I'm an Eleventh by blood, so that's always been my team. But Apollo, Evie—they've become family. Ulysses, too."

"Ulysses?"

"Yeah. He'd come by and check on us while Evie was detained. Bring us little things to make us feel better. He's a good dude."

"See that?" Jonah looked around the table. "That is the problem with these fucking Spirit Guides. The world is not black and white.

They've been on their own for so long that they don't seem to get there is such a thing as human complexity."

"They were never human, J," Spader reminded him.

"Neither were Apollo and Zeus," Jonah countered. "I'm just hoping cooler heads prevail while we try to put something together to give us clues on Ange De La Mort."

"The best thing for you to do is to stay in France with Evie, J. If things break bad, you don't want her alone." Reena shook her head. "You know what a loner she is."

"She is," Jonah agreed as he continued to eat. "But she's met some people. Had a guy she was talking to before we made things official."

"What?" Terrence sat up straight. "No, she didn't?"

"Yeah, she did. Some baguette bitch with an aristocratic background."

"Seriously?" Spader sat forward. "You're not shitting us?"

"No," Jonah replied, still salty about Pierre the Prick. "He was this uber rich dude named Pierre, whom she had a few dates with."

"How far did it go?" Spader demanded.

Jonah grimaced. "Just this once, but that's all you get," he murmured. "It didn't go any further than third base. She did him, he did her, the end."

"Son of a—" Spader balled his hands into fists. "I was right *here*, tossing my line for Eva to catch all this time, and then she hops a plane across the ocean to get Inspector Clouseau off?"

"Spader?" Jonah said in a dangerously calm tone. "How many times today must I threaten your physical life? Anyway, she was trying to convince herself to sleep with him, but the party got crashed by yours truly."

"I gotta say, your timing was impeccable. If you'd waited another week, things might've been different."

"Yeah," Jonah muttered. "Because I would have killed him."

"Jonah!"

"Don't you 'Jonah' me, Liz." He focused on what was left of his stew. "Dude had no business messing with my Eva."

"In fairness, that was before you two became an item."

"Not the point, Re. He just wanted to screw around."

"How do you know that?"

"Because she isn't with him. Never really was." Jonah waved a dismissive hand. "It doesn't matter now, anyway. Ancient history."

"And now, she's on fire."

"What are you talking about, Terrence?"

"Cause you and Eva are burning a hole in that bed every night, aren't you?"

"Not answering that, Terrence."

"Oh, come on!" He laughed. "You gotta give us something! We've waited three damn years for this to finally happen. And you gonna leave us hanging? That's not right!"

"Gentlemen never kiss and tell."

"You shared quite freely about Lo," Terrence reminded Jonah.

"Lo was a friend with benefits," Jonah replied. "Eva is my twin flame. *Huge* difference."

"That is just the sweetest thing," Liz teased. "So, is the wedding going to be in France? Or here? Cause I'd like a heads-up before that happens."

"That'll be awhile, Lizzie-Beth."

"Wait." She sat up straight as a plank. "I was just trying to get under your skin. Are you screwing with me? Or are you two that serious already?"

"We're not making wedding plans any time soon," Jonah told Liz, "but I can definitely see it happening down the line. We're just taking it one day at a time, like everything."

"Well, we're happy for both of you. Sucks that Evie isn't here, but maybe we can come to France? It'll be like one big family vacation."

Jonah considered Reena's suggestion, but he knew a trip like that wasn't going to happen any time soon. Not until Eva was ready to drop the Lea persona. In the end, Jonah said the only thing he could think to say. "Let's take it one day at a time, Re. That's the only thing we can do right now."

———

Jonah got back to Marseille two hours late—with his travel bag, beloved bookbag, and a container of chicken stew Terrence had insisted on sending back with him. After putting the food in the fridge, Jonah headed upstairs. He knew where Eva would be and he was right.

"Hey, babe." He sat the bags on the bed before he approached. Eva's entire face lit up when he stepped on the balcony to kiss her. "How was your day?"

"Fine." Eva stuck her bookmark between the pages, then tossed the book on the table. She wrapped her arms around his waist and rested her head against his stomach when he stopped in front of her. "How are things at the estate?"

Jonah hesitated, but not enough to make Eva suspicious. They were not addressing the bullshit right now. "Everyone is good."

"Well, you haven't missed anything here. Got work taken care of so we can focus on the weekend. I haven't been home long."

"How's Theia?"

"Same." She shrugged. "No surprise there, right?"

"Connor grumbling about your sabbatical?"

"Of course," Eva replied. "He tried to coax me in to do a few promo tours. I flat out refused, and there wasn't a damn thing he could do about it. When I shot Connor down, he just grumbled and said, 'Fine'. Felt good to put my foot down. He'll see me early in the New Year and not a second sooner."

"I'm proud of you for that."

"For putting my foot down?"

"Yeah. I know you're all about the show ... how much you love it."

Eva stared out at the sea and linked their hands together against the tabletop.

"I do love *Grave*, but I realized something when I was ... away. I can't let Theia or the Council keep running me into the ground. I think it was so easy for me to trust Joey like I did because I was just exhausted. That weakened my judgement. I don't want that to happen again. And.."

"And?"

"And I don't want to miss moments like this for anything in the world. Just sitting here, taking it all in, being with you. I love this more than anything. Even *Grave*."

Jonah pulled Eva closer to him. "Eva, my love, I have watched you for a while now. Fulfilling all your requirements dutifully. Doing the damn thing day in, day out. But I've been concerned. Not about your abilities, not at all. But about the fact that perhaps the issues you've had mentally, physically...was because of your schedule. You're the crown jewel, but you're treated like a foot soldier. When you've been at peace, though? You're a different woman. Perfect example is eating. Do you realize that you've eaten at least half your meals every night this week? And you almost ate your entire portion of the pasta-bake I made last night. I wondered if your body responds to everything better when you're at peace. Even food."

"Maybe." She smiled up at him. "I am at peace here. I am. It's crazy how everything that surrounds us can end up affecting us. Even when we don't realize it. Your writing is a perfect example."

"Pardon?"

"I think that the peace you feel now is what's broken your writer's block. Jonah, you may not realize it, but over the past week, I've seen you change. You laugh more. Smile more. You seem like a weight has been lifted off your back and I love that. I love seeing you so happy."

"*You* are what is making me happy. Trust and believe that."

"You make me happy, too."

Jonah just held her. He knew that the time they had here in Marseille was going to be precious. And when they were forced to go back to the real world, they would do what had to be done and come right back. In less than a week, Marseille had become more than just a place on the map. It had become a sanctuary. *Their* sanctuary.

Jonah watched the ocean over Eva's head and thought about Minako and the assassin. He hoped cooler heads would prevail, but they weren't going to jump into this fight. And if that fucker dared to come after him or Eva?

There would be hell to pay. Absolute hell.

FIVE

EVA MCRAYNE

ONE YEAR LATER

I STARED at my reflection and tried to get used to being my old self again. The glamor spell I had used to change my hair to red and my eyes to blue had been deactivated, so Lea was gone. Eva was back.

It was strange to see the gold again. After a year of being blissfully happy, I was almost afraid to return to the woman I used to be. I busied my hands by piling my hair up on top of my head. I was pinning the bun in place when Jonah came into view. He placed a kiss on the back of my neck, and I smiled a little.

"There's something I haven't seen in a while."

"Eh, you weren't missing much." I turned around to smooth out his blue button-down shirt. "I don't want to go."

"Then don't. Tell Apollo you aren't ready."

"No." I kissed him quickly. "No, I've been away far too long already. It's time to make my grand entrance."

"The Council will be excited to see you." Jonah rubbed his hands up my arms and I moved even closer to him. "And you talked to Connor?"

"Yeah. He wants to know where I'm going first, then said he didn't give a damn as long as an episode came out of it."

Jonah grimaced. "Connor can shove it up his ass. You've done so well, that business didn't even go down in your absence. Plus, Nemesis' new album just went quadruple platinum; Theia Music Group is almost as shiny a diamond as *Grave*. Bastard would have been fine if you had more time."

"I know, but I can't hide away forever. We'll do what we have to do and go home. That's the game plan." I took a step back. "Let's go. I don't want to keep Apollo and Ulysses waiting."

Jonah took my hand and we headed out of our suite at the Garden of the Gods. The one thing that stood out to me the most was how nothing had changed. The same faces, the same furniture, the same threats.

I tightened my grip on Jonah's hand without realizing it. He glanced down at me but didn't comment. Maybe he thought I was nervous, but I wasn't. I was afraid. Returning to Eva meant that Hera could find me. Her followers could find me. Would they force me to take Hera's poison? Or had she found yet another way to end me?

"Evie?"

"Hmm, what? Sorry. Wasn't paying attention."

"I can tell. You almost walked by Apollo's study."

"Oh." I smirked. "Whoops."

Jonah cut his gaze at me, but I ignored him and knocked. The door swung open to show my father sitting at his desk. Ulysses was standing close by.

"Eva?" Apollo's face broke out into a huge grin. He met us in the center of the room to sweep me up in his arms. "How glad I am to see you!"

"Thanks, Daddy," I hugged him back. "How are things?"

"For Olympus?" He pulled back, then shook Jonah's hand. "We have much to discuss. Jonah, glad to see you."

"Always an honor and a pleasure, sir."

"Sit. Tell me of Gaelic country."

"It's called France now," I responded drily. "And it's beautiful. Thank you again for the house."

Jonah raised an eyebrow at me. I hadn't bothered to mention the house was a present from Apollo. He had told me when I reached France to find a place to ease my mind and he would make sure it was mine. He made good on that promise.

"Yes, well." He sat on the edge of his desk as we joined him. "You are welcome. It is high time you found refuge away from the world, Eva."

"What's going on? I know there has to be something."

"Indeed."

Apollo and Jonah looked to each other. Ok. So that meant they were hiding something from me. Something I wasn't going to like.

"What are you hiding?" I focused on Jonah. "The both of you."

"Eva, there have been some interesting events since you left." Apollo crossed his arms over his chest, then raised a hand. "Calm. I can see you're getting upset."

"I'm not upset. I'm *confused*."

"There's an assassin on the loose, Evie." Jonah leaned forward to clasp his hands on his knees. "He's an Eleventh. Been killing Olympians for a while now."

Hera. That was the first name that came to mind. She was looking for me. Or, rather, her assassin was. I gripped the armchair until my knuckles went white.

"You knew about this?"

"I consulted Jonah on the matter." Apollo brought my attention back to him. "And I ordered him not to speak with you about it. I did not want your solitude disrupted."

"Jonah doesn't take orders."

I glared at my father and tried to determine if he was lying to me or not. Apollo liked Jonah. He'd cover for him in a heartbeat.

"He will when he knows it's for your own good and if he wants to keep his girl's father happy."

Oh. Ok. That made sense, but I still didn't like it. "Well, I know now. Is he still out there killing people?"

Apollo steepled his hands. "The last person to fall was about three months ago. A girl named Nidia. She was one of Hestia's maidens, very young, only seventy-five years old. She had a cover identity among the mortals as a nurse. She didn't report into work, mortal authorities were alerted. Ulysses' wife Merrill—call her Merri if you meet her—was undercover as one of them. She was garroted almost to the point of decapitation."

I felt my hands tighten once more. I had to stop that before they noticed. "That's brutal. But how does this killer know his victims are Olympian?"

"Pardon?"

"He has to get the information from somewhere. If this maiden was undercover, there would be no way to know she was attached to Olympus … unless he got that information from an inside source."

I froze as this conversation triggered something in my memory bank. I grabbed Jonah's arm to get his attention. "Is this why Spader asked me about the Olympians hierarchy?" I demanded. "I *knew* that question was random!"

"Yeah." Jonah patted my hand, and I loosened my grip. "We were brainstorming that night."

"You should have told me."

"Baby, you know me better than that. I was trying to maintain your sense of peace."

I closed my eyes and pinched the bridge of my nose. I wasn't mad at Jonah. I couldn't be when I would have done the exact same thing. "Ok. Let's talk about the details. Game plan." I shifted the conversation to what mattered. "What do we know about him?"

"Next to nothing. He's male and his aura is white."

"How common is a white aura, Jonah? And what abilities are attached to it?"

Jonah looked at me, and I could tell he was trying to keep his expression stoic. "White auras are a dime a dozen. Apparently, this guy is a career assassin, and hides in plain sight. White auras share some traits with red auras, weirdly enough … they can will themselves to not be seen. If this guy has that trait, it's easy for him to kill and slip away."

"Can I see the files?"

"They are gruesome, Evie."

"Not all that worried about gruesome things. I want to see the information."

Apollo willed a file and passed it over.

I flipped it open then looked up at him. "This is on the killer."

"Yes."

"I want the ones on the victims."

"Is that important?"

"It is if we are going to find this guy." I passed the first file over to Jonah. "Anyone who's ever been exposed to *Sherlock Holmes* knows to look at your victim first."

"Eva's not wrong," Jonah said as he put on his reading glasses. "And Apollo, how have the meetings with the more cooperative of the 11ths been going? It's my understanding you guys have been convening at different points over the months?"

Oh, that was low, and Jonah knew it. I shifted against my seat and he grinned. He knew the effect his reading glasses had on me. I loved it when he looked so damn smart. He always put them on to read in bed, until I couldn't stand it anymore. And I couldn't do a damn thing. Not with my father in the room—my father who was speaking. I had to focus on that.

"Very well, actually. Those who are allies to us have been training with our spies in hopes of finding out who the assassin is."

"And relations with the Curaie?"

Apollo's expression darkened. I couldn't help but notice the sunlight dimmed as well.

"As strained as ever."

"What does that mean exactly? Y'all aren't still threatening a stupid war against each other, are you?"

"The Spirit Guides want to make a show of force." Jonah flipped through the file as he spoke. "Olympus is growing and thriving. Meanwhile, the ethereal world is kinda stagnant because the same old talking heads are in charge. The ethereal world needs changing, and they don't want to admit it. *No one* in the ethereal world wants war, Apollo. Jonathan and the Protector Guides he trusts will have told you that. It's why the people working with your friends are trying to get leads on Ange De La Mort. We don't want the Olympians riled any further."

"The Council is opposed to war as well, son, although there are those who wish to overthrow your Curaie to put new Spirit Guides in power. Ones who wish to see our worlds even more conjoined."

"Can I just say that the talk of war is absolutely ridiculous?" I crossed my ankles and leaned forward. "How many lives would be lost? And for what? Because both sides are too damn stubborn to work together to find a murderer?"

"No. Because the Curaie have insulted us. It would be an act to defend our honor."

"Insult." I snorted. "Look, y'all are all mad because I was imprisoned. I get that. I appreciate that. But honestly—"

"The Curaie doesn't want the two of you together."

Jonah's head snapped up.

Mine began to pound between my ears when the blood rushed to through. "Excuse me?"

"The Curaie doesn't want the two of you together. They feel that Jonah is consorting with the enemy. A criminal." Apollo sneered at uttering the final word. "I am surprised you haven't heard of this, Jonah. They have made their demands to separate the two of you very loudly and very clearly."

"I *had* heard of it, Apollo," Jonah revealed. "I have friends in the Curaie, after all."

"And your stance?"

"You know my stance, sir." Jonah took Eva's hand. "Last time I checked, my parents were in the ground. I don't give a fuck about anyone's approval."

I squeezed Jonah's hand and looked Apollo square in the eye. Gold on gold. "And your stance, Daddy?"

"Not that it matters, but I am thrilled." He relaxed as he spoke. "For one, I can see how good the two of you are for each other. And two, I am fond of Jonah. The urge to strangle him is less than it would be with a stranger."

"Thanks," Jonah deadpanned. "Appreciate that."

"At any rate, your relationships are your own. Politics has no place in the bedroom when emotions are involved. Dare I say, I'd draw up a contract of consummation for you today if I thought you would go for it."

"A what?" Jonah asked.

"A marriage contract. One that would bind your souls together forever more."

We both stared at Apollo in silence. That word hadn't come up between us. I didn't know if it ever would. Marriage seemed so fragile compared to what we had.

"You don't want to get married? You've been together for over a year now."

Jonah and I looked at each other. I was the one who spoke first.

"Please, don't mistake me, I would love to become Eva Rowe someday. But right now, we're in a good spot. We're solid. I'm not saying that marriage would break what we have, but I think we both have too much going on at the moment to actually walk down the aisle."

That much was true. I wasn't opposed to marriage, but I was happy where we were. I didn't see a reason to change it. I had a feeling I would take Jonah's name in the future, but not now. Not when there were threats and a damn ethereal government trying to separate us.

Apollo nodded. "Very well. That is most understandable. I'm optimistic things will be righted, but we'll remain wary and cautious, nonetheless. It was a pleasure to see you, Daughter Mine. Now, if I could have a moment alone with Jonah?"

"Are you kicking me out?" I teased. "You haven't seen me in two years!"

"Drop in the bucket given our lifespans, Evie," Apollo smiled as I stood. "We shall have dinner tonight to catch up."

I started towards the door and waved for Ulysses to stay put when I heard a knock. I opened the door to see a man dressed in Agema gear. He bowed at me, so I stepped aside.

"Othys?" Apollo approached us. "What is this about?"

"An emissary was found deceased less than an hour ago, milord. The assassin."

"Is the crime scene still intact?"

"Yes, Representative." The Agema threw cold eyes at Jonah. "It was another ethereal beheading."

"Don't you dare."

"Pardon?"

"Don't you dare look at Jonah like that," I snapped. "He isn't out there murdering people and neither are the other Elevenths who are our allies. Apologize."

The Agema didn't want to. I could see it with how he lifted his chin with a pride that just pissed me off. "My apologies if I implied anything improper, Blue Aura."

"You're damn right you implied something improper, Agema," Jonah grunted.

Othys narrowed his eyes. "My name is not Agema."

"And my name ain't Blue Aura," Jonah shot back, "yet here we are."

"I believe your point has been made."

"Where's the crime scene?"

The Arena looked to Apollo. "Milord, may I be blunt with the Representative?"

"Why are you asking him when I am literally in front of your face? Spit it out already."

"Very well. That crime scene is no place for a woman." He met my gaze. "The victim was tortured prior to her beheading and it is quite disturbing."

"No place for a woman," I repeated. "Are you kidding — how do they still make misogynistic —"

"The victim," he dared to cut me off, "has an appearance similar to the Representative, Lord Apollo. Same stature, same build, same coloring, save the eyes. I believe the sight would be enough to send anyone — warrior or not — into shock."

I closed my eyes for two reasons. One, because the information was more than gruesome. Two, because here I was, once again, in the presence of a man who was a fucking pig. Any woman with any brains could relate to this. Having to work twice as hard to get half the respect. As Jonah would say, Swell.

"Your stance is something I don't appreciate. You think I can't behold a crime scene, or even talk about it. Were I a *son* of Apollo, you'd have had no hesitation. It's sexist and you need to check it."

Othys inhaled and exhaled very slowly, an indication that he was frustrated. "I'm of a different time than you. When I was a young man, earning my keep and paying my dues—"

"Women knew their place and didn't question anything," Jonah shrewdly supplied.

"Exactly," Othys said without thinking, then froze.

I was done. "Get out."

Othys blinked. "What?"

"I realize I have an accent," I told him, "but it isn't *that* thick. Leave. I desire the aid of an Eleventh."

"You don't have the--"

"She does, boy." Apollo's voice was quiet, but they caught every word. "My daughter has the might of the sovereign Lord of the sun behind her. And she asked you to depart."

Othys sat there, seething. Jonah stepped forward, ready for anything. One of the things I loved about him.

"Do we need to sing it for you, pumpkin?" he demanded. "Get!"

Othys glared at Jonah, then at me. "Look into dyeing your hair," he advised. "The blonde illustrates you as vapid and tedious."

Without warning, my father struck out like a serpent, hitting Othys just once. The blow was enough to knock him flat on his ass, bloody and groaning.

"Look into that injury," my father advised. "The blood illustrates you as weak and fragile."

"Thank you, Daddy." I crossed my arms over my chest. "That was very much appreciated." Apollo shook out his hand and I smirked. "Been awhile since you laid somebody out?"

"Not as long as you might think," he grumbled. "But I don't see a need for you to go to the crime scene."

"Why?"

"Because I haven't seen you in two years and I wish to spend time with my youngest over dinner. A crime scene will surely interrupt that."

"It's not because I am a woman, is it?"

"Eva, you have more strength than any male who has sworn his allegiance to Olympus. I am not worried about you in that regard. Now, go. Rest. I'll send the tailors in at noon."

"Tailors? Why?"

"We are going to have a bit of a ball tonight to welcome you home."

"Fabulous," I deadpanned. "I think I would rather go see the corpse."

"Of course, you would." Apollo went back to his desk as a Keeper I didn't recognize helped the asshole out the door. "Jonah, please make sure Eva allows them entry when they arrive."

"Of course, sir," Jonah nodded. "I got it."

Apollo vanished, and Jonah looked over at me. "Time to be the Superstar again, eh?"

I rolled my eyes. "I'd rather punch chauvinists and investigate corpses."

"Maybe you'll get to punch a chauvinist while being the superstar," Jonah teased me and I stuck my tongue out at him.

In truth, I was relieved that Othys had given me something to strike out against. Kept me distracted from the fact that the newest victim was proof that Hera was behind the assassin.

Why else would he go for someone who looked like me?

"What's on your mind, Evie?"

"Pardon?"

"What's on your mind?" Jonah smiled as he took my hand. "You're a million miles away."

"I'm concocting a theory. We'll talk when we get to our room."

"Will we, though?" Jonah made his voice provocative. "Or will you be so frustrated about Othys that you'll need to purge emotion?"

"You have something else in mind then?" I linked our fingers together as I gave him the most innocent look I could muster. "The Gotch Bible?"

"I mean, we could—"

"Jonah!" I laughed. "You're not supposed to turn it around on me like that!"

"Well, how about this?" Jonah suggested. "We get to our room, and I'll turn *you* around. Sound good?"

"Is that a new Gotcha move I don't know about yet?"

I jumped when he goosed me on the side. "I'm only teasing," I laughed again. "Please, don't tell me to 'get'. I don't think I could stand it."

Jonah laughed. "Switching gears only for a second, I just got an alert before we left the chambers. Minako is supposed to meet with us."

"I remember that name," I mused aloud. "I hung up on her a year or so ago."

"You recall that?" Jonah asked, mystified.

"I've always had a good memory," I pointed out, "and it's only sharpened since I've been around you."

Jonah smiled at that. "Well, yeah, you hung up on her. No one could blame you for that. But Minks is actually one of the people in the Curaie that actually has a goddamn soul and is not a hardline automaton. She's a part of the group of Elevenths and spirits that Jonathan rounded up to liaise with the Olympus free of Spirit Guide stupidity. She'll help get things done."

"We'll see."

"You should give her a chance, Evie."

"I'm all for giving people chances, but anyone who is associated with the current Curaie support abuses that I can't."

"What abuses? If you mean the Plane—"

"No, handsome, not the Plane." I stopped at our door and grabbed the knob. I leaned against it to push it open. "I'm talking about in the jails."

"What did you see in the jail?"

"I'm not going to tell you." I entered the room and kicked off my heels. "Seriously, Jonah. You're better off not knowing. But I want you to know two things. One, I wasn't harmed in any way because of my position with Olympus. And two, if I give this Minako the cold shoulder, I have my reasons."

Jonah bristled at that. I felt the air in the room change as a result. Tense. Heavy.

CINDY D. WITHERSPOON & T.H. MORRIS

"If you won't tell me, then tell Jonathan."

"No."

"Yes." Jonah stepped forward and spoke in hushed tones. "It could prove fruitful in getting rid of the current Spirit Guides in the Curaie."

I looked into his eyes, confused. They could do that? How? "Is that what they're trying to do?"

Jonah got even quieter. "There are rumblings. Jonathan and many other spirits and guides, not to mention many Elevenths, are not pleased with how the Spirit Guides are handling things. It started with their treatment of you. Everyone knows harmony is the best way to do things, and they're choosing to be cunts, which puts us all in danger. So ... big change could be on the horizon."

Jonah sighed. "Eva, a while ago, Jonathan made some choices to keep us safe from Spirit Reapers that were ... questionable. I didn't even agree with him. Long story. But the Curaie took huge issue and invoked confidence. They gave Jonathan a vote of no confidence and ousted him. Things got worked out in the end, but that's what they did to muscle him out. Well, the same confidence vote can be invoked on *them*, too. The Protector Guides, other Spirit Guides, Elect Spirits and Very Elect Spirits can do it. Yeah, they've been in power for ages, but if they keep fucking up like this and putting us in danger, their tenure won't be enough to keep them in power."

I knew no one could hear us, but I wasn't taking any chances. I grabbed Jonah's hand and pointed to the bed. "Let's lay down, handsome."

Jonah gave me a strange look before he took off his shoes, then his shirt. I stripped down too, and we slipped under the covers. I pulled them over our heads before I returned to our conversation. It was harder than I thought, given how close we were to each other.

"So, there doesn't have to be war for that to happen."

"No." Jonah shifted so that his mouth was next to my ear. "Not at all. Just a vote of no confidence."

"And I have to talk to Jonathan?"

"Yes," Jonah replied. "Tell him everything. I mean absolutely *everything*. See, Eva, you're jaded and attached to this, which I understand completely, so don't get me wrong. But what you didn't know is that the ethereal prison system is run like its own little fiefdom. Spectral Law? Networkers ... well, let's say seventy percent of them anyway? They have no idea what goes on in there. Minako didn't even have the job she has now when they took you away. She hadn't left Sanctum yet."

"Why is it like that? Why be given so much autonomy?"

"Initially, it had to do with reducing corruption," he began. "With the Deadfallen disciples and the Reapers and rogue sazers and shit, all the branches being interconnected could lead to dirty mother-fuckers slipping in the ranks with no one being the wiser. Its why ranks are tight. Elite. It's also why you see Networkers sometimes use outside specialists, like Felix. The problem is that guards in the jails know that they are pretty much Alpha. Most of them have little to no compunction about what they do."

"Ok, so how do you know all this?"

"I asked around. Did some research off the record. I generally avoid matters associated with the Curaie, but here, I learned a thing or two. But I have no idea what goes on in the jails. No one would talk about *that*. Not even you. So, there is a disconnect ... not a lot of people outside that circle know. But you know who does know? The Spirit Guides that head the Curaie. Don't think for one *second* that they don't monitor and police the aspects of the ethereal world and not know everything that goes on. So, that means they're aware and turning a blind eye. It means they were more concerned with making an example of you than they were with keeping the ethereal world safe. That's a powerful weapon against them in the hands of people we trust. And I trust Jonathan wholeheartedly."

"So, the people who would have a vote in this ever get together?"

"What do you mean?"

I brushed a palm over his chest as I put my thoughts in order. The tattoos that meant so much to him. The one he had gotten in France of the Sibyl's Phoenix over his heart that meant so much to me. "I'm willing to go before them to talk about what I witnessed. If it means making it stop, then I am willing to do that."

Jonah nodded. "I don't know all the play-by-plays; what I just told you is the extent of my knowledge, pretty much. But Jonathan will know. You can contact him whenever you want, just like I can contact Apollo now. Reach out when you have a free moment."

"I'm free right now."

"No, you're not."

Jonah threw his arm around me and buried his nose into my hair. I mirrored his movement by holding him as close as possible. I felt tears sting my eyes as I remembered what Apollo had said. The Curaie wanted us apart. They were trying to separate us. I would start a war with them on that fact alone.

"You ok?"

"Thinking about the possibility of war."

"It's never gonna happen, baby."

"It will if they try to take your away from me." I held onto him tighter. "I'd start the damn war myself if they ever tried."

Jonah snorted, but the action was void of mirth. "Eva, I've already made it crystal clear what'll happen if they try to split us up."

That's what I was afraid of. More than anything. I knew exactly what Jonah would do. Images from the vision Jonathan had shown me years ago danced behind my eyes. I had to ask him, though I already knew the answer. "You would really go Dark Blue for me?"

"Without hesitation," Jonah responded. He was dead serious. "I'd do anything for you."

I closed my eyes as he said the words I knew he would say. I understood all too well the depth of his emotion for me. I knew it because mine were just as deep. "Jonah, you can't go dark blue." I whispered. "You can't. Not even for me."

"Yes, I can. I will."

"No, my love. You would lose everything. You would lose yourself." I pressed a kiss against his heart. "I can't let you do that. I've seen what can happen. I don't ever want you to be like that."

"What does that mean?"

"Jonathan showed me a vision once. It was horrible, but it showed me how important it is for you to remain balanced. It's so *very* important." I swallowed. "Please. Promise you won't? No matter what happens in the future?"

"What vision?"

"It's not important … because it will never happen."

Jonah raised up, so I took the opportunity to change the subject. I pressed a kiss against the side of his throat and trailed my hand downward.

"What do you think you're doing?" He sounded amused. "We're having a very serious conversation."

"Working out those frustrations we talked about. I think you're right. This is a much better way to do it than talking."

Jonah nudged the side of my head, then caught me up in a kiss that made me forget all about the current turmoil in our worlds. Because there in that bed? Nothing else mattered. Not the Council. Not the Curaie. Nothing but us.

SIX

JONAH ROWE

THE MEETING HALL was crammed full of creatures and beings by the time Jonah and Eva made their entrance. Jonah would have taken the opportunity to introduce himself to most of them. One of the most enjoyable parts of being at the Garden was the numerous cultures he was exposed to. Except, this meeting wasn't one to be enjoyed. He and Eva had woken up not to tailors coming to prepare them for the party that evening, but to Ulysses, who announced an emergency meeting had been called. Eva was required to be there.

Which meant Jonah was, too. He wasn't going to let her out of his sight as long as there was a damn assassin on the loose.

Eva stopped at her seat before the Council and kissed him on the cheek. "Meet me here when this is over?"

"I'll be here." Jonah went to find a seat close by, but it was harder than he thought it was going to be. He lowered himself into a chair three rows back from Eva. There were two nymphs in front of him, whispering to each other.

"The Council must see reason," the nymph with dark curls pulled up on her head was saying to the other. "If we ever hope to keep our traditions alive, we must have our purity restored."

That got Jonah's attention. What purity? The Olympians were the most diverse group he had ever come across.

"Indeed," the second nymph in a matching gown agreed. "'Tis a pity Zeus has allowed a half-breed into the ranks of royalty."

"She is his blood."

"So? Do you know how many of Zeus' children he had cast aside? They have the royal birthmark. She does not."

Jonah felt fire in his blood. Even in the Golden City, there were Mean Girls? As he turned to excoriate them, someone took hold of his arm. It was a tall woman with striking eyes and faint scars on her forehead and jaw. Her jet-black hair was pulled away from her face as she glared at the nymphs, now gaping at her in apprehension.

"You're aware that talk like that will get you pitched into Tartarus," the woman said. "And two dainty little things like you? I'd bet gold that you will be there by dawn tomorrow. I can arrange that. Just keep calling the Representative a half-breed while her father is in the room."

The nymphs paled and scurried off. Jonah regarded the woman when she seated herself next to him. "I could've handled that on my own," he said, "though their response to you made me laugh."

"It was nothing," the woman said. "Nymphs need to be reminded of their place, same as everyone else."

"Guess so," Jonah muttered. "I'm Jonah Rowe."

"Oh, I know," the woman smirked. "Demetria. Demetria Wellington Barlowe."

"Nice to meet you."

"You as well, Jonah." The woman situated herself so that she was twisted towards him. "Are you here to speak? Or just observe?"

"Observe, for now." Jonah studied her. "What is your role in all this?"

"To observe." The woman gave him a tight smile. "Despite the conflict at the moment, there are many who are grateful you are here. I am one of them."

"Me? Why me?"

"Because you are an example of good in the ethereal world. One that the Traditionalists have a tough time turning people against."

"What the hell is a Traditionalist?"

Demetria didn't answer immediately. She seemed to weigh her words. "Your file says you like history. So, think of your American Civil War. The Confederates who wanted no change. Traditionalists are just like that. Consider them Confederates, just Olympian."

"So, they are diehards who are stuck in their ways?"

"Yes. The old ways. The ones where Olympus was run solely by men, women were property less valuable than land, and there was no intermingling with other beings."

"Intermingling?"

"Yes. Having relationships with mortals or ethereal beings that could taint the bloodline."

Jonah glanced over at the Council. "What did these fuckers think of Hera? Demeter? Aphrodite? Artemis and Athena? Were they the exception or something?"

"They are gods, but not even they are exempt from the judgment of the masses. Hera, however, is still seen as the Queen. Thus, she has her fair share of supporters."

"How could people think this way? After all this time?"

"Simple. Times may change, but the values of immortals do not. Their beliefs tend to remain the same, no matter how many centuries pass."

"Well, they can shove it up their immortal asses because it is going nowhere. Even when I'm long gone, Eva will still be there. Thriving. Winning. And they won't be able to do fuck-all about it."

"Hmm."

"What was that for?"

"Two reasons. One, do you truly believe that Eva would continue to live without you? And, two, do you really think Apollo would watch as she withered away in her grief?"

Jonah swallowed hard. It was a sore subject. Eva would never touch it. She insisted they never talk about it. "Demetria ... it sucks. But it's reality. We Elevenths do have longer life expectancies than Tenths, but ... but it's just reality. I've made my peace with it."

"No, you haven't," Demetria said immediately.

Jonah started to protest, but then sighed. "Fine. No, I haven't. But it's just real life."

"All rise for the Olympians Council!"

Jonah and Demetria stood with the rest of the crowd while the gods filed in. Zeus was last. He made his way to the center throne and motioned for everyone to sit down.

"We meet today due to the current conflict that has arisen between the ethereal beings and ourselves." Zeus scanned the audience and his gray eyes stopped on Jonah. "I am disturbed by talk overheard in these halls."

"May I speak, milord?"

An Agema approached the Council. Zeus sat on his throne.

"Where is Telamon, Thrys?"

"On duty, Lord Zeus." The Agema kept his eyes forward. "I am allowed to speak in his place."

"Then speak and be done with it."

"We ask that the Representative be stripped of her title."

Zeus sat up straight. "Pardon?"

"We ask that the Representative be stripped of her title," the man repeated. "She is the source of our current conflict and despite that, beds our enemy. She is a disgrace to Olympus."

"A disgrace?" Eva hadn't quite seated herself before she shot back to her feet. "How dare you! The Ghostly Ones are not our enemy. The Spirit Guides currently ruling the Curaie are. And even then, their actions are questionable, but not worthy of warfare."

"My point has been proven, Lord Zeus. She has been tainted by her exposure to the Ghostly Ones. Her power must be purged."

"*You* have been tainted, Thrys!"

Jonah shouldn't have done it. He should've stayed quiet. He shouldn't have made a scene. It went against decorum. But that bastard threw Eva under the bus. *Fuck* decorum.

Jonah's outburst caused stares and mutterings, but Thrys looked scandalized.

"How dare you, filth!" he whispered. "I don't know what you're used to in that cesspit you call the ethereal world, but here —"

"Put your thumb back in your mouth and shut up," Jonah

growled. "You call us trash. It's a known fact that the Keepers, Agents of Olympus, and"—Jonah gave a protracted gasp—"Agema all have Elevenths in their ranks. Are they suddenly trash now? Are you going to request *they* get kicked out, too?"

"Lord Zeus, this boy's outburst is proof enough of—"

"First off, don't call Jonah a boy." Eva made her way over to the soldier. She jabbed him on the chest with her finger. "And I'll tell you right now that the ethereals have more integrity in their little fingers than you do in your entire body."

"You conduct traitorous behavior and dare to flaunt it on these sacred halls," Thyrs snapped at her. "And you dare to insult me? If not for your blood, you would have been strung up for your actions."

Apollo stood up from his throne, but Eva never gave him a chance to speak.

"You want an example of trash? Look in the mirror. I have never been so ashamed to look at someone wearing my family's armor." She turned back to the Council. "You all know my words are the truth. But if you even consider placating the words of the Agema, I will resign. I refuse to be associated with any organization that allows such division."

"That won't be necessary, Evie." Zeus focused on the soldier. "My granddaughter is right. You and those like you are a scourge upon Olympian ideals. Apologize."

"I am allowed to have my opinions."

"Your opinions, yes. But you claim to represent my most elite soldiers. In that regard, you will apologize to both Eva and Jonah."

Jonah stayed still. He waited for the asshole to make a move.

The Agema member stared at Zeus, then did something completely unexpected: he spat at Eva's feet before he turned on his heel and marched from the room.

Jonah saw red and charged. He wasn't a fast runner, but he caught Thrys within seconds. When he tackled him, they crashed through a wall of hardened glass. They slammed onto earth in a rain of noise and shards. Jonah was ready for a fight. He was ready to batter Thrys for daring to speak to Eva like that and then spit at her.

But there was no need.

Thrys was immobilized.

Seriously. This big, hardened soldier was barely conscious. Dazed and groaning.

That made Jonah even angrier. He was Billy Badass talking to Eva, but couldn't be bothered to stay strong enough to be cognizant once Jonah got hold of him.

"Jonah!"

Eva slid to a stop next to him, followed by Ulysses and several Council members, including Zeus. Jonah stared the soldier down as Ulysses and another man in a Keeper's uniform lifted him to his feet.

"Take him below," Zeus ordered. "Then come back inside. We have much more to discuss."

"Wait. I got something to say first."

Jonah grabbed the rounded collar of the bastard's chest plate and pulled him forward. Thyrs' head was hanging, but Jonah knew he could hear him.

"Disrespect the Representative again, and I will end you." Jonah pushed him back and turned towards Eva.

She stepped forward to examine the cuts covering his arms and face. "You need medic." She took his hand and turned it to further examine him. "You could have all kinds of glass in you."

"I'm fine," Jonah told her. "You wouldn't believe the things we learned to shrug off during Thor's survival training. I'm good."

Eva wrapped her arms around him and hugged him gently. "Thank you, handsome. That was very sweet of you to do."

Jonah hugged Eva. "You never have to thank me for that. I will *not* tolerate that petty, xenophobic shit."

Apollo strolled forward and extended his hand.

"If I didn't respect you before, I'll respect you forever now. Thank you for defending my daughter's honor."

Jonah took the hand the god offered and shook it.

Apollo clasped him on the shoulder. "Come. Sit with Eva."

"I can do that?"

"Yes. I want to make it perfectly clear where our alliances are."

"Thrys can't be the *only* dissenter, man," Jonah said. "I don't want to cause anymore drama. "

"*You* didn't cause drama, Thrys did," Apollo told him. "Now, sit down. If anyone else has a problem with it, they can discuss it with me."

"Come on." Eva pulled him over to her seat, but ignored the extra one a nymph pulled over. Instead, she pushed Jonah down and sat right on his lap. She wrapped her arms around his neck and grinned. "Best seat in the whole damn place."

"You know this is gonna cause a scene."

"Do I look like I care?" Eva pressed a kiss right on his mouth. "Let them talk. They're just jealous that their man isn't as good as mine."

"That would be accurate, Representative."

Demetria was back. Eva narrowed her eyes at her.

"And who might you be?"

"Oh, babe," Jonah said in a calming tone, "this is Demetria. She's cool. Frightened off some mouthy nymphs who were throwing you under the bus."

Eva stiffened and Jonah swore he saw recognition in her expression. What the hell was that about?

"Demetria. Of course. Tell me, how's your father these days?"

Her eyes flashed and Eva smiled sweetly as the hall got itself back in order.

"I don't know what you mean, Representative."

"Sure you do. Tartarus? Charged with attempted murder?"

"Excuse me."

The woman stormed off and Jonah narrowed his eyes. "Evie?"

"What? I didn't like her."

"What happened?" Jonah wanted to know. "Did she rub you the wrong way? You've met her before?"

"Not exactly," Eva replied. "Her name isn't Demetria; she's a spy for Demeter named Alexa. Alexa Alexius."

Jonah stared as the pieces fell into place. Cyrus had a daughter?

Eva nodded. "Yup. It's my understanding that she's his oldest."

"Why would she use a fake name?"

"Probably because Alexa Alexuis is a little tedious?"

"You're so mean, Superstar."

"No, I'm not. I don't trust her."

"You don't even know her. She did defend you."

"An action I am sure she wouldn't have done if you weren't sitting there."

"You think so?"

"Pretty sure," Eva replied. "Word in the halls say she has it pretty bad for you."

"Evie, you can't get all rankled every time a woman shows interest in me."

"You're not the one who can go all caveman," Eva pouted. "Besides, I know she has an ulterior motive."

"You do?"

"She's a spy," Eva replied. "There, I win."

"Order!" Zeus stood before his throne. "Poseidon, it is your turn to speak, brother."

Poseidon rose from the table and Eva winced each time his cane cracked against the floor. When the old god stopped in front of her, he tapped her once between the eyes. "You must do a task for me."

"What sort of task?" Eva seemed as confused as Jonah. "What will you have me do, great Poseidon?"

"The Titans have tainted my waters. They are attempting to awaken the great beast below."

"What great beast?" Eva frowned. "I'm not clear on your meaning, milord."

"My waters are being tainted and that is an insult to me." He chewed on his lip for a minute before he continued. "It is well known to those of us on the Council that our enemy has captured the human heart. Men who were once our allies turned against us. They fell behind the single god the Titans created. They taught their children through fear that we did not exist. And that weakened us greatly."

"Ok." Eva nodded. "I understand that much."

"Yet, man continued to be superstitious. That became our crutch until our little Sibyl came along." Poseidon gave me a toothless smile. "They continued to build shrines. Pray for a successful harvest.

Hang horseshoes over their doors for luck. The village of Minami-hama was no different. Each house had a shrine to me. Each prayed that the fish would come to them. Or that their businesses would bring prosperity."

Jonah exhaled slowly. It seemed as if they were being sent to Japan then.

"Your shrines are being destroyed?"

"Yes. By Titan magicks."

"What does this have to do with the assassin?" Jonah threw out the most obvious question he could think of. "Are they related?"

"Indeed. We are convinced that whoever has cast the ethereal assassin upon us wants us weakened by war. Mix that with the use of Titan magick, and we believe that our enemies are once again attempting to strike us."

"Tell us about these barriers."

Poseidon knocked his cane against the floor. "You see, Ghostly One, the great monster is restrained by four very crucial barriers. The first is located in South Island, New Zealand. The second is in Madagascar. These barriers were attacked through natural disasters. Weakened when the Titans used magick to call forth both fire and water."

"Attacked, but not destroyed," Eva pointed out. "Right?"

"Wrong." Poseidon shook his head. "Each barrier was a town that continued to use shrines. When the disasters occurred, the inhabitants found that the main god on their alters was damaged. Minamihama, Japan was the third barrier. You will go there to witness the disgrace firsthand before you travel to the fourth and final barriers."

"Ok." Eva shifted her weight on Jonah's lap. "So, where is the fourth barrier?"

"Poveglia Island." Poseidon tapped his cane against the floor once more. "Surely you've heard of it?"

"I tell ghost stories for a living. Of course, I've heard of it." She raised an eyebrow at him. "Poveglia was never a civilization, per se. It was a sanctuary for those who had the plague. Then it served as a mental institution. And it has been abandoned for a very, very long time."

"The mad see more of the world than you give them credit for." Poseidon stopped tapping his cane. "You will find my shrines buried in the rubble. But they are there."

"Ok. So, how can Eva stop the barriers from breaking? Is this going to be like Romania?"

"No, Jonah. This is nothing like Romania, because the barriers are already cracking," he shrugged. "But she can vanquish the monster that will arise from my waters."

"And then what?" Eva shook her head. "How in the hell am I supposed to stop a sea monster?"

"Decapitation." Zeus sighed. "It is the only method we did not try when the great beast threatened us before."

"Wait, what?" Jonah frowned. "You mean you've fought this thing before?"

"Why do you think there are barriers?" Zeus focused on Jonah, then waved a hand at Poseidon. "Take a seat. I believe it is my turn to address our Sibyl."

This was not going to be good. Jonah could feel it. Eva swallowed and waited for her grandfather to speak. She didn't have to wait long.

"The great beast is known as Typhon, the father of monsters." Zeus dropped his hand. "He was created by Gaia and Tartarus as a punishment for the Titanomachy. I fought him myself. Nasty beast."

"How did you defeat him?" Eva spoke her words slowly and it dawned on Jonah what she was about to face. "You said decapitation was the only thing you didn't try."

"That's true. I overwhelmed him with my lightning. Blinded his eyes while Hermes knocked him back. The beast was contained under the sea and has been for centuries."

"And Eva has to fight him … why?" Jonah frowned at the Council. "Why can't Olympus just rebuild the barriers?"

"Because the beast will always be used as a threat if he is not extinguished." Zeus shook his head. "The Titans never imagined that we would see such a resurgence. And we are seen as weak for not going to war with the Curaie as soon as they stole you from us, Eva. I am certain that is the reason why they are hellbent on raising the monster now."

"You will need to speak with Chronos, Eva." Apollo sat back on his throne. "Since you have garnered a relationship with him, he is the only one who can tell you how to best defeat Typhon."

"Then it is settled." Zeus tapped the table. "Eva, go to Seattle and see the old man. From there, you will travel to Japan, then Italy. We will join you on the island before the fight."

"Maybe I can make this into some *Grave* episodes. Garner more support for our side."

"That's a fabulous idea, my dear." Zeus beamed down at her. "The more who see you victorious, the less who will question your standing within the Council."

"I don't think a few fights is going to help with the Agema."

"The respect of warriors is always found on the battlefield."

"I'm going, too." Jonah placed his hand on Eva's lower back. "There's no way you can ask Eva to do this without as many allies as possible."

"Jonah?" She looked at him. "Are you sure? I really don't want to see you get hurt—"

"Your assistance is much appreciated, Jonah," Apollo cut in. "Although your Curaie won't like it."

"I don't give a damn about the Curaie. I do give a damn about Eva getting ambushed."

"You may assist, but this is a battle only Eva can wage."

"Yeah? Well, she can wage battle all she wants. I'm going to be there when she does."

"Wait," Eva frowned. "No offense, because I know I need all the help I can get, but why are ya'll tagging along all of a sudden?"

"It's been too long since I have shed blood, Evie," Zeus grinned. "And your Pappy Zeus is ready to steal some of your thunder. This meeting is adjourned."

"Long live Olympus," Eva muttered along with everyone else. She waited until Zeus said his goodbyes before she turned to Jonah. "You up to meeting Chronos? He's a bit ... prickly."

"Eh, he can't be the worst family member of yours I've met."

"He's a sweetheart, really. But you have to get through his armor to see it."

"That explains where you get it from," Jonah teased her before he heard Apollo call out to him.

"Jonah, I wish to speak with you."

The conversation that had been delayed by the Agema in Apollo's office was going to happen after all.

"I'll be right there, sir." Jonah squeezed Eva's arm. "See you in the room?"

"Yeah, handsome. I gotta make some calls and get the ball rolling if we are going to be filming in Japan." Eva disappeared into the crowd and Jonah crossed over to Apollo.

"Let's do this in my office."

"Ok," Jonah frowned. "Does this have to do with the monster?"

"I have news on that, yes, but what I wish to discuss with you is far more important."

Jonah and Apollo walked the rest of the way in silence. Once they got to Apollo's study, he shut the door and moved to stand in front of Jonah.

"You've been with Eva for a year now."

"Yes, sir."

"And all of your previous arrangements have ended?"

"Yes, sir," Jonah tucked his hands in his pockets, a bit irritated by the questioning. "Why do you ask?"

"Because I want you to understand something." Apollo crossed his arms over his chest. "My daughter is exceedingly important to Olympus, but she is even more precious to me."

Jonah nearly smiled when the irritation vanished. This wasn't the first time he'd gotten the dad speech, but he was sure it would be the last.

"Eva is precious to me, too."

"As well she should be." Apollo's expression remained serious. "And she should stay as such because—while I have the utmost respect for you and all you have done—I will always hold a bit of hatred for you. You remain devoted, treat my daughter with the utmost respect, and take care of her? That hatred remains small. Yet, if you *ever* break her heart, I will break *you*. Are we clear?"

Jonah nodded. Not out of fear, but deference and respect. "We're clear as a sunny day, sir," he said. "But for the record, I'm never breaking Eva's heart. Ever." Jonah swallowed before his next words. "The only thing that will separate me from her is when I pass into Spirit. And even then, I'll love her still."

Apollo gave Jonah a weird smile. An unreadable smile. "Glad to hear it son. Glad to hear it."

Jonah glanced down at the carpet, then looked up to meet Apollo's gaze.

"You mentioned a marriage contract earlier that binds souls together. What did you mean?"

"Exactly what I said." Apollo moved over to his desk.

Jonah followed.

The god pulled out a thin sheet of gold and passed it over to Jonah. "The magick contained in this document will bind two literal souls into one for all time. The bond between the names signed on it can never be broken. There is no divorce in Olympus, Jonah."

"What happens when one of the two passes into Spirit?"

"I do not know. Only immortals and those with enhanced lifespans have ever signed the document."

"Ok. What happens if the two aren't compatible?"

"Then their lives are filled with conflict forevermore. That is why it is so important to know that the person you sign this document with is your true soul twin." Apollo took the sheet back when Jonah passed it over. "I think you already know the answer to that."

"I've always been leery of marriage, sir." Jonah sat in the chair across from Apollo. "I have. Always seems to cause more trouble than it's worth."

"You have only experienced marriage in the mortal realm, son. A marriage of souls is a completely different undertaking."

"I understand that it is different." Jonah clasped his hands together. "But there is still the fact that I will pass into Spirit. I'm thirty-four years old. If I'm lucky, I have another good fifty years before I have to say goodbye to Eva."

"Are you certain about that?"

"What do you mean?"

"Jonah," Apollo leaned forward. "You are well versed in ethereality, but you forget that you sit before a god who is fond of you. A god who wishes to keep his youngest daughter happy. You have options others do not."

"Like what?"

"Immortality, for one. A snap of the fingers and it is done. Or an enhanced lifeline much like the nymphs and the Keepers. But that choice is your own. I cannot make it for you."

"Immortality? I'm not of royal blood. I thought that was the requirement? Everyone else is enhanced."

"I see you're reading those books I sent to France last year."

"Guilty," Jonah smiled a little. "I couldn't help myself."

"It will serve you well to learn all you can about our affairs. Especially since the prophecies have begun to fall into place."

"What prophecies?"

"I am not allowed to share them. Only know that you are on the correct path." Apollo leaned forward. "As for your previous question, immortality can be granted to you as long as a contract is put in place to bind you to another immortal. So, you have much to consider, Jonah."

"It appears that I do but, um, didn't you have something else for us to talk about?"

"Ah, yes, Typhon." Apollo tapped his fingers against the top of his desk. "I want you to understand why Eva must deal the killing blow."

"Ok. Why?"

"Because Zeus has decided she will be his successor. A bold move given the other children he could have granted the honor to. But he believes that Olympus needs to move forward. Become more progressive in its mindset. You and Eva will be the perfect pair to take on such a challenge."

"He can't just make an announcement? A decree or something?"

"No. There are far too many who disagree with Eva's rise

already. With this battle, and by defeating the monster that Zeus himself only captured, there would be no room for questions."

"Mmm." Jonah nodded. "Such a victory would make Eva like Teflon. Dissenters would bitch at their own risk."

"Exactly. We will support her, but there is more."

"More?"

"Indeed. You've heard of the Traditionalists, correct?"

"Unfortunately. Don't know that much though."

"They are supporters of the ancient ways and led by a pair of cousins: Ajax and Achilles." Apollo clasped his hands together. "Ajax is the commander of Zeus' Agema forces, which is why two of his men responded to Eva the way they did today. Achilles has kept a low profile on the earth plane, but his influence is still great."

"What does this have to do with Typhon?"

"We are going to request Achilles join you and Eva in Italy. Perhaps if he witnesses her victory firsthand, he will change his ridiculous stance."

"If I may, sir, that could backfire. He could just as easily sabotage Eva's efforts, then sing to the highest mountains that he always knew Eva would choke."

"That is why we are going to ensure that she doesn't. And Jonah, I ask that you share none of this with Eva. I do not want to put more on her mind than is already there."

"Aw, man." Jonah grimaced. "You know lovers have no secrets."

"It's not a secret," Apollo replied. "Keeping your loved ones in a sharp state of mind leading up to important events is an act of grace."

"Do you know how much trouble I nearly got into because I didn't tell her about the assassin? If you hadn't stepped in, she'd have me sleeping out in the hallway tonight "

"I doubt that very much," Apollo laughed. "But have no fear. Our conversation will be safe."

"Alright. Anything else?"

"Only that if Achilles mouths off, don't go with him through a wall." Apollo appeared amused as he stood.

Jonah did as well.

"They are made of stone and marble in Italy."

"I make no promises," Jonah said, mirth and seriousness mixed together. "This Achilles is *the* Achilles from the stories, right?"

"Indeed."

"But he was a hero," Jonah said. "How did he go from hero to asshole?"

"At that time, Ares' shrines burned brightest," Apollo began. "No one had an issue with the god of war being the crown jewel, as the tools to get him there were warriors. But there are those who don't care for Olympus returning to prominence by way of the primadonna sun god and his golden daughter. People feel that if the shrines that shine brightest are the ones at Delphi, Olympus looks weak."

"The Titans think Olympus is weak, Achilles thinks Olympus *looks* weak. Where does it end?"

"On the battlefield. In Italy." Apollo clasped Jonah's hand again and shook it. "I shall let you return to Eva. You will head out with her tomorrow to see Chronos?"

"Yeah. That's what Zeus said. But I thought he was in Alaska, not Seattle."

"Chronos is moved every century or so," Apollo explained as they walked to the door. "It is for his safety and ours."

"Is he still a threat?"

"'Tis a Titan, son," Apollo murmured. "Threats are all they are."

"Eva feels they are very close." Jonah rested his hand on the doorknob. "They even wrote to each other while she was in France since she couldn't visit him."

"Perhaps … Chronos is drawn to Eva as we all are. But I take no chances with him. Have a good evening, Jonah. Consider our discussion here today."

"Will do, sir," Jonah said. "And please keep me posted on how the liaisons are going."

"Of course. If all goes well, there will be no need for secret liaisons."

Jonah threw Apollo a wave goodbye and stepped out into the

hall. He was surprised to see Eva sitting on the bench across from the door. "Eva? What are you doing?"

"Minako called." She passed him her phone. "Asked you to call her back."

"You talked to her?"

"No. She left a voicemail. Couldn't get through on yours."

"I'll call her back when we get to the room." He helped her to her feet. "You sure that's all?"

Eva cut her eyes up at him as they walked, then exhaled. "No. The suite was giving me the creeps. Felt like someone was watching me. Ulysses checked it out, found nothing, but I still didn't want to be in there alone."

"You know I got your back," Jonah promised. "Always."

"As I have yours." Eva stepped ahead of him to weave through a crowd in the middle of the hallway. When they were side by side again, she continued. "What did Apollo want to talk to you about?"

Jonah knew the question was coming, but he thought he'd have a few more minutes to prepare for the answer.

"He gave me the dad speech." Jonah smiled. "It was about time."

"The dad speech?"

"Yeah. He threatened life and limb if I ever broke your heart. I promised that he would never have to do that. It's a tradition of sorts."

"How is that a tradition?"

"Just is. I'm surprised it took him this long."

"Probably because this is the first time he's seen you since we got together."

"Point."

They entered their room and Eva froze in the middle of it. "Do you feel that?"

"Feel what?"

"I don't know. The air ... feels wrong."

Jonah frowned. In his training in the Glade, he'd heard of this feeling. Never experienced it though. "Eva get down!" Jonah tackled Eva to the floor and not a second too soon.

A dagger with a scarlet-covered blade missed them by inches, impaling the wall near Eva's linen closet. Jonah turned to see a figure in the corner who definitely hadn't been there before.

The person was in a full-bodied cloak with gloves that had strangely wicked tips. A hood shadowed the head, with the face obscured by a form-fitting mask that gave nothing away save the ice-cold eyes trained solely on them. Another red blade was already in hand.

This had to be Ange de la Mort. At long last, he'd come for his final target.

Jonah scrambled up and grabbed Eva's arm.

"Eva, we got to move!"

Jonah shoved Eva in front of him, towards the door, as he tried to initiate the Astralimes. Nothing. He grabbed the doorknob seconds before he felt something slice into his shoulder.

No, not something. A dagger. Fire raced from the wound and into his blood. He staggered back as Eva yelled out his name. Everything else was foggy. Jonah barely recognized the impact of his body hitting the floor. He saw Eva drop down next to him. He tried to tell her to run. He tried to warn her when he saw the assassin appear behind her.

He released a silent scream as a thin wire wrapped around Eva's throat. She was so focused on checking him over that she hadn't been watching out for herself.

The assassin jerked her to her feet and she clawed at the wire. Thin trails of blood began to seep from the wound as Eva gagged, gasping for breath that was being stolen from her.

The assassin whispered something and Eva stopped clawing at her throat. She willed a dagger in her hand and thrust it backwards. She missed, but her action was enough to make the bastard release the garrote.

Jonah struggled against the effects of the fire. He had to move, dammit. He had to balance this out. The more he focused on that, the more he could move. But he was struggling to keep his focus on that instead of the fight playing out in front of him.

The bastard had his hands back on Eva. She struck out with her elbow into his throat in two rapid shots before she kicked him square in the stomach.

The assassin dropped back, then rushed her again. He slammed her into a mirror that resulted in the glass shattering around them. Eva had gotten her hands on his hood and had jerked it off. When the bastard reared back to punch her, Jonah got a good look at just who the Ange de la Mort really was. Pierre Bernard. The baguette bitch.

The rage was instant. This fucker had nearly caused a war. Could still cause one. Jonah's rage was so strong, it burned through the sedative. He made his way up to his feet and stumbled over to them. Pierre was so focused on his target, he didn't notice Jonah until he was picked up by his collar and thrown off Eva.

"You wanna fight, Frenchie?" Jonah popped his neck muscles. "Let's go."

Eva was angry as hell, but she was injured. Jonah noticed that her ankle was sprained, possibly broken. She was still trying to catch her breath, despite the wire hanging around her throat. Jonah wanted more than anything to check on her, but his entire focus needed to be on Ange de la Mort.

Pierre.

The bitch boy cast hateful eyes on Jonah, unpleasant surprise giving his features a sharp edge. "So, it was a flesh wound. Inconvenient, but no matter. You might have burned through as only your balance will allow, Blue Aura, but you're still flesh and bone."

Jonah charged Pierre with a roar, and they slammed into the wall. Pierre barely even registered the pain as he gave Jonah two quick body jabs, then kicked him away. Jonah made the mistake of putting weight on the arm that was cut. The poison may have no longer been a factor, but it remained sore, and gave out on him.

Pierre took advantage of Jonah's disorientation and gave him a roundhouse, tumbling him to the ground. "I must admit," he sighed. "I expected more from the big bad Blue Aura. No hit has ever been a challenge, but I at least expected more resistance than *this*."

Jonah ignored the jab. He was still stunned that this baguette-eating coiffed fucker was a seasoned assassin. "What the fuck is wrong with you? You realize your actions could cause genocide?"

Pierre scoffed. "I don't give a shit. I just go where the money is."

"So, you're an assassin and merc on top of being an ass," Jonah snarled. "How much are you getting paid for Eva?"

"True businessmen don't discuss transactions," Pierre replied. "However, this isn't business, it's personal. Imagine my surprise to discover the contract was the same bitch who got me off. Terribly, I might add—"

"Mother—"

Jonah was on his feet before he realized it. Pierre threw a serving tray but Jonah swatted it aside before throwing his forearm full force into Pierre's jaw. Blood flew, but Pierre parried Jonah's next hit and attempted a chokehold. Jonah had practiced chokeholds and submissions for far too long with Reena to ever get caught in one long-term; then Pierre surprised him by restraining his leg when he tried to rake his shin.

"Nice try, Blue Aura," Pierre hissed, "but I'm inveterate at this."

Jonah struggled, but Pierre expertly tightened his grip. Jonah's oxygen was more constricted, and he tried to grind out a gasp that wouldn't come.

"You've quite the nerve, Blue Aura." Pierre sounded angry now. "Dining on *my* leftovers. She wasn't even worth it."

Jonah felt his breath failing as he swung his elbow behind him.

Pierre hooked the arm with his free hand. "What part was unclear, boy?" he hissed. "I can read your every move."

Jonah felt himself fading as instinct overtook him. He let ethereality flow into his free limb until his fingers stung. Then he reached back and tapped Pierre's face. One infinitesimal moment of contact was all that was needed.

His finger sparked Pierre's face and the assassin flew back like he'd been shot, falling into a chair before the thing collapsed under his weight.

The sudden rush of air gave Jonah a headache, but he paid it no mind. "Read *that*, bitch," he snarled.

Pierre growled like an inhuman beast and charged Jonah. Jonah expected that move and sidestepped the assassin, slamming an elbow into his back and shoving him to the ground, where he began to drag him along the floor into the minefield of glass that had been broken earlier. Pierre roared at the pain, which gave Jonah sick pleasure. Pretty Boy wasn't pretty now.

Pierre produced another dagger and ran it across Jonah's forearm. Jonah gritted his teeth and his grip slackened. The bastard took the opportunity to yank Jonah down onto the glass-studded floor with him. He mounted him and the two men grappled. Pierre freed one arm then slammed it into Jonah's chest. The man was stronger than he looked.

He slammed his forearm into Jonah's chest again, but Jonah absorbed the pain just like Thor had taught them, grabbed a shard of glass, and ran it across the side of Pierre's face. Pierre hissed but focused entirely on Jonah as though nothing had happened.

His mistake.

Somehow, Eva managed to get to her feet and slammed one of Jonah's batons across the back of Pierre's head. He howled and loosened his grip, which freed Jonah to wrest free his arms and hook his bleeding opponent into a guillotine chokehold.

Pierre swore and struggled fiercely, but Jonah locked his legs around his waist and held him fast. The assassin roared and fought. Jonah held him, tightening with each protest. Then Jonah saw another red blade come into form in Pierre's hand, like the poison-laced one from earlier.

"No!"

Eva grabbed Pierre's knife hand at the wrist and pulled it back from making contact with Jonah's skin. She twisted the wrist to an awkward angle, until it snapped. Pierre grunted weakly as Jonah had tightened the guillotine to the point that his own arms were hurting from pressure.

Then Pierre gave a final ghost of a wheeze and his entire body slackened.

Ange de la Mort was no more.

Jonah wrested himself free of the now physically lifeless body and lay on the floor. He was in pain and bleeding, but he'd won. As

Thor said a time or two, injuries weren't the focal point. Survival was.

Eva crawled to him. Her adrenaline was likely all gone, as she winced and favored that ankle. "Jonah, are you okay?" she asked breathlessly.

"Peachy," Jonah murmured. "How are you?"

Eva winced again. "No runway walks for a while."

Jonah tried but failed to snicker. "Thank you for your help, Superstar."

"It's like you said," Eva told him, "the way you control a knife fight is to control the knife hand."

"You remember that?"

Eva rearranged her weight so as to reach her phone. "I remember everything you say," she answered. "Now, I'm gonna call for help. They should be able to get in now that he's gone."

"Wait a second."

Jonah reached for Eva and tilted her head up. He unraveled the garrote, then winced at the cut it made. "You sure you're ok?"

"Fine, though I'm a bit disappointed in myself. I should have been able to take him out."

"That's what teamwork is for." Jonah dusted glass off his arms. "Honestly never thought that bastard could be an assassin. He seemed too fragile."

"Me, neither."

Eva stood and went over to the phone. Jonah heard her make the call for the Keepers. Within seconds, Ulysses was walking through the door with Apollo. Both stopped to survey the mess and the corpse.

"Ange de la Mort," Eva pointed to Pierre. "In the flesh."

Apollo glared at the lifeless body. Ulysses' eyes narrowed.

"Eva, is this the man you were seeing prior to Jonah?"

"I don't want to talk about it."

"Evie, you should. Maybe you know something and you don't realize it."

"Obviously not, or I would have killed him in France," she

huffed. "Can you just make him disappear? I want to get Jonah taken care of. He was the one who took him down."

Ulysses sighed and snapped his fingers. Two other Keepers appeared.

"Takos, Merikos," he said, "take this one to the furnace—"

"Wait," Jonah winced as he grabbed his own phone. "Just wait a second before you do that." He hit a number on speed dial and placed it to his ear. "Minks? Come to the address I just texted you. I'm about to get you a promotion."

"Jonah? Where are you?"

"I'm at the Garden of the Gods. The assassin? He's physically dead."

The line went silent.

Jonah frowned. "Minks? You still there?"

"Yes." She cleared her throat. "But I am not allowed to walk on any grounds held by the Olympians. Direct orders. Can you meet me somewhere with the body?"

"No," Jonah insisted. "You haven't come here because someone told you that you couldn't. Nothing is binding you. Get here, now. The Curaie is going to look *profoundly* stupid if they punish the investigator bringing them proof that one of the most notorious Eighth Chapter criminals, who's eluded capture for so long, is now in Spirit and no longer a threat. Know what I mean?"

"Jonah—"

"Get here or don't. He's dead and I'm trying to help you."

Minako sighed. "What're the coordinates?"

"I texted them to you," Jonah repeated. "Now, do you want to be a game changer, or do you want to keep acting like you're still living at Sanctum Arcist?"

That struck a chord, like Jonah knew it would, and Minako responded. "I'll be there soon. And stop saying 'dead'. You know better."

Jonah disconnected before he could say that the bitch was dead again. There was no satisfaction in ending a life under normal circumstances. But this time? There was.

"Minako will be here in a moment."

"We will allow her to collect her evidence before I heal you both."

Jonah nodded just before the winds picked up. Minako stepped out of thin air and surveyed the scene. When her eyes fell on Pierre, she frowned.

"This is Pierre Bernaud," she said. "The Fortune 500 CEO. He was Ange de la Mort?"

"Time out," Jonah looked at her, "how did you know about him?"

Minako looked downward. "I um ... I was a huge fan of his wine. I have a few bottles in my house."

"Smash them and come find me, girl," Apollo said. "I have ale that is leaps and bounds above the contributions of this filth."

Minako threw Apollo and Eva an awkward glance, then focused on Jonah. "I need to take photographs of your injuries, Jonah."

"Ok."

"Do you want to do this in front of an audience?"

"We can step out." Ulysses took Eva's arm. "If Lord Apollo wishes it."

"Indeed. We will stay out in the hallway."

Jonah couldn't help but notice how Eva and Minako had avoided each other. So the second the door closed, he focused on his friend. "Eva isn't your enemy, Minako."

"No, but what she represents is something that is an enemy to my leaders."

"I thought you wouldn't be controlled again." Jonah pulled his shirt over his head as Minako began to snap photos of his cuts. "And yet, here you are."

"I'm not being controlled." She leaned in to take a close-up of his throat. "I am doing what I have to do to survive. I have bills to pay and, if I'm honest, I enjoy my job."

Jonah let that linger until she was finished. When Minako passed him his shirt back, he shook his head.

"Keep it as evidence. It's cut all to hell anyway."

Minako dropped the shirt in a bag and went about taking photos of the room, then the body. She got on the phone and within seconds, the corpse vanished.

"Sent him to the morgue," she explained. "I'm going to get started on my report. Thanks again, Jonah."

"Hold on." Jonah narrowed his eyes at her. "Eva was the target. She had her throat cut. Busted her ankle and god knows what else. Shouldn't you document her injuries, too?"

"Jonah, she doesn't exist to us." Minako held up her hand when he started to protest. "She doesn't. Remember how I told you she was an unmentionable? That goes beyond just saying her name. We are not to recognize her at all. So, even if she was the target? Even if she had been the one to stop the assassin? It wouldn't be recognized by the Curaie."

Jonah sneered. "I mean no harm, Minako, but that's stupid. And if you're buying that, *you* are stupid too. Sorry, not sorry."

"They have their reasons, Jonah. You may not like them, but it's true. And it's not just with her. It's with anyone who has been imprisoned. Criminals are banished. Their existence is erased. It's just protocol."

"Whatever, Minako. You got your assassin. Your case is now closed."

"Jonah, you can't get mad at me for doing my job."

"I'm disappointed, not mad. I thought better of you than how you're acting right now."

Minako rubbed her hand over her eyes, then dropped it. "I am sorry that you feel that way."

"Yeah," Jonah said, looking away from his friend, and slightly saddened by the fact that it seemed like that needed the term "former" in front of it. "I know you are. Now go forth, further your career. I wish you the best."

Minako frowned slightly. "Are you saying goodbye?"

Jonah looked back at her. "I'm saying that he'd be so proud of you right now."

"Who?"

Jonah's expression towards Minako became slightly wistful.

"Gamaliel Kaine, of course. He'd be so proud of you. And the fact that his indoctrination was lifelong."

Minako's lips parted slightly. Jonah's words clearly stung. But Jonah didn't care. He was stung, too.

"And the irony of it all?" He added one last thing. "Kaine created that little Sanctum Arcist because *he* was disillusioned with the Curaie as well. Funny, huh?"

Minako arranged her things and rose. There might have been tears in her eyes. "Goodbye, Jonah."

"Mmm-hmm." Jonah turned away from her and threw a half-hearted wave. "Bye."

Jonah waited until she vanished before he went to open the door. Eva must have noticed something was wrong because she quickened her steps back to his side.

"Jonah?"

"We're good to be healed, though I think we'll have to bunk somewhere else for the night."

"The Curaie member is gone?" Ulysses furrowed his brow. "She failed to speak with Eva."

"Yeah." Jonah decided to save the truth for later. He'd talk to Apollo about it. "Had to get back."

"Very well then."

Apollo clasped Eva's arm and she erupted in gold before the god did the same to Jonah. When the light cleared, neither had a scratch on them.

"We'll take the room next door." Eva linked hands with Jonah. "Thank you."

The two of them went across the hall and Eva shut the door behind them.

"Ok, handsome. Spill it."

Jonah sighed and decided to level with Eva. "The Curaie considers you persona non grata … no surprise there. But what *is* surprising, unpleasantly so, is that your status with them means you don't matter. Even though you were the target, you didn't matter. That's why Minako didn't come to speak with you. You're a nonentity."

Eva's eyes flashed, but they softened when she realized there was more. "You called her 'Minako', not 'Minks'." Did this end your friendship?"

Jonah inhaled deeply and at length. "I don't want anything more to do with her. We know who our friends are among the Curaie. She is no longer one of them."

Eva stepped forward and wrapped him in her arms.

"Jonah, you don't have to lose your friendship with Minako. You don't. People can have different opinions on things, but if there is common ground, you shouldn't throw that away."

"She made it clear that you don't matter, Evie. I won't stand for that."

"Minako is just following orders. She is doing as she must." Eva pulled back a little. "So, if she repeats what the Curaie says now, then she will repeat it once leadership changes hands."

"I can't believe you are defending her."

"I'm not defending her, per se. What I am doing is trying to keep you from throwing away a friendship that means something to you. Please understand that."

Jonah sighed. He didn't appreciate Minako's stance and, now, moments removed, he realized he'd said some hurtful things. Still, Eva was his entire world. To have her treated like this was unnerving and infuriating. But he didn't want to lose his friend. Not after every-thing. "I hurt her, Eva."

Eva hugged him again, unfazed. "In emotional situations, we say shit we don't mean. Clearly, Minako is a good friend because you're hurting. And if she is as good a person as you say, she's hurting, too. We'll just need to give it time. This shit will be sorted out. One way or another."

SEVEN

EVA MCRAYNE

"Chronos is in a hell of a mood today, Representative."

I took my visitor's pass from Glinda at the front desk and snapped it onto my blouse. She passed one to Jonah with a sniff. Chronos must have hurt her feelings or something. Glinda was too damn sensitive anyway. Most nymphs were.

"He's always in a hell of a mood." I took my bag back and slipped it over my shoulder. I fluffed out my hair. "Rec room or private room?"

"Private. He hasn't left it in three days."

"Thanks."

I started down the hallway with Jonah right beside me. We stopped at the elevator and I watched the button with the reversed arrow light up.

"So ... what should I expect?"

"With Chronos? I have no idea. He's always been a bastard, but he's warmed up to me. Mainly, because he recognizes his own stubborn nature."

"When did you start coming to see him?"

"Not long after I found out about him. Three years, I think."

"And you haven't seen him since you were detained?"

"Not in the flesh, no. But as soon as I was released, I started writing to him. We kept in touch through letters. I'd send him trinkets or little rocks I found in France. Chronos seemed to enjoy that."

I stepped into the empty elevator and pressed the button for the basement. "I know you're tough, Jonah, but don't let Chronos get under your skin. He'll act crazy, forgetful, downright mean, but it's all an act. He knows exactly what he's doing."

"So, why do you come here?"

"Because it's awful to be locked away, don't you think? Shielded from the world and people. Thrown in isolation because of who you are."

Jonah didn't say anything, but he placed his hand on my lower back to lead me out when the doors pulled open. I resisted the heat that rushed through me.

Focus, I told myself. *Don't get distracted.*

I stopped in front of a door labeled B4 and knelt to put my hand on the food tray someone had left behind. It was still warm. I picked it up, then knocked.

"Fuck off!" Chronos' voice boomed through the door.

I shifted the weight of the tray, then shook my head when Jonah offered to take it from me.

"My lord," I called out. "You have five seconds to open this door before I pitch a fit so epic, you won't ever recover."

Two seconds later, Chronos jerked open the door with a grin so big, I thought it was gonna sprain his face.

He pulled me into an embrace that made me nearly drop his tray. "Evie! I didn't think you were ever coming back!"

He released me and I looked him over. Chronos appeared to be thirty-eight with a head full of strawberry-blonde hair that I'd convinced him to keep cut. He was lean, but I knew it was only because he refused to eat more often than not.

His grin fell when he saw Jonah standing behind me. "Who the hell are you? What are you doing with my Evie?"

"Chronos, meet Jonah. Jonah, Lord Chronos. My lord, Jonah is my boyfriend and you will be nice to him. Understand?"

"Why should I?"

"Because I asked you nicely and that is enough."

Chronos huffed, then stepped aside. "Leave that shit outside. I'm not eating it."

"Yes, you are." I brought the tray inside his room. It was a wreck. "What the hell have you been doing in here? Having ravers?"

He dropped down in his chair with a pout. I sat the tray on his side table, then pulled it in front of him.

"Eat, milord. Glinda told me how you've been acting out."

Chronos glared at me and I glared right back until he took the lid off his tray. He picked up a plastic fork then began to eat. "I am the lord of time and you are an impertinent girl—"

"One who just loves you to pieces." I patted his arm. "Now, why are you so sour? The dreams again?"

He cut his gaze over at me, then over to Jonah, who had stayed close to the door. "Can I trust him?"

"I do."

"That doesn't mean I can talk in front of him."

"I give you my word. Now, what's wrong? You're a wreck."

"I'm trapped in this damn cage. That's what's wrong!"

"Nope."

"What the hell do you mean, *nope*?" He clattered his tray against the table. "You try being locked away."

"I was, remember? But that's not what's wrong." I studied him for a moment. "Were you truly afraid I wasn't going to come back?"

He hunkered down over his tray as he ate. I patted his arm again.

"Well, I'm here now and our visits can resume. So, talk to me. What's wrong?"

"Memories. I can't shut them out."

He'd grumbled the words, but I'd heard him.

"And don't you dare say they're a result of my meds. I'll bite the very soul out of that damn nurse if you do."

"No, you won't," I laughed. "You're too much of a germaphobe. You wouldn't risk having contact with them."

He grumbled again as he dug into his green beans.

"Jonah is a Ghostly One, milord." I waved Jonah over from his spot by the door. "Jonah, come introduce yourself to Chronos."

Chronos froze, then turned cold eyes up at Jonah. "You a Ghostly One? You one of them bastards responsible for locking up my Evie?"

"No, Jonah was not." I glared at my great-grandfather once again. "Not every Ghostly One is bound by the Curaie."

"Yeah? Let *him* tell me that."

Jonah narrowed his eyes and I knew that Chronos had gotten under his skin. Everybody being written off due to the actions of a few had always been a pet peeve of his.

"Not every Eleventh Percenter is the same, man," he said, "just like not every Olympian is the same."

"I'm no Olympian, boy."

I interrupted their little tiff. "Chronos, behave. Jonah is exceedingly important to me. He has saved my physical life more than once. Apologize, please."

The ancient god grumbled once more as he took another bite of food. He wiped his mouth before he spoke.

"I am sorry, Ghostly One. If you have saved my Evie, then I suppose you are a good sort."

Jonah regarded the Titan. "Apology accepted. If Eva has taken a liking to you, I figure you can't be all bad."

"Why would I be all bad? Because I'm Chronos, the Big Bad Titan?"

Jonah shook his head. "Please stop jumping to conclusions, dude. It's an expression."

"I need your help." I tapped his arm and he turned to look at me. "Typhon is breaking loose."

"How the hell is Typhon loose?"

"Something has broken the barriers. I have to fight him, Pappy."

"No."

"I don't have a choice."

"Yes, you do." He narrowed his eyes. "Say no and run. That is the best thing you can do."

"What kind of hero would I be if I did that?"

"One who is physically alive."

"Look, I am going to fight him. Either you help me or not."

"Evie, you can't. You can't. Zeus—the fool that he is—couldn't defeat him. Why do you think you can?"

"Because I have more than Olympus on my side. I have Jonah."

Chronos gave Jonah an appraising inspection.

Jonah didn't seem to mind. He'd told me previously that he had gotten used to people doubting and second-guessing him all his life. I thought that was sad. He told me he used it to his advantage.

"Tell me boy," he said at last, "what do you know of Typhon?"

Jonah rocked back on his heels. "Father of all monsters, youngest son of Gaia and Tartarus, hundred dragon heads, personification of volcanic activity—"

"As I suspected," Chronos interrupted him with an impatient wave of his hand. "You know nothing. Spouting attributes and accolades is impressive, boy ... if your goal is to make a fool of yourself. You know the who. You know the what. But you are wholly unaware of the why."

"What are you talking about?" I asked, curious now. "What do you mean when you say the 'why'?"

Chronos returned his gaze to me. "Typhon exists for one reason, and one reason only. Because someone coaxed Gaia and Tartarus into conceiving him."

"What!" Jonah straightened, taken aback. "Who would do such a thing?"

Chronos raised an eyebrow. "If you want that information, you need to do something for me."

"I'll help you regardless, Pappy." I tapped the back of his hand. "All you have to do is ask. What can I do for you?"

Chronos glanced down at his hands before he lifted his head. "There was a Titaness I loved once. Eurynome. I wish to know how she is and if she is happy."

"Eurynome?" Jonah blinked. "Zeus' wife?"

"What?" I frowned as I tried to recognize the name Chronos had said. I got nothing. "That can't be right, Jonah. Hera was Zeus' wife."

"Hera was Zeus' seventh wife, Superstar. Eurynome was the third. She was there long before Hera."

Chronos looked at Jonah, stunned. "How do you know these things?"

Jonah shrugged. "If there was any benefit to growing up with no friends, it was that I had a lot of time to read."

Chronos was silent.

Jonah sat near him. "The nightmares are from losing her, aren't they?" he asked gently. "But why now? You've been here forever. Why are you hurting so badly for Eurynome now?"

Chronos twisted his fingers in his lap as he studied them. "I loved that girl," he finally muttered. "I loved her the most and she's gone."

I clasped his hand and he stopped fiddling with his fingers.

He studied me as he continued. "When you love someone ..." His voice caught before he tried again. Chronos turned his focus onto Jonah. "When you genuinely love someone, it is like a knife to the throat when they are gone. Time made it a little easier, but not much. One day, you will know my words to be true, Blue Aura."

"I understand exactly what you mean." Jonah cleared his throat as he met my gaze. "That's why I am here. Now, Eurynome can't be gone. Immortal means immortal. Where is she, Chronos? Was she punished, too? Was she in the war, or was she a peaceful Titan, like Calypso and Eos?"

"She was peaceful. That's what saved her. I tried." He swallowed his emotions, but we still heard them. "I tried to save her from the madness. Zeus stole her from me. A prize from the war. I despise him more for taking my sweet Eury than for anything else."

"Do you think we could find her?" I asked. "Surely, she would come—"

"No!" He looked at me with pure fear. "Please, Evie. Please. I can't let her see me like this. Not this broken shell. Please."

"Ok," I responded softly. "Ok, Chronos. Calm down. We can make you and this room presentable, but you have to be calm."

Jonah, without warning, grabbed Chronos with blue-gleaming fingers. The Titan gasped, but then some of the focus came back into his eyes. He looked over at Jonah.

"What did you do?" he demanded. "Did you fix me?"

"Of course not," Jonah answered. "Your pain runs deep. It'll take months, at minimum, for my balance to be permanent. I just gave you a boost. Good for ... forty-eight hours, give or take? Enough to see Eury. Now, where is she?"

"I can't leave here," he grumbled. "These walls are my prison."

"Then we will go find her."

Chronos looked at me with a twisted expression I couldn't put a label on. "You would do this? You would bring my Eury to me?"

"Of course, you deserve to be happy. You deserve to be loved no matter what happened in the past."

"Her name is Sara now. Sara Milton. She works as a nurse at Seattle General."

I got out my phone and did a quick search. I found exactly what I was looking for, then stood up. "Excuse me for a second."

It didn't take long to talk to the Titaness. She was elated and promised to be at the facility in thirty minutes. When I returned, I noticed Jonah and Chronos glaring at each other. I focused on Chronos first.

"Let's get you cleaned up, my lord. Eurynome can't see you like this." I gave Jonah a curious look before I pushed Chronos towards the bathroom. "You go shower and shave. You have twenty minutes before she gets here, milord."

He glanced around the room, but I waved my hands to shoo him away.

"Go. I'll straighten up the mess."

"You gonna push everything under the bed?" Chronos grinned.

"Don't question my methods," I joked. When he closed the door, I turned towards Jonah. "Did he say something to you? You look upset, Jonah."

Jonah scoffed. "Just an old man trying to give free advice. Whatever. Let's clean this pigsty."

"You sit." I waved him back into the chair. "I got this."

I started picking up the clothes and tossing the magazines Chronos had ripped to shreds.

"You talked to Eurynome?"

"I did. Found her number on Google." I swept the contents on Chronos' nightstand into the trash can. "She was shocked, of course.

She had no idea that Chronos was here. That, I'm sure, was done by design. Zeus didn't want anyone to know he was still alive."

"I wonder if she even loved Zeus?" Jonah mused aloud. "I mean, I'm not a traitor or anything, never that, but the gods have done their fair share of questionable things, too. I hope Zeus didn't marry her just to flick off Chronos."

"It's possible. The stories I've managed to read illustrate how love and sex are often used as a weapon. What better way to cement his victory over Chronos than by taking away the woman he loves?"

I pulled out the extra sheets and pillowcases.

"Let me help." Jonah took the sheet from my hands. "Least I can do."

"You've done so much already, Jonah." I studied his face and settled on his eyes. "Truly. I can't thank you enough for being here."

"There is nowhere else I'd rather be. Chronos, like the rest of them, ain't perfect. But a lot of it came from pain. Pain has a way of making things seem rational."

"I can think of somewhere else you would rather be." I shook out the flat sheet next. "That three-story bookstore I am going to take you to when we leave here. I'm just going to sit at the coffee shop downstairs and let you run wild."

"Nope," Jonah responded. "Life is more fulfilling and fun with you anyway."

"It's more fun with you too, handsome." I blew him a kiss across the bed. "And that other word you used."

"Fulfilling?"

"Uh-huh." I threw the dirty laundry in the basket located at the back of the closet. I returned then started making the bed. "You make everything exciting. More real and satisfying."

Chronos shuffled out of the bathroom before Jonah could respond. He had changed into a fresh t-shirt and lounge pants worn by the patients. We heard a knock on the door and I went to open it. On the other side was a petite woman with black hair piled up in a bun on top of her regal head.

"Representative, you said —"

"Eury."

Chronos choked out her name and I stepped aside as the two of them stared at each other. The newcomer dashed into the room, then the two of them crushed each other in a hug that was full of laughter. Joy.

I moved over next to Jonah and wiped at the tears forming in my eyes.

He glanced down at me before he whispered. "You alright?"

"Yes," I whispered back with a nod. "I'm just happy for them."

"We'll come back around six." Jonah tightened his arm around my waist. "We can speak then, sir."

Chronos barely heard him. He barely noticed us at all as he focused on the woman who had been lost to him so long ago.

———

We returned to Chronos after spending the day walking the streets of Seattle. He was in such high spirits that he was almost unrecognizable.

Jonah released my hand and extended it to Chronos. "Who are you and what did you do with the cranky curmudgeon who lived here?" he teased.

"Silence, boy," Chronos said, but his tone and expression were so warm as he took Jonah's hand, that it wasn't even a jab. "I am thankful for all that you have done for me. May the Fates smile on you always."

The Titan released Jonah's hand and seated himself, inviting us to join him. "I am not going to stall time; it's never been how I do things. I vowed to give you information if you helped me, and so I shall."

I took Jonah's hand again. I felt like I'd need support for whatever Chronos was about to tell us.

"You know my story. I could keep you here for years on end, detailing how my actions in the past were far just and noble but, time locked away, if nothing else, leads to perspective. And if my words can help you at all, then I consider it the beginnings of work … chipping away at the masterpiece that is my redemption. Now then, I told you that someone coaxed Gaia and Tartarus into conceiving Typhon."

"You did." I didn't want to rush him, but I *did* want to rush him. The lord of time was nothing if not vexing when he got longwinded. Believe me. "Who would do such a thing?"

"Someone who wanted a god more powerful than Zeus in existence."

"Who is this god?" Jonah asked. "What would he have to gain by having someone more powerful than Zeus in the mix?"

Chronos smiled without mirth. "It's a goddess, boy. She's my third eldest daughter."

Jonah's eyes widened and his face went white. That scared the hell out of me.

"Who are you talking about?" I frowned at Chronos. "Who is your third daughter?"

My great-grandfather eyed me again. "Which of my daughters are you most familiar with, my girl?"

Now, I was the one who paled. My voice came out in a hoarse whisper. "Hera."

Chronos nodded. "Yes. That bitch is the reason Typhon lives. She was angry at Zeus' indiscretions and wanted to put him in check. Typhon was the result."

I couldn't breathe. I thought I was going to pass out from lack of oxygen.

Jonah must have overcome his own shock because he wrapped an arm around my waist to hold me upright. "Breathe, Superstar."

I tried. It came out in short gasps as I sat down. Hera was so hellbent on seeing me dead that she was willing to unleash a monster onto the world? She was willing to kill untold millions just to put me in the grave?

I forced myself to count backwards and focus on the numbers. I raised my head when my breathing went steady. "Why?" I managed. "Why would she hate me so much?"

"I adore you, child, but it is not you who has captured my daughter's hatred. Not the way you think." Chronos took my hand to study my palm. "Hera has always had a secret hatred for her husband.

Always. She shrouded it with devotion, but as Zeus' power waned, so too did her patience. She began to interact with other pantheons in search of power."

"I know that," I whispered. "She infiltrated the Native American pantheon. That's how she turned a former acquaintance of mine into a skinwalker."

"Hera's goal with you was to see the curse of the demigods come to pass."

"The what?"

"The curse of the demigods," he explained. "Have you ever wondered why you are in constant danger? Why you are always a target?"

"Yes."

"There is your reason. And it will always be so. Any person who is half-man half-god will suffer from that fate. Gaia herself put it into motion in the hopes that her offspring would stop consulting with mortals. As you can see, it didn't work."

Jonah bristled. "So, Gaia had a grudge against demigods as well?"

"At one time, yes," Chronos answered. "Mortals, too. ...There was a reason the first Four Ages were called the times when men were free of knowledge."

"You said that, Chronos," Jonah murmured. "According to lore, anyway."

"Guilty," Chronos concurred. "As I said, I was far from a just being. Eventually, Gaia warmed to mortals like many beings in many pantheons, but those incantations she put in back then were ancient. Powerful. Likely to never be undone. But Hera's hatred of demigods is absolute.

"She is the goddess of marriage and family, so the gods having half-mortal offspring is the biggest slap in the face there is. She experiences blood rage in regard to faithlessness, and gets especially irascible when her colleagues' shrines are enriched through the actions of demigods, as she has no demigod children herself—plus, she prefers the old ways when gods were superior and consorted with no one else. Look through history and you will see examples of her anger and jealousy everywhere. But you, dear Eva ... you have aroused her ire more so than even Heracles."

"I don't understand." I leaned back and rubbed my forehead. "I didn't know her prior to Elliott."

"Ah, but she knew of you. See, Hera made a declaration about seven hundred years or so ago, after Zeus got caught with an aristocrat in Prague. No god shall consort with humans. He seconded her decree since he was tired of hearing her bitch at him."

"And?"

"And Apollo broke that decree. Since you were the result, Hera focused her hatred onto you."

"Do you really think she raised Typhon just out of spite?"

"It's possible." Chronos patted my hand. "'Tis why I want you to run. If your Ghostly One knows what's best for you, he'd take you to another realm and vanish."

"I couldn't live with myself, safely in another realm, knowing it was in my power to end Typhon once and for all."

"You won't be able to live with yourself if you face him, period," Chronos told me. "Because my dear, it's suicide."

I glanced over to Jonah, who had pressed his hand over his mouth. He caught my eye and gave me a quick shake of the head. I knew that meant we'd talk sooner rather than later.

"I am being sent to Japan. Something about Poseidon's shrines being disrupted as part of the barriers breaking." I focused on the information I needed instead of the ominous words Chronos had spoken. "Is there a connection?"

"Aye. Where the monster treads, the powers of the gods are weakened. They may help you, but they risk their existence as well."

"The gods can't pass into spirit."

"They very much can, child. They very much can."

"What?" Jonah said, stunned. "I thought immortal meant immortal."

"It does," Chronos responded. "Until it doesn't. Gods don't pass like mortals do, but it can happen. How do you think other pantheons weaken to nothing?"

I needed to talk to Jonah. I needed to tell him to run as far away from Typhon and the Olympians as possible. I wanted him with me —there was no one else I trusted by my side. But I wanted him alive. Healthy. Not fighting against Hera's creation.

I had other things to tell him. Just in case I failed. I needed to tell him about my will. I needed to tell him that the Olympians who remained would either leave me to rot on Poveglia or send me into the ether ... with fanfare and a grave covered in golden roses.

I couldn't. Not with Chronos present. I had to seem confident. Sure that I could beat the father of monsters.

"We'll be fine." I settled on that phrase. "All of us. So, tell me how to kill him so we can get this done."

"Aim for the spine," Chronos grumbled. "The head that reacts is the head you have to cut off."

"Why didn't Zeus do that before?" Jonah wanted to know. Maybe knowledge gathering would help him power through his nerves. "Why did he just kill him instead of banishing him?"

"Typhon's vulnerabilities weren't common knowledge," Chronos replied. "Hera would've seen to that. Plus, as I said, Zeus is a fool."

"Anything else I need to know, aside from running away like my hair is on fire?"

"No. Just ... don't go, Evie."

I stood and he did as well. My talk with Chronos had done nothing to ease my mind. I pulled him into a hug and he held me so tight, I tapped his arm to get him to let up a little.

He whispered words in an ancient language that I didn't understand before he released me. I kissed him on the cheek and gave him my love. When Jonah and I reached the door, Chronos called out to us.

"Take care of her, Ghostly One. Otherwise, your days will be dark ones."

"I always will, Chronos, and I respect your caring for Eva's well-being," Jonah replied. "But all due respect, please don't threaten me. I don't respond well to that."

Chronos looked over Jonah, then smiled at me. "I like this one," he said simply.

I rolled my eyes and blew him a kiss goodbye.

As we walked to the front desk, Jonah nudged me with his arm. "This one? How many people you bring to see Chronos?"

"Just you." I hooked a hand around his arm. "You ok? You handled him very well."

"Once I pegged him for a lovesick dude, it was fine," Jonah answered. "You have no idea how much sex can purge negative emotions."

"Oh, I do, handsome." I made my voice provocative. "I do."

Jonah grinned at my tone. "When do we have to be in Japan?"

"Tomorrow." I tossed my visitor badge on the desk, then grabbed the front of Jonah's shirt to pull him towards me. "Which means we can find a nice room in here in Seattle for the night if you are interested."

"Baby, I'm never *not* interested," Jonah said. "Let's go!"

I laughed when he initiated the Astralimes. He nipped at my nose as we emerged in an alley not far from downtown Seattle. As we walked, we discussed the city. He had been here before because of Vera Haliday, but his memories weren't good ones.

I wanted to change that. I *would* change that. No matter what happened in Italy, I wanted Jonah to remember this city in a good light. Just as I wanted him to remember me.

———

"You ready, Superstar?"

"I suppose." I turned from the mirror to kiss Jonah quickly. "Joey just texted me. He is at the hotel."

Jonah's expression darkened.

I went back to brushing my hair. "You gonna be ok around him, handsome?"

Jonah hesitated before he answered. "I have my balancing power to fall back on in the event of issues. Besides, the Curaie may have turned a blind eye to him, but courtesy of Hermes and Patience, his life has been pretty fucked up, too. I'm kinda loving that."

I gave him a small smile before I tossed my brush in the bag and Jonah spoke again.

"So, what are you going to be doing for the show?"

"We're going to investigate the legend of a spirit hitchhiker." I locked our hands together. "You can ride with me when we do that part."

"You're going to drive?" Jonah raised his eyebrows as a small smile played on his lips. "You sure?"

"How hard can it be? It's just on the different side of the road." I gave Jonah a shrewd expression. "Besides, I know you don't trust Joey to drive."

"Not in the slightest, " Jonah answered.

"Do you think he's still using, handsome?"

"I wouldn't be surprised, but I don't know how he could afford it."

"Let's get this over with." I squeezed his hands. "I am ready to go back home. I miss our little house and the sea and peeking in your writing room to see you lost in another world."

"I miss that, too," Jonah stated, "but not as much as I miss you coming in just to distract me."

"It doesn't work," I laughed. "You keep on writing."

"Like hell it doesn't."

Jonah initiated the Astralimes and we appeared in the lobby of the hotel we would be staying at for the next three nights.

I spotted Joey Lawson for the first time in over a year leaning against the front counter and flirting with the clerk. He looked good. Relaxed and tanned. Designer clothes that seemed right out of a magazine. Jonah tensed up beside me again.

"I don't think it worked." I whispered to my beloved. "Or maybe, he has another benefactor."

Joey spotted us and came over with a smug smile.

"Baby girl!" His voice was boisterous. Jubilant. "Look at you!"

He opened his arms wide for a hug, but when he stepped in, I calmly raised a hand and placed it on his chest. I took a step back for extra measure.

"Nah, Joey," I said, "I'm good."

"Hey, J. Didn't realize you'd be with us for this." Joey extended his hand, then dropped it when Jonah didn't take it. "Ok. So, I wasn't expecting this to be so awkward."

"A lot has changed in the past year. A whole lot."

Joey frowned slightly. "You're still hung up on that drug mess?"

Jonah stared back at him. "Yes, Joseph. Very much so."

Now Joey looked unpleasantly surprised. "Joseph? It's like that now?"

"It's been like that for a year," Jonah informed him coolly. "You are the only one who it's a revelation to, believe me."

Joey turned his focus onto me. "Listen, there's so much we need to talk about. I need to speak to you alone, Evie."

"If it has to do with *Grave*, then great. If it has to do with anything else, I'm *not* interested."

"Come on, Evie!"

"No. I lost six months of my life because of you," I snapped. "I think that you should consider the fact that I am speaking to you as a blessing.

Joey looked scandalized. "I had a human moment and you hold it against me?"

"You had an asshole moment," Jonah corrected him. "And yeah. It's gonna be held against you for a long time."

"Alright. Fine. You gonna tell me what we're doing?"

"Not right now." I took Jonah's hand, then squeezed it. I was proud of him. He hadn't reached for his batons once. "Go rest up. We'll meet you back here at midnight."

Joey gave us one long look before he noticed our hands. He raised his eyebrows and, unfortunately, Jonah noticed.

"You got a problem, Joseph?"

"Nah, man. No problem. Glad to see you finally added Eva to your list."

Jonah bristled, and focused. "Thank you. I wondered what wayward dude you're screwing now. The getup and tan are a dead giveaway."

Joey's eyes flashed, but Jonah was stone-cold calm. Joey couldn't hurt him, even in his dreams. "Oh and if you're inclined to go snitch to

Conner that I'm here with Eva, two things: one, he already knows and, two, Apollo put the fear of God in Conner right after Eva got locked up for you. So, the iron fist he once had over her? Hell and gone. Sorry."

Joey stiffened but didn't say anything. He stormed away, but I didn't relax until he was on the elevator.

"You did so well, handsome." I leaned up to give kiss Jonah a quick kiss. "Balanced?"

"Like you wouldn't believe, baby."

I led Jonah over to the desk and took the key the woman gave me. I passed it over to him, then led the way upstairs. "Have you ever been to Japan before, Jonah?"

"Nope," Jonah replied. "I'm excited about it though. You?"

"A few times. Tokyo is a souped-up New York, but Kyoto is lovely. Maybe we can come back on vacation someday. I think you would love the historical aspects of the country."

"If you ever let me leave the bedroom," he teased as we found our room on the second floor. He unlocked the door, then held it open for me. "Ladies first."

I strolled inside, pleasantly surprised by the oriental decor with small western touches. "Oh, this is lovely." I faced him. "And so are you. Why would you ever want to leave it?"

"I wouldn't," he grinned. "I was just stating fact."

"Jonah, I want you to listen to me." I kept my eyes trained on his face. "Listen. If anything happens to me—"

"It won't."

"If it does, I want you to be prepared for that." I tightened my grip on his hand. "I want you to go to Charles Stephens, my lawyer. He has a copy of my will, which leaves everything to you. I want you to take everything, Jonah, and then find a way to escape the earth plane. Promise me?"

"Eva, I don't want to think like that. You've thrived over monsters before; why can't you do so now?"

"I'm not saying that we won't beat him, but I do want you to be ready for any outcome. Please. Just promise?"

"How long have I been the benefactor of your estate?"

"For two and a half years." I dropped his hand. "What belongs to Olympus will go back to the coffers. Everything else goes to you."

Jonah sighed. "Eva, my love, may I say something? You always, and I do mean *always*, shut me down when I mention my mortality. So, how can you expect me to be receptive to you talking about ... any outcome?"

"You have a point. A good one. But—"

"But we're going to get through this. We'll get through this and anything else that our enemies throw at us." He stepped closer to me and ran his hand over my hair. "So, don't talk about your life ending."

"Jonah, if it comes down to me and you, I'm sacrificing myself. You must know that. I don't want to imagine a world without you in it. Ever."

Jonah pulled me against him. He held me so tight against him, I had no choice but to hold him back. "My feelings exactly. I'm a lot less significant than you are, Eva. A house of people needs me. An entire *kingdom* needs you."

"And I need you more than any house or any kingdom."

"We'll take him down. Easy. And when this is over, we'll keep living. You'll keep doing *Grave*. I'll keep harassing Joseph. It'll be fun."

I just held him. I didn't know what else to do. I didn't know what else to say. Jonah was the most valuable asset I had. My most valuable treasure.

"You wouldn't consider staying off the battlefield, would you?" I rested my chin against his stomach as I looked up at him. "Somewhere safe. Where I can wrap you in bubble wrap or something?"

"Not a chance," Jonah smiled, but was dead serious. "Chronos said you have to perform the kill, but it'll take a team to get close. You'll have one."

"You didn't—"

"You're right, I didn't," he told me. "They volunteered. Everyone on my call back to the estate: Terrence, Reena, Spader. Liz wanted to come, but bless her, she's trying to get on as a member of the Green Team, which is the name of the medical practitioners at Spirits of

Mercy. That's the biggest ethereal hospital in the Southern United States. But she did make us promise to contact her if we needed the assistance of a Green Aura. But Terrence, Reena, and Spader? They're pooling funds as we speak—for tickets to come here."

"I'll pay for their tickets." I released him. "Get them on the phone. Find out if they want to meet us here or in Italy, and use my credit card."

"Are you sure?"

"Yes." I willed his phone in my hand and passed it over. "Have them meet us in Venice on Thursday. That will give us time to know what we are dealing with."

"Yes, ma'am." Jonah kissed me quick. "It sounds like a plan."

Jonah's phone rang in his hand and his expression darkened when he looked at the screen. He answered so that I knew exactly who was on the other line.

"Minako. What can I do for you?"

Jonah went silent, then rubbed his forehead. "You were there—"

Another round of silence. Jonah looked up to the ceiling, then responded.

"Alright. I'll be there in less than five minutes."

He disconnected and I tilted my head at him. "You have to go?"

"Yeah. Minako needs me to give a statement about the fight with that French bastard." Jonah tucked his phone in his back pocket. "I'll be back as soon as I can."

"Ok."

"Are you going to be ok with Joseph if I don't make it back by midnight?"

I snorted. "Of course, I will be. Don't worry about me, handsome. I can handle it."

Jonah leaned forward to kiss me goodbye. Within moments, he was gone. I stared at the spot where he had been as I considered what we were going to do tonight. I considered Jonah's question about Joey. Before the shootout at LaGuardia, I trusted Joey with my life. Now, I knew better.

EIGHT

JONAH ROWE

JONAH WASN'T happy to leave Eva in Japan with only Joseph as back-up. As if the disgraced cameraman could actually back her up. But Minako had dropped a bomb on him that he couldn't ignore. She'd told him that the investigation into the assassin had uncovered disruptions in the spirits in Japan that could not be explained. When she had mentioned something about shrines, Jonah knew he had to go back to the estate. Minako had no idea about Typhon, and they sure as hell didn't need Curaie agents on the battlefield in Italy.

Jonah used the Astralimes to the hall that led to Jonathan's study. It was easier that way. He didn't want to run into any of his family members while he was there. They'd hold him up and he needed to get back to Japan as soon as possible. But he had to do this first. No matter what had happened between himself and Minako.

He knocked on the door and stepped in to see the room was full. Minako, Jonathan, Reena, Terrence, and Spader all sat around the office. Fabulous.

"Hey, people."

"Jonah, you're just in time." Jonathan gestured to the empty seat next to Reena. "Please, join us. Minako was just getting started."

Jonah took the seat, then leaned forward. He clasped his hands together in his lap. Minako threw him an awkward look before she spoke.

"Protector Guide, we have gotten reports from spirits that the seas are angry." Minako frowned. "And they tell us of shrines being disrupted and that the assassin was a cause of it, but we are at a loss. I was hoping we could put our minds together to figure this out."

The Protector Guide sat back and steeped his fingers. "Where did this information come from, Minako?" he asked. "Poseidon himself?"

"No," Minako answered, "it came from Delphin and the Nereids. They met with us when the Spirit Guides refused to see them."

Of course, the leaders of the Curaie would refuse to see representatives of the Olympian Council. It was yet another snub against a group who were supposed to be their allies. Instead, the old guards kept pushing and pushing. Maybe they wanted a war, after all.

"Delphin?" Jonah asked. "The dolphin thing?"

"Delphin can take human shape, should he wish to," Minako said. "And he got it from a couple of Nereids that the shrines they've been assigned to have been desecrated."

"How have they been desecrated?"

Minako pulled out her phone and typed in a code. She pulled up a file and passed it over to Reena in response to her question. Jonah leaned over her shoulder to look at the image of an altar—or, at least, a table that used to be one. The cloth was ripped to shreds. The offering bowls were shattered. There was obvious water damage to the walls behind it.

"No wonder Poseidon isn't happy." Reena whistled before she stiffened next to Jonah. She turned to him and narrowed her eyes. "You knew about this already."

"Guilty," Jonah shrugged. "What I can't figure out is how the French bastard is tied to all this."

"Once we had his corpse, we raided his homes," Minako explained. "We found documents detailing the disruption of the shrines. Since the Olympians had contacted us prior to the assassin's passing, we recognized the connection between the shrines and him."

"Eva was right. This was an inside job then."

"What do you mean?"

Jonah ran his tongue over his teeth. "She is in Japan right now to see the disrupted shrines for herself. It has to do with a monster being set loose upon the world."

"A monster?" Minako sounded skeptical. "A *real* one?"

"Apparently so. Typhon. He was bound in a prison under the ocean. Something has broken the barriers of that prison in an attempt to get him free. We just don't know why. Not really."

"Who do you think could have caused this?"

Jonathan looked over the picture. "The first thing that comes to mind is pettiness and sabotage. Minako; have you heard of anyone under the sea causing strife?"

"Most recently, a river god by the name of Scamander made waves, no pun intended, by defecting to the Titans," Minako replied. "Scamander's scope is small; he's just a minor river god, after all. But Poseidon was pissed because it put him in an awkward position, as Scamander is married to Rhode, one of Poseidon's daughters."

"So, he's a possibility." Reena tapped her fingers against her chin. "Who else?"

"Given the scale of the vandalism, we aren't sure." Minako frowned again. "You see, it's not just one or two shrines that have been destroyed. So far, there have been three. Spread out around the coastlines of the world. The most recent was in 2011. Minamihama. The entire town's population was swept away in a tsunami."

"That's a natural disaster. They happen all the time now, thanks to global warming," Reena pointed out.

"True, but surveillance of the town that remained found that every citizen had an altar to Poseidon. And every one of them had been destroyed in the exact same manner."

"Ok." Spader dropped down in the chair next to her. "So, now, I get to ask the million-dollar question: is this Scamander dude powerful enough to do that?"

"That's a good question," Jonah nodded. "I mean, he might be a minor god, but he is still a god. Maybe he has enough hatred towards the Council that he would work with the Titans to raise the monster?"

This was good. Better than thinking that Hera, damn her to hell, could still be plotting and scheming despite the state they had put her in.

"Scamander is strongest in his domain, which is rivers," Minako said. "He's a dampened deity in a true ocean. He's been fickle and petty since forever. He joined the Trojan War just because Achilles insulted him. He tried to kill Achilles in the Trojan War but failed three times."

"Can we see a map of the places you described?" Reena parked herself next to Spader as Minako took her phone back. "I want to see if there is a connection."

"Sure."

Minako fiddled with her phone, then passed it back to Reena. Where the image of the altar had been before was now a map with three red dots. One was in New Zealand. The second was in Madagascar. And the third was in Japan.

"Over the past ten years, each of these locations has suffered the same fate." Minako leaned forward. "The only town not to rebuild was Minamihama. It has been abandoned by the Japanese government completely."

Ten years? Hera hadn't been after Eva for that long. Hell, Eva hadn't been the Sibyl that long. She'd had the role for eight years, not ten. Jonah frowned as he considered his conversation with Chronos. Maybe Hera's true motive was to get back at Zeus? The ancient Titan had said something about how deep her hatred ran for her husband. That made sense.

"Ok. Here's what I don't understand." Spader crossed a leg over his knee. "Why is the Curiae involved? Especially now?"

"Because, with the threat of war with the Olympians, they are looking for *any* reason to blame the Council for wrongdoing. And since the spirits are angry," Minako repeated, "the energies in these lands have begun to affect Eleventh Percenters. Some have become more prone to violence. Outbursts of anger. It's caused quite a bit of discord amongst our people."

"Ah." Jonathan nodded. "Minako, be frank with me. The Curaie knew it crossed a line when they imprisoned the Representative of

Olympus. Now, they are looking for any reason to point fingers back at the Olympians. This is a perfect opportunity."

Minako nodded. "You guys are the best at making connections, so I came here."

"Answer me this, Minako," Jonah said. "Are there *any* connections you know of between ethereal humans and the sea? It might help to determine a source."

"The only connection is the energies of the sea and how it affects us," Minako responded. "Think about it. When you are by the sea on a clear, calm day, how do you feel? Have you ever been next to the sea during a storm? It affects us so much more than the average Tenth."

Jonathan nodded. "I believe conversations are in order. Scamander is in the wind, so that's not a possibility. Where is his wife, Rhode? Do you know, Minako?"

"She works as a marine biologist under the name Himari Naka-mura. She's at Waseda University in Shinjuku City."

"I was going to head back to Japan after this meeting," Jonah said, "but do you want company in Shinjuku City? Maybe if we figure this out, it can help Eva in her investigation."

"I think we should go after Rhode ourselves." Reena stood. "Things are okay here in Rome, right, Jonathan? That way, we don't have to add any more to Eva's plate than what's already on it."

"I agree," Jonathan stated. "It's quiet here. Go on and see what Rhode has to say. If her estranged husband *is* the guilty party, he will have hell from two different realms."

Minako pulled up the coordinates on her phone, texted them to the group, and then pocketed her phone.

"I'll see you at this location in less than five minutes."

"Where are we meeting?"

"In the common area of the uUniversity where Rhode works." Minako gave them a small salute. "I will see you there."

"I'm going to change." Spader yawned. "I'll come, too."

"This makes more sense than us trying to spend money on airline tickets." Reena began to initiate the Astralimes. "We can be there in seconds."

Jonah initiated the Astralimes as well. When he stepped out onto the campus, next to Reena, he felt a force so strong, he damn near fell to his knees.

"Jonah?" Reena caught him. "What the hell? What's wrong?"

Jonah felt like he'd just been slapped by a brick. A dozen bricks. He tightened his eyes and lost his breath all at once. "The balance," he gasped. "This ... place is all ... all out of whack ... how is your essence not overloading?"

"I don't know." Reena hooked his arm around her shoulders. "I'm taking you back home. You can't be here."

She pulled them both through the Astralimes and back into Jonathan's study. She lowered Jonah onto the sofa as Jonathan stood.

"What's wrong?"

Jonah took some time to collect himself. It literally felt as if he'd been pulled up from underneath the water and could breathe once more. "We touched ground at Waseda University," he began. "And I just ... it was like the air turned on me."

"You damn fool," Spader scoffed as he returned. "Why didn't you wait for me?"

"Your presence would have made little to no difference, Royal," Jonathan said. "*This*, however, will." He held up a long chain about the length of a rosary. "If you want to help your Eva, you, like Reena, will need a dampener."

"A dampener?" Jonah rubbed his face before he took it from Jonathan and slipped it on. "Jonathan, why? What the hell is so wrong in that country that I need a dampener for balance?"

"That is what you were searching for before you got derailed." Jonathan clasped him on the shoulder. "Now, you are prepared, son."

"Yeah," Spader agreed. "Now, let's go as a group."

Another set of steps and they were back in the common area of Waseda University. Reena and Spader gave a wary eye to Jonah, who was equally as leery. But Jonathan's dampener worked perfectly. No constriction. No compression. All was well. He nodded.

"Did the trick," he said. "I'm great."

"Awesome," Spader said. "Now, this Rhode lady ... how does a Greek goddess pass for a Japanese biologist?"

"You've never seen her, dad," Jonah said. "Gods can look however they choose, and Poseidon resembles a Japanese man. It only makes sense that he has offspring who look Japanese, too."

"Uh-huh," Spader said. "Next question. Who here can speak and/or read Japanese?"

"You don't have to be able to do that."

They turned to see Minako approaching.

She gave them a small smile. "English is taught in the schools here. I bet most of the students can speak English better than you can."

"So, how do we find her?"

"Easy."

Minako headed over to a table where two girls were giggling with their heads together. She began to speak with them in rapid-fire Japanese. When the three women bowed to each other, Minako trotted back over to them.

"Rhode is in the science building." She turned towards her right. "We're lucky she's here today. The girls said she only comes on campus twice a week."

"Huh?" Jonah looked surprised. "What kind of George Jetson job does she have?"

"On campus, J," Minako smiled at him. It was a little less uneasy now. "She researches underneath the ocean the other days."

"Then we *are* lucky."

"It's my specialty, Minks." Spader threw his arm around her shoulders. "I'm everybody's lucky charm."

"So you say."

She laughed as they walked in front of Jonah and Reena.

Reena tucked her hands in her pockets and bumped Jonah with her elbow. "You ok? We can handle this if you aren't."

"I'm ok." Jonah ran his fingers along the chain. "I really am, thanks to Jonathan. I have to say, I had no idea what it's like for you without one—until that moment."

"Like a soccer kick to the head." She gave him a quick smile. "You know, I've never been to Japan before. Always wanted to come here. Maybe when we get whatever Greek hell this is over with, I can bring Kendall here."

"Kendall's wanderlust is legendary," Jonah said. "Were it up to her, the two of you would likely be on voyages every month."

"She does love to travel," Reena chuckled. "But there are times where I have to rein her in. Who the hell wants to go to Iceland in January? Really?"

"Kendall is an interesting woman," Jonah said. "I mean, she likes Baja in the dead of summer. So, maybe it's a thrill. But I love her need for a thrill. Matches my own."

"You think so?" Reena smirked at him. "Fine. Then I'm volunteering you next time she wants to tour Egypt in August."

"I'm game," Jonah responded. "I've wanted to go to Egypt since having to do a report on the country in eighth grade."

"You say that now. Wait until you're on the back of a camel under a sun that is so hot, your hair is on fire." Reena reached up to muss his hair with a grin. "While I stay at the estate with this little thing called air-conditioning."

Minako stopped in front of a building and frowned at the Japanese characters over the door. "This is it. Her office is on the second floor."

"Lead the way, Minks."

The group followed Minako up a wooden staircase to a second floor filled with students milling around. Jonah flashed back to his own college days back in South Carolina as they wove through the crowd to stop in front of a door. Once again, the signage posted was in Japanese. Minako read it, then knocked.

A woman responded and Minako opened the door. When they stepped inside the tiny office, Jonah got his first look at Rhode. She was tiny—not even five foot—her black hair so dark, it gleamed blue under the lights.

"May we converse in English?"

"We may." Rhode eyed them from her spot by the window. "What can I assist you with?"

"We are seekers in a sea of chaos."

"Then may your sea calm so you will find what you seek." Rhode raised an eyebrow as she finished the phrase. "What are you? Keepers? Agema?"

"Neither. My name is Minako, and these are my friends. We are Ghostly Ones. We have come to humbly ask your assistance, daughter of Poseidon."

"My assistance?" Rhode snorted. "You have come to the wrong place. Olympus has no use for the likes of me."

"Good thing we ain't here for Olympus then," Spader stated. "We just said we're Elevenths, didn't we?"

Rhode scoffed. "So, we have a smart ass in our midst. Great one, American. Did you spend all day practicing it?"

"Hold on there, honey," Spader snapped. "I wouldn't talk, seeing as how you're Greek and posing as a Japanese woman —"

"Arguments help nothing, Spader," Jonah interrupted. He'd be damned if they got distracted by spats and snags. Not when Eva needed them. "Rhode, we know your husband defected to the Titans. We need to ask you some questions that could benefit us concerning another matter. Are you willing to talk to us?"

Rhode looked at him, her expression unreadable. "Yes, certainly." She coughed. "Pardon me for that. I need a quick drink of water. Throat's parched."

Jonah was slightly impatient by this time but shrugged. "Do what you have to do."

Rhode nodded and opened a bottle of water. She lifted the bottle to her, and then suddenly, its entire contents lifted from the bottle and exploded in a wave.

The daughter of Poseidon had just morphed bottled water into a wave strong enough to slam Jonah and his friends back against the wall of the office and down to the floor. The entire place was now a wasteland of soggy and drenched papers and equipment.

Dazed, Jonah groaned on the floor as Rhode grabbed keys and hightailed it out of the room. Spader attempted to give chase, but immediately slid and ended with his face planted on the floor, making him curse in the process.

"Get that bitch!"

"On it!"

Reena rushed from the room while Minako clutched at her head. She rose from her knees with a wince. "Damn Greeks are always so feisty."

Jonah forced himself to his feet, then helped Minako up.

Spader waved him off. "I got this, brother."

Jonah snorted as Reena came back into the room empty-handed.

"She's gone. Ran right into the crowd and I lost her," she huffed. "*Now* what do we do?"

"All is well," a voice said. "I got it."

They turned. A burly black man was now in the office with them, a bound and gagged Rhode in tow. He left her where she was to aid Minako to her feet.

"Who the hell are you?" Jonah asked.

The man snorted. "I am Delphin, god of dolphins and general of Poseidon's armies. Nice to know I wasn't the only one on Rhode's tail."

Reena looked over the oddly colored chains that bound Rhode. "What are these made of?"

"They're infused in freshwater," Delphin explained. "Rhode, as a daughter of Poseidon, is strongest in seawater."

"You can't do this!" Rhode cried. "I'm guilty of nothing!"

"And you proved that by attacking people and fleeing?" Delphin asked. "Wait till we get you to a much dryer setting. Then we'll talk all about it. "

"I panicked, alright?" She wiggled against the chains. "It has been centuries since anyone associated with Olympus has knocked on my door. I didn't know what to do."

"We told you—"

"Lies. You told me lies!" Rhode spat. "If you were not affiliated with Olympus, why was he asking about the Titans?"

"Rhode, if you have nothing to hide, then what's the harm in speaking with us?"

She gazed at the newcomer, who shrugged.

"Your choice. You know we are going to find him eventually."

"Will Scamander be harmed?"

Delphin sneered. "Scamander is a traitor, a liar, and is currently working with our greatest enemy. Yes, Rhode. He will be harmed. You know as well as I do what happens to traitors."

She paled at that, then looked away. "I have done nothing. I know nothing. If you force me to speak against my husband, I will only tell you lies."

"No, you won't," Spader declared.

Rhode turned her angry eyes to him. "Why are you so certain, Ghostly One? Is this some ethereal hypnosis trick or something? Because I am a child of the sea. Like the tide, my mind is far too changeable for such mental manipulation."

"Nobody's fucking with your mind, Lady in the Water," Spader told her. "I know you won't lie for Scamander because you love him too much to dig his hole even further, and screw yourself in the process."

She blinked as she stared at Spader. She opened her mouth then shut it.

"Well?"

"I don't know anything," she whispered. "Truly, I don't. It has been years since I last saw my husband. Well, I haven't seen him since he joined the cause against us."

"Then why did you run?"

"To escape this conversation. To escape the blame that would surely fall upon my shoulders since my husband and I are bound as one through the golden contract of Olympus."

"Wait, what golden contract?" Spader looked intrigued. "Is it really gold?"

"Aye. And it bounds two souls in marriage. It makes any pair a singular. Each responsible for the other and their actions." She looked at us curiously. "You do not know this? You must not be true Olympians."

"We're not," Jonah responded. "We're Elevenths, like we said before. But Delphin, can you appeal to Poseidon? It's not right that Rhode should have Scamander's actions wrapped around her neck."

"Treason is a matter for the crown to handle." Delphin pointed his finger skyward. "*That* crown."

"But Rhode is *Poseidon's* daughter," Reena said. "He wouldn't leave his own kid for Zeus to hang out and dry because her husband is scum. No one blamed Zeus for Hera, did they?"

"I'm going to change tactics here." Jonah stuffed his hands in his pockets. "You know this area well, correct?"

Rhode snorted. "Better than anyone."

"So, what's going on with the spirits here? Why are they going so postal?"

"I don't know, Ghostly One. Spirits are not in my realm of expertise."

"You don't know anything, then? Nothing about the spirits, nothing about your husband?"

"I don't. Test me if you like, but my existence has been dedicated to the animals who live beneath the waves."

Delphin narrowed his eyes at her, then sighed. "Alright. Let's go."

"Where are you taking me?"

"We are going to speak with Zeus on your behalf. You know as well as I that all decisions regarding marriages and treachery go through him." Delphin bowed his head to the group. "Thank you, Ghostly Ones. Perhaps we will see each other again soon."

Delphin left with Rhode.

Spader shook his head.

"What?" Jonah asked.

"She was damn useless," he remarked.

"Not really," Minako said.

"What are you talking about?"

"She was completely oblivious," Minako advised, "which means Scamander could have made her an unwitting accomplice at any time. Hide stuff in their home, hiding places in plain sight ..."

Jonah stiffened. "Like this office. Let's sweep it."

Reena, Spader, Minako, and Jonah got to work. The group searched through the shelves and the desk without any results. Jonah was running his hands along the sides of a drawer to see if it had a false drawer when Reena piped up.

"What's this?" She held up a flyer. It was written in a language that Jonah had never seen before.

"It's a piece of paper, Re. So?"

"So, it's not in English or Japanese." She frowned as she set the book aside. "I wonder what it says."

Minako looked at it with a frown. "Looks like Hebrew. Who among the Greeks is Jewish?"

"No one," Jonah muttered as he took the flyer from Reena's grasp. "If Scamander defected to the Titans, could they be using Hebrew as a code?"

"Ok. So, my next question." Reena crossed her arms. "Who do we know who is Jewish?"

"Ben-Israel," Spader answered instantly. "He is an atheist now, but was raised Jewish. Had a bar mitzvah and all."

"Back to the estate?"

"Yeah. See you guys there."

Jonah initiated the Astralimes and appeared in the gardens where he knew he would find Liz Manville. She and her sister Nella were covered up to their elbows in dirt and chatting happily while they worked.

"Liz? Hey," Reena jogged over as the others appeared. "Is Ben-Israel home?"

"Yeah." Liz squinted against the sun as she looked over to them. "He's on cleaning duty in the infirmary. Why?"

"We need his help. Thanks!"

The group went inside and upstairs. They found Ben-Israel bobbing his head to the music blaring through his earphones. Jonah tapped his shoulder and he jumped.

"J?" He tapped his earbud to turn it off. "What's up, brother?"

"Ben-Israel," Jonah said, "I need a favor. I know you're a non-believer, but you were raised in the Jewish faith. Would you happen to still speak and understand Hebrew?"

"Bits and pieces," he answered. "But if you're looking to be converted—"

"No, it's not that." Jonah took the paper from Reena. "Can you read this for me?"

Ben-Israel frowned as he took the document. He scanned it. "Give me a few days. It's been a long time, guys."

"Alright. Thanks, man."

Minako led the group into the hall. She sighed as she turned to them. "I'll update my people and keep digging."

"What should we do, Minks?" Spader followed behind her. "Sit and wait?"

"Yeah," she sighed. "That's all I got at the moment. You guys are amazing. Thanks for the help in Japan." She gave them a mock salute and vanished.

The group looked at each other.

"Sit and wait?" Reena asked with a sigh. "Really?"

"It's all we can do for now, Re," Jonah muttered. "Let's hope Ben-Israel can decipher that paper sooner rather than later. Otherwise, I think we'll all go stir-crazy."

Spader sighed softly and tugged something from his pocket. "Cards, anyone?"

NINE

EVA MCRAYNE

"AND GO!"

I waited until the red light on Joey's camera went solid despite his command. My cameraman had been a little too excited about our current location. Not because of the ghosts, mind you. But because he was in Japan. The land of ancients and androids.

"Welcome to another international episode of *Grave Messages*!" I smiled at the camera and extended my arms towards the bay we were standing in front of. "We are in northeast Japan, visiting a town called Ishinomaki."

I grinned wider when I realized I had pronounced the word correctly. Thank all the gods for Google Translate.

"What's so special about Ishinomaki? Well, my dear viewers, that's why we are here. Did you know that this town was devastated in the 2011 tsunami? It's true. According to Japan's Reconstruction Agency, the damage came out to around 300-billion dollars. Over 230,000 homes were lost. Over 15,000 people died."

I leaned against the car behind me to cross my arms over my chest. "Now, I have complete and utter respect for the ghost stories based out of the Victorian Era. But tonight? I'm hoping to capture evidence of spirits who lost their lives during a more modern tragedy.

Will they come through? Will I be ignored? There is only one way to find out."

I pushed away from the car. "You see, there have been numerous reports of spirits appearing on the side of the road. At the Ishinomaki Station. When the cab drivers speak to them, they all request to be taken to various districts that were destroyed. Some want a ride to Minamihama, which is still abandoned. Tonight, Joey and I are going to play the part of cab drivers. Each of us will have our own cab. We'll drive along the main road leading to Minamihama to see if we can pick up phantom fare."

I gestured to the camera. "Joey, give me that. It's your turn to talk."

Joey passed the camera without complaint.

I almost fell under the weight of the stupid camera, but I managed to steady it on my shoulder and train the lens on him.

Joey was grinning. Light. Not at all like the Joey who had stormed away from me and Jonah at the hotel earlier that afternoon.

"Howdy, folks." Joey gave the camera the biggest smile he could muster. "Since Evie is great at bringing out the ghosts, but not so great at the technical aspects, she demanded that I explain how we were going to be filming ourselves in the cars."

"Demanded?" I snorted. "I asked very nicely, thank you."

"*Demanded.*" Joey stressed the word as he opened the car door. "Inside each vehicle, I've wired up several cameras. We've got one here on the dashboard, one on the rear window, and we are going to be wearing our body cameras. Just in case."

I moved as close to Joey as I dared until he took pity on me and took the camera back. I mouthed my thanks as I shook out my shoulders.

Joey held up his hand, lowering each finger to signal for silence. Silence helped him mark the video for editing purposes. When he folded his hands into a fist, he sat the camera on the passenger seat and pressed a button I couldn't see. "You sure about this, Eva?" Joey glanced over at me. "I don't like us going in separate vehicles."

"Joey, if someone wants a taxi, which one are they going to pick? One that is empty or one with a passenger already in it? I'll be fine."

"I'm not worried about you," he grumbled. "You're not the only one who is going to be driving by themselves."

"You ready to go?" I tucked a loose strand of blonde hair behind my ear. "Fingers crossed, we can get the footage pretty quickly."

"You still gotta fill an hour," Joey reminded me. "You don't want to find the ghosts too soon."

"Yeah, yeah." I watched as he lifted his camera off the seat. "Ready?"

"As I'll ever be." He wrapped me in a one-armed hug. I started to push him away, but decided not to piss him off. I'd tell him not to touch me later, when we weren't filming. "Go get 'em, tiger."

Joey released me with a long look to the bay waters behind us. I had to admit, this country was one of the most beautiful places I'd ever seen. Yet, I was far too familiar with the fact that beauty could hide the ugliest truths. I shut the passenger door before I jogged around to the other side of the car.

"Stay behind me," I called out to him. "I don't want to get lost."

"Yeah."

I knew right then and there that Joey was nervous. There was no smart remark about my driving. He didn't roll his eyes. Or tell me how bossy I was. Joey threw a single wave at me before he folded himself up in the driver's seat of the car behind me.

"It'll be fine." I breathed in the sea air as Chrono's warnings played in the back of my mind. "It'll all be fine."

———

We spent the next two hours driving up and down the same streets in the hope of catching sight of anything out of the ordinary. Which was saying something given that we were in Japan. A country known for its strangeness.

I was flipping through the radio stations for the fiftieth time when I saw the shadows shift about two hundred yards ahead of me. I put on my emergency lights as I slowed down. I glanced up to see Joey slow down with me and breathed a sigh of relief when I saw the woman standing on the side of the road. It wasn't until I had closed the gap between us that I got my first good look at her.

Japanese. Small. She looked to be in her early thirties. I pulled to a stop and waited until the car door opened. The lady got in the backseat before she spoke.

"Please take me to Minamihama."

"Minamihama?" I gave myself a mental congratulation for the second time for my correct pronunciation. "Ma'am, are you certain? That area was abandoned years ago."

"Yes," she whispered in her native language. "My family is waiting for me."

For the first time in a long time, I didn't know what to say. So, I released the brake and began to drive. I could hear Joey in my earpiece as he asked me if I was ok. I tapped the brakes twice to respond before I heard the woman behind me spoke again.

"Am I dead?"

I adjusted my grip on the steering wheel as the woman's timid voice filled the car. I cleared my throat before I responded. "What happened to you?"

"Nature's vengeance," the spirit whispered. "The sea was angry."

I waited for her to continue, but the woman had other plans. I felt her icy touch against the back of my neck. I tried to pull away, but her grip tightened. Within seconds, I felt her fear. I was hit by the strongest sense of claustrophobia I'd ever experienced. I felt water filling my lungs. I felt myself choking. Gasping for air that wasn't there.

I released the steering wheel to claw at my throat as rancid seawater began to flow out of my mouth. The spirit began to whisper words I couldn't hear as I lost control of the car.

I couldn't breathe. I couldn't see. My only focus was on the fire filling my chest. I was drowning. And there was nothing I could do to stop it. I don't know what happened next. I couldn't explain it in a million lifetimes. One second, the life was choking out of me. The next?

The car slammed into the rental car Joey had been driving. And I do mean slammed. I jerked forward against the seat belt and bashed my face against the airbag. Somewhere, amid the madness, I felt someone grab my arm. I felt the seatbelt fall away.

I hit the asphalt with a tortured gasp as I tried to breathe. I was rolled over and pulled up just enough to release the rest of the disgusting seawater that was pouring out of my mouth.

"It's ok, Eva." Joey's strained voice cut through the rushing in my ears. "I got you. It's going to be alright."

I reached up for him and clutched his shirt when the air began to rush back into my lungs. It took a minute, but once I got my bearings back, I looked up at him. And winced. Joey's face was black and blue from the impact. He had a massive gash down the side of his right cheek.

"Joey, oh my god," I whispered. "Are you …"

He didn't respond right away. He was too busy looking over my injuries. I narrowed my eyes at him when his mouth set in a hard line.

"What?" I sat up with a hiss and cradled my left arm. "What's wrong?"

"This was a stupid idea, Eva! Stupid!" Joey snapped. "We could have been killed! Ok. Not you. But me!"

I opened my mouth, then closed it. I decided not to face him, so I looked at the remains of our cars and shuddered. Both were totaled. Both were smoking. Crumpled. But if Joey hadn't reacted? If he hadn't put his car in front of mine?

I would have ended up in the ocean. Fitting, considering how it had been seawater that had stolen my breath away.

He stood up and offered me his hand. "That was just a ridiculous thing to do."

I sighed as I let Joey lift me, and hugged myself when Joey gave me a pointed look. "What do you want me to say? I fucked up. I'm sorry."

"Eva, look." Joey ran a hand through his hair. "We've had our issues. We gotta talk about them without Jonah present. He's made it clear how he feels about me and—"

"Later." I turned away from him. "Let's document what happened. Then, we'll call the cops."

"Yeah. Ok."

I could tell that Joey was still aggravated, but what was I supposed to do? I couldn't take back the accident.

So, instead, we put our game faces on. Joey filmed the cars. I talked about what I had experienced when the ghost touched me. How I felt like I was drowning. Then, my cameraman joined me on the screen to talk about his own experience.

"I saw Evie start to swerve." Joey leaned forward to rest his elbows on his knees. "I didn't think. And yeah, I know I was a total badass. But I wasn't worried about myself."

"My hero,," I teased him before I faced the camera he had set up. "So there you have it, folks. The ghosts are just as active in this foreign land as they are in the U.S. But that is only one tale. The legends of spirits in Japan are just as ancient as the country itself. And we've only begun to scratch the surface."

"No wonder their cartoons are so damn good." Joey grinned when I punched him on the shoulder. "What?"

"Anime aside," I rolled my eyes at him, "we found what we were looking for. Until next time, guys. See you then."

"See ya." Joey waved at the camera and counted to ten under his breath before he stood up.

Me? I got on my phone and called the U.S. Embassy, who was less than thrilled that I had decided to keep filming instead of reporting the accident immediately.

Whatever. We were fine. The cuts and bruises only made for good television. My highest rated episodes were the ones that put me in the hospital. And besides, it's not like the road was heavily traveled. We hadn't seen a soul aside from the ghost woman all night. An extra hour wasn't going to hurt anything.

"Joey, the cops are on the way." I stood up and stretched. "Did we get enough footage to make this a solo episode?"

"'Fraid not." He sighed as he packed the tripod back in its bag. "If we are going to make this a full hour, we need another location. And I sure as hell don't want to do this again tomorrow night."

"Ok." I glanced down the dark road. "Let's go explore the old town. Or what's left of it anyway."

"We can. But not tonight. Don't you want to go back to the hotel?" Joey gave me the most pitiful set of puppy dog eyes in existence. "My face hurts, Eva. Bad."

"You do look pale," I admitted. "Fine. Let's deal with the cops. Then we can crash. The rubble will still be there tomorrow night."

"That's my girl!" Joey turned around when the night lit up with blue and red lights. "And look. Calvary's right on time!"

It was time to charm the hell out of the Japanese authorities. And if anyone could do it?

We could.

———

It took three hours to get through the red tape all foreigners had to go through when they had an accident. We had to fill out paperwork. Give statements. Joey even downloaded our footage onto a flash drive and handed it over to prove that I was driving safely before I got attacked from behind.

By the time we reached the hotel, I realized just how exhausted I was. My entire body hurt from the wreck. My nerves were shot as I remembered the woman's fear. How the water had felt when it filled my lungs. She had died a horrible death.

It was one that would stick with me for a while. No matter how much I tried to forget about it.

I shut the water off from my shower as soon as I could. Don't get me wrong. It felt divine. But I didn't want to think about what I had experienced. I didn't want to think about the spirit or my current fight with Joey. I shouldn't be so nice to him, but what choice did I have? I didn't want the rest of the world to know that he had gotten me thrown into an ethereal prison because he was a damn drug trafficker.

The truth was, I didn't want to think about anything even remotely related to the reasons I was in Japan. No Council. No ghosts. No television show. No Joey. I wanted to close my eyes and shut it all out.

I sighed when I dropped down on the bed. I began to pull my

hairbrush through my hair as I considered how much my life had changed in the past few years. I was famous. My face was every-where. *Grave Messages* was the most successful paranormal show of all time according to the critics. Why?

Because I put my neck on the line every episode. I didn't settle for the basic locations. I didn't settle for legends that every town had. I had dedicated my life to my success as Apollo's Sibyl. And the results were mind-blowing.

Now? I had Jonah. I had the one soul I loved more than anyone else in existence. My deal with Hera flickered in my mind. Maybe she'd forgotten about it.

Even I knew how stupid that sounded.

"Beware of the sea."

I jerked up as my heart began to pound. I searched the shadows of my room before I clamored up to my feet.

"Who's there?" I willed my sword into my hand and turned in a slow circle. I was alone. "Dammit, I know I heard you."

I felt a cold breeze across the back of my neck. I whirled around to see the woman from the roadside staring at me with empty eyes.

"Beware of the sea," she whispered again. "The waters are angry. Monsters are waking. Beware, Sibyl. Beware."

I scrambled back when she disappeared. I didn't think as I grabbed my phone. I needed to get through to Jonah. I needed to know what the hell her presence meant here. So far away from the road she haunted. I stabbed my thumb against the power button and frowned when the device remained black.

So, that was weird. I knew that spirits liked to drain batteries for energy. I grabbed my charger from the bag and jabbed it in the phone … and raised an eyebrow when I felt something wet on my thumb.

I tugged the back off my phone, then groaned aloud. It was soaked. Small droplets of water pooled up against the battery compartment. I'd have to call Apollo to get a new one.

Later. I'd deal with it later. I tossed the ruined phone in the trash. I could use Joey's phone to call Jonah.

I jerked my hair up into a ball on top of my head, grabbed my key, and stormed out of the room. I would eat something. Get some sleep. And tackle my damaged phone and a mysterious Japanese spirit tomorrow.

As I approached Joey's room, I couldn't get the woman's voice out of my head. I couldn't get her warning out of my ears. I shuddered as I raised my fist to knock. Her eyes had been so empty. So hollow. As if the ghost was a shell of the person she had once been.

"I don't know, man. They were all over each other this morning. Said they were in love. That's all I know."

I swear, my heart stopped when I heard a familiar voice filter through the door in response. Cyrus? He was supposed to be in Tartarus. Had Apollo released him?

I couldn't make out his words, but I didn't care to hear them anyway. I rapped my knuckles loudly against the door. I started to do it again when Joey scrambled to open it.

"Eva? What are you doing here?"

"Where is he?" I pushed past Joey to see his empty room. I whirled around to face my best friend. "I heard Cyrus, Joey. Where is he?"

"Eva, I was alone." He pointed to the television. "Maybe you heard the television."

I studied Joey, then sighed as I rubbed my hands over my face. I don't know why I was so on edge, but he didn't deserve to serve as the brunt of my frustration. Cyrus wasn't here. He was still locked away.

"Thanks."

Joey came up to run his hand along my arm. He pulled me into a hug and I recognized the gesture for what it was. A truce. I hugged him back before I pulled away. "I'm still mad at you, Joey."

"Can we just take this one day at a time, please?" Joey ran a hand through his hair. "Seriously, Eva. The last time I really saw you, I was in a lot of emotional and physical pain. I didn't have time to explain anything. We need to talk about what happened."

"Not now. Not while we are filming." I rocked back on my heels. "Listen, can I borrow your phone? Mine is full of seawater."

"Yeah, of course."

Joey went across the room, then returned with his cell. I pulled up his contact with Jonah and started a text conversation.

Hey, handsome, it's Eva, not Joey. My phone got damaged, so I won't have one until I talk to Apollo. Facetime?

See you there.

I pulled up the app and, soon, Jonah's face filled the screen.

"Hey." I dropped down on the edge of Joey's bed. "How goes it?"

"Jesus, Superstar." Jonah winced as he leaned closer to his camera. "What'd you get into a fight with?"

"Airbag. I had a run-in with one of the hitchhiker spirits. I'm ok," I threw in. "Promise. I'm going to catch a few hours sleep before we go into the abandoned town to look at the shrines."

"You need me, Superstar?"

"I always need you," I admitted. "Did you get your statement done?"

"No. Minako had something else connected to Typhon. Thought I'd stay here for a bit longer to make sure she and the Curaie don't show up when Typhon breaks loose."

"Why would they show up in Italy?"

"To point fingers since something Olympian is fucking with Elevenths," Jonah explained. "There is evidence of spirit corruption affecting the Elevenths in the area. Turned out a river god named Scamander has defected to the Titans and is now in the wind, but his wife was available. Thus, Shinjuku City. As I said, she tried to run, but it turns out she was innocent. She ran because she thought that since Scamander had fled, she'd get caught holding the bag. "

"I wonder if the spirit I encountered tonight was connected to this ... effect on Elevenths in the area."

"What do you mean?"

I explained to Jonah what happened during filming. How the spirit wanted me to take her to the abandoned town. I told him about how she touched me so that I experienced her death by drowning, which was how I wrecked the car.

"She showed up in my room here not too long ago." I tapped my fingers on my knee. "Weird since the spirits aren't supposed to leave the roadway. But she gave me a message before she disappeared.

Something about the sea being angry and monsters waking up. I'm ninety-five percent sure it's related to Typhon."

"Anything else?"

"Not yet. We're going to shift through the ruins tomorrow night. If I get anything, I'll pass it to you."

Joey gestured to me he was going into the bathroom. I waited for the door to shut and then heard the water come on before I spoke again.

"Listen, there's something else weird going on. When I got to Joey's room, I could have sworn I heard him talking about me and you to Cyrus. I confronted Joey about it, but he swears all I heard was the television."

Jonah's face darkened, though I could barely see the change in him. His eyes always gave him away when he was irritated. "I told you not to trust Joseph, Superstar." Jonah growled a little. "You think Cyrus got released from Tartarus?"

"I don't know." I glanced back at the closed door before I turned back to my love on the screen. "If he had been freed, Apollo would have warned me. And no one—not even Cyrus—can escape from Tartarus. That place is on total lockdown."

"Ok." Jonah mused over that. "Eva, you said you overheard some of it. Did you just hear Cyrus? Or was Joey responding?"

"He was responding."

"What did Joey say exactly?"

I opened my mouth to speak, then shut it before I shook my head.

"He was saying that we were all over each other this morning." I sighed. "I don't know, Jonah. I don't. We've been taking shots at each other all day. After the wreck, he lambasted me for putting him in danger. I apologized and thought we were back on common ground. Now, I'm not sure what to think."

"I seriously doubt it was the television you heard." Jonah shifted in his seat as he went back to our conversation about Joey. "We can contact Apollo. See what's going on."

"No. I think I'm going to play nice with Joey at the moment. See if I can catch him in anything sketchy. If he's truly in contact with

Cyrus, that means he has become my enemy. And that would explain his cushy lifestyle. Maybe he'll slip up."

"I don't like it."

"I don't either. But I don't have much of a choice, right?" I pushed a rogue curl that fell out of my bun behind my ear. I heard Joey getting closer to the bathroom door, so I changed the subject. "I don't know what we'll find in the town tomorrow, but maybe I can research crime reports and numbers tonight to get the lay of the land."

"If possible, look for crime reports that don't smell right," Jonah suggested. "When Creyton blocked the paths way back when, Elevenths and Tenths started acting out of character due to spiritual imbalances in the areas. So, look for reports of violent crimes from citizens that had no police record prior to a few weeks ago. Sudden behavioral changes equal disruption in the Spirit world."

"Consider it done, handsome. I'll email you the files as soon as I have them."

"You think the cops will work with you on this?"

"Sure. I'm a favorite since I decided to keep filming for an hour instead of calling in the accident," I joked. "They love me. The U.S. Embassy, too."

Joey came out of the bathroom, toweling his hair. He dropped down on the bed next to me and stretched out on his stomach as he leaned into me to see the screen.

"Hey, J. Eva tell you about how I saved her from trying to drive on water?"

"Yes." I rolled my eyes at him. "You know I tell Jonah everything."

Jonah tensed and he flipped off the lights. I wondered if he did that so he didn't have to bother with maintaining a poker face over the app.

"Appreciate your heroics, man." Jonah didn't bother to hide his sarcasm. "Who'd have thought you're a guardian angel as well as a damn drug trafficker?"

"Right? I'm amazing, I know." Joey sounded lighthearted. Completely oblivious to Jonah's passive-aggressive remark. I wondered if I really was overreacting, being suspicious of him. "Anyway, I'm about to call room service. What do you want, Evie?"

"Eh, I'll just steal your toast."

"Ok." Joey got up and I made a face at Jonah.

I saw his smirk. "I guess that's my cue, handsome. I'll call you as soon as I can." I blew him a kiss. "Love you."

"Love you back, Superstar," Jonah said. "About to watch a basketball game. The Charlotte Hornets are playing the Memphis Grizzlies. On paper, the Grizzlies are no threat, but they can be deceptive. Gotta watch 'em."

It took me a minute, but I caught onto the veiled reminder to watch my back around Joey. I nodded. "I gotcha. Enjoy the game, Blueberry."

I disconnected with Jonah and logged out of the app before I passed the phone back to Joey.

"Throw it back in my bag, will you? I'm gonna use the landline."

"Sure." I got up and slipped his phone into the side pocket. I winced when something sharp pricked my finger. "Ow." I lifted my finger up to the light to see a drop of blood on the tip. "Joey, did you break a lens in here or something?"

"No, why?" He shot up as I reached into his bag again. "Evie, don't! I got it."

Joey was too little, too late.

I pulled out the thin syringe I had poked myself on. It had been used. Hell, there was still some cloudy liquid in it tinged with blood. I stared at it before I raised my eyes up at my friend. "What is this?"

"Evie—"

"What the hell is this, Joey?"

"You know exactly what that is." His eyes flashed. He snatched the syringe from my hand and dug around for the cap. "It's no big deal."

"Yes, the fuck it is. After everything we went through, you are using *again*?"

"You know what? Just leave."

"Joey!"

"I mean it, Eva. You don't give a damn about me. Not so long as I follow you around and make you look good," he snapped. "So, go and be the goddamn hero somewhere else. Enjoy your time with Jonah until he drops you again."

"Excuse me?"

"You heard. You know you're nothing more than an easy lay and you got the audacity to come in here and judge me?"

I shoved him back, then grabbed a bag of needles from the pocket.

"Give me those!"

"You want to ruin your god-damn career, fine," I hissed at him. "But you are not going to ruin mine, understand? This shit will get us banned so fast our heads will spin."

"You don't know what you're talking about." He jerked the bag out of my hand, then stormed over to the door. "Leave. I'll see you tomorrow."

I had to calm down. How could I play nice with someone who was so damned determined to piss me off? Maybe Jonah had the right idea, after all. When I didn't move, he jerked open the door.

"Bye, Eva."

I took longer than necessary to leave. My mind was racing. Joey used to have a heroin problem. It appeared he still did. He'd been trafficking cocaine with his former boyfriend, Pedro, which is how I ended up in prison in the first place.

Had he been using it on location? When he was driving?

I pulled my keycard out of my back pocket, then re-entered my room. I sat on the edge of my bed as I realized the one thing Jonah had tried to warn me about.

Joey could very well be dangerous to me. Very, very dangerous.

———

I was not ashamed to admit that I was thoroughly creeped out as we walked through the abandoned streets of Minamihama. Especially at night. The entire town had been devastated by the tsunami and Japan had no interest in rebuilding it any time soon.

Odd, in my opinion. Especially since Japan was one of the most populated countries in the world. Surely there was a reason why this single spot of land continued to go unused.

"Are you getting the heebie-jeebies like I am? Or is it just chilly tonight?" Joey stopped and panned his camera around the broken buildings. "'Cause I'm feeling freaked out right now, Evie."

"Yeah." I moved ahead a few more steps, then crossed my arms over my chest. Joey was in full charmer mode tonight. I wondered if he knew how bad he'd fucked up or if he was actually sorry for the fight between us. And I had to play along since the camera was rolling. "God, Joey. Could you imagine the panic that had to have happened that day? So many people. Just … gone."

"I'm more worried about rats." He glanced over at me. "And street gangs that may have set up shop here. But ok. We can worry about the dead people too."

"You're so mean," I teased as I continued forward. "I have no idea why I put up with you, Joey Lawson."

"Cause I'm awesome?" He snorted. "Seriously. Be careful, Evie. I don't want either of us to get hurt."

"We're fine." I glanced over. He sure as hell wasn't worried about me getting hurt last night. "Besides, when did you become such a worrywart? We've been to worse places than this before."

He fingered the bandage along his cheek as if he were considering my question. "Gee, I don't know. Maybe since you rammed a car into mine?"

I started to respond with a quick retort of my own when I heard a soft crying noise just to my left. I frowned and turned towards it, then held up my hand when Joey started talking again.

"What? True story. I got it on film and everything."

"Hush." I dropped my hand. "Do you hear that?"

Joey was quiet for a minute or two as the crying resumed. I saw his eyes go wide when he grabbed my arm.

"No. No way in hell." He shook his head. "We are not going to go see what is up with that."

"Yes, we are." I twisted my arm until he let go. I was still too pissed at him to let him touch me for long. "Or you can stay here. Give me the handheld."

"Evie, sometimes I think you take this whole ghostbuster thing a little too far."

"Come on, chicken." I grinned at the camera. "You wanna get this on film or no?"

He gave me a hard look, followed by a deep sigh, when I crossed the road. I had passed two houses by the time he caught up with me.

"Are you doing this because I snapped at you after the wreck or because of our little tiff last night?"

Little tiff? Is that what he wanted to call it? Really? When I didn't answer, he threw up his free hand.

"Fine. But if you fall through a bunch of busted-up stairs, I won't save you. I'll just leave you to the rats."

"And the street gangs?" I gave him my most innocent look as I stopped in front of a house that had fallen in on itself. "Don't forget about the street gangs."

I faked a laugh when he started to grumble to himself, but my laughter died in my throat as I climbed over a plank of wood that had fallen over the door. I reached in my back pocket, pulled out my phone, and turned on the flashlight app. The place was a wreck. But that wasn't the worst thing about it. Water had destroyed the structure. It had washed the furniture all over the place. I ducked past a series of spider webs to see books laying on the floor. Pictures that had managed to hang onto the walls were crooked and wilted in their frames. I lifted the light and shivered when I noticed the kitchen.

A pot laying on its side by the oven. Scorched walls meant this house had burned as well as flooded.

"Evie, there's no one here." Joey had managed to make it to my side. I could see the reflection of his camera light blinking against the walls. "Can we go now?"

"In a minute." I turned to face him. "I want to go upstairs."

"Of course, you do." He glared at me. "But at the risk of sounding like a broken record ..."

"Let's go." I slipped past him and studied the stairway that was just off the front door. It looked less than sturdy, and I knew that most of the upper floor had fallen in. So I was careful. I hopped over the last broken step and gestured for Joey to do the same. "We need to get the address to this house before we leave. I want to know about the family who lived here."

"Noted." Joey stopped on the landing behind me and whistled.

The upper floor wasn't broken up into rooms. It was a single loft. And just as I had suspected, the entire right side of the floor was caved in. I swept my light through the darkness to take it in.

"What's that?"

I jerked when Joey broke the silence. Despite my bravado, I wasn't kidding when I said this town creeped me out.

"What?" I turned to see that he was pointing against the far-right wall. I swept my thumb across my screen to brighten my light and aimed it in that direction. A small table had been set up, covered by a teal blue cloth and dotted with figurines. "Joey, I want to get over there."

"Baby girl, *how*?" He sounded exasperated. "Do you not see the big hole in the floor?"

"Yes. I also see that spot is the only one untouched in this whole house." I shifted away from him and winced when the floorboards creaked. I was one hundred and ten pounds max. Yet, I didn't know if the boards were going to support me or not. "Give me the camera."

"You're going to fall and bust your head in."

"I'll survive it." I took the camera from him, then held it out in front of me. The night vision Joey was using was ten times better than my flashlight. "I'll be right back."

I held onto the walls and tried not to think about how slimy they were. I stopped only when I reached the remains of a mat and pressed down on it with my toe.

The floor cracked. It honest-to-god *cracked*.

"I'm fine." I called out before Joey could have a heart attack. "Promise."

I didn't wait for him to respond as I tested the floor next to the hole I'd made. Then the next board when the first was sturdy enough to hold my weight. After what felt like forever, I stopped in front of the makeshift shrine.

I kept the camera trained on it as I studied the figurines. Fish. Mermaids. All in a semi-circle around the statue of a man who held a trident over his head. Except he wasn't standing. He was face down. A massive crack along his back.

I frowned and made a mental note to check out the superstitions of fishing villages. I knew enough about magic to know that shrines or alters were not to be messed with. And the smallest symbol could have the biggest impact. I knelt and lifted the figurine.

Poseidon. I recognized the white beard and the jagged crown from the books Cyrus had forced upon me. Funny, how he looked nothing like this in real life.

"Joey," I brushed the dust off the statue's face. "We gotta go check the other houses."

"Why?" He frowned. "What did you find?"

"A broken god." I glanced back at him over my shoulder. "A very broken god."

TEN

EVA MCRAYNE

IT TOOK another hour of walking to get back to the car. Just long enough for me to want to strangle Joey and throw him in the ocean if he sang the *Gilligan's Island* theme song one more time.

"Joey." I dropped down in the car and pulled my new phone out of the glove box. Apollo had gotten it to me right before we left for the ruins the night before, thank Olympus. "Can you turn the radio on, please?"

"Why?" He opened the back door to put his camera in its bag. "You don't like my singing?"

"No. It's not your talent." I tapped the screen and pulled up my messages. Two texts from my personal assistant. Three from Connor. A sweet text from Jonah, wishing me the best on location. I replied with a quick summary of what we found then promised to call him as soon as I could.

Next, I pulled up the first text from Connor that demanded I call him immediately. I ignored it and opened the second one. Another demand for a phone call.

"So, Connor wants you to call him," I muttered to Joey as he put the car in drive. "Like, yesterday."

"Right." He glanced over at me and shook his head. "Has anyone told you that you are a horrible, horrible liar, Evie?"

"Oh, come on." I dropped my phone into my lap as I gave him *my* version of puppy dog eyes. "Joey, you know he's going to yell at me about the car wreck. Can't you do it? You are so much better handling him than I am."

"That's because I'm respectful." Joey turned his focus onto the road. "And because I don't do everything in my power to piss him off."

"Yeah? Well, I can't help it if he's too easily triggered." I shrugged. "Please? I'll buy you something."

"Bribery will get you everywhere, my dear." He grinned. "I want something fancy."

"New iPad?"

"Nope. I don't know yet. I'll put it on your credit card the second I decide."

"How the hell do you know my credit card number?" I narrowed my eyes at him. "Have you been going through my purse?"

"God, no! I'd like to keep my hands, thank you." He chuckled. "It's not my fault if you leave your mail all over the condo."

I rolled my eyes at him, then opened the first message from my assistant. I hadn't had much contact with Jaclyn Williams since she took the job. And to be honest? I didn't see a reason for her to be attached to me. I did just fine on my own.

Well, sorta. She did fend off all the crazy offers I got from the Hollywood crowd. I hated doing promotional work. And that fact was so well known, it made me an even hotter commodity. I pulled up the message and began to read.

Eva –

I wanted to let you know I have put my resignation in. I'm moving back home to Hawaii to take care of my mom. Connor has another girl lined up for you though. Her name is Ariel Pendergrass.

I will pray for her. She is going to need it.

J.

"Well, hell." I sighed. "Jaclyn resigned."

"Your assistant?" Joey slowed down as we came upon a red light. "I'm surprised. That girl has been with Theia for over five years. What'd you do to run her off?"

"It wasn't me. Her mom." I frowned as I pulled up the next email. "She's moving back to Hawaii to take care of her. Said she'd pray for the new girl."

"As will we all," Joey teased. "What else did she say?"

"Nothing, but at least now I know what Connor wanted me to call him about."

"So, I don't get to do it?" My friend sighed. "And I was so looking forward to spending your money."

"No, you can still call him."

I responded, but I wasn't paying any attention to Joey as I read the next message. This one was from the new girl.

Eva –

I'm sure you've heard the news by now. And since you're across the world from me, I thought an email would suffice. My name is Ariel. I've had over ten years' experience dealing with the best divas Hollywood has to offer.

That being said, I admire your commitment to being a massive pain in the ass to anyone who tries to help you. And despite your current filming schedule, I have made arrangements for you to do a little promotion in San Marco tomorrow morning. You will be doing a photoshoot for Valor – the infamous clothing line by Wells Cole.

I know you're in the middle of closing this email out, but don't give up on me just yet. This one is for charity. All profits go to kids with cancer. And you'll do it for the kids, right?

Can't wait to meet you. I'm sure you're an absolute blast.

Ariel P.

I know my jaw was hanging open as I read her message, but damned if I couldn't close it out. I read it three more times before I realized Joey had parked the car. He didn't say anything. My cameraman just stared at me, his eyebrows raised. Finally, I found my voice.

"Oh, hell, no." I looked up at him. "Joey, how illegal is murder in California?"

"That depends." He tilted his head to the side. "How good are you at getting caught?"

"Oh, just," I sputtered. "Just read this."

Joey took my phone and read through the email before he burst out laughing. Even my deadliest glare wasn't enough to get him to stop. At long last, he got a hold of himself and grinned. "I like her already. She's spunky."

I snatched my phone back and hit the reply button, but Joey grabbed my hand before I could type what I wanted to.

"It's for the kids, Evie. We have time for you to do a quick photo-shoot." He grinned. "You're just mad because she got you where it hurts."

"I do not like being commanded, Joey." I pouted. "And I am not a pain—"

"Right." He drew out the word. "So on that note, I'm going inside. Are we leaving at the same time tomorrow?"

"Hell if I know. I haven't gotten that far." I closed out the screen then opened the last email from Ariel. It contained the details for our flight. "Good lord."

"What?"

"Better sleep fast." I cut my eyes over at him. "We're leaving at six tonight."

"What?" Joey sat up straight. "But I'll just be getting in good and deep then."

"Yeah, well. It's for the kids," I reminded him sweetly. "So, go. Pack up and grab some shut eye. I have a feeling that we're going to need it."

———

Through my time with *Grave Messages*, I'd gotten used to the grab-it-and-go lifestyle. Filming seasons were like that. We bounced from airport to hotel to location and back so fast, it made my head spin. So, I shouldn't have been in such a horrible mood when we checked into the Hotel Royal San Marco.

Maybe it was my lack of sleep. Or maybe it was because I was being forced into doing a photoshoot right after I'd nearly killed Joey in Japan. Or had my head spun about by Poseidon's riddles. I hadn't even had the chance to do the research I'd promised for Jonah. And I always kept my promises to Jonah.

Always.

I threw my arm over my eyes when I heard a knock on the door. "Go away." I called out. "I'm not here. Leave a message."

"Ms. McRayne?"

Who the hell was that? I sat up with a frown. I counted to ten before I tugged my ponytail free and forced my body to get off the bed. I made it to the door, then jerked it open to see a man standing there.

A very big man. I raised my eyebrow as I took him in. Perfectly trussed blonde hair. Sea-green eyes. Muscles that didn't seem to appreciate being confined by the suit he wore. I felt like I should have recognized him, but I was drawing a blank.

"That's me." I leaned against the door. "And who are you?"

"Wells." He gave me a dazzling smile. "Wells Cole. I heard you and your cameraman had arrived. I wanted to see if you would join me for a late dinner. We could discuss the shoot tomorrow."

Oh. He was here about the Valor shoot. Ew.

"I don't think you're going to get Joey up and about. Poor thing is dead tired. To be honest, so am I," I responded before I thought about it. "What time?"

"It's just after eight now. Would you prefer I return in thirty minutes?"

"Not really. No offense, but I'm not really in the mood to deal with business. I just got checked in."

"Then you must eat. I'll be back in a bit." Wells gave me another smile before he disappeared down the hall.

I watched him go before I closed the door. I nearly screamed in frustration. What in the hell was up with people commanding me lately?

At that exact moment, my phone rang against the comforter where I had left it. I stormed over to see Jonah's picture on the screen and, suddenly, my bad day got brighter.

"Hey, handsome." I dropped on my stomach as I answered. I put him on speaker before I continued. "If you don't have the best timing on the planet, I swear."

"Hey," Jonah chuckled. "That bad, huh?"

"You have no idea," I groused. "You're not busy, are you? I'm sorry I haven't gotten those crime statistics to you yet. I haven't stopped for two days already."

"Put it out of your mind, baby. You've got enough to deal with and I can do research just as good as you can." Jonah rustled something on his end of the line. "Now, what's up? Bad flight? Or is Joey being an ass again?"

Jonah had no idea how much of an ass Joey had been the other night. I hadn't been able to talk to him since it all happened.

"No, the flight was standard." I rubbed my thumb over the spot where I had pricked myself on Joey's needle. "As for Joey ... I think he's using again."

The line was silent for several seconds. "What happened? Did you find him on the floor or something?"

"No. Nothing like that. I put his phone back in his camera bag the other night and pricked myself on one of his damn needles. I confronted him about it. He got pissed and told me to leave. We haven't talked about it since."

"You pricked yourself?" Jonah sounded instantly alarmed. Almost scared. I didn't like that tone one bit. "Eva, get that checked out. He might have something, like HIV or something."

"I'm fine, Jonah." I shook the hair out of my eyes. "Immortal, remember?"

"You really think immortality is gonna help if you catch one of his damn diseases?"

"Would it make you feel better if I got checked out?"

"Yes."

"Then I'll call Hecate. See if she can fit me in." I pinched the bridge of my nose with two fingers. "At any rate, that would explain why he acted so funny at the airport. He was coming down from a high."

"He's not safe to be around Eva." Jonah sat at his desk chair. I heard the old wood creak when he leaned back in it. "Not if he's using. He's a danger to himself, and to *you*. He operates delicate machinery. He does most of the driving. That can't happen, Superstar. He needs to go."

"I can't fire him, Jonah. I don't have that sort of power. And if I turn to Connor, he'll laugh since lunch for him is a salad and a snort of coke." I shifted to pull the hotel pillow under my head. "I can take over the driving."

"What about his gun, Eva?"

"He can't have it in Japan. I don't think he has it with him."

"Then he needs to be sanctioned," Jonah said. "Something has to be done. Eva. I care about *you*. Your safety. You encounter enough dangers as it is to have a damn junkie be a liability. Leak it to *TMZ*. Spread it as an anonymous source. Make it so big that Connor can't ignore it without losing face. Do *something*."

I thought about Jonah's words. I really did. It took me a minute to come up with another idea. One that didn't threaten the reputation of the show I'd dedicated my life to.

"What if I held an intervention for him?"

"You really think he is going to listen to you?"

I thought back to my argument with Joey. I remembered how shocked I had been by his reaction.

"Maybe."

Silence on the line again.

"Didn't you mention that he had twin younger sisters who idolize him for whatever reason?"

"Yeah, Leah and Rachel," I replied. "I've never met them though.

Joey's family are all Catholic. They don't seem to care too much for the pagan influences of the show."

"Catholics, huh?" Jonah responded. "Get *them* involved. I hate to play that card, but nothing humbles a stubborn person like shame and guilt. He acted pissy towards you? Let's see him act pissy towards *them*."

I sat up with a grin. "You think that'll work?"

"It's worth a shot, Superstar. Get his folks involved, too."

I tapped my chin. "We can stage it in Wyoming. I'm sure there's an actual rehab in that state that doesn't cater to celebrities."

"And make him pay for it. His fuck up, he pays the price."

"Hell, if he can afford heroin, he can afford rehab, right?"

"Yeah. Exactly." There was a shifting on Jonah's side of the line. "What'd he say to piss you off?"

"You don't want to know, handsome."

"Yeah, Eva," Jonah spoke the words slow. "I do."

His tone made me nervous for Joey. I remember all too well how Jonah and Cyrus had been around each other. I considered my next words very carefully. Truly, I did. But in the end, I told Jonah everything. I always told him everything.

"Alright," I sighed. "Joey said I didn't care about him as long as he did his job to make me look good. Whatever. But the thing that set me off was that he called me an easy lay. Asked me how I had the audacity to judge him. Then he kicked me out of his room."

I heard Jonah's growl in the back of his throat. I almost regretted telling him. Almost.

"Fucking junkie," was all he said. "That's big talk coming from a guy whose longest relationship was the length of his bedroom to the front door."

"Either way, I told him he was going to ruin his career. He got lucky with the trafficking mess. He didn't believe me."

"Still think you need to put him on blast with *TMZ*, babe."

"I can't risk putting *Grave* in a bad light, handsome. I just can't. If this gets out, the press will have a fucking field day questioning every aspect of what we do."

Jonah grumbled something I didn't quite catch.

I continued. "It may be awhile before I can call you back." I sighed softly. "You've heard of Wells Cole, right? Gonna be doing a charity photo shoot with him tomorrow. He's persistent about having dinner to discuss it tonight. I wanted to let you know in case the paps throw their usual shit into the mix."

"Wells Cole? The model and actor?" Jonah scoffed. "He makes bad action movies."

"Got it in one." I hid another yawn behind my hand. "He's more than just a bad actor though. He is the founder of that athletic line, Valor. My new assistant was nice enough to schedule a damn photo shoot in the middle of my filming schedule."

"New assistant?"

"Yeah. Jaclyn quit, so I'm stuck with a new one. A damn overzealous one by the sounds of it."

"Who is the new blood?"

"I haven't met her in person yet." I flipped my hair over my shoulder. "I'll do some digging though. Her name is Ariel Pendergrass."

"Mmm." Jonah didn't sound thrilled. "Be wary of new people."

"I'm suspicious of everyone … except one person."

"Tell me more about this new assistant. She set you up to have dinner with Cole?"

"No, she set me up to do a charity photoshoot. He's the one insistent on a meeting tonight." I ran a hand through my hair. "Since there is no way in hell I'm letting him in my room, he suggested dinner. But I don't want to do anything that may make you think I'm screwing around on you. So, I wanted to run it by you first. Say the word and I won't go, babe."

Jonah's brief silence made me antsy. So much so, I started to tell him I didn't want to go anyway.

But then he answered. "I trust you, Eva," he said. "I know you aren't going to do something you shouldn't."

"How about I skip dinner? We can make use out of this big ol' bed."

"Give me two minutes and your location."

I gave him the name of the hotel and my room number. "See you soon, handsome."

Jonah disconnected and I ran to the bathroom to splash water on my face. I looked a mess, given my day going between airports, so I did what I could with the brief amount of time I had. I wasn't expecting to see Jonah tonight, but I was thrilled.

I had just finished combing the knots out of my hair when I heard a familiar footstep in my room. I opened the bathroom door and leaned against the door frame as I took Jonah in. He looked good as hell in his jeans and t-shirt.

"Did you really come to see me?" I teased. "Or try out that bed?"

"You, of course." Jonah was giving me such a greedy look that I nearly abandoned teasing him. "What good's the bed without you in it?"

I met him in the very center of the room as the two of us clashed together with the usual frenzied passion that tended to drive us. I was just getting Jonah out of his shirt when a knock at the door resounded around us.

"Ignore it."

I gasped as Jonah grabbed my hips with both hands to pull me flush against him. When the insistent knock happened a second time, I groaned.

"If that's Joey, I'm kicking his ass," Jonah grumbled against my throat.

I muttered under my breath too before I pulled away from him. "My money is on Wells. He said he was coming back. I completely forgot about him."

After I made sure Jonah was decent, I opened the door.

Wells Cole raised an eyebrow at my appearance.

"I thought you'd be ready by now."

"I'm not going to dinner. I'm busy."

"I don't understand." He frowned. "It is very important—"

Jonah must have come into view because Wells' expression darkened a little.

"Wells Cole, meet my boyfriend, Jonah Rowe. Jonah, Wells."

I saw Wells' expression go damn near arctic as he regarded

Jonah. I raised an eyebrow at that. Who the hell did this guy think he was?

"Pleasure to meet you," Wells said casually. "You are indeed a lucky man." He extended his hand, but Jonah didn't take it.

"Nah I'm good, actually." Jonah placed an arm around my shoulders and I leaned into him. "Eva and I are occupied. See you when we see you."

"One would think that you would like an idea of what you will be doing tomorrow." Wells studied me. "One of the reasons I was so excited to contract your services was due to your professionalism. I see now that I was mistaken."

"What can I say? Even the Sibyl needs a night off now and then." I shrugged. "What time do I have to meet the driver in the morning?"

"Four a.m. in the lobby."

"Then I'll get back on the clock at 3:59. Good night."

"I was also wondering if—"

"See, um, Wells?" Jonah piped up from his spot beside me. "That moment that Eva said 'good night' was when we were done with you. Now, go on. Get."

Jonah closed the door in Wells' irritated face, and turned to me. He looked vexed, but I didn't give him a chance to say anything else. I pushed him against the door and lost myself completely in the man who I could finally call my own.

ELEVEN

EVA MCRAYNE

"Can't we just stay like this forever?" I muttered against Jonah's shoulder after he dared to suggest we get up and shower. "I don't want to move."

Jonah laughed as he ran fingers through my hair and down the arm I had laying across his chest. "Don't you feel a mess, baby? You don't want a shower?"

"No." I drummed my fingers against Jonah's chest in time with his heartbeat. "I don't."

"You just said you didn't want to move." He adjusted his head against the pillow. "One would think you'd be worn out by now."

"I'm tired." I pushed hair from my face. "But a good sort of tired. Like when you get finished at the gym, I'm sure."

"Better."

"Better?" I leaned up on my elbows to see his face while I teased him. "I wasn't expecting you to ever say anything was better than one of your gym workouts."

"Um, Eva? I love exercise as much as anyone, but when it comes to sex with you, there is no question or comparison."

"Not even with your Gotch Bible?"

I burst out laughing as Jonah growled playfully and rolled us so that I was beneath him. I wasn't used to this. I wasn't used to being so damn happy.

"Ok, ok!" I gasped. "You made your point!"

"Good to know." Jonah kissed me until I moaned. "And for the record, it's the Gotch Bible."

"That's what I said—"

I froze as I felt a set of eyes on me. Not Jonah's either. I turned my head towards the window and saw nothing.

Jonah noticed the change in my demeanor. He lifted up to follow my gaze, then he looked back down at me.

"Eva?"

"Did you feel that?" I met his gaze. "I just had the craziest notion that someone was watching us."

"Stay here. I'll check it out."

"Jonah—"

I flipped over on my side as he got off me. Jonah snagged his batons from their place on the nightstand. I was bad, I know. I admired the lines of his lean frame as he checked the doors. The closet.

"Have I ever told you how hot you are when you go into protector mode?"

That earned me a look of exasperation.

I just grinned. "Come back here. Everything's fine. I'm just jumpy, is all." I reached for him. "I'm not used to being so happy."

"Jumpy or not, it was worth a look." He came back to the bed and kissed me. "Since I'm up, I'm going to go take that shower. I have to be back at the estate soon."

"Do you really have to leave?" I frowned. "It's so much better when you're here."

Jonah didn't want to leave; I could see it written all over his face. He ran a hand through his hair and I felt guilty for even asking. I knew he had responsibilities that didn't involve me. I started to apologize when he spoke.

"I need to see if Ben-Israel deciphered something we found at Waseda University. I can come right back after that. Tomorrow night?"

"That'll give me time to do this damn photoshoot with Wells." I squeezed his hand. "I'm just being greedy, is all. You go do what you have to do, handsome. I understand better than anyone that you have a ton of shit on your plate."

I got up on my knees and threw my arms around his neck. I placed a kiss beneath his Adam's apple and grinned when his pulse quickened.

"I love that I can do that to you."

"I've changed my mind. I'm not leaving. I'll just call."

"Jonah!" I laughed. "If you have to go, you have to go. I'll be waiting for you right here."

"Exactly," Jonah replied. "I'm not willing to leave you here."

"I don't want you to skip important things." I ran my palm up his side. "And whatever you found in Japan is important."

Jonah tried to glower, but didn't work because he knew that I was right.

I kissed him quickly. "Go. Take your shower. We can meet back up when you're finished at the estate, ok?"

"Alright, fine."

Jonah disappeared into the bathroom and I fell back on the bed with a sigh. I didn't know what the hell I was getting into with Joey. With the possibility of Cyrus being free. With Typhon and broken shrines. I felt as if I had a million pieces to a million different puzzles and none of them wanted to fit together.

I rolled over, onto my side, and spotted something small on the window sill. The same one where I could have sworn someone was watching us earlier.

What the hell?

I crossed the room to see the tiny glass figurine of a peacock. I froze as I studied it. I knew exactly what that meant. Peacocks were a symbol of Hera.

I guess she hadn't forgotten about our arrangement.

I ignored the figurine and pulled the note beneath it closer to me. I was convinced I was going to choke as my heart rose to my throat. Written in perfect calligraphy, the ancient language of the gods spelled out a very simple message for me.

You are out of time.

———

"Are you certain that you want to spend time on Poveglia?" Wells wiped his mouth with a napkin before he continued. "The island has quite the reputation for being dangerous."

I remained silent as I had throughout most of our meal. I wasn't a fan of Wells Cole. During the photoshoot, he'd been too demanding. Too touchy-feely. I'd asked him to stop multiple times, but he would laugh at me. Told me to relax and enjoy the shoot. His words hadn't made me feel better. They had pissed me off. But I kept my mouth shut for the most part. It had been a charity photoshoot. I had told myself that I would never see him again after it was over.

Yet, here I was, sitting at a dinner table with the man I had come to despise so quickly.

"That's why we're going." Joey released an exaggerated sigh. "Where there's danger, Evie is there with bells on." He decided to change the subject. "How'd the shoot go?"

I made a face at the topic.

"Wonderful. Eva is a natural."

"I was frozen solid. There's no way Giorgio didn't pick that up." I took a bite of my salad. "I'm pretty sure I'll be blue in those proofs."

"They are beautiful." Wells grinned. "I'm sure this will be our most successful campaign to date."

I bet so.

"Just as I'm sure Poveglia is going to be one of my most successful episodes to date," I shrugged in response. "I can't wait to fight something. It'll take the edge off."

"I understand that need for carnage far too well." Wells sipped his wine. "My days in the field are over. I've accepted that."

I raised my eyebrow at that one. Such an odd statement from a man who was a business model.

"Eva has a good head on her shoulders," Joey piped up. "But you should have been with us in Japan."

"Joey, now is not the time—"

"She *totally* freaked out when a ghost touched her."

"Joey!" I stiffened. "What the hell?"

"Relax." He laughed. "I'm just teasing you. Though you got to admit, the ghost thing was creepy."

Wells was looking between us, his expression stoic before he stood up and shut the doors to the private dining room we were in.

"Did Poseidon appear?"

I narrowed my eyes at him and put my hands in my lap in case I needed to have my sword handy. I'd been on edge since I'd found the note in my room the night before. And Wells was an unknown element. An element I didn't like in the least.

"What do you know about Poseidon?" I asked my question slowly. Carefully. "Why do you care?"

"Because I have had dealings with him in the past." Wells dropped back down in the chair next to mine. "Relax. I am not your enemy."

"Then, who *are* you?"

"My legal name now is Wells Cole." He gazed at me intently. "But in times far gone, I was known as Achilles."

I took a deep breath and tried to relax my shoulders. I couldn't do it.

Finally, Joey broke the silence that had fallen around us.

"Achilles? The soldier? Dude," the cameraman grinned. "That's awesome. Now I *know* you have to come to Poveglia. Somebody has to keep Eva in line."

"I'll be fine." I kept my eyes on the man next to me. "Why are you so concerned about Poseidon?"

"You should always be concerned when Poseidon's name comes up." Wells—no, Achilles—picked up his wine glass and gestured. "Do you not recall the stories regarding his volatile nature? He can turn on you in a heartbeat, dear girl."

I opened my mouth, then shut it before I could say something that would make me look like an idiot. The truth was, I didn't know much about the god of the sea at all.

"Look, it doesn't matter. What does matter is that Poseidon's shrines have been disturbed, and—"

"Poseidon's shrines were disturbed? That is quite serious."

"Yes." I bit back my irritation at being interrupted. Maybe that was my problem. Wells reminded me too much of Cyrus. "And the Council is convinced that Typhon is being set loose."

"By whom?"

"No clue. Hera is a suspect. So are the Titans, but I don't think so. I haven't seen any evidence that they are involved."

"What do you know about the Titans, Eva?"

"Not much," I admitted. "I know about the war between the Titans and the Olympians. I know they lost."

"That is all?" He looked at me in surprise. "Did your Keeper not train you on these matters?"

"Look, my Keeper ..."

"Cyrus Alexius," Achilles butted in once again. "I have encountered him in the past. Yet, he is not here now. Why?"

"I don't need some overhyped babysitter," I bristled. "But for your information, Cyrus is in Tartarus. I have a new Keeper now."

"And that would be ...?"

"Ulysses of Athens."

"Then you should be well versed on the Titans. And all of the gods. Especially those that sit on the Council you serve."

Achilles looked between the two of us, then rubbed his hand over his face. When he dropped it, he spoke.

"Very well. Yet, this would be so much easier if you knew the basics." Achilles took another sip of his drink before he continued. "Titan magicks are far more powerful than the Olympians. They pride themselves on their abilities to manipulate the world around them."

"That means they focus on the elements." I shrugged when he looked at me, surprised. "What? I graduated from the Academy. I'm not completely stupid."

"Regardless." He gave me a cold look. "The Titans may have lost the war, but they have been far from quiet. The lands they control are called Territories. Each numbered to warn those of us with Olympian blood to steer clear."

"Why?" I went back to picking my salad. "If the Olympians won, then why are there areas that are off-limits to us?"

"Because of the magicks I spoke of." Achilles snagged my wrist and reminded me of how much he had put his hands on me earlier that day.

I pulled my arm back so that it was out of his reach.

"The effects can range from illnesses to a complete elimination of your immortality if you stay in their lands for too long."

"Really?" I frowned at him. "How is that possible?"

"A simple enchantment of the soil." He sipped wine. "And if you are unknowledgeable of those locations, then so much the better for your enemy."

"Ok," I breathed. I mean, what else could I say? I had no idea that the world was a literal chessboard for me. "You said the Titans had been less than quiet. What did you mean by that?"

"They are the force behind the monotheistic religions that dominate the world today."

"Wait," Joey frowned. "I was raised Catholic. There is no way the Greeks had anything to do with what I learned."

"You are wrong." Achilles leaned back in his chair. "The Vatican is the headquarters of Titan forces. Why do you think it is a city-state? Its highest positions are held by beings far older than the religion itself."

"Listen." Joey leaned forward. "Don't get me wrong. If you're really Achilles …"

"It makes sense," I interrupted. "Sorry, Joey. But I'm with Achilles on this one. Think about it. If the gods get their power through believers, and those believers stop paying homage to them, it's a surgical strike. And it has been damned successful."

"Until you came along," Achilles responded drily. "To think, Apollo's little girl with a television show has disrupted centuries of work."

"I don't think I've been that effective," I snorted. "Churches are still filled to the brim every Sunday. Especially where I come from."

"No, they aren't." Joey pushed his plate away. "But I don't think you're the sole reason for that, Evie. The Church itself is to blame for its decline. As the times change, so have attitudes. People our age and younger don't like to be told how to live our lives."

"You have a very valid point, Joey," Achilles nodded. "Yet, it cannot be disputed that the old temples have gained more attention since *Grave Messages* has been on the air. Apollo himself enjoys quite a bit of power now. More so than he has since his heyday."

The room grew quiet as we got lost in our own thoughts. Our dinner was supposed to be a way to unwind before I meet with the Council in the morning and our following trip to Poveglia. Now, we were discussing religion and the fact that Wells Cole was not in fact a simple man, but a soldier renowned for his actions in Greece.

I was done. I wanted to go to my room and crawl into the bed. I took the napkin from my lap and stood up. Joey and Achilles joined me less than two seconds later.

"Listen." I rubbed my forehead. "I am supposed to head out to Poveglia first thing in the morning. If you wish to accompany me, you are more than welcome to. If you want to stay out of the drama that is my life, that's good too. I can't blame you. But right now? I think I just want to go to bed. Today has been quite exhausting."

"Of course, Eva." Achilles offered me his arm. "I will walk you back to your room."

"No." I glared at him. "I'm not comfortable with you coming anywhere close to my hotel room."

I slipped out of the dining room and took the back stairs to my floor. This hotel catered to the elite … celebrities that didn't want to be photographed every moment they stepped out in public.

Celebrities like me.

Thank the gods for peace and quiet. I relished the silence that surrounded me when I entered my room. I kicked off my heels and pulled my hair free from the top knot it was in. I considered texting Jonah. He'd said he was coming back tonight. Maybe he got caught up at the estate looking into those spirits in Japan.

I didn't want to think about it. I didn't want to think about restless spirits or broken shrines. Not tonight. I wanted to relax. I needed to curl up in the bed and take my mind off everything so that I could focus on my meeting in the morning.

Yeah. Right. Even I knew better than that. Especially since my mind kept going back to what Achilles had said about the Titans. How they had been the primary source of shoving pagan religions into the shadows to weaken the Olympians.

I made up my mind to research the rise of monotheistic religions as I approached my closet. And I would. But not in the evening gown I wore. I needed sweats and coffee for this kind of research. I opened the door and bent down to reach for my luggage.

Only to cry out in pain as someone struck out. My head snapped back as I landed on my back. I didn't stay down for long though. To do so would mean my ass would be handed to me. I rolled to the side and scrambled up to my feet to see a man stroll out of the closet.

"I didn't realize this room came with a personal maid." I spat blood out of my mouth as I willed my sword into my hand. "Do I have to tip you? Or can we just call you busting in my face as even-steven?"

My newest opponent was my height and skinny, but when I threw a punch at his jaw, I realized he was as hard as granite. I hissed, then drew my hand back as he shook off the hit. I moved to strike again, this time with my sword, but the man was quick.

He grabbed my sword wrist, then slammed his hand against my elbow. I cried out for a second time as I felt something snap in my arm. He jerked me forward and slammed his head against my nose, then dropped me.

I landed flat on my back as the man looked down at me with such hatred, any normal person would have backed down. Too bad for him I wasn't anywhere close to being normal. I smiled and licked the blood off my teeth.

"I gotta say, you're pretty pathetic." I forced myself to sit up and ignored the fire that ran up my injured arm. "I mean, you had a surprise drop on me. You should have wiped me out right then and there. That was such a wasted opportunity on your part."

"You have yet to pay the price, Sibyl." The man's right hand shimmered as a wicked ax appeared in his grasp. "I will not walk away until your debt is paid with your head."

"My head, huh?" I kept my eyes on the ax as he crept forward. I knew now exactly who had sent an assassin to my door. Hera. "You know, my publicist can hook you up with as many headshots as you want. There wouldn't be nearly as much blood involved."

"Bitch—"

He swung the weapon in a wide arc. I let instincts take over and dropped back flat against the carpet and kicked his knee—then again, until he stumbled away from me.

The Titan clamored back, but I knew he wasn't done. When he swung a second time, I rolled to my feet. I used his momentum against him. I kicked him in the gut but caught his uppercut right in the mouth.

Dammit. Just *dammit*.

I jerked up my sword with my good arm and prayed I wouldn't have to use it. I wasn't ambidextrous at all. I lunged forward, determined to bash his face in when he swung at me not once but twice. Both strikes meant to cut me in half before I got too close to him. As the stranger raised his weapon for a final strike, I thrust my sword forward. I twisted it as deep into his abdomen as it would go.

His grey eyes widened with shock as he dropped the ax onto the floor next to me. The stranger stared down at my sword before I whispered in his ear. "Send Hera my regards. And tell her to send a professional the next time instead of insulting me with such a rookie."

My attacker vanished without a single word. I wiped my sword clean on the side of the ruined dress and willed it to disappear. Hotels tended to frown on the presence of such weapons, after all. And I couldn't be too careful.

Despite the man's disappearance, his ax remained. I lifted it and winced. The damn thing was heavy. Solid metal. Engraved with symbols I didn't recognize.

I tucked it away in the back of my closet, cradling my arm against my chest to keep it still. But damn, it was hard. I had too much to do. I didn't have time to waste waiting on my arm to heal. And my enemy had broken it. I'd caused enough broken bones during my time as the Sibyl to know what one sounded like. And the fire I felt?

Ow. My only saving grace was the rush of sheer anger that filled me moments later. I closed my eyes as I felt Cyrus' presence. Even now, I recognized it.

"You sent me to Tartarus."

"You dropped me off a cliff." I was surprised at how cold my voice sounded as I faced the closet door. "How the hell did they let you out?"

"Bitch, you will pay for the time you have stolen from me!"

I turned to head to the bathroom when Cyrus grabbed my broken arm. Right at the elbow. Black spots danced in front of my eyes from the pain before I whirled around.

"Don't touch me!" I shoved him back, but I closed the distance between us to shove him again. "Who do you think you are? What makes you think you have the right to touch me?"

"You can't get rid of me so easily, Eva." I saw his jaw twitch, which meant he was as angry as I was. "I'm bound to you through an oath—"

"Oh, fuck off!" I hissed. "You aren't bound to me anymore. Ulysses has stepped in to take over the role—"

Cyrus caught me off guard when he lashed out to wrap his hand around my throat. He cracked my head against the wall, hard enough for stars to dance in my vision.

"What courage you have now!" He ignored my attempts to claw at his hand. "Is this because of Rowe? I'd heard that you threw yourself at him enough that he finally decided to add you to his list of whores." Cyrus tightened his grip until I couldn't breathe.

I had to get him to let me go. I didn't have a choice.

"You stupid, stupid girl." He released a hard laugh. "Have the warnings I've given you not sunk in? Have you forgotten them already?"

I felt a rush of fear flow through me when Cyrus produced a dagger in his free hand. He pressed the tip of it beneath my right eye, hard enough to draw blood.

"Let," I choked, "go—"

"You believe it is so simple to replace me? To have me thrown away in Tartarus and Rowe will protect you?" he snarled. "Very well. But you have signed his death warrant. And your own."

Cyrus willed the sword Jonah had made for him and pressed the blade against my throat as he released his grip. I could breathe, but I was afraid to. I felt a trickle of blood run down to my shoulder as I squeezed shut my eyes.

"There is a bounty on your head now." He pressed the blade harder into my skin and I felt the blood pool around the blade. "I plan to claim it."

TWELVE

JONAH ROWE

Jonah didn't hear back from Ben-Israel for nearly twelve hours after he returned from Italy. But instead of going straight back to the hotel room in Venice, he decided to keep himself busy with the library and working out. Hell, he'd nearly ditched the idea of coming back to the estate in the first place. When he went back to Italy, he wasn't going to be able to leave Eva again. That was for sure.

"Stop doing that."

Jonah looked up to see Reena narrowing her eyes at him.

"What? I thought you needed help building this thing?"

"This thing is my easel. And you have that smile that tells me your mind is not on building it."

"Guilty." Jonah shrugged. "I'm doing my best, Re."

"Uh-huh. So, how was Italy?"

"What?"

"Italy. You know, that country you disappeared to last night? It's across the ocean. I'm sure you've heard of it."

"Funny."

"I thought so." She chuckled, then abandoned her saw to sit on the floor next to him. "I wanted to talk to you anyway."

"About what?"

"You never did tell me how you and Eva made things official." Reena rested her chin in the palm of her hand. "And it's been what? A year?"

"It just ... happened." Jonah allowed himself a smile at the thought of Eva. "Seriously, we stopped lying to ourselves and just bowed to the truth. We've been in love for a while. Felt like a weight off my back, too, when I finally said it."

"Yeah?"

"Yeah." Jonah went back to lining up the two pieces of wood until he realized that Reena was still sitting there expectantly. "What?"

"That's all I'm going to get? It just happened?" She snorted. "I want details, dammit."

"You're expecting girl talk?" Jonah laughed. "It may have escaped your notice, but I'm a dude."

"And for a dude, you suck at gossip." Reena grinned. "You seem happy. Actually happy."

"I am, Reena." Jonah sat down again next to her. "Eva truly brings out the best in me. I don't have to walk on eggshells when I talk to her. Not every word is a trigger. She helps me look forward to the days. All of 'em. Just hearing her voice makes me smile. Eva is it. Truly."

Reena's expression softened as she squeezed his hand. "I'm glad, J. I am. I can't think of two people who deserve to be happy more than you guys."

"You two gonna sing 'Kumbaya' next or something?" Spader came in with a grin.

Terrence was right behind him, with a box of donuts. "I got dibs on the chorus if you do."

"Not now, Spade." Terrence ignored Reena's glare at the donuts. "And ease up, Re. We're celebrating. J's home and all is—relatively —right with the world."

"Relatively," Jonah grinned. "Japan is still up in the air, ain't it?"

"Not right now." Terrence popped open the top of the box. A sweet smell filled the air, nearly masking the wood laid out in front of them. "Right now it's all about carbs and calories."

Jonah took the donut Terrence passed him and raised his eyebrows at Reena while he bit into it.

"So, what were you two talking about?" Spader grabbed his own donut out of the box. "Looked serious."

"Jeva."

"Jeva?" Jonah nearly choked on his food at Reena's response. "What the hell is that?"

"The nickname that the media has given you and Evie," Terrence grinned devilishly. "Nice one, Re."

"The media?"

"Yeah," Reena laughed. "You haven't been online over the past few days. There are pictures of you and Eva in Seattle all over the news."

Jonah shook his head. "Nosy asses. Whatever. I'm happier than I've ever been. They won't take my shine."

"Take your shine? They are basking with you." Terrence grinned wider. "You're on top, brother. They ain't trying to knock you down."

"Jeva, though?" Spader scoffed. "Sounds too close to java. They could've come up with something better than that."

"You mean, like using our actual names?"

"That's no fun." Reena grinned wider as she saw the opportunity to tease him. "They could have gone with Eonah. Or Mowe. Or Jova."

"Not Jova," Spader joked as he started his second donut. "Sounds too much like that old car from the 70s."

"Y'all are crazy," Jonah muttered, but then he laughed. "I guess we'll have to go with Rendall for you, Reena. Terrence, well ... it's to be determined. And Spader? Well, you date so many women that I'd run out of breath trying to come up with a portmanteau for *you*."

"Nope. We aren't Brangelina status," Reena chuckled. "You never did tell me about Italy."

"When did you go to Italy?"

"Last night."

Spader scrutinized Jonah before he burst out laughing.

"J can't tell us shit about Italy, Re," he managed. "He can't because he didn't see a damn bit of it outside of Eva's hotel room.

Jonah smacked Spader.

He yelped and Jonah shrugged again. "Nothing personal," he told him. "For one, you're drooling over my girl. And two, it's none of your business."

"Dammit, J," Spader rubbed his arm. "Your 'principle' hurts like a bitch."

"At least it wasn't the back of your head this time." Jonah tightened a screw before he continued. "Anyway, you're not getting any details about my time with Eva. It's personal."

"How did things go once you saw Joey again?"

The mention of the cameraman jogged Jonah's memory and gave him the perfect way to change the topic of this conversation.

"Eva found evidence that he's using again."

Jonah's friends went silent as they looked at one another, then back at him.

It was Reena who spoke. "When you say *using*, you better mean a new type of camera?"

"You wish, Reena," Jonah muttered. "But no. Not this time. He is back on the horse. Heroin. He tried to gaslight Eva and put her down to take the heat off him."

"Jesus." Terrence whistled. "How long?"

"No idea."

"She can't call her boss and get him yanked?"

"No."

"Wait. You said that Joey wrecked into Eva's car in Japan to keep her from going into the bay, right?" Spader finished his donut. "Think it was heroics? Or was he high as shit?"

"High as shit, I'm sure," Jonah answered drily. "But Eva said Connor wouldn't bat an eye, as *he* is a functioning addict himself. I told her she ought to leak it to every tabloid and gossip rag in existence. Let it take on a life of its own. I told her it needs to be made so big of a deal that Connor couldn't ignore it without losing face."

"She won't." Reena picked up the flathead screwdriver and tapped it against the floor. "Eva won't risk anything coming back on *Grave*. That show is her baby."

"So, he gets off scot-free again?" Spader demanded. "Who are these people? Aren't they held accountable for *anything*?"

"I wouldn't give a damn if I knew Joey shot up on his time off." Jonah took the screwdriver away from Reena before the tapping noise drove him insane. "But you know it doesn't start or stop when the cameras are rolling."

"He went to rehab once. Maybe this time it will stick."

"Fine." Jonah noticed he was tapping the screwdriver himself now, so he lowered it. "But if his mouth gets him in trouble again, all bets are off. Just saying."

"At any rate—"

Reena stopped when Ben-Israel poked in his head.

Jonah perked up.

"Hey guys. Got a minute?"

"Sure, man." Jonah abandoned the easel, then gave Ben-Israel his full attention. "You got anything on that document?"

"I think I deciphered it." He joined them in the room. "It's a call to action. Whoever wrote this put out a hit on somebody."

"Do you know who?" Reena frowned. "Does it say anything about disrupting energies?"

"No." Ben-Israel sat the paper on Reena's desk, then pointed to a series of characters in the center of the page. "See this? It means bounty. Looks like they are offering two million."

"Two million?" Jonah murmured. "Dollars?"

"Yeah." Ben-Israel shook his head as Reena and the rest of the group crowded around him.

"What?"

"It doesn't make any sense. Not really." He ran that same finger under a line of text. "See this? It stands for 'bird'. And this? Whore. So, I'm thinking the target is a woman."

"Bird?" Jonah repeated. "Whore? Almost makes me think someone was targeting prostitutes or something. Don't know about that bird thing though."

"Could it be related to Zeus?" Ben-Israel wondered aloud. "Eagle and all that?"

"Possibly. Doesn't Zeus have an entire harem on the earth

plane?" Reena tilted her head as she followed Ben-Israel's finger. "Could be an attack on them."

"It's not clear at all." Ben-Israel leaned over the document. "It talks about breaking an oath but there's no clear distinction on who is being targeted." He began to read aloud. "As an oath has been broken, we shall gather. But it has been foreseen the whore has deceived us. Bring the bird—no, wait … phoenix's … head to our Lord's house to receive two million dollars. You will be crowned as a son of god."

Ben-Israel stood upright. "There's more, but that's the main paragraph."

Jonah's entire body went ice cold. "Phoenix. This is a hit on Eva. Why would he leave it in his wife's office?"

"That's pretty easy." Reena shook her head. "It's a misdirect. Scamander hoped all this would fall on Rhode."

"Why would the Titans use Hebrew?" Ben-Israel frowned. "Aren't they better versed in Latin? Maybe it's not from the Titans at all."

"I can assume it's possibly not Titans," Jonah said. "I wonder how old this is. Could this be the assignment that the Ange de la Mort was working on?"

"There's no telling, Jonah." Frowning, Reena tugged at her ponytail. "This could been months old for all we know. Or years."

"I gotta go." Jonah took a step back. "I'm going to give her a head's up about this."

"Be careful, brother."

Jonah snorted as he initiated the Astralimes. He appeared in the lobby of a grand hotel. The place looked ancient but well kept. It butted up against a canal. He headed over to the front desk and the woman beamed at him before she spoke in rapid-fire Italian.

"Can I help you, sir?"

"Yes," Jonah leaned against the desk as he responded in kind. "I'm with Theia Productions. Miss McRayne called me to bring her a particular camera. Can you tell me what room she is in?"

"Of course!" She typed something into the computer. "She is on the third floor. Room 3678."

"Thanks."

Jonah headed towards the elevator, a bit shocked it was that easy to get the information for one of the most famous women on the planet. He was going to have to talk to Eva about the security measures being taken when she stayed at hotels.

The elevator doors opened on the third floor and Jonah frowned as he headed towards Eva's room. It was quiet. Too quiet.

He stopped in front of the door and knocked. "Eva?"

Nothing. Jonah narrowed his eyes as he focused until his hands stung with blue current. The resulting click told him that the lock had been electric and he was now free to enter the room. When Jonah stepped into the room, he froze as he took in the sight before him: Cyrus Alexius, the traitor, had a blade to Eva's throat.

"One step forward, hero," Cyrus spoke calmly, sounding almost rational. "And the whore will lose her head. Leave now, or I will take yours next."

Cyrus yelled when Eva released a flash of fire against his side. He dropped the sword seconds before she ducked beneath his arm. She cracked her elbow against the back of his head twice before Cyrus dropped to sweep her legs out from under her. Eva's head cracked against the floor, but she rolled back to her feet.

Jonah rushed forward as Cyrus swung a punch at Eva. She blocked it before she grabbed Cyrus by the front of his shirt to head butt him away from her. He snarled as his head snapped back and he grabbed her by the shoulders; Eva released a choked cry when his knee connected with her stomach.

Eva staggered back from Cyrus' strike, clearing the way for Jonah to slam him full on in the face with both batons. He fell to a knee, and vanished.

"God …. dammit!" Jonah snapped. "What the hell—"

He shut up when he heard Eva coughing, and filed away his anger as he dropped down beside her. "Are you ok?"

"Fine," Eva managed before she became overcome with a coughing fit. She fell back on her ass and leaned her head against the wall. "Just ... need a minute."

"Eva, what the hell happened?" Jonah asked as he tried to check her injuries without touching her. "Jesus ..."

"Man ... came out of the closet. Won that fight." She closed her eyes and swallowed. "Cyrus came after."

"What *man*?" Jonah demanded. "What do you mean?"

"Someone tried to kill me," Eva answered. "He had an ax. I handled that, then Cyrus came from nowhere. I don't know how he even found me. Apollo broke the bond—"

"Joseph," Jonah growled. "You were right. You did hear him talking to Cyrus the other day."

"Maybe. I don't know that for sure." Eva cradled her arm against her stomach. "It's possible Cyrus was following the assassin. He said something about a bounty on my head."

"How? How did he get out of Tartarus?"

"I don't know, handsome. But the timing is pretty convenient, don't you think?"

"You think it's connected to the mess with Typhon?" Jonah ran his hand tensely over his head. "You said the first attacker left his weapon?"

"Yeah. Put it in the closet. It's heavy as hell. You can't miss it."

Jonah got up and pulled out the axe. It was silver, carved with symbols. "I think you're right, Superstar." He balanced it with both hands. "See this? The inscription states it was blessed in a cathedral at Vatican City."

"Fabulous. Now, the Catholic church is trying to kill me?" Eva released a dry laugh. "My enemies' list just keeps getting longer and longer."

Jonah grimaced. "Not necessarily. It is possible that the assassin is of the Titan contingent in the Vatican, but it doesn't mean the Vatican is behind the hit. And Cyrus is involved, and we know it's not about money with him."

"It wasn't the Titans who put out the hit."

Eva stood slowly, bracing herself against the wall. She stumbled over to the dresser to pull open the top drawer with one hand.

"What's up with your arm, Superstar?"

"Broken." She lifted up a card, then turned towards him. "I got this last night. Found it after you left, handsome."

Jonah sat the ax aside, then took the card from her. *Your time is up.*

"What do you make of it?"

"Does it matter? The hit is out there. Now, I need to figure out how to stop it." Eva grabbed a pair of pants from her luggage, then seemed to think better of it. She dropped them and snagged a t-shirt instead. "Thanks, Jonah. You saved my ass tonight."

"But?"

"No buts. I'm beat all to hell and exhausted." She turned back towards him. "I am going to go take a shower. Clean up and wait for my healing to kick in."

"Do you want me to call Apollo?"

"No." She went into the bathroom.

Jonah waited until he heard the water start before he headed away from the closet. He froze when Eva pulled open the bathroom door. Jonah gave her an innocent look. There was no way for her to hear him.

"Can I get you to unzip me, handsome? I can't reach the back of this dress one-handed."

"Oh, yeah." Jonah approached her, relieved. "I got you."

Eva turned around and Jonah pushed her hair out of the way before he tugged down the zipper. "Anything else?"

"No, thank you." Eva gave him a small smile before she went back into the bathroom.

Jonah counted to twenty before he slipped out of the room. He heard the man shuffle behind the door with zeal, for whatever reason.

"Nico?" he asked, his voice falsely husky and provocative. "That you?"

Jonah palmed Joey's face when it appeared and shoved him back. He staggered, then fell to the floor.

"Nah, I ain't your plaything, asshole," he snarled. "I'm someone else."

"Jonah? What the …?" Joey rolled to his feet as Jonah shut the door behind him. "What are you doing here?"

"You got one second to answer my question." Jonah stepped farther in.

Joey stepped back.

"Did you tell Cyrus where Eva was tonight?"

"No, dude." Joey shook his head. "I haven't seen Cyrus in ages. Isn't he in prison or something?"

"Try again. Eva heard you talking to him in Japan." Jonah crossed his arms over his chest. "What is he offering you in exchange for information? Heroin? Money? What?"

"Look," Joey raised his hands. "I don't know what's going on, but there's nothing I can say to help you."

"When it comes to addiction," Jonah snapped, "the first thing to go is the truth. Now answer the question or I'm breaking your jaw."

"Fine." Joey looked down at the floor and ran his hand through his hair. "Cyrus was my dealer before it all went to hell. I got my fix, he got information. But I haven't said shit to him in awhile. That much is true."

"Did you invite him in here, yes or no?"

"No! I told you that already." Joey began to clench his hands into fists. "You think I want Eva hurt? Hell, no. What happened at the airfield was an accident—"

"How do you know she's hurt?" Jonah asked quietly.

"Dude, it's Cyrus. We both know their history. If he's free, and he finds out about the two of you screwing, he'll go ballistic. And Eva can't get hurt. We got too much shit to do for the show."

"Yeah, the show." Jonah was so disgusted, he didn't know what to do. "That's *all* you care about."

"Look man, I didn't tell Cyrus that Eva was here!" Joey snapped. "I told him to meet me in the sauna tonight, but he insisted on the room, and—"

Joey froze. He realized his mistake a second too late.

Jonah popped his neck as he sized Joey up. The man was a marksman, not a fighter. Should be easy.

"Jaw or wrists?" Jonah whispered. "I really have no preference."

"Wait! Just ... just wait for one damn second!" Joey hastily held up both hands. "You break my wrists, I can't do the show. You know that. Plus, you break my jaw and I won't be able to help Eva with the commentary shit."

"Don't really give a fuck about the show right now, Joey."

"You don't, but Eva does. Come on. You want to beat the shit out of me? Do it after we're done in Italy."

"Are you proposing I let you off without a hitch, Joseph?" Jonah demanded. "Are you kidding me? There's no way in hell—"

A realization hit Jonah like a brick. Cyrus was supposed to meet Joey tonight. Joey thought Jonah had been one of his lovers coming to see him. Cyrus ... *and Joey*?

"You and Cyrus." Jonah stared at him, still stunned. "How long have you and Cyrus been screwing on the side?"

Joey's silence screamed the answers he wouldn't say out loud.

Jonah let the final pieces fall together in his mind. "You two have been together since the beginning of *Grave*." Jonah nearly spat on him too. "Does Eva know?"

"No." Joey took a step back. "Not together. We just screw sometimes."

Jonah gritted his teeth and grabbed Joey by the throat. He lifted him up until they were nose to nose.

"You little bastard," he hissed. "Eva loved you. Trusted you. Lodged you rent-free. And you're *fucking* the man who abused her, and is trying to kill her? Even after you let her take the fall for your goddamn crimes?"

"J, man, let ... up ... can't answer ... q-questions ... if I can't ... b-breathe."

Jonah let up on Joey's throat.

The man stumbled back in a coughing fit before he could answer any questions. "Don't know what to say." Joey managed. "Shit just ... snowballed, alright? I wasn't expecting things to happen. They simply did."

Jonah said nothing.

Joey tried again. "I know it looks bad. I know. But I'll figure out a way to make it right. I will. Just don't tell Eva. She's pissed enough as is."

"It doesn't look bad, Joseph," Jonah grumbled. "It *is* bad. Let's start with you answering some questions."

Joey dropped his hands and tilted his head back. "You want the truth, you gotta promise not to get pissed at me."

Jonah released a long, loud exhalation. "I can't promise anything. That is the best I can do. Now, when did you begin your arrangement with the Keeper?"

"About four years ago. We'd dose up, then screw."

"Where was Eva?"

"Asleep. Or at the office."

"When was the last time you met up?"

"Two days ago." Joey cut his eyes over at Jonah. "In Japan."

"What sort of information did Alexius ask for?"

"Everything, really. What Eva did with her day, who she talked to, where she went. It was nothing, usually."

"Usually?"

"Yeah. Sometimes it broke bad, but not all the time."

"Mmm-hmm," Jonah said softly. "And at what point did you tell Cyrus about Eva and me being a couple?"

Joey opened his mouth, but Jonah waved a hand. "Before you ask the obvious question, I'm aware that you called Eva an easy lay," Jonah told him. "You'd only say that out of spite. Only this time, the spite wasn't yours."

Joey sighed. "As soon as it happened, okay? After I saw you two in the lobby together."

Jonah tightened his fists. It was taking every ounce of restraint he possessed not to attack Joey. He was suddenly acutely aware of how punchable Joey's face was.

"Surely you know that Alexius doesn't give a damn about you? He's been playing you like a fine tune from the moment this arrangement began. And *all* the things he's done for you in order to get information? All the favors and perks? They'll vanish the second he no longer needs you."

"I figured he'd kill me before that happens." Joey shrugged. "I'm not an idiot. I'm just trying to get what I can while I can."

"So, you know Cyrus is a threat to you?"

"Yeah, dude. I've seen him beat the shit out of Eva just because she didn't get home from work fast enough. You think he'd hesitate to run me through? Hell, he finds out I'm talking to you and he probably will."

"So, you've witnessed Eva being abused, too? Why didn't you tell Apollo? Why didn't you tell the Council?"

"What the hell was I going to say to them, Jonah? What?" Joey glared at him. "And how? I can't just pick up the damn phone and call them."

"You got Apollo's speed dial the same time Eva did, bitch." Jonah glared right back. "As for what you would say? It's damn simple: 'Apollo, Cyrus is battering your daughter. She needs help.'"

"Look, it's not like I didn't do anything. No, I didn't step in. But I bandaged her up when she would let me."

Jonah struck out with a haymaker punch that connected with Joey's nose. The cameraman dropped to his knees and cradled his face. It took every ounce of balance Jonah had not to finish the man off. It was bad enough that Joseph was the reason Eva had been taken away from him. Now, to hear all this made the images of violence Jonah had gone to Siberia to control rush forward in his mind.

"Joseph Lawson, you are nothing to me," Jonah said in a measured tone. If he got louder, he'd likely make this ten times worse. "Not family, not a friend, not *human* ... nothing. The only single, solitary reason that you're making it to tomorrow is to do what you have to for Eva. And then, you're going to tell her everything. I'll be damned if you force me to have *this* shit on my conscience!"

Agonized and anguished, Joey opened his mouth to protest.

Jonah grabbed his head and forced it back so that Joey began to choke. "Everything," he whispered. "And then you're going to leave and go to rehab, go to Wyoming ... go to hell, for all I care. Right now, you are a danger to Eva. That means that I am a danger to *you*."

"If ... if I tell Eva, I'll lose everything, man."

"When," Jonah seethed. "Not if. *When* you tell Eva. You ain't got a choice."

Joey took a ragged breath, then adjusted himself to lessen the pain. "I'll figure something out."

"You did this to yourself. You realize that," Jonah snapped. "How the hell could you be so stupid, Lawson? How?"

"Have you considered something?" Joey stared at him. "Don't go off half-cocked and think! This is gonna break Eva's heart, Jonah. It is. You know how fragile she can be. If she knows that I went behind her back, it'll crush her. I've done a lot of shit, but I don't want to be the one to do that to her."

"So, by keeping *your* secret, I spare her?" Jonah scoffed. "If you think I'm letting you off the hook in some twisted, manipulative way to save Eva's feelings, you can go to hell with glass-infused drawers on. You made it about *you*, again. Eva will be fine. Why? Because she has people that care about her, and will see her through every step of the way. She deserves *far* better than some junkie loser who forgot everything she did for him the second he bent over to be a traitor's bitch."

"You and the rest of the Elevenths aren't much better," Joey retorted. "You're not. You're gonna stay every step of the way, huh? Until another piece of ass comes along to distract you. Vera, Persephone. You say you got my number? I got yours, too."

"Keep running your mouth, Joey," Jonah smirked. "You got lucky, you understand me? But if you aren't fucking squeaky clean from here on out, that luck is gonna run out."

———

Jonah slammed the door behind him.

Eva looked towards the door and gave Jonah a knowing look. He gave her a small shrug in return."What? I wanted to check out the security measures here."

"Uh-huh," She reached for him from her spot on the bed. "Come here and say hello properly. You're the best thing that's happened today."

"That's good to hear." Jonah sat next to her on the bed and she rested her head against his shoulder. "What all happened today?"

"Wells Cole is none other than Achilles. And an ass." She looped her arm through his. "I don't like him."

Jonah stiffened as he remembered what Apollo had said. Achilles was a Traditionalist. Eva was being saddled with the man to prove that the values the ancient asshole had were false.

"Why don't you like him?"

"He's an ass, he's demanding, and he was way too touchy-feely." She sat up with a frown. "All through the damn photoshoot."

Jonah raised his eyebrows at that. "What'd you say?"

"I told him to stop, obviously. I'm not a fan of being manhandled." She snorted. "He told me it was just because of the poses for the shoot and to relax. We got done not long after that."

Jonah gave Eva his full attention. "You made it clear to this motherfucker that you weren't comfortable with him touching you, yet he continued anyway?"

"Yes and no. I didn't bash his face in on set." Eva sat up. "I thought I'd never see him again but he showed up at dinner last night. Told me who he really is. Now, I think we are going to be stuck with him on Poveglia."

"Call Apollo now and get rid of him," Jonah said instantly. "He's one of the main ones in Traditionalist shit, remember? Let's also not forget that they're akin to white supremacists, just with golden tans. Call Daddy Gold. Or if you're uncomfortable with that, call Hermes. He'll do something shady and no one will be the wiser."

"What are you talking about?" Eva frowned at him. "Achilles is a Traditionalist?"

Dammit. Jonah forgot that Eva hadn't been part of that meeting with Apollo. And he wasn't supposed to let her in on that.

"The point is he put his hands on you," Jonah pointed out. "Call Apollo. Achilles is here to prove you can't defeat Typhon because you are a woman."

"Is that right?" Eva's eyes flashed. "I knew I should have decked him."

"So, call Apollo—"

"No. I'm not going to run to the gods every time I have a problem, Jonah. You know me well enough by now to know I don't do that." With a huff, Eva stood. "And now? Now, I'm pissed off. I'm going to kick Typhon's ass and then, Achilles' ass for thinking I couldn't do it."

Jonah shook his head. "Eva, this isn't the time for dick-measuring. Achilles is here only to prove you as second-class. That is dangerous; he could very well sabotage you, simply to prove his outdated point. Don't keep him around—and potentially exacerbate the danger—so as not to give him the satisfaction."

"Do you really think that he would try to sabotage this?"

"Yeah. I do."

"Fine." Eva willed her phone in her hand. Two rings later, Apollo answered. She didn't give him a chance to speak. "Hey, so I need you to get rid of Achilles. Now."

"Eva? What has happened?"

"Oh, nothing much. Had a photoshoot with him this morning. He had a field day groping me, then told me to get over it when I called him out on it. Now, he wants to go to Poveglia and I'm pretty sure that if I kill him, it's going to defeat the purpose of proving his stupid ideals wrong."

Since Apollo was on speakerphone, Jonah heard his sigh, which put him on edge. It was a they-were-going-to-have-to-tolerate-bullshit-of-some-sort sigh.

"I'm sorry. Daughter mine, the answer is no," he said. "Achilles is a necessary evil. The world isn't as simple as only working with people who are nice to us."

"Ok, so how am I supposed to handle him?"

"With as much grace as you can muster."

"Can any of the gods strike him down?" Jonah spoke up. "Not smite him, per say. But do something?"

"Not until the battle is over, son."

"That reminds me." Eva glanced over at Jonah. "Cyrus attacked me last night."

"Pardon?"

"Cyrus. I thought he was still in Tartarus."

"So did I," Apollo growled. "I'll look into Alexius. Perhaps you were attacked by an imposter."

"No. It was him. Before him appeared a Titan assassin," Eva responded drily. "It's been a great day. Really. Achilles, Titans, Alexius. Not sure how much more fun I am going to be able to take."

"You are selling yourself short, Eva," Apollo said. "It seems to be that every challenge that's ahead of you, you simply knock it down."

"Have you been reading those motivational books Celesta likes again, Daddy?"

Apollo laughed and Jonah simply rubbed a palm along his forehead.

"I can't kick his ass either, can I?"

"No. We cannot give Achilles any ammunition."

Jonah glared at the phone. "So ... he gets a pass. We know his opinion of us, but we have to respect him?"

"I never said respect him, Jonah. But don't give him anything to take back to his followers to use against you."

"I would expect you to defend yourself, Jonah."

"Does that mean I get to punch him in the face for this morning?"

"No, Evie. The time for retribution has passed. However, keep that in your arsenal."

THIRTEEN

EVA MCRAYNE

I SHOULDN'T HAVE BEEN SURPRISED to find the sun shining as we crossed the waters to Poveglia Island. I should have taken it as a sign that my father was looking out for me. That he would keep his word to be by my side in two days to fight the biggest threat I had ever encountered.

I meant that literally. The pictures I found online this morning of Typhon were only sketches, but he was huge, his head up to the clouds.

I kept telling myself this was going to be fun. I loved a good fight. But there was a weight in the pit of my stomach. One that I couldn't explain.

"You are anxious."

I glanced up to see that Achilles had come up beside me. He squeezed my hand tightly against the rail when he looked out over the water.

I jerked it away, then wiped it against my jeans. "I'm not anxious."

"Then you are a fool. Typhon will not go down easily."

"What is the real reason you are tagging along with us?"

Achilles raised his eyebrows at me.

I tucked my hand under my arm in case he tried to grab it again.

"You question my motives? If Typhon is not defeated, then we will all suffer."

"You don't think I can take him down?"

"No," Achilles chuckled. "No, I do not. It is clear that you rely on many fighters to weaken a beast before you strike the final blow."

"That's not true."

"Of course it is, *plat*. Do not allow Apollo's dreams of glory for his line shield you from the truth."

"What did you just call me?"

"*Plat*." Achilles didn't seem to be joking. Granted, I could have heard him wrong since the blood had rushed straight to my ears. "'Tis a term of endearment."

"Calling me 'property' is *not* a term of endearment," I spat.

"Ah, I am impressed. You know the native tongue then."

"Yes, and if you keep calling me that, I'm going to cut yours out!"

"Oh, calm yourself. You modern women are far too ignorant of your place in the world."

"Achilles, how much do you weigh?"

"Why do you ask?"

"Because I need to know if I can throw you overboard by myself or if I need to get help."

Achilles laughed at me. He actually laughed as if I were joking.

"Of course, you would need help," he stated. "You believe you are strong, but alas, you will find you are much better suited in the home. Not rushing after monsters with an army and the gods behind you."

"The…" I stopped myself. I had to tell myself that Apollo said I couldn't get rid of him. "Excuse me." I turned on my heel to walk as far away from him as possible.

"We are not finished with our discussion."

"Yes. Yes, we are."

I moved to the other side of the ferry and spotted Joey working with the equipment. I turned to my right to stay away from him when I spotted Jonah coming up from the bottom of the boat with a picnic basket in hand.

"Oh, thank Olympus," I breathed when I approached him. "Quick. Tell me something smart."

"Um, why?"

"Because one conversation with Achilles and my brain cells are dying."

Jonah raised an eyebrow and looked over my shoulder. "What did the golden grand wizard say this time?"

"You really don't want to know."

"Yeah, I do."

"No. I already want to throw him overboard. You might actually do it."

"You sure you don't want me to check him?"

"I'm sure," I insisted. There was no way Achilles would make it onto the island if Jonah knew the nature of our conversation. I was sure of it. "I'm more interested in checking out what you have there."

Jonah snagged my hand, then pulled me over to a bench. He passed me a thermos and I uncapped it to inhale the heavenly scent of caramel coffee.

"I had the hotel pack us breakfast," he explained. "Since I don't like the other two, I forgot to order them anything."

I chuckled before I sipped the coffee.

When I offered Jonah some, he shook his head. "Nah, I got my own. I don't want my teeth to rot."

"Hmm." I sipped again. "I'm so lucky you like me."

"I got you a bagel, too, though I doubt you'll eat it."

"You eat it. I'm too anxious."

"Nutrients will calm your nerves," Jonah said. "You know you'll need to be at peace before—"

"That is modern day, pussy-foot nonsense."

I swear Jonah's neck popped when he jerked his head toward the unexpected, undesired voice.

Achilles took the bagel Jonah had set out for me and tossed it overboard. "Telling her to eat bread and be calm before a fight to death. Gods on high, this might very well be the reason many women have forgotten their place. Because they've been trying to pick up the slack for bitch-boys like your ass, Blue Velvet. First bagels, whatever next? Vol-au-vents and tea?"

"Now, wait one damn second—"

"What did you just call me?" Jonah sat down the thermos, then got to his feet.

I stood, then placed my hand on Jonah's chest as a silent reminder of what Apollo had ordered.

"Say that again, asshole."

"What would be the point?" Achilles glanced between us, then smirked. "Honestly, how can one respect you as a man when you hide behind a woman?"

"Achilles." I managed an even tone instead of screaming. "Leave. Do that right now."

"I don't think so." Achilles leaned back on his heels. "Tell me, Eleventh, do you accompany Eva to all of her locations? Such knowledge will be useful."

"How the hell is that useful?"

"Because I would like to know how weak the two of you are. Does she depend on you for every fight? Or is it the other way around?"

Jonah bristled and bolted forward, though I blocked him. This fucker had some nerve.

"And how does that work with you, Wells?"

Reena had joined the party. Achilles looked at her, not hiding disdain.

"I don't believe anyone was talking to you, woman," he said coldly.

"But this woman is talking to you," Reena said conversationally. "Now, how weak are you? Are your victories due to any real skill or profound talent? Or is it just dumb luck, due solely to your mama dipping you in the Styx? Except for that heel, of course."

She pitched a dagger at Achilles' left heel. He yelped and scrambled back.

I gave a smug nod.

"My question has been answered," she declared. "Now fuck off unless you want me to keep playing footsies."

Achilles seethed, but I just shrugged. As he limped off, I clasped hands with Reena as Spader and Terrence came up behind her.

"Just in time," I grinned. "You guys honed in on Jonah, didn't you? I know you didn't get on the ferry with us."

"Damn skippy." Spader rocked back on his heels. "Jonah is like a damn beacon."

"Never mind the tracking apps on our phones." Terrence rolled his eyes. "Anyway, what's up with the pig?"

"Achilles is someone we have to be nice to, so don't kill him. Especially you, Re."

"Why would I kill him?"

"Because he believes our place is in the kitchen," I responded drily. "Just steer clear. Per Apollo, we can't kill him until after the fight with Typhon."

Reena gazed coldly after the bastard. Jonah was still angry. I could feel it radiating off of him. But I knew that was nothing next to Reena. She had been owning men for the better part of her life.

"I'll make no promises," she said at last. "If I accidentally step on his foot in the battle, or he trips over my socket wrench ... shit happens, you know?"

I grinned. "Yeah, I suppose it does."

"So, Joey's here, right?"

I nodded. "Other side of the boat."

"How's that going?"

"So far, it's tolerable." I tucked a strand of hair behind my ear. "We haven't really spoken much."

"He's still alive, so good on you, J." Spader pulled out a deck of cards and started flipping them between his hands. "I thought you would have wrung his neck by now."

Jonah freed himself from me, though it was free of force or contempt. "It's taken every ounce of restraint I possess, man. I mean, first the botched drug thing, then the fact that he's Cyrus' slave ...

when exactly did Joseph become the poster child for fuckups at every turn?"

"That's easy," Spader murmured. "Joseph is one of those lapdogs in need of an Alpha to hold his dick for him. Pedro snuffed it, and he was in need of a new master, so enter Cyrus. He didn't just become a fuckup, dude. He's always been one, but was able to keep the mask up so long as the right people held his hand and kept his nose clean for him."

"What are you talking about?" I turned to Jonah, then looked at Spader. "You said Joey is Cyrus' slave?"

Jonah's face twisted, which meant he wasn't supposed to tell me that. Was that another order from Apollo?

"Jonah?"

"I wanted Joseph to tell you," he sighed, then met my eyes. "I confronted Joseph last night when you were in the shower. Found out that he and Cyrus have been screwing on the side. Cyrus was giving him heroin in exchange for information on you."

I stared at Jonah, suddenly sick at the thought of how long Joey had been stabbing me in the back. He'd been my closest friend, my confidante, for years. He'd bandaged me up after Cyrus knocked me around. And the whole time he was feeding all of my secrets to my enemy?

"Eva, sit. You look like you are about to pass out."

I didn't answer Reena. Instead, I turned on my heel and stormed the length of the ferry. Joey looked up when I stopped in front of him.

"What did you tell him?" I whispered.

"Eva, what are you—"

"Cyrus!" I yelled and grabbed him by the front of his shirt. "What did you tell him?"

"Everything!" Joey snapped back. He wrestled himself free from my grasp just as Jonah pulled me back. Joey smoothed out his shirt before he glared at me.

"What did you expect, Eva? Really?"

"I trusted you!" I tried to pull free, but Jonah had my arms tight.

"Gods dammit, Joey! You were my family! You saw what he did to me and you fucked him?"

"Yeah. Well, guess that was your mistake, huh?"

I wanted to cry. I wanted to break down, say fuck the monster, and leave. I couldn't do any of those things.

"You're right," I managed when I was sure my voice wasn't going to break. "You're right. That was my mistake. But it is one I won't make again."

Joey shrugged. "Still as self-righteous as ever, huh?"

I managed to do what Jonah always said and filed my bile away. Temporarily. "No. Just righteous."

"Whatever, Eva. I've made my mistakes—"

"And how many times have I paid for them?" I responded bitterly. "How many times did I get the hell beaten out of me because of something you told him?"

Joey rubbed his forehead with tense fingers, then dropped his hands.

When he didn't respond, I laughed, though there was no mirth behind it. "Yeah. Ok. I am done. Outside of *Grave*, I don't ever want to see you again, understand?"

"Whatever. Don't get too pissed. We're shooting the intro in less than twenty minutes." And just like that, Joey dismissed me. He sat back down to adjust the knobs on his camera.

"Come on, Evie." Jonah wrapped his arm around my neck. "You left your coffee behind. Let's go grab it."

I let him and the others lead me away. When we returned back to the bench, I sat down and twisted the thermos in my hand.

"So, Joey was fucking Cyrus?" Reena demanded. "How long?"

"Not now, Re." Jonah sat beside me. "Later."

I didn't look up as my mind replayed the last five minutes on a twisted loop.

"No. Go ahead." I met Jonah's gaze. "Please. Tell them everything. I have a feeling it's the only way I am going to get the truth."

Jonah sighed, and told Reena everything.

When he finished, Reena scoffed, "That bastard didn't make a mistake. He *is* a mistake. Jonah, I'm glad you called us. Legit. Not that I question your abilities or Eva's, never that. It's just that I wouldn't want you two on your own with a traitor strung out on drugs and a chauvinistic prick who can be killed by being shot in the foot."

"Need to have someone behind us I trust, Re." Jonah shifted and clasped his hands together. He brushed his shoulder against mine. "Evie, I know it's a lot to take in. Especially now."

I didn't respond. I was reeling from the revelation that Joey had stabbed me so easily in the back while smiling to my face.

Spader was the one who broke the silence. "You sure we can't just give him to Typhon? We'll throw Achilles in, too. Like a buy-one-asshole-get-one-free."

That was supposed to make me laugh. I couldn't. I closed my eyes and forced myself back to center. I had to focus on the show. On the Council's orders. My broken faith in Joey didn't matter at the moment. "Let's just get this over with." I said at last. "I really, really just want to go home and hide away from the world."

"Rome ain't the same without you, Evie. It'll be good to have you back."

I didn't have the heart to tell Terrence that Rome wasn't my home anymore. Not as long as Hera kept sending assassins after my head.

"Yeah." I cleared my throat. "I'm sure it's a lot more peaceful."

"We're here." Joey stopped when he saw us. "You ready?"

"I don't have a choice." I stood up, then passed Reena the thermos. "Guard this with your life."

"What's in it? Some secret weapon?"

"My coffee. Much more precious than any weapon."

"Allow me to help you unload the bags." Achilles came around the corner. "Granted, there aren't as many as I would have suspected."

"Not yet." Joey gave me a look that I ignored. "We need to film, real quick."

"He's right." I looked up to Achilles. "It's part of the introduction. I always talk about the history. I wanted to start that on the ferry."

"Of course." He gave me a blinding grin. "Shall I be on film with you?"

"I need to introduce everyone as guests on the episode. There is no way you guys won't end up on camera." I fell into the roles I knew best: the producer, the host. It was easier than being myself at the moment. "Joey, you got the mask?"

"Yeah." He gestured for us to follow him. When we came upon the pile of bags, he pulled out a box, then passed it over. "Be careful with this thing. The museum will be pissed if you drop it."

"Thanks for jinxing me." I headed back outside where the crew members had huddled close to the back of the boat. "I want to do this up front, so the island is in the background. Then we need to find out why the natives are so damned scared."

"Is she always this demanding?" Achilles strolled up next to Joey. "Or worse?"

"Worse," Joey responded when he pulled out his camera.

Say what they will about my antics, but I always got the job done. I walked over to the rail, then gestured to the group to join me.

"The world knows you as Wells Cole." I looked up at him. "So, that's what I'm going to call you on film from here on out."

"Very well."

"Stand next to Jonah. Jonah, hold this." I passed him the box. "I'll take the mask out when I'm ready."

"Are you going to get started? Or spend what little daylight I have chatting?"

I ignored Joey when I got into place between Jonah and Achilles. Spader, Reena, and Terrence flanked us. "And you say I'm demanding."

I waited until he counted down on his fingers. When he dropped his hand, I put on my biggest smile. "Last time, it was Japan. Today? Italy. But the two are more connected than anyone could imagine. I know. It sounds crazy. What could these two countries possibly have in common?"

I paused for a second. "We'll get to that before the show is over. I'm sure you've noticed that we have guests with us. The first is a man I am sure you will recognize. Jonah Rowe has helped me keep my sanity on more than one occasion. Our second guest is Wells Cole, the brilliant mind behind Valor, who was kind enough to help us explore the most haunted patch of land in Europe. Then there is Reena, Terrence, and Spader. All dear friends of mine who I trust with my life."

I gestured to the island behind me. "Poveglia Island is one that very few paranormal shows have been able to document. So, I consider this episode a huge honor. You may have heard that it was the home of an insane asylum. That's true. Located between Venice and Lido, it was the perfect land to dump souls no one wanted to deal with. Souls that are said to remain."

I turned to Jonah and opened the box. I pulled out the mask and said a silent prayer that Joey hadn't jinxed me. I held it up to the camera. It was frightening. White, despite its age. It reminded me of a bird's skull. The eyes were circled in red paint. The seams were stitched together with thick, black slashes of leather.

"This is the mask plague doctors would wear to protect themselves from consuming the 'bad air' believed to surround their patients. See the beak? It would have been filled with herbs, meant to protect the doctor from the smell. This would be the last thing plague victims would have seen when they were dropped off on Poveglia."

I stared at the mask as the world seemed to shift. In that instant, I was no longer on a ferry. I was on the beach, staring out at a blood-red sky. A figure in long black robes stood across from me, his face hidden by the grotesque relic in my hands.

"Evie?"

I blinked and the image was gone. I stared at Joey before I found my voice. "The Isle of the Damned. That is the name that was given to Poveglia in 1776 when the land was converted to a place … when the Magistrato alla Sanità deemed it a sanctuary for those affected by the Black Plague. The doctors would take them. Dump them on shores covered with the bones of those who had died before."

I put the mask back in the box and wiped my hands on my jeans. I didn't know what that image was. I didn't want to find out. "In 1805, the sanctuary status became official. Hundreds were deserted on these shores. The sick. The mentally ill. Political enemies. It was a death sentence. This continued until the government decided to make the island into a mental asylum. Buildings were erected to house patients from 1922 to 1968. Once the hospital was closed, the land was used for farming, until it was auctioned off in 2014."

"Farming?" Joey broke in. "Eva, are you serious?"

"Yeah." I glanced to the island behind me. Its beauty was suddenly alarming. I couldn't find it in me to say that it was fitting, given how rich the soil would be—considering the whole island was a graveyard. "Farming. A sign that life can flourish in the darkest of places."

———

Poveglia Island had been all but abandoned since the 1990s. The buildings even longer. So, it was no surprise to find that they had collapsed in on themselves. We hiked through the foliage in silence, which gave Joey a chance to film our surroundings. Not that there was much to see: shells of what remained, empty windows that seemed to scream against the daylight, a pitiful excuse for a grave-yard that was right behind the buildings.

"It's too quiet."

I jumped when Joey spoke from his spot behind me. I pushed a branch out of my way before I decided to speak to him. "I thought it was supposed to be quiet. We're the only ones here."

"That's just it. That's exactly what it feels like."

I stopped to face him. Achilles came up behind him and dropped the bag he was carrying.

"There's no animal sounds." Joey frowned at me. "No birds. Hell, I haven't seen the first spiderweb. This place should be full of them; given the trees. Spiders, snakes …"

"It is strange." Jonah stretched out to grab the limb above him. "Wildlife can thrive in the harshest of climates. It's like the animals abandoned the island, too."

I looked at the group that surrounded me, torn between agreeing it was creepy and telling them that I was just thrilled that I hadn't stepped on a snake. Instead, I shrugged. "We are almost to the main building. Let's get there and set the gear down. We still need to figure out where we are going to film tonight."

"Maybe that's why the locals decided to farm here," Joey spoke again as we reached the set of cobblestones that hadn't been shrouded by the grass. "No wildlife meant that their crops were safe."

"I think it was a stupid decision on their part," I snorted. "Poveglia was a dumping ground for the plague. Who's to say that it's not still here?"

"You mean, like tuberculosis in old hospitals?"

"That's exactly what I mean." I started searching the ground for cobblestones. For a path to follow. "Thank god you had all your shots."

"It's no secret how contagious the Black Death was. Nor why the humans were so frightened."

"You lived through the actual Black Plague epidemic, didn't you, Achilles?" I glanced past Joey to see Achilles nod.

"Yes. I was in London at the time. A military strategist for King Edward III. When the plague began to ransack the palace, I relocated to Russia."

"When was this?" Terrence hacked at a patch of overgrown vines ahead of us. "Do you remember?"

"1360."

"Why did you leave?" I spotted another patch of cobblestones and headed towards them after I squeezed Terrence's forearm with silent thanks. "You are an immortal. You wouldn't have died."

"No. But I would have contracted the illness and survived. A far more dangerous proposition, since I would have been exposed as an immortal."

"Dude, it's not like you couldn't have fought them off." Spader came up beside me as we reached a clearing. The main building to the hospital seemed to loom over us. "Right?"

"Yes. But you learn to adapt as the times change. And you learn that it is easier to stay in the shadows so that questions aren't raised about your longevity."

Achilles may have been answering Spader's question, but his response was directed at me. I couldn't explain it, but I wasn't comfortable with their conversation. I didn't want to think about the fact that I would still be around after everything I had known had passed away. So, I did what any reasonable girl would do.

I changed the subject. "The west wing is pretty much shot." I pointed to the skeleton of bricks to my right. "But the center section looks safe enough. Let's set up there."

"Lead the way, Superstar."

Thankfully, my companions stopped talking when we climbed up the hill. The closer I came to the building, the more I wanted to run away from it. I chastised myself as I shoved open the weathered wooden door.

I had been in worse places than this. I wasn't going to let the past scare me off. Hell, the horrible stories were why we were here in the first place. When I stepped inside, I froze. Nature's destruction was gone. The gray and white floors gleamed as nurses lounged next to a small desk. I looked to my right to see men dressed in suits pass each other on the stairs. People in wheelchairs passed by an open doorway across the lobby.

Ok. This was way too weird for my liking. The island was abandoned. I'd seen it with my own eyes. Read countless papers and articles about its abandonment. What I was seeing now shouldn't have been happening. These people shouldn't have been here.

"Hello?" I moved towards the desk where the nurses were still chatting. "Excuse me, but what are you doing?"

They turned towards me, their faces blurred in shadow, their eye sockets empty. I stumbled back when the one closest to me opened her mouth.

Black wisps of smoke seeped out as she spoke. "Welcome to Poveglia, Sibyl," she screeched in my head. "Welcome to hell."

I stumbled back. Smacked right into Achilles, who grabbed my arms as the horrible scene faded. The room we were in was crumbling. The paint peeling off the walls in long curly strips.

"What the hell, Eva?"

"I ... you didn't see that?"

"See what?" Achilles turned me around to examine my face. "You're pale."

"I think I just met the welcoming committee."

"What did you see?" Jonah frowned at me. "I tried to use spectral sight but got nothing."

"I saw it too."

Joey looked like he'd had the fright of his life. He was shaking when he hit a few buttons on his camera. "Here. I got it all here. Couldn't see it unless I looked at the screen."

Achilles kept his hand on my arm. He reached over with his free hand to hit the triangle in the center of the camera screen. I could see myself open the door. I saw the room change from the rubble to pristine condition.

I couldn't watch anymore. I focused on Joey instead. Reena, Spader, and Terrence crowded around Jonah. I was glad they were here for him. I was glad they would be able to protect him.

"What was that?" Joey ran his hand through his thick dark hair. "Eva, we've seen some crazy shit before. But that …"

"Welcome to hell," I repeated the nurse's words when the film ended. "I think that says it all."

"Yeah. So, when do we get to go home again? There's not enough liquor in Europe to deal with this level of crazy."

"Three days." I turned away when he took back the camera. "I still have to deal with the big bad monster, remember? But I can call the boat for you."

"No." He shook his head. "No way in hell can I leave. Contract."

"I have the strangest feeling we're going to catch more glimpses like that. We can do voice-over work to splice them into the episode."

"Thank god we have a two-hour time slot. I don't think that's going to be enough time. Poveglia may have to be a two-parter."

"Maybe." I picked up his camera bag from where he'd dropped it. "Want to use what little daylight we have to talk about where we are now? You can be in the shot with me."

"That means I would have to set my stand up."

"No, it doesn't. You can just put the camera on the counter. It's high enough."

"How about we unpack instead?" Reena glanced out the shattered windows. "We need to use the light for more than filming."

"Yeah, ok."

I started pulling our supplies out of the backpack I'd carried. Bottled water. Dry food. We had packed for camping. If we weren't going to film anything anytime soon, then I was going to make myself useful. I had to. I couldn't get the spirit's screeching out of my head.

"You're awfully quiet, Jonah." I tilted my head up when he came to stand next to me. "You alright?"

"Yeah." He reached in the bag and began to help. "Kinda bothers me that I couldn't use my abilities."

"It has to be the island." I handed him the next bag we needed to work on. "Think about how dark the history is here. I'd be more surprised if you could use your abilities."

"Eva, I need to speak with you."

Achilles came up beside me and I shook my head.

"We've got too much to do at the moment. Later."

"I only need a moment." Achilles stuffed his hands in his pockets. "Surely, you can spare me that much?"

"At least you're asking permission. Wouldn't want you interjecting yourself into her space. You know, like per usual."

I snapped up my head at Jonah, whose nonchalant expression did nothing to hide the aggravation in his tone.

"I was unaware that your services included acting as a guard dog, Eleventh."

"Hey!"

I whirled around, but Jonah was quicker than I was.

He tossed the gaff tape back in the bag he was working on before he faced off with Achilles. "Call me a dog again, Abercrombie, and we will have a problem. The fact that you feel that harassment and invasion of personal space can be explained away is very telling."

Achilles didn't even acknowledge him as the tension in the room rose tenfold.

I pinched the bridge of my nose between my fingers before I broke the silence. "It's warm, but I still think a fire is a good idea, so we don't have to rely on the flashlights. Right now, I'm thinking that we just build it in the middle of the room."

"We need firewood." Achilles looked between me and Jonah. "I will be more than happy to go."

I watched Achilles leave, then turned back to the task at hand with only one thought in mind: I wanted to be anywhere else but here.

FOURTEEN

JONAH ROWE

Of all the places Jonah had been during his life, none of them had been as depressing as Poveglia Island. If Hoia-Baciu Forest had been the home of forgotten monsters, then this accursed place was the home of forgotten people.

"Hey, you ok?"

Jonah dropped another match on the wood they had piled in the center of the room. "As good as can be expected, Reena. You?"

"Fine. I'm worried about Eva though." She poked at the fire with a stick. "She hasn't said much since we got here."

"You noticed that, too?"

"Yeah. I think it's the Joey factor." Reena glanced over the large room and then back to Jonah. "She was crushed by what you told me."

"I wasn't going to tell her." Jonah sat back as the flames erupted. "I only told Terrence and Spader when I called this morning, so they would give you a heads-up. I guess they didn't."

"No, we didn't really talk." Reena cleared her throat. "I was saying goodbye to Kendall."

Jonah shared a small smile with her. Reena bumped his arm.

"At any rate, she knows now. We just gotta keep her from casting everyone in the same light."

"What do you mean?" Jonah raised his eyebrows. "She knows she can trust us."

"Under normal circumstances, yes. But these circumstances are most definitely not normal, J."

Jonah straightened. "Reena, Eva knows we would never do to her what Cyrus and Joseph did. We're the closest allies she's got now."

"I hope so, but how many times has she been betrayed now? Three?"

"Three times too many."

"True. Maybe I should go talk to her. We can have girl talk. I can see where her head is at."

"Reena, do you even know how to have 'girl talk'?"

"Shut up." She laughed. "Fine. We'll just talk."

"Let me do it." Jonah sighed. "I want to run something by her anyway."

"What's that?"

"I didn't tell her about Joseph. But before that, I didn't tell her about Ange de la Mort. I want to make sure she knows I'm not keeping anything else from her."

"Oh." Reena winced. "Was she pissed?"

"Nah, Apollo covered for me."

"You're lucky. Usually, the dad is the first one to throw you under the bus."

"Yup," Jonah agreed, "but Apollo totally covered my ass. I want Eva to know she can trust me completely."

Reena nodded. "Lover's Lesson Number One."

"Huh?"

"Lover's Lesson Number One," Reena repeated. "It states that lovers have no secrets."

"Are they really secrets if I was told not to say anything?"

"Flip it around. How would you feel if Eva found out that your former best friend had betrayed you and if she kept the existence of an assassin after your head from you?"

Jonah thought about it, then stood. "I'll go talk to her now."

"I'll be here."

Jonah headed across the room to the sleeping bags where Eva, Terrence, and Spader were playing cards. He stopped behind Eva. "Whatcha playing?"

"Not strip poker, which is what I suggested," Spader muttered. "Just regular poker."

"You're just mad because you owe me three hundred bucks." Eva chuckled. "Which I want in cash, by the way. Actual cash. Not that fake movie money you try to pass off as real."

"I've done no such thing," Spader said with innocence. "I'm an honest guy in all my transactions."

Jonah stepped back.

Spader frowned. "Why did you do that?"

"Oh, no particular reason," Jonah said casually. "I just didn't want to get hit by lightning was all."

"Do you want to play, handsome? I can deal you in."

"Actually, I was hoping we could take a walk. I wanted to talk to you for a minute."

"Talk, huh?" Spader used air quotes. "Cause if he's about to break up with you, Evie, I'm still available."

"No one is breaking up with anyone," Jonah grunted. "I just wanted to speak to my girlfriend, one on one. That is literally all there is to it."

"I mean, you never know ..."

"How mad would Jonathan be if we left Spader here?" Eva stood up, then dusted off the back of her jeans. "Like, on a scale of one to ten?"

"Jonathan doesn't like abandoning people," Jonah said with mock sadness. "We're stuck with Spader."

"Be that way," Spader gave them a smirk. "One day soon, you'll be glad I'm around."

Eva dismissed Spader with a wave, then looped an arm through Jonah's. He nearly sneered at Achilles who watched as they headed outside. Once they reached the beach of ash and bone, Eva stopped and tilted her head back to meet Jonah's gaze. "What's up, handsome?"

"I wanted to make sure we were good." Jonah tucked his hands in his pockets. "I don't want you to think I'm keeping things from you after what you found out about the assassin and, now, Joseph."

Eva crossed her arms over her chest, then shook her head. "You are worried over nothing."

"You're not upset?"

"No, because I understand your motives. You wanted to protect me. I'd have done the same thing if our roles were reversed."

Jonah couldn't convey his relief at that. Still. "I'm grateful for that. Even so, I just wanted you to know that I didn't want any secrets between us. Joseph is proof positive that they only lead to horseshit."

"I don't want secrets between us, either." Eva's expression softened. "I tell you everything."

"Everything?" Jonah shook his head. "You never told me what Achilles said this morning."

Eva opened her mouth, then closed it. She cleared her throat. "You make an excellent point." She took both of his hands. "So, I'll swear it on the Styx."

"What?"

"I, Eva McRayne, Representative of the Olympian Council, swear on the Styx to never keep secrets from Jonah Rowe. No matter what the outcome may be."

A wave crashed against the shore and Eva looked that way before she grinned at him. "I think it worked."

Jonah glanced at the water. "That is still so weird to me. That whole Styx oath thing. As for the redneck traditionalist Olympian ... I wonder if being dipped in the Styx caused psychosis of some kind."

"It's possible," Eva admitted. "He seems unhinged in more ways than one."

"Like how?"

"Well, his nickname at the Garden is the Savvy Savage, which I found rather stupid until I heard the stories." Eva kept hold of

Jonah's right hand as they walked. "He was gruesome even after the battle."

Jonah stepped closer to Eva and spoke in hushed tones. "Is it true that he cheated on his wife ... with his sister?"

Eva's mouth twisted. "According to the rumors, his sister was the other woman for the long-term."

"Ew," Jonah hissed, repulsed. "Guess he *is* an Olympian redneck. Traditionalist right down to keeping it in the family. Jesus."

"They told us at the Academy how common that used to be." Eva wrinkled her nose. "So, I wasn't surprised when I heard that."

"What else did you hear about him?"

"He used to buy women. Kept a harem of sorts. He still does, but calls them mistresses. Houses them all over the world."

"Oh, that I knew," Jonah said. "It was a scandal that kinda came to light after his *Final Son* movie came out. Apparently, he had sex houses or something. But the lead whistleblower had a psychotic break and nothing came of the investigation. Convenient, no?"

"Very convenient," Eva agreed as they started walking again. "The sooner he is away from us, the better."

Jonah tucked his hands in his pockets before he spoke again. "His sister, though? Really?"

"Yeah." Eva made a face. "His honest-to-Olympus sister. Apparently, they were in love, but their father married her off to an elder Senator. She killed herself on the wedding night."

"Seriously?"

"Yes," Eva nodded. "She opened her veins in the bathhouse when she was supposed to be readying herself for the wedding night. According to Medusa, it was a gruesome discovery. She was so pale from all the blood loss that she looked like a marble ghost in a sea of red."

"That's a pretty vivid description, Superstar."

"Yeah, well, I was there once myself a time or two. I can be poetic about it when it suits me."

Jonah nodded, sobering. "I'd pity him were he not a dick head."

"I pity the sister." I studied the gray sand beneath my feet. "Her actions were questionable—not to mention beyond gross—but people don't suicide themselves for no reason. She must have truly felt like there was no way out. I can relate to that, and I hope she found peace in the next life. Or more peace than she'd ever have, being with her sick brother."

Jonah nodded as he came to a stop. "That's a good point."

"Was there anything else you wanted to talk to me about? Or just the secrets thing?"

"The secrets. I feel horrible that I didn't tell you."

"Well, don't. And you don't have to worry about me keeping things from you either. I swore on the Styx, after all."

"Glad that's done, " Jonah said. "I also want you to have this." Jonah produced a mesh, sheer top.

Eva regarded it. "What is that?"

Jonah stretched it out. "Its an invention of Hephaestus; he made them for all of us. Its weaving makes us all less vulnerable to the fangs of Typhon's monsters. And it'll also make it almost impossible to stab us. And since ..." Jonah shook his head. "Since fucking Cyrus is around again, I wanted you to have yours long before the battle."

"You really are in deep with my family. Apollo, now Hephaestus?" Eva leaned up to kiss him on the cheek as she took it from him. "Thanks, handsome."

"Yeah, well, you never know. And since Joseph has been feeding him information, I have a feeling he's gonna show up when we least expect it."

Eva stripped off her shirt, then put the mesh on. She slipped her shirt on top of it. "Can you tell I am wearing it?"

Jonah shook his head, fascinated. "I'd be none the wiser. Hephaestus is freaking amazing!"

"He really is."

"How does it feel?"

"I barely feel it at all, to be honest," she admitted as they started walking back. "Is this new body armor common knowledge? Or is it secret?"

"Why do you ask?"

"Just curious if I should say anything about it to the others or not."

"Well, it was a gift for us in the inner circle," Jonah answered. "But for obvious reasons, Joey is unaware."

Eva nodded. "I won't say anything then."

"How are you feeling about the whole Joseph mess?"

"Hurt?" She shrugged as she looked out, over the sea. "Disappointed? Angry? I really don't know, Jonah."

"Evie, this isn't your fault."

"I'd like to think so, Jonah. I would. But what's the old saying about … if everyone has an issue with you, then maybe you're the issue?"

"I don't—"

"There you are." Joey came down the walkway with his camera in hand. "You ready to start filming this yet?"

"Yeah," Eva nodded. "The sooner the better, right?"

Jonah followed Eva up the path and stopped at the door when Reena beckoned him over. "So?"

"So, what?"

"How'd it go?"

"Great. She's not pissed at me. Swore on the Styx to not hold secrets from me. I gave her the mesh piece."

"Good. I'm glad you two made that pact."

"Um, I didn't."

"You didn't? But you just said—"

"Eva did. I got distracted." Jonah sighed. "Then Joseph grabbed her to film."

"She didn't bring it back up?"

"Not really."

"You should do it sooner rather than later," Reena pointed out. "It's not a good look, J."

"Suspend the lecture, Re," Jonah said. "The only thing that stopped me was the distraction from Joseph."

"You sure, J?" Spader asked shrewdly. "Because the whole 'I didn't get the chance to' is the oldest trick in the book to weasel one's way out of shit."

"Don't start with me, Spader. Not today."

"Just sayin'."

"Guys?" Eva approached them. "We're going to do a walk-through. If we're not back in two hours, come find us."

"Eva, hang on really quick." Jonah walked over to her. "I never actually joined the pact with you. I'll do that now. I, Jonah Rowe ... um, I don't have a fancy title like you, I'm ... just Jonah ... swear on the Styx ... not to keep secrets from you, barring surprises or presents. But all else is fair game."

"Jonah—"

"No, I didn't do it before and I should have and I'm—"

He didn't get to finish. Eva launched herself at him, then kissed him square on the mouth. When she pulled back, he grinned. "That seal it or somethin'?"

"Something." She kissed him again. "I am just touched by how sweet that was."

"But?"

"But presents and surprises don't count, silly man," she laughed. "So, you aren't going to get a free pass with me anyway."

Jonah grinned widely. "Good to know that, then! I'm thankful we're on the same page, my love."

"Can we get started, please?"

Both Jonah and Eva turned to glare at Joey before she kissed him once more, then repeated her instructions. "Two hours. If we aren't back by then, come find me."

"I'll certainly come look for you, Eva—gotta have you safe. Joseph, I'll take either way."

"Thanks," Joey responded drily and Jonah resisted the urge to give him the finger. "Come on. Let's go."

Jonah released Eva and she blew him a kiss before they disappeared from the room.

"You wanna follow them, J?"

"You know I do."

"I don't blame you," Achilles spoke up and Jonah turned towards him.

He'd almost forgotten about the asshole.

"I don't. 'Tis like sending two children off to scour the woods alone."

"Nah, the kid is still here," Jonah spat. "We're heading out. You go—well, go to hell for all I care. Bye."

"You have dislike for me, Blue Aura? Whatever for?"

"The list is too damn long, man."

"I got something." Reena crossed her arms and faced off against Achilles. "You have no respect for women. Why?"

"I have the same respect for women as I do for all fine creations. But those creations must be cared for. Cultured. They must be molded into effective members of society."

"By staying in the kitchen?"

"By taking care of the next generation, yes. It is men who are to provide, protect, and preserve the bloodlines. It is women who are meant to nourish that bloodline and ensure the following generations adhere to our gods and our traditions."

"Statements like that are why this world is as fucked-up as it is," Reena muttered. "No wonder your movies and your clothing line suck. Because you're a chauvinistic pig, surrounded by yes-men who believe the same way you do. It's disgraceful."

"Believe whatever you like," Achilles shrugged. "I am one of the wealthiest men in the world. If I am surrounded by yes-men—as you call them—then I must be doing something right."

"Re, don't even bother," Terrence scoffed. "Dude is not worth your time."

"I believe I know what your issue is, Reena."

"Is that right?" Reena raised both eyebrows. "Please, enlighten me."

"You've never had a man actually take care of you, so you've convinced yourself that the only person who will ... is you. As such, you've taken on a man's role. On the battlefield, the bedroom, you get the idea."

"Yeah, ok," she scoffed in return. "Are you offering or something?"

"Not in the least. I only associate with Olympians. Elevenths on the very rarest of occasions."

"And also Tenths," Jonah added.

Achilles' smug smile faded immediately. "Excuse me?"

"Oh, you know," Jonah shrugged, "we know all about the women you have in those sex houses. How many kids did you father? Nine? Ten?"

"That's right!" Spader whistled. "Damn, dude, with numbers like that, the fact you're still wealthy is a damn miracle!"

"Not that it is any of your business, but what offspring I have that is proven to be mine, I take care of." Achilles glared at them. "Did I not just say that it is my role as a man?"

"Dude, despite all of this—"

Terrence stopped when a loud scream echoed off the brick walls. The four of them looked at one another before they bolted in that direction. Even damnable Achilles joined them.

Jonah nearly bowled Joey over as he stumbled up the path. Despite the darkness of the island, Jonah could see the cameraman's clothes were soaked with blood.

"Where's Eva?" Jonah grabbed Joey by the shoulders. "Where is she, dammit?"

"Cemetery .... Cyrus ..."

"It's northeast, Jonah!" Reena took off in that direction.

He dropped Joey and headed after her.

A trek that felt like forever was only five minutes, but once they reached their destination, Jonah saw no one. "Eva!" He yelled. "Eva, where are you?"

The group spread out among the small tombstones and the weeds. It wasn't long before Spader yelled out. "Over here!"

Jonah ran through the stones before he slid to a stop. Up ahead, he could see Spader was cradling a limp form in his arms.

"Is she—"

"She's alive." Spader sounded strained. "But she's hurt, man. *Bad.*"

Jonah was instantly enraged, and he nearly forgot about Eva. He laser-focused on Joey. "You!"

Blood roared in his ears and all his judgement evaporated as he charged the cameraman. Jonah straddled the bastard, and proceeded to throttled him.

"Jonah! Stop! Hold on, man!"

Jonah heard Terrence's words but they didn't compute. His eyes were only on the bastard he was choking—who was increasingly turning blue. "You did this," Jonah whispered, rage engulfing his entire being. "It was you, you spying junkie!"

"Jonah! Let him go!"

Jonah barely felt hands on him. He barely heard the voices yelling at him as Joseph Lawson choked. But Jonah became all too aware when he was slammed against a headstone, away from his target.

"Calm down, J!" Terrence had him by the shirt and forced him back. Farther away from Lawson. "Calm the fuck down before you do something we all regret!"

"Let me fucking go, Terrence!"

"Balance first!" Terrence hissed in his face. "Eva needs you, man. She don't need you getting hauled off because you murdered the asshole on camera. Focus and balance, Jonah. Do that now."

As if to reiterate his point, Terrence grabbed Jonah's face and forcibly turned his gaze to Eva. Spader was still cradling her, looking more solemn than Jonah had ever seen him. Achilles was attempting to help, but Spader angrily batted him away, placing a shirt to her injury.

She looked frail. Fragile. Hardly the badass he knew her to be. Instantly, the rage ebbed away. Joseph could still rot in hell, but Eva needed him. "Alright, back up," he told Terrence. "I'm here. I got it."

"You sure?"

"Yeah. Thanks."

Jonah pushed past Terrence and dropped next to Spader. "What's the damage?"

"Wicked gash across her eye, J. We need Liz or Apollo. Like now!"

"Her regeneration?"

"Not doing a damn thing."

"Give her to me, Spader."

Spader shifted Eva off him and Jonah took the rag. He started to lift it when Achilles spoke.

"Lord Apollo is on his way."

"Uh-huh." Jonah's eyes never left Eva. "Thanks for being useful for five minutes."

Joey rose, looking incensed, but Reena grabbed his shoulder so tightly that he yelped and winced.

"If you're thinking of retaliation, let it go, or we won't pull Jonah off of you next time," she promised. "If you want to say anything at all, you'll tell us exactly what information you gave Cyrus to exploit, and exactly what he did to Eva."

Joey must have tried to respond, because he made a raspy noise, but no words came out.

Jonah wanted him to say something. He wanted an excuse to wrap his hands around Joey's throat again.

"Come on, baby," Jonah whispered instead, focusing on Eva. "Wake up. Heal. Do something!"

"Achilles spoke of the traitor." Apollo stepped through the group surrounding them. He knelt next to Jonah. "Eva?"

"Alive."

That was all Jonah could manage as Apollo lifted the blood-soaked rag to expose the lengthy wound that ran from Eva's left eyebrow to her cheek.

"Is she going—"

"Where is her sleeping equipment?" Apollo cut off Reena as he placed a hand over the wound. Gold erupted from his palm. "I will transport her there. Then I need to know everything that happened."

"We don't know." Spader glared over at Joey. "He was with Eva, alone, and then we heard a scream and—"

"Soon, Royal, soon." Apollo gathered up Eva and stood. "Lead the way."

Jonah rose and followed Apollo. He focused on Eva. If he looked back at Joseph, he'd throttle him again. "Cyrus is no longer Eva's Keeper, so these wounds will all heal, no problem, right?"

"Not necessarily, son."

Whereas Jonah had been enraged before, now he was frozen. Chilled to the bone by Apollo's response. "Excuse me?"

"You heard me, Jonah. The magicks that tie a Keeper to the

Sibyl are not so easily dismissed. I will heal her appearance, but I do not know how her sight will be affected."

"But ... but you're the *god of healing*!"

"Even the gods have their limits." Apollo approached the first sleeping bag he came to. "Especially when the magicks used are primordial in nature."

Jonah's insides felt as if they were filled with lead. He gritted his teeth, then relaxed his jaw enough to speak. "If you can't heal Eva, then heal Joseph. He can barely talk because I strangled him. Fix his vocal cords and find out what he snitched to Cyrus."

Apollo raised his eyebrows, then beckoned for Joey to step forward.

The cameraman looked like he was about to bolt; Reena grabbed his arm. "Go. Do the right thing for once." She shoved him forward.

Joey looked as though he wanted to be anywhere else on the planet than there, in that moment. Jonah was forced to pocket his hands, or else he'd strangle the quivering bastard and see it through to the end. First, he got Eva locked up for months. Then, he admitted to spying on her. Now, he'd gotten her gravely wounded. If he got off for this one, Jonah was going into full Charles Bronson mode from *Death Wish* with nary a regret.

Apollo snapped his fingers, and Joey coughed. Even the bruises on his throat were gone, which made Jonah a little salty. The bitch didn't deserve to be unmarked. Eva was hurt, after all.

"Your vocal cords are healed, boy," Apollo murmured, his golden eyes staring daggers through the tech man. "Speak, knowing that you are only living and breathing because I'm allowing it."

Joey stared at the group before he swallowed. "I told Cyrus we were coming here. That's true. But that was before he tried to get Eva in Italy. I haven't talked to him since the day before all that happened. I swear."

"You told him about Poveglia?" Apollo raised an eyebrow. "What else?"

"About the monster. The episode. That Jonah and the Elevenths were going to be with us. That was it, sir. I swear. I had no idea he would—hell, could—hurt her like this."

Apollo's glare didn't diminish. "What have you to gain from betraying my daughter, boy?"

"Um, is it really betrayal—"

Apollo took a step forward.

Joey took a step back. "Ok, ok." He held up his hands. "Dope, mainly. There were other favors. Money. A place to live after I got kicked out of the condo. I had to survive while the show was on hiatus."

Apollo tilted his head, and then slapped Joey. The blow knocked him off his feet.

"Dude, my god!" Spader exclaimed. "Pun intended!"

Apollo gave Spader a quelling look before returning his eyes to Joey. "You dare lie to a god?"

"I ... I ..."

"Silence, you filth," Apollo snapped. "You are a liar. Money and favors for survival. I have it on good authority that your story was accurate until about two months before Eva's release. At that point, you began living off the charity of a benefactor. So you weren't suffering anymore, boy. So, once again, what did you have to gain from betraying my daughter? Since you weren't grasping for alms and scraps anymore."

"My benefactor—"

"Name. *Now*."

Joey sat up and put his head in his hands. Finally, he dropped them. "Promise me protection and I will tell you everything. If you don't, you can go ahead and kill me. I'm a dead man walking anyway."

"Are you serious?" Jonah demanded. "You were living off someone new? You were still betraying Eva, even after you were back on your feet?"

Apollo gave Jonah the same quelling look just like he'd given Spader. "Talk, Lawson." His voice was quiet. Menacing. "If you do that, I'll promise you that I won't smite you myself. Probably. Now, who is your benefactor?"

"No." Joey seemed harder, darker than Jonah had ever seen him. "You want something that I got? You gonna have to give me something in return. I want protection from the benefactor and from the Elevenths."

"Boy, I will —"

"Smite me? Yeah. Go ahead. My life is gonna be over anyway if you don't agree to this. You can help me go easy." Joey folded his arms over his chest. "So, what'll it be? Information? Or my death?"

Apollo inhaled deeply, then extended a hand. Joey's whole body was bathed in golden light, but it was far from warming. It was harsh. Blinding. Apollo rose his hand, and Joey rose in the air as though by levitation.

"Know this, boy," he whispered. "I am Apollo, god of medicine, the healing arts, and prophecy. I bow down to no one, least of all, an impertinent, traitorous mortal such as yourself." He stepped closer to Joey. "We gods are forbidden to interfere with free will, strictly speaking. But with you, I don't give a fuck what rules I violate." His hands gleamed brighter, and Joey coughed. "Now give me a name. I, Apollo, Fourth throne of Olympus, order you to answer."

"Hera." Joey's answer was immediate.

Jonah looked at Apollo in shock. He'd broken an unwritten rule amongst gods and forced Joey to answer. "It's Hera. She hired Ange de la Mort, as well."

"What is Hera's reasoning?"

"Eva ... made a deal. She broke it."

Now, they were all looking at Joey in shock. If the name Hera hadn't rocked them, the fact that Eva had been in contact with the evil bitch had.

"You lie —"

"No. Cyrus ... told me. Eva told Hera she would give up her life for the antidote to free Jonah from Persephone's evil. Hera didn't make her swear on the Styx. Fucked up. Eva didn't take the poison. So Hera ... sent assassins."

Jonah looked at Eva's slumbering form in horror. They'd made a pact of no secrets.

"Boy," Apollo rasped, "you are telling me that my daughter volunteered to suicide herself in exchange for freeing Jonah of bewitchment?"

"Yes."

"Disgraceful," Achilles chided, regarding Eva with disgust. "Utterly disgraceful. Why did she renege, boy?"

"Because Jonah needed her and she got sent to the ethereal prison," Joey replied. "Then, she ran. Hera couldn't have that. She wanted the bitch dead. By any means necessary."

"What happened tonight?" Apollo continued his questioning. "What was your roll in tonight's attack?"

"Get Eva alone. Away from the Elevenths. Cyrus attacked her from behind. Plan was to stab her in the eye, then dump her in the ocean. He missed."

"Why did he miss?"

"Eva fought him off ... for a few moments, anyway," Joey answered quietly. "He tried to gut her, but the blade wouldn't go through her shirt. Eva tried to stab him, but he blocked it and tried to get her again. She tried to block him. The aim knocked her off kilter, and instead of stabbing her in the eye, he grazed it and scarred her face."

"Why did he run?" Reena demanded.

"He fled because Eva got a lucky shot," Joey said. "She jabbed *his* left eye. Completely ruptured it. He vanished."

"Is there anything more the rest of you wish to know before I turn him loose?" Apollo was pale. His eyes blazing. "I will answer for this, so make use of it."

Jonah stepped forward. "When did your friendship with Eva end, Joey? When did you turn on her?"

"When she didn't notice me," Joey stated solemnly.

"What?" Spader cried. "But you're gay!"

"It was never about sex, Spader," Joey muttered. "And Eva didn't even notice me. At first, I was hurt. Then, I was resentful. Then, it became hate. Strong hate. I'm glad she got locked up. She deserved worse. She was all depressed and mopey when Cyrus ignored her. Next, she turned around and did the exact same to me? Fuck her."

Jonah's fists balled up before he knew it.

Reena wrapped an arm around his wrist to pull him back to the task at hand.

"You said Eva offered her life in exchange for Jonah's. But they were just friends back then. Why would she do that?"

"Friends? Please. That bitch has been head over heels for Jonah since she met him. I tried to stop her. Even went so far as to tell her about all the women Jonah was getting on the side. Reminded her that she was better off alone. Didn't fucking work though. Jonah gave in and added her to his list of fuck buddies."

"Back to the suicide pact, Joey."

"I don't know anything else about it. Just that she didn't do it. The plane to New York wasn't supposed to make it that far. I know that much."

"Excuse me?"

"The plane—we'd rigged the equipment cases with dynamite so Albertson couldn't get his hands on it. Bomb didn't go off. Fucker died anyway though."

Jonah couldn't feel anything. He was numb to his bones. He couldn't even feel his fists. Spader walked forward and spat in Joey's face.

"You are a bona fide piece of shit, Lawson," he whispered.

"Yeah," Joey said, his voice level. "But at least I'm honest about it."

"How necessary is Lawson to Eva's show?"

"He's got a contract and it's ironclad." Reena sounded like she was going to be sick. "So, I think we are stuck with him. For now."

Apollo pulled Joey forward and whispered something in his ear. The cameraman slumped forward and Apollo released him. Joey hit the floor with a thud.

The god turned on his heel, then sat on the ground next to Eva's unconscious form. He turned those blazing eyes up at them as he rested his hand on her forehead.

"If any one of you are considering betraying my blood, it would be in your best interest to leave."

None of them said a word.

Finally, Jonah found his voice. "What's going to happen to Lawson?"

"I do not know as of yet. I will have to speak with Zeus first. For now, he is safe, Jonah. But that does not mean he won't feel my wrath before the end of his days."

"I like the sound of that," Jonah muttered. "Just one thing. What did you tell him?"

"He's been bewitched to be nothing but a model citizen to all of you," Apollo said. "When Typhon is dead, the spell will break."

"Oh, now." Achilles shook his head. "That's serious infractions, Lord Apollo. Zeus will have to punish you for such actions on mortals."

"Achilles," Apollo said, eyes on Eva, "was anyone talking to you?"

"I mean no disrespect, milord."

"I don't believe you are quite that stupid, Achilles." Apollo glanced at the group. "Go. Attempt to rest. We won't know anything more about Eva's injury until she wakes."

"Come on, J." Spader stopped beside him. "You look like you need a case or three of joints. We'll stay close by the entrance."

"I'm not leaving Eva."

"Jonah, go partake in calming vices," Apollo commanded. "Cyrus will not return here, I've seen to it with my powers. And as I've stated, when Joey wakes up, he'll be nothing but a model citizen. Now, go."

"But—"

"The second she awakes, you will know it, son." Apollo never took his eyes off his daughter. "So, go."

Jonah nodded, then followed the others outside.

Reena pulled out her joint and lit it before she passed it to Jonah. "Here. You get first dibs."

Jonah took it and pulled so hard, he feared he'd burn through the whole thing. "Keep it coming," he told her. "I still want to kill Joseph. Even if he's mind-fucked into being a lapdog for the next two days."

"We brought plenty. Figured we'd need it." Spader lit another one for the rest of them. "You, um, you need to talk about what we just learned in there?"

"Nope," came Jonah's response instantly. "I need to talk to Eva and Eva alone."

"Dude, are you angry at her?" Terrence asked.

"Damn right I am," Jonah grumbled. "To use her physical life as a bargaining chip for *my* ass? I ain't worth that."

"Are you serious?"

"Damn right, I am."

"You have a woman who loves you enough to sacrifice herself for you and you're pissed?" Spader whistled. "You got that twisted, J. Especially since you would have done the same thing if roles were reversed."

"That's not the point."

"Sure, it is."

"Eva should have told me. We agreed to no secrets—"

"Yeah, like two hours ago. Then she got pulled away and hurt." Reena blew out smoke before she continued. "You have every right to be pissed, Jonah. But if I didn't respect Eva before, I sure as hell do now. That was an act of love before she knew you loved her back."

"But, Reena," Jonah grimaced, "Now she has a psychotic, disgraced goddess on her ass who's sent not one, but *two* assassins for her, and who knows what else? I wouldn't have let Eva do this shit. Not for me. She's more valuable to the world. I'll be gone one day, remember?"

"No, Jonah." Reena shook her head. "No. *You* don't understand. Eva may be important to the world, but to her? You *are* the world. And she was willing to put up with ethereal prison, Hera, and these assassins just to keep you safe."

Jonah stood there, silent. The anger was still there, but he didn't know what was more prominent in his mind: the fact that Eva was brave enough to do that for him, or the fact that she loved him enough to do so, even when he'd been screwing Persephone. "Fine. I ain't gonna argue. But put Typhon aside ... what will we do about Hera? Will she keep sending assassins?"

"I don't think we need to worry about Hera, man." Terrence pulled on the weed. "You saw the look on Apollo's face. That bitch's ass is grass, and Apollo is gonna smoke it just like this weed."

"It's true. He was pissed."

"In all fairness, Apollo reacted as the rest of us did." Terrence pointed out. "Except, the target is his kid. That's a whole different level."

"Yeah, but don't forget about Cyrus." Spader shook his head. "For one, how'd he get out of Tartarus? And two? Why? You'd think once he was free, he'd be hell and gone."

"Because of me."

They turned as Apollo approached.

The god nodded. "'Tis true. Alexius has despised me since his capture. Since he couldn't take that hatred out on me, Eva became an easy target. He simply wrapped that hatred in words like 'duty' and 'honor'."

"Why?" Spader asked again.

"Because Eva has my blood and, so, she was the next best thing. A representative of myself and the Council Alexius believed had betrayed him."

"And you found this out, how?"

"Through Alexius himself … the first time I had him tortured after he tried to end my Eva's life." Apollo turned to Jonah. "She is stirring, so she will be awake soon."

"Jonah, let that woman rest," Reena told him. "She's been through a fuck ton in a short period of time."

"Really, Reena?" Jonah asked, irritated at the chide. "I truly didn't know that."

"You're going to go over with guns blazing and—"

"No, I'm not."

Jonah passed her the nub that remained from his smoke and slipped past Apollo. He made his way over to the sleeping bag and sat next to Eva's head. He didn't need the light to see the gash was gone, or how fragile she still seemed. How delicate.

He lifted her up enough to put her head in his lap. Jonah stroked her forehead and considered everything they had learned over the past twenty-four hours. Joseph had betrayed her. Set her up to be murdered more than once. Cyrus—bastard that he was—hated Apollo enough to take his rage out on the woman who just happened to share DNA with his master. The fact that Eva loved him enough to sacrifice herself for him.

Jonah didn't know what to think. He didn't. As Reena had said, it was so much in such a short period of time. But the more he caressed her face, the more he relaxed. The more the anger began to seep away.

"Your anger is to mask fear, son." Apollo stepped forward. "You are afraid of your own passing, yes. But I believe it is more than that. I believe you are as afraid of losing Eva as I am."

"Of course I am, man," Jonah declared. "I wasted valuable time not knowing what I wanted, and it ... *she* ... was here in my face the whole time. Now we're together, and all these fuckers come out of the woodwork at once? Not to mention Eva put herself in Hera's crossbars, just for me? Yeah, I'm scared. Out of my mind."

"I am not allowed to share the words of the Fates, but I will tell you that your fear—while honorable—will be put to better use on the battlefield."

"What does that mean exactly?"

"You have already learned to hone your anger to your advantage, yes?"

"Yeah."

"So, do the same with your fear. Hone it. Shift it into energy to ensure success." Apollo sat next to him. "And once the battle is over, decide what you wish for your future to be."

"I wish for Eva to be my future."

Apollo nodded, pleased at that response. "Then it's high time for more responsible choices. Choices such as not forgetting your training and letting your emotions run you, or damn near murdering mortals. No matter how tempting they make it." Apollo threw a glance in the direction where Joey was, but returned his focus to Jonah. "You can't go around acting as though you don't matter. You always have, in more ways than you know. And my daughter will sacrifice everything for you. Including herself. You wouldn't want to nullify her contributions for you by being reckless and cavalier, no?"

Jonah swallowed that. There was more truth in it than he liked, so he changed tacks. "I'm sorry Joseph made you resort to breaking

Olympian rules. That was ... a little scary. You said you had to answer for it ... what's gonna happen to you, dude? Is Zeus going to ... is he gonna actually punish you?"

"No. Not when he hears the motivation behind my actions."

"What's going to happen to Joseph once this is over? Surely, he will have to answer for his crimes."

"He will, though I am certain the Council will take his mortality into account which means he will not be sent to Tartarus." Apollo clasped his hands together. "Unfortunately."

"Which means, what?"

"Lawson will give up the information needed and he will be admitted into a rehabilitation facility. When Eva is forced to work with him, he will be monitored closely."

Jonah felt the sneer on his lips, but smoothed his expression. That was too damn nice. "Those drug charges should count for something."

"They will," Apollo promised. "Rehab will happen, whether he's jailed or not. As challenging as it is, Jonah, we can let Joseph deter us. Mind your anger, and use it."

Jonah sighed. "Fine. I got it. And Apollo ... that other thing?"

The god smiled and passed Jonan two tickets.

Jonah nodded excitedly. "Thank you, sir."

"Not at all."

Eva turned over in Jonah's lap and slept. Jonah stroked her head again and pulled out his phone. Three rings later, someone picked up. "I thought you hated me now, Jonah."

"Shut up, Minako," Jonah said impatiently. "I'm busy right now. Something kinda big. Well, big is an understatement, but that's not the point. If I make it out of this, I want to meet up and talk. Hash things out."

"Where?"

"Front row of *The Electric Funeral*."

Silence. Jonah knew there would be.

"Are you trying to bribe me with tickets to my favorite band?"

"Uh-huh," Jonah said with no shame. "You in?"

"Of course, I'm in!" Minako cried. "It's *The Electric Funeral*!"

Despite everything, Jonah smiled. "I thought that would be your response. The plan is next Friday. Meet me at the estate at six."

"I'll be there!"

Jonah disconnected the phone and Apollo nodded. "Better?"

"Better. I hate to leave shit like that hanging for too long."

"That is understandable." Apollo was silent for a moment. "What are your plans after Typhon is defeated?"

"France," Jonah responded immediately. "Eva is happiest there. I'll meet up with Minako, but aside from that, we're going back to Marseille for awhile."

"She will go as herself, I hope. Once this mess with Hera is squared away, she will have no reason to hide."

"You think that's the real reason for her disguise?"

"I do. She was running for her life, Jonah. If she had come to me from the beginning, there would have been no need for all that."

"How is Hera still a threat?" Jonah wanted to know. "She has almost no power."

"She still has her mouth and her mortal money, Jonah," Apollo advised. "Both are all that's necessary to be dangerous."

"Yeah, but—"

Eva groaned and Jonah moved his hand. She jerked upright and Jonah caught her before she fell to the side. "Evie? Take it slow. You don't want to move too quick."

"Jonah?" Her question was slurred. She blinked, as if disoriented. "Daddy? What ... what's happened?"

"Calm, daughter." Apollo placed golden hands on Eva once more. "Slow and steady. A lot has happened. What exactly do you remember?"

"I ..." She placed her hand on her face. "A cemetery? There were stones. And I was fighting. I *think* I was fighting."

Apollo nodded. "You were indeed fighting. With Alexius."

"Cyrus?" Eva whispered. "How did he find us?"

"Not yet, baby." Jonah pulled a water bottle from the closest bag and opened it. "Get your bearings first. How do you feel?"

"Dizzy. My face hurts."

"Where?" Jonah asked. "Maybe I can balance your equilibrium."

"I … wait." Eva frowned, then closed her eyes, as though there were bright light in her face. She opened one eye, then the other. "My eye." Her voice one step below panic. "What's wrong with my eye?"

"Evie—"

"Why can't I see?" She turned to Apollo. "What happened to me?"

"Evie, calm yourself. Alexius injured you."

"But … he's not my Keeper anymore. You can fix it."

"No, dear girl." Apollo kept his hand on her arm. "Not even I can override primordial magick."

Eva began to gasp for breath. She clutched her throat. "I can't … I can't do this. I can't—"

"You can and you will. Breathe. You'll pass out if you don't."

"I can't …"

Jonah reached out and placed his hand on the back of Eva's bowed head. He hated balancing people without permission, but Apollo was right. She had to calm down. After a moment, she shuddered.

Jonah met Apollo's gaze, then nodded. "Eva, how do you feel?"

"Tired. So … damn … tired." She dropped her hands. "What can I do, Daddy? How can I do this now?"

"You will do your very best, as always," Apollo answered. "You have support and you have my blood. You can and *will* do this."

"Perhaps I can be of assistance."

Jonah sneered at the hated voice and turned to see Achilles at the entrance of the tent.

Achilles met Jonah's gaze with that smug smile. "A little known fact about me is that I have many Laistrygonians among my staff," he began. "I train them and give them direction and purpose, something they can lack in these modern times."

"So what?" Jonah snapped. "That doesn't have shit to do with anything."

"In addition to the Laistrygonians," Achilles went on as though Jonah hadn't spoken, "I've also trained a great many of their cousins, the Cyclopes. So I have a background with training soldiers with the

223

limitations and spatial orientation associated with only having one eye. If you'll have me, I can extend my skills to the little lady here."

"Little—"

"Are you not small, Representative? In size and stature?" Achilles approached the group and knelt next to Apollo. "You could benefit from my knowledge."

Eva glared at him.

Apollo simply sat back.

"The battle begins in just over twenty-four hours. Will you have the time?"

"Plenty of it. We can begin in the morning."

"Why?" Eva seethed. "Why would you help me?"

"Because I am loyal to the Council we both serve. If you listen to my instruction, then I can assist you. If you do not, then you will fail. Those are your choices."

Eva hesitated before she extended her hand. "Very well."

Achilles shook it. "You can see nothing?"

"Not from my left side. No."

"Then we shall strengthen that." He turned to Apollo. "I am going to go to New York tonight, but I can use shadow travel to be back at dawn."

Apollo nodded. "I, too, need to depart. The Council must be made aware of these new developments."

"Ya'll are just going to leave?" Jonah stared at them. "We have twenty-four hours—"

"Perhaps, you and yours should retreat for the night as well." Apollo gave Jonah a pointed look. "As long as you return by dawn to begin training, I see no reason why you can't go home."

"I'll take Eva to the estate."

"You can't." She turned towards him. "Jonah, I still have a year before I can go back. You go home. I'll just ... I'll stay here or something."

"Then I'll stay with you, then," Jonah stated. "You guys can go recharge. We can get Ulysses to bring us some supplies or something."

"Jonah, go get some creature comforts—"

"Don't need too many creature comforts," Jonah told Eva. "Thor's boot camp taught me to be a total minimalist, should I need to."

"Um, suggestion?" Reena shook her head. "Go to Marseille. The condo. Get away from this horrible place. Jonah doesn't have to come with us to use the Astralimes."

"I swear, for two brilliant people, ya'll can be so damn dense." Spader snorted. "We leavin' Joey behind?"

"No harm will come to him." Apollo stood. He reached down and pulled Eva to her feet, then caught her when she seemed unsteady. "Take it easy tonight, dear girl. I mean that."

"I don't think I have a choice."

"Fine," Jonah said. "Eva, I'm sure you don't have an appetite, and I don't either. Let's just go to the condo and drink our calories. I'll make superfood smoothies."

"What?" Reena perked up. "You're serious?"

"Yes, Reena, I make your smoothies," Jonah told her. "Hell has frozen over. Damn shame Typhon couldn't be frozen inside it."

Everyone else laughed. Everyone, except for Eva, who hugged Apollo goodbye before she turned to Jonah.

"Ready, Superstar?"

She nodded, then took his hand. Jonah waved to the others before he initiated the Astralimes. Within seconds, the horrible island became Eva's condo in L.A.

"Do you want that smoothie now or ..."

Eva shook her head, then stepped forward to wrap her arms around his waist.

"No," she finally muttered. "No, I'm fine. I want you, and a shower and bed, in that order."

Jonah raised his eyebrows and she turned on her heel to head towards the stairs. When she passed the sofa, Eva cracked her hip against the edge of it. "Dammit," she muttered. "I was closer than I realized."

"Ok." Jonah came up behind her to clasp her shoulders. "I really think you need to take it slow. Shower first. Then we will see how you feel."

"I'm fine."

"Uh-huh. You're a mess, and you're covered in dirt and ash, but you're fine?"

Eva stopped at the bottom of the stairs. She took the first step, then stumbled when she missed the second one. If Jonah hadn't been holding her, she would have fallen face-first onto the carpet.

"Ok." She breathed before she twisted around to sit on her butt. "So my perception is off. I'll get there."

"Yes, you will," Jonah agreed. "But no one is expecting it to be immediate."

"It has to be, handsome," Eva replied. "I'm fighting the father of monsters soon, after all."

"Not alone." Jonah sat on the stairs next to her. "You'll have all of us with you."

Eva studied him, then closed her eyes.

He squeezed her hand against her knee. "Baby, don't worry. He'll be in the ocean. I can shock him straight to hell if I have to."

"That's not a bad idea." She opened her eyes again. "But that's not what I was thinking about."

"Yeah?"

She sounded sad when she spoke again. "I can only see half of you now."

Jonah grimaced. Hatred for Cyrus fought sympathy for Eva. "Baby, it's just been one night. Maybe something that can be done. There are other realms, other schools of thought, treatments ... maybe something can be done."

"Maybe. We'll cross that bridge when we get to it, huh?"

"Yeah, we will." Jonah stood and offered her his hand. "What'd you say we get off the stairs?"

"Why? I can't run into anything if I sit here." She took Jonah's hand and let him lift her. Eva held onto the banister and the two of them made it to the top without any more stumbles.

"So, that was progress."

"It was," Jonah agreed. "Let me help you with the shower."

"I don't need help."

Jonah stopped in the doorway of the bedroom and watched Eva

head to the closet. She stripped off her ruined shirt and then the mesh armor he had given her right before her fight. It had probably saved her life.

Jonah shuddered at the thought of how close Cyrus had come to being successful. One slip, and Eva wouldn't have merely lost her sight.

He crossed the room when she didn't come out of the closet, then snagged one of his shirts she had folded up on top of her own.

Eva jumped when he brushed against her. "Sorry," she muttered. "I didn't realize you were there."

Jonah tilted up her chin in the light so that he could take a good look at her face. It was still perfect, save for the thin white scar that now ran through her damaged eye, from the eyebrow to her cheek. He ran the flat of his thumb along the line without thinking and Eva swallowed.

"Is it bad?"

"Is what bad?"

"The scar."

"No," he answered truthfully. "It's barely noticeable."

Eva took the shirt with a sigh. "At least there's that."

"Baby, listen—"

"What?"

Jonah didn't want to tell her what Joey had said, but she needed to know. "We promised no secrets, so I am giving you the option. We learned some things—horrible things—about Joseph. Do you want to know them now or later?"

Eva seemed to weigh his words before she spoke again. "Later. I can't take much more tonight, handsome. I just can't."

Jonah nodded, filing it away. "I'll respect that. But just a heads-up. When you see Joey next, he'll be docile. He'll be helpful, subservient ... he'll basically be kissing all of our asses until Typhon is gone. That will be due to ... to the terrible things."

Eva rubbed her forehead and then dropped her hand. "We promised not to keep secrets from each other anymore. I ... I have one that I have to share with you. Two, actually."

Jonah tensed. He couldn't help it. He knew about Hera, so that wasn't going to be a surprise. But what was this second secret? He'd been so sure that Eva told him everything. Apparently not. "Eva—"

"No. Let me give you the same option. One secret is not something I am proud of. Something I did when reacting to an emotional situation. The other is not bad, per se, but I can see where you would think I had overstepped my boundaries. Do you want me to tell you?"

Jonah regarded her, and braced himself. "Tell me the second one. I'm ready."

"First, know that I am not a stalker."

"Ok."

"I pay a landscaping company to go out every week to take care of your grandmother's grave and the surrounding cemetery. They put fresh flowers on her grave every week. Keep the entire place looking nice." Eva tightened her arms around herself. "The church thinks the money that pays for the service comes from a federal grant, so they don't have a problem with allowing the landscapers to do their thing. I started that not long after we returned from Romania."

Eva cleared her throat before she continued. "She took such good care of you, Jonah. I just ... I wanted to make sure that she was taken care of to the best of my ability. Please don't be upset. I'm not trying to intrude and if you want me to stop it, I will."

Jonah frowned. "Baby, why would I be mad by such an act of charity and kindness?"

"Did I mention that it seems kinda stalkerish? I know how precious she is to you, Jonah. I guess I'm just afraid that you would see that as me intruding on those memories."

"Baby, not at all!" Jonah exclaimed. "I love it! Matter of fact, I'm thankful you saw fit to provide blessings to my memories! Thank you ... so much, my love."

Eva smiled. "There is, um ... one more thing. It's not actually a secret; my investigators did the work because they vet people who come into my circle. I know where your siblings are."

Jonah blinked. "What?"

Eva nodded. "You have two brothers and three sisters. I've got their names and locations in a safe in Malibu. I just kept it for ... for if, or when ... you ever wanted it."

The next question came out before Jonah could stop it. "Have you met them?"

"No. I never went that far. And the only reason I had them found was because I know how important family is to you, Jonah. Even the ones you haven't met yet."

Jonah thought about that. To be honest, it didn't require much thought. "Not ... right now. I'm good with the family I have at the moment. But ... maybe … one day."

"I am leaving that completely up to you."

"That secret wasn't bad, Eva. What is the first one?"

"The first one *is* bad."

Yeah, she was going to tell him about Hera. "Go for it."

"When we figured out you were being poisoned, I began asking around for people who could help me get the antidote." Eva shifted her weight on her heels. "Um, Hera was the only one on the earth plane. So, I went to her and found out she had actually helped Persephone craft the black roses poison, and she had the antidote. I told her I would give up my life in exchange for it."

"Why?" Jonah finally got to ask the question that had been plaguing him since Joey had spilled the truth. "Why would you do that, Eva?"

"Because ... even then ... I loved you. I couldn't stand to see what the poison was turning you into. And I knew that if Persephone had been successful, you were going to be lost to your family forever. So, I accepted Hera's poison and got the antidote. I had to save you, Jonah. I had to."

Jonah remembered his anger from before. He couldn't bring himself to feel it now. "Eva, I'm grateful you saved me. I am. But Hera wanted you gone. She could have betrayed you. She could've done anything. I'm ... I'm just scared what else she'll unleash on you."

"I don't care what she does to me." Eva reached out and grazed his arm with her fingers, then dropped her hand. "I don't. I would make that deal again in a heartbeat if it meant you were safe and living your life freely, Jonah. You deserved so much more than to be a slave to Persephone. I would have paid any price to make sure that didn't happen."

"But Eva, you bargained with your *life*."

"If you weren't here, I'd have no life. So, that is a moot point."

Jonah considered Apollo's words. Reena's words. Eva had just proved them right. "I love you too, Eva," he said. "I'm just ready for these bastards to get what they deserve. Ready for Typhon to be gone. Ready to come back here to Marseille and just chill the hell out."

"Me, too," she whispered. "I miss our routines and our traditions. I miss our life, Jonah."

"Same." Jonah ran a finger down Eva's cheek. "I look forward to you not needing a disguise though."

"Yeah? I thought you liked Lea?"

"She's alright." He smiled a little. "Like you more though."

Eva stepped into him and wrapped her arms around his waist.

He held her as tightly as he could in return. Jonah couldn't stay angry with her. Not after what he knew now. It was an astounding thing to be so loved. It was a feeling he had never expected to have. "Go. Take your shower." He finally released her. "It'll make you feel better."

"You need one as bad as I do."

"I need Gotch Bible first," Jonah said. "Need to purge some anger. Then I'll shower."

"Alright. I know better than to get between you and the Bible."

Jonah waited until he heard the water running before he went over to the nightstand to grab a deck of cards. He wasn't kidding when he said he had a lot of anger to work out. Anger that he couldn't take out on Lawson. Or the damn Keeper.

So, he tore himself apart. Eva took a while in the shower. That was good. It gave him time. And when he heard the hairdryer kick on, he was sweating from exertion. Jonah returned the cards and headed towards the now open bathroom door.

Eva stood at the counter, wearing nothing but his shirt as she worked the hair dryer around her wild blonde curls. When she realized he was staring, she flipped off the dryer. "What?"

"You're so beautiful, Superstar."

"For a lion? Sure." She smiled. "You want to take your shower in peace? I can move to the bedroom with this."

"Nah, you can stay there," Jonah laughed. "I don't have anything you haven't seen before."

"Hmm, but I love it every time I see it."

Jonah grinned as he slipped past her. He stripped off his shirt and tossed it in the hamper. "I called Minako."

"Good." Eva turned the dryer on low and went back to work. "How did that go?"

"I needed a peace offering, so Apollo got me two tickets and backstage passes to see her favorite band, The Electric Funeral," Jonah answered. "She heard that, and things were right as rain."

"When's the concert?"

"I'm going to meet her at the estate. We'll leave from there."

"Good. You deserve a night out, handsome. It's been too long."

"Maybe. What do you think you'll be doing that night?"

"Dunno. Work? Research?" She finished her hair and hid a yawn behind her hand. "I'll figure it out when the time comes."

Jonah made a face when she kissed him on the cheek. "I'm all sweaty, Evie."

"Ok, ok." She laughed as he turned on the water. "Enjoy your shower. I'm going to go lay down."

"I won't be long."

"Take your time. Enjoy it." Eva slipped from the room and Jonah stepped under the spray.

Say what you would about modern life, but nothing beat a hot shower after a workout. Or after the island of hell.

By the time Jonah finished and got ready to rejoin Eva in the bedroom, he could see that she had fallen asleep while she waited. He went through the condo, checking the locks and shutting off the lights. When he finally slid into bed and pulled Eva flush against him and kissed the side of her head.

"You're safe, Superstar," he whispered more to convince himself than to her. "You're going to be just fine."

FIFTEEN
EVA MCRAYNE

TRAINING WITH ACHILLES wasn't so bad. He was infinitely patient with me. Even more so with Joey when he and Jonah switched sparring partners. He showed my friend the basics while Jonah worked with me on my balance, which was good.

Good but useless. By the time I was back sparring with Achilles, the immortal got the drop on me every time he came at me from the left. It didn't matter what I tried to do. Nothing he told me to do seemed to work.

I grunted when I hit the sand again. I was seconds away from telling him this wasn't working. I had the words on the tip of my tongue when he broke in to interrupt me.

"You aren't listening to me."

"Yes, I am," I snapped, then shoved myself back to my feet. "I am doing everything you tell me to do. It's not working."

"Do you want it to work?"

"What is that supposed to mean?"

"Eva, I've known you for what? A week? Less? I can already see the denial on your face. You think it's easier just to ignore your injury. To go on as you did before. You can't do that. If you don't adapt, you will fail."

Ok. Achilles had me there. How he was able to see right through me was more than a little unnerving. Was I that easy to read?

Achilles clasped his hand around the back of my neck and gave me a light squeeze.

"Slow down right now. Pay attention to what I tell you. You can't go on autopilot now."

"Fine." I blew a strand of hair out of my face. "I'm sorry I snapped at you. I'm just very frustrated at the moment."

"Of course, you are." He released me. "Stand still."

"What?"

"Stand still. Get a feel for your surroundings. The energies of the environment."

"I'm not going to have time to stop when something attacks me." I tried not to glare at him but dammit, I wanted to. "And if you tell me it's something that gets better with practice, I'm going to hit you."

Achilles laughed at my temper. He reached out and put his hands over my eyes so that I had to close them. "Stand still." He stressed the words as he repeated them. He also removed his hands.

For once, I did what I was told. I froze in place. The winds were stirring. I could feel them. Yet, it was more than that. There was a charge in the air. One I hadn't noticed before. I jumped when I felt that same charge shift seconds before Achilles caught my shoulders from behind.

"Good," he breathed next to my ear before he released me. "Try again."

I closed my eyes once more. This time, the energies around me seemed to spark. I ducked down and slammed my boot into his knee. Achilles dropped his shield as he lost his balance. When he caught himself next to me, I grabbed his shirt, then rolled the both of us until I was on top of him.

"So, that's a start, right?" I climbed off him. "Let's go again."

"Give an old man a minute." He sat up to look out over the water.

What choice did I have? I lowered myself next to him.

After a moment, he broke the silence. "Is it true? You can absorb the knowledge of the gods?"

"You heard about that, eh?" I folded my arms around my knees.

"Yeah. Only when I have no choice though. I don't go around just stealing power."

"What do you learn?"

"Everything." I looked over at him. "But I've learned how to compartmentalize the information. I only access what I need. I push the rest back. I would go crazy if I didn't."

"You have the secrets of the gods at your disposal and you've never accessed them?"

"If you mean about their little dirty secrets, no." I wrinkled my nose. "Ew. No. I am not the least bit curious."

Achilles studied me for a minute. "You are quite an interesting creature."

"Why? Because I'm not nosy?"

We sat in an awkward silence for a few minutes before Achilles decided to speak again.

"I want you to absorb my power, Evie." He turned his head towards me. "I want you to use my knowledge on the battlefield."

Ok. That was a first. I had always stolen what I needed. I had never once been asked to take the information.

"Achilles …"

"This is too important to wrestle with semantics. You must succeed in this matter. You must be the leader the Council knows you to be."

"You don't think I can do it on my own."

"No. Quite the opposite. You are already great. Your stories are already legendary. I only want to expand your knowledge."

"I don't know if this will work."

"How does it work exactly?"

I extended my hand. Achilles placed his on top of mine and I squeezed it. "Achilles." I focused on him. On who he was. What he was. I was so sure this wouldn't work.

I cried out when his memories slammed into my brain. A millennium of war flickered through my memories. The scenes were horrible. Full of rot and bodies and blood.

I loved it. No, *he* loved it. Achilles lived for the victory. He lived for the destruction. Had lived for the power he'd gained. War was a game to him. One he was damn good at.

I shoved the memories to the back and focused on his knowledge. Like Athena, he was one hell of a fighter. He understood how important the environment was to victory. I knew at once what he had spent the morning trying to teach me. Not to mention the strategy. Achilles was a master of it.

I felt his grip loosen so I dropped his hand. He was staring at me with a strange look. Something close to awe.

"Eva ... I felt you. I felt you in my head."

"Really?" I took a shaky breath. "You didn't lose anything. I swear. You won't have any bad effects."

"What did you see?"

"War." I choked on the word when the memories tried to resurface. I shoved them back in their box. "Battlefields."

"Then you understand." Achilles grinned. He seemed thrilled. "You understand how important—"

"Yeah." I stood, then headed towards Jonah. "I got it. I got everything."

"Hey!" Achilles came up behind me.

I stopped when he appeared in my line of vision. "Are you alright?"

"I will be. That move tends to take a lot out of me." I swallowed my unease. I couldn't explain it. I didn't want to explain it. I chalked it up to the war scenes. I wasn't kidding when I said they were gruesome.

"Come on." I moved around him. "Let's go get our dueling duo. I need to review the cameras. Make sure everything is set up before the big day."

"I would prefer it if we sparred a little longer. You need all the practice you can get."

"No, I need a break." I resisted the urge to wipe my hand against my pants leg. He thrived on the victory, yes. He lived for the thrill of war. But his obsession? What kept him coming back time and time again? The screams of the men he had been able to torture after his victories? This was the basis of his nickname: the Savage. It wasn't his rage. It was his cruelty. And I was sickened by it.

"I'm going to get Jonah. Take a walk."

I crossed over to where Jonah and Joey were sparring. I watched them counter each other and pride replaced the sickness in my stomach. Jonah was amazing to watch, that was true. But it was his restraint against a man he didn't care for that was most impressive.

When they came to a stop, I called out, "You up for a break, Jonah?"

"Absolutely." Jonah immediately ceased. "Go sit down. Take five, Joseph."

Joey nodded. "Good idea, Jonah. I will." And he jogged off.

Jonah watched him, his face inscrutable.

I nudged his arm. "Is that bewitchment he's under still weird to you?"

"Like you wouldn't believe," Jonah answered. "Let's sit down though."

I snagged his hand and pulled him over to the dock. I tested the old wood before I sat on the edge.

"How are you doing?" Jonah sat next to me. "With the asshole?"

"I suck." I gave him a small smile, then glanced behind me to make sure Achilles was nowhere close. Still, I leaned in and whispered, "He had me absorb his knowledge. He's one screw up immortal, Jonah. Seriously screwed up."

"We know he's the equivalent of a racist," Jonah replied. "Does he have PTSD, or something?"

"No. He's a sadist. Is that the right word?" I frowned. "Anyway, he's not just a racist. Or a misogynist. He's twisted. Gets off on torturing people. That's where the 'Savage' moniker came from."

Jonah eyed me, then looked over in Achilles' direction. "So, he wasn't in it for duty. He just loves carnage."

"Yeah," I told him. "I think that Styx water at birth might have made him crazy."

Jonah grimaced. "That's the same thing I said, dammit."

"That's not all I got."

Jonah turned his head into mine.

I whispered again. "His whole family—parents, siblings, cousins —were all Eleventh Percenters. He is, too, but he denies it to himself. He believes his family's ethereality is a curse that was placed upon them."

Jonah stared at me, just like I knew he would. But the look on his face was not just that he was unnerved. It was something like ... concern? "Eva, we need to steer clear of him."

"I mean, of course, but— "

"No you don't get it." Jonah quieted his voice. "It might not have been the Styx water that makes him ... crazy."

"I don't understand."

"Jonathan told us about psychosis that can be engendered when an ethereal being denies their ethereality," Jonah explained. "Ethereality is like any other living thing ... it needs expression. Exposure. When that doesn't happen, it turns inward, and fucks things up. Eva, you know as well as I do, how toxic it can be to deny parts of yourself. Denying ethereality is the same. But it carries consequences that can translate into really bad shit."

"He's done some really sick things," I admitted. "But what do you mean? What consequences?"

Jonah sighed. "Have you encountered someone who's had a psychotic break?"

"I've had them myself."

"Ah." Jonah looked sheepish. "Sorry, baby. Well imagine that, but ... perpetually. No relief. No light on the horizon. Ethereality will turn bad if it isn't used, same as everything else. If Achilles is denying his, and has been for centuries, then he's not only a misogynistic xenophobe. He's also a basket case."

"Basket case? Is that a technical term?"

Jonah chuckled before he threw his arm around my shoulders to pull me into him. He kissed the side of my head. "The point is, we need to be hell and gone from that guy. You said his whole family was ethereal?"

"Yeah. Which makes his anti-ethereal stance make even less sense."

"Alright, *plat*," Achilles called over to me. "Your break is over. Come back."

I stiffened.

Jonah noticed. "You ok?"

"I will be. Once I can shove a dagger through *his* face." I turned at the waist to yell back. "No! And don't call me that!"

"I feel like I'm missing something."

"You are. *Plat* is Greek for property."

Jonah rose to his feet, then turned around. "You just called Eva property?"

"Yes. That's what she is, after all."

"Keep that to yourself. Unless of course that means I get to call you an incestuous psychopath."

"Say whatever you like. It does not make my words less true."

I stood and placed my hand on Jonah's arm.

He ignored me. "How the hell is that true? Eva is—"

"Property. The property of her father, at the moment. But when Apollo sees fit, he will relinquish her to a man's household for some sort of gain."

"Oh, thank you," I responded drily. "I am now on the level with cattle."

"Not cattle. You do have a royal bloodline, so your children will as well. That alone makes you more valuable." Achilles shrugged. "'Tis true. If this were the golden age of Olympus, you would have been married at the age of twelve. Apollo has been forced to adapt to modern times, though I am sure he is weighing the offers he has had for you."

"My God, asshole," Jonah muttered. "The small dick energy is strong with you."

Achilles' eyes narrowed. "Are you questioning my manhood?"

"No," Jonah scoffed. "Why question something I know full well doesn't exist?"

"Your insults mean less than nothing to me, Blue Aura. You have already proven what I already know of your kind."

"What is that, exactly?"

"That you are weak in mind and spirit."

"Now, wait just one damn minute." I glared at Achilles. "I won't stand here and let you speak to Jonah like that."

"You're still untamed, Eva." He appeared amused. "You speak out of place and defend someone who has no issue with hiding behind a woman. Perhaps I will approach Apollo myself and make an offer on you. I could put you in one of my houses in Europe."

I felt my lips part to speak, but the words wouldn't come out. I couldn't settle on anything bad enough to call him.

Finally, I found my voice. "If you ever—and I do mean ever—attempt such a thing, I will find a way to end you. I don't care how immortal you are."

"And you speak of my kind?" Jonah said heatedly. "*You* are am Eleventh, you little fool. Calling me weak ... that's a stretch coming from a man who denies his true nature and doesn't acknowledge five of his kids."

Achilles turned cold eyes on me. "You divulged the secrets of my mind without permission? You said you did not seek out the memories, only the knowledge."

"I tell Jonah everything," I shot back. "Can you blame me? I'm no better than a breeding cow in your eyes."

"At least a cow would remain silent on things that do not concern them!"

"You wanted me to absorb your mind. I did, unfortunately," I snapped. "You didn't want me to know your secrets? You shouldn't have offered them up."

"Don't get mad at Eva for leaving yourself wide open," Jonah growled. "If you were that guarded, you shouldn't have volunteered your shit. As for you being a horrible father, everybody knows that. The youngest is just fourteen months. You claim to be so superior and noteworthy, yet your trifling ass doesn't have the power to produce a fucking child support check."

"You don't know me, you bastard!" Achilles charged Jonah.

Jonah sparked his electricity so hard that it sounded as loud as a leather whip.

Achilles yelped and fell back on his ass.

Jonah took one step forward, not even pausing to let the blue current recede from his hands. "An experienced Eleventh could have blocked that," he whispered. "And I know exactly who you are. I've hated men like you my entire life."

"Back away from me, Ghostly One." Achilles willed his shield in his hand and stood. "If you wish to spark the war between our kind on these lands, I will happily do so."

"Oh, for the love of ..." I stepped forward to focus on Achilles. "First off, you started this shit. Second, you exasperated it. Turn around and walk away."

"You cannot order me —"

"I outrank you with both the Council and by my blood, Achilles." I stood as close to Jonah as I dared, but the charge coming off of him was making my hair stand out from my head. "So, yes, I can. And you have to follow those orders. Now, leave."

Achilles was angry, but he rose. He sized up Jonah before he glared at me.

"Your lessons are at an end," he grumbled. "I will stand my ground in the final fight, but I will no longer assist you individually."

"Oh, no." I responded drily. "I can't be around you anymore? Poor me. What *ever* will I do?"

Achilles stormed back to the main building and Joey gave us a curious look before he went to follow him. It wasn't until they were both out of sight that Jonah relinquished his ethereality.

"You ok, handsome?" I studied his tense expression. "I don't think I've ever seen you spark like that."

Jonah must have recognized the concern on my face because he pulled the electricity back, then tapped his hands against his pants legs to get the last few sparks to fade. "I'm fine. I *really* don't like bullies. And when those bullies happen to be terrible fathers, that makes it ten times worse."

"Is he really that bad of a dad? I don't pay attention to celebrity gossip, having seen myself there so much."

Jonah ran his tongue along the inside of his cheek. "Put it to you like this, Evie. He's got two boys ... one in Wilmington, North Carolina, and the other in San Diego. Same age, same grade. Don't even know they're brothers. And that's just *two* of his kids."

"I hate to say this, but I think they are better off without him as an influence in their lives."

"Yeah. Still."

I took Jonah's hand and squeezed it. "I'm going to finish that walkthrough when it gets dark. Want to come with me this time?"

"I'd love to," Jonah replied. "Might get some pointers myself. I'm ready to get this over with though. Ready to see people get what is coming to them."

"Like Joey?" I pulled Jonah back to the edge of the dock and sat down. "What happened, Jonah?"

"I thought you didn't want me to tell you."

"I didn't. Not last night. I'm better now. More calm about things."

Jonah sighed and told me everything—from Joey's admission of betrayal, to Apollo's breaking Zeus' sacred rules and magically forcing Joey to answer his questions, to the horrible things Joey admitted while under Apollo's control, which resulted in his temporary bewitched subjugation. When he was done, I was silent for several moments, which seemed to alarm him.

"Do you need weed?" he asked. "I brought my stash—"

"No." I shook my head. "He'll do whatever we say right now, right?"

"Until Typhon is defeated. Why?"

"Because I'm going to tell him to walk into the fucking ocean."

"Baby, sit down." Jonah grabbed my arm when I started to stand. "There is absolutely nothing—"

"I trusted him, Jonah!" I pulled away my arm, but sat next to him again, and buried my face in my hands before I started laughing. The sound was harsh. Jagged. "I should have known. I did know—long before the drug deal went bad. I told Spader and Terrence he was going to abandon me because everyone fucking did. But to know all this? Even now, it still hurts."

"I know, Eva," Jonah pulled out his pouch and lighter. "I ... I almost killed him. I nearly strangled him. Terrence had to throw me against a tombstone."

"You almost killed him?" I felt the blood drain from my face as I realized how close I had come to losing the man I adored. "Jonah, no. You can't do that. You could've turned dark and I would have lost you."

"I need us to *lose* Joey," Jonah grumbled. "He betrayed you to Cyrus, Eva. With no remorse. He will pay. In some way, shape, or form."

"But you can't cross that line, Jonah. Promise me."

"Eva—"

"No." I grabbed him as if I had already lost him. "Please! Not over Joey. Don't let him take you away from me, too."

Jonah sighed. "Fine. I'm good. I'll just be proactive in making him pay through means that won't taint my soul. Deal?"

"Deal."

"Evie, why are you so afraid of me going dark?" He picked up something from the sand, then chucked it into the waves. "You said once that Jonathan showed you a vision, but you never told me what that vision was."

"Jonathan asked me not to tell you. He said it would be too upsetting for you." I crossed my legs beneath me as Jonah continued to throw bits of rock at the ocean. Rock or bone. There was no way to tell for sure. "But if we have no secrets, then I can tell you. My question is: do you *really* want to know?"

Jonah must have thought about it, because in the end, he took a hit and shook his head. "No. I don't. I'd rather not have the thoughts in my brain to give life to. I'll respect this secret, baby. But I'm good."

"I'm so glad you said that." I leaned over to rest my head on his shoulder. "I want us to give life to positive thoughts, too. Your birthday is coming up. Trips we want to make. Things like that."

"Agreed," Jonah said. "And your anniversary as the centerpiece of *Grave* is coming up, too. So, think about what you'll want to do for that one."

"Quit."

"What?" Jonah gave me the look of utter surprise that I expected. "Are you serious?"

"Ok, maybe not quit, but scale it back. Twenty-two episodes is a lot for me to balance with the Council."

"You mean like specials?" Jonah asked. "Like a dozen episodes a season?"

"Fifteen is the standard for most shows. Connor pushes for twenty-two because it gets more money from the streaming services," I explained. "And before, I was good with that. But I'm not doing *Grave* for the money anymore. And I have someone who I want to be home with. Besides, if the Council keeps throwing shit at me like Typhon … and then I have to go deal with murder victims? I think I'm going to burn out."

"Well, good thing Apollo terrified Connor by doing … whatever." Jonah grinned. "Since that time, Connor hasn't shot down a single idea you've had. He used to revel in doing that. What did Apollo do?"

"No clue." I shrugged. "I really don't want to know, either."

"I'm glad he did it, whatever it was," Jonah said. "He completely neutered him. It's beautiful. "

"You've never been the biggest fan of Connor, have you?" I teased.

Jonah scoffed, "Hell, no. He's an ass."

"I'm not going to dispute you there."

"So, now what, Evie? What do you want to do?"

"Spar? Practice my balance?" I sighed. "The fight is tomorrow and I still feel so … off."

"Since Achilles is off pouting and pissy—a matter on which I have no fucks to give—you want to call in a favor?" Jonah suggested. "Polyphemus, maybe? He owes you for clearing his forges of that rogue mania, and you know he'd do anything for you after that. He's a Cyclopes, too, so he's proficient with range of perception and motion. You think he'd come in, one night only, to give you tips?"

"I was kinda hoping that you would spar with me." I gave him a small smile. "But I understand if you don't."

"Baby, of course I will," Jonah replied. "I just brought up Polyphemus in the event that you felt I wasn't … experienced enough to help."

"How can you even say that?" I stood and Jonah did as well.

243

"Let's find a spot away from the main building. I don't want an audience for this."

Jonah grinned. The two of us headed down the beach and away from the asylum. The farther away we were, the better. Except, it wasn't a private spot that stopped us. It was Hephaestus and Poseidon, coming from the opposite direction.

Gods dammit.

"Hello." I managed a small smile as they approached us. "Fancy seeing ya'll here."

"We've come with armor for your people, Representative." Hep smiled brightly at me. "Where is everyone?"

"Everyone is out and about, but they're all within reach. You're more than welcome to do one of your beacons and get everyone here. Except Achilles. If you brought goodies for him, hand them over personally."

"Why not show us around, Eva?" Poseidon tapped his cane against the beach. "The battlefield won't be far from here. I can sense it."

"Um, sure," I glanced at Jonah, who was absolutely unreadable. "Although ... I am not sure exactly where it is going to be. There is no way for me to know, really."

"Let us meet the others."

Hephaestus beckoned for us to follow him. I sighed as I walked back alongside Jonah. We came up on Terrence, Reena, and Spader first, just inside the ruins.

Jonah stepped forward. "Hey, guys," he announced. "This is Poseidon and Hephaestus. They've come to armor us up some more. My lords, these are my two best friends, Terrence Aldercy and Reena Katoa, and also Royal Spader. We tolerate him."

"Oh, ha-ha," Spader muttered. "You should be a circus clown with the jokes."

"I could've easily said you're like the little brother I never wanted."

"Funny."

"I thought so," Jonah grinned before he turned back to the gods who had joined them. "How does this work exactly?"

"I've studied your folders." Hephaestus grew serious. "I shall will your new armor and weapons onto you now, so that you may have them before the battle. I want you to get comfortable in them."

My uncle reached for me first and I stepped back. "Nope. I'm good. You can just will the pieces." I gestured towards my crew. "Start with them."

"You don't want to put your armor on, Evie?" Hephaestus grinned. "You look smashing in it."

"Not yet. Get the others squared away first."

"Very well." Hephaestus looked at Jonah and his friends. "I've made you armors that have elements of your aura colors. Just stand still. They'll appear on you in twenty seconds."

I leaned against the stone wall and whistled when their armors began to appear. Reena's armor fit her like a glove and glowed a soft yellow in the late afternoon sunlight. Terrence was more bulky, but when he realized that his knuckles had spikes attached to them, he grinned like a kid at Christmas. Spader's armor had been styled with coat tails of all things, and his helm had a shield that slid over his eyes. But I didn't pay much attention to them. Instead, I was awestruck by Jonah's armor.

The metal was light—much like Keeper armor—and possessed the same sheen of blue as his aura. The armor emphasized his shoulders and lean frame. On his head, there was a helmet that only exposed his eyes. Weighted gloves and boots completed the look.

"Evie, stop drooling." Spader gave me a crooked grin. "We know we look good, but you might slip in that puddle you're making."

"Oh, you're still here?" I blinked in his direction. "I barely noticed."

"Lies."

"How does it feel?" Hephaestus broke in. "Can you move well?"

Jonah walked around a bit. "It fits like everyday clothes," he marveled. "Dude ... it smells like a new car in here!"

"Wait till you fight in it," Hephaestus grinned. "You'll be in for a ride."

"Impressive, but it begs a question."

Everyone turned. Achilles was back, looking irritated and spiteful. He folded his arms across his chest as he scornfully looked Jonah up and down.

"I mean, is it functional, or just fashionable?" Achilles went on. "We're in for a huge problem if it's just the latter."

Hephaestus growled. "It's been awhile since I've seen you face to face, Ghostly One. Are you still wearing the same armor from your honor guard days prior to Troy?"

"Absolutely. Why fix something that has worked for centuries?" To prove his point, Achilles tapped his shoulder.

I rolled my eyes. "Whatever. Just don't get stabbed in the foot."

That earned me a glare. Hephaestus cleared his throat, then tapped my shoulder. I growled a little as he beamed at me.

My t-shirt and jeans became an elaborate armor ensemble of white with faint gold accents. On my head sat a golden laurel crown. The set was gorgeous, sure. But I felt like an idiot. "Change me back. I look like a wannabe Barbie in this."

"The Royal armor was designed by Zeus himself. You wouldn't want to hurt his feelings, would you?"

"No, but you may as well put a damn spotlight on me. I'm gonna stick out," I pouted. "Let me wear Keeper armor. It's all black. Simple."

"No can do," Poseidon shook his head. "You're about to fight the mighty and feared Typhon, my dear. Leave the wearing of subpar battle armor to Achilles."

"Fine. But change me back."

"Can we at least see it?" Spader stepped around Hep and the others joined him. "Oh."

"Shut up, Spader. If you say one word about medieval Barbie, I'm getting your blood on my sword."

"Um, is armor supposed to make you look like that?"

"Like what?"

"Like you could kick my ass and I'd enjoy it. Sorry, J. You can smack me for that later."

Jonah pitched a baton.

Spader yelped and ducked. He narrowed his eyes.

"You're gonna pay for that, " Jonah said, "so you may as well get it over with now."

"If the petty exhibition is quite over, can we get back to the tasks at hand?" Achilles snapped. "This behavior only reiterates what I've said about you people all along."

"Silence," Hephaestus barked. "You and your compatriots in Olympus are acting in a manner most incongruous with the Mount's true sentiments. Progress is necessary, not your outdated stance."

"Progress for the sake of progress is whimsical nonsense," Achilles fired back.

Hephaestus shrugged. "I wouldn't expect you to understand Olympian matters. After all, you are not truly an Olympian."

Achilles bristled. "I am as Olympian as you are—"

"You are no such thing, boy," Poseidon interrupted. "You may have been amongst us all this time, but you have never been one of us. All you ever were was a warrior from the sticks."

"How are any of these insults beneficial to the battle we wage tomorrow?" Achilles snapped back. "'Tis bad enough we will become nothing but fodder for Typhon."

"You really don't think I can beat him, do you?" I crossed my arms over my chest. "You're right. I can't. Not alone. I need as many capable warriors as I can get. If you keep acting the way you are acting, then I don't need you on the battlefield."

"You are not a soldier," he seethed. "You are a woman who has been forced into a man's role."

"A woman who had your own knowledge. So, if you have no faith in me, then what you're really saying is that you have no faith in yourself."

Spader whistled.

I raised my hand before he could speak. "That being said, your sword is necessary. Your mouth is not. I don't want to hear another word from you until I have no choice but to speak to you. Am I clear?"

Achilles was beyond pissed. I could see the tips of his ears turn red. His jaw tightened and I knew he wanted to put me in my proverbial place.

"Don't speak. Just nod yes. Then get out of my sight."

Achilles gave me a curt nod, then stormed out of the room.

Hep clapped me on the shoulder but he didn't make my armor vanish. Dammit. "Spoken as only a queen could."

"I'm no queen, Hephaestus."

"Of course not." He gave me a grin I didn't like. "You reminded him of your status just the same."

"That was perfect, Eva," Reena told me. "That bastard needed to be knocked down a peg or two ... or twenty. I don't think I've ever seen someone so content in being an asshole through and through."

Jonah and I shared a look. He knew exactly what I was thinking. Achilles was crazy. A twisted soul. He knew why, too.

I would let him handle telling the others. I had a show to do. "Alright, Hephaestus. In all seriousness? Get me out of this thing. We're going to be filming in half an hour and I have to go find my cameraman."

"Maybe you should keep the armor on —"

"No chance in hell, Spader."

Hephaestus sighed, then tapped my shoulder. My normal clothes appeared and I felt better. Less gaudy. He did the same to my companions.

"Thank you." I shook out my shoulders. "I know Joey came in here. Does anyone know where he went?"

"Yeah," Terrence said, "he's just sitting in his tent, looking chilled as can be, waiting for someone to give him an order."

"Sucks that the spell is broken once Typhon is gone," Spader ruminated aloud. "I kind of like him like this."

"Thanks." I turned to Poseidon and Hephaestus. "You two gonna stay or will I see you back here tomorrow?"

"I will be back tomorrow." Poseidon rapped his cane against the floor. I knew that was a habit of his, but it really grated on my nerves. "Before the battle. How is your injury, Representative?"

"I'll be fine."

"And the rest of you? Are you prepared?"

"As ready as I'll ever be, sir," Jonah replied.

"I'm game to throw down whenever, wherever," Terrence declared.

"I'm always ready, Lord Poseidon," Reena told the gods. "And it doesn't hurt that I'm the brains to keep rashness from these guys in check."

"I don't need the pep talks," Spader replied. "I'm just ready for the victory weed I'll be smoking after we win."

Jonah was instantly alert. "Stupid bitch. She's coming here."

"You think so?"

"Damn straight," Jonah spat. "She's famous for her gall and ego. She wants to see us fall, Eva. What do you wanna bet Cyrus ran to her and snitched once you gouged out his eye and turned him into a fucking pirate?"

"Then we'll take her down." I shrugged. "Though I don't know how. You would have thought she'd learned her lesson by now."

"So, why'd you deal with her, Evie?" Spader piped up. "Really?"

"You know why." I squeezed Jonah's arm as I slipped past him.

I had to go get Joey and get started. Then, I was going to curl up in my damn sleeping bag and pass out. That was the plan. That was what I could control.

Everything else could wait.

SIXTEEN

EVA MCRAYNE

THIS WAS IT. My own personal D-Day was beginning. I'd been in plenty of fights before. My mouth got me into plenty of them. And I had done what I needed to do to survive. But I was pretty damn sure this was the first time I would have to fight wearing armor. I glanced down at myself. Running my palms over the sleek white material. I had no idea what it was made of.

Hephaestus had done his little magic trick to outfit the four of us. He had accepted our thanks before he vanished back to Olympus. Now, we were doing nothing but waiting. Well, most of us. Achilles had done nothing but watch me all morning. I didn't like the look in his eye, but what could I say? I didn't want him to know how disturbed I had been. And I hated the fact that I had his memories in my head … memories and knowledge I was going to have to call upon.

Use what you have to use. Discard the rest.

I clung to the words I had told him before I took what he had offered. Really though. You'd think I would have learned by now. Nothing was free. Nothing was without its consequence. Especially when it came to the immortals I surrounded myself with.

I was fumbling with my gloves when Jonah approached me. He took the strap I was struggling with, then slipped it into place.

"I'm going to stay to your left and protect the side you can't see." He kissed the top of my head. "And don't go crazy for the show. Get in. Get the job done. Then we come home."

"Jonah, promise me something?"

"What's on your mind, Superstar?"

I pulled back and unclasped the chain around my neck. It was the dragon pendant he had given me for my last birthday. I loved it. Never took it off ... until today.

I stepped back into his personal space and put it in his palm before I closed his hand over it. "Keep this safe for me." I studied his eyes for a minute. "It's precious to me. I don't want anything to happen to it during the battle."

I wasn't going to tell him how afraid I was. I wasn't going to burden him with the fact that I still didn't know how I was going to manage this. He was going to be on the battlefield with me. That scared me more than anything. I wanted him safe. I needed him to be safe.

Jonah looked down at our hands before he kissed me. I closed my eyes and relished in how that single, simple act of affection made me feel.

"You are going to make it through this and I'm holding you to that. Don't make me have to go down to hell to bring you back again."

"I'll do my damnedest, Blueberry." I bowed my head, then looked up at him with a small smile. "I don't think either of us would be welcome down there anyway. You kicked too much ass last time."

"Damn straight, Evie." He rested his forehead against mine. "Damn straight."

"How long are we stuck here again?"

Joey had approached us. I was so wrapped up in Jonah, I hadn't noticed.

"Too damn long."

"Jeez, you're grumpy this morning." Joey threw an arm around my shoulders and I shrugged him off. "Some daughter of sunshine you are."

I ignored Joey and approached Apollo, who was watching the sky from the windows facing the beach. I frowned up at the sky with my father and wondered exactly what he was seeing. "What's wrong?"

"The sea is angry." He narrowed his eyes and scanned the horizons through the gaping windows. "The barrier is breaking."

"How long?"

"Soon, child. Too soon."

The sea was churning. The waves slammed against the old dock with enough force to send a sheet of spray into the air. But that wasn't the most frightening part. The sea was receding. Pulling back to show the bedrock beneath.

This was bad.

It was made even worse when the room flashed gold and two more gods appeared. Two. Not eleven. I stared at Zeus and Poseidon when they approached me.

"Did Hephaestus make that suit for you, Evie? There is nowhere near enough gold on it."

"Not all that worried about my outfit at the moment, Pappy." I studied them. "Where is everybody?"

"They aren't coming." Apollo glanced over at Zeus before he took me by the arm. He led me deeper into the room. Away from the rest of the group. "There have been developments."

"More? I heard about Hera last night."

"It appears that Hera was responsible for Alexius' release from Tartarus as well as Typhon."

"She hired two assassins, freed the Keeper, and Typhon?" I couldn't keep the sarcasm out of my tone. "Glad to know she's been keeping busy."

Apollo ignored my jab. "At any rate, we believe she will appear at the battle today. We hope to catch her in a trap."

"Ya'll focus on that. I'm gonna have my hands full."

Apollo gestured over to Jonah and the Elevenths. They joined us and I rolled my eyes as Spader tried to check me out without Jonah noticing. I didn't have time for his antics today.

"We need to strategize." My father focused on the group. "If Hera appears, we will need people to restrain her. Currently, the plan is for Zeus to grab her. But if he is busy, are there any ethereal methods that can be employed to keep her from escaping?"

"I can try a Mind Cage," Jonah suggested. "She isn't at full strength, so it could work … at least until Zeus takes her down."

"And we can knock the ever-lovin' hell out of her, too."

"I hope it won't be necessary, Terrence." He began to say more but was interrupted when Zeus whistled for him.

"Apollo, get over here."

My father clasped my shoulder, then went across the room to join the others.

It was Reena who spoke. "Can I ask, or was that top secret?"

"Hera is the one who freed Cyrus from Tartarus.."

"What?" Jonah hissed. "How?"

"Excuse me?" Reena's eyes widened when I shushed them. She lowered her volume and tried again. "Seriously?"

"Yeah." I turned to Joey with my next question. "Is everything set up?"

I knew that it was. Joey had set up the cameras when we first got here. So, when he gave me a look, I knew exactly what he was trying to say. So, I asked something else.

"Where are you going to be?"

"On top of the main tower. The stairs are rotten, but I can get up there. I will be able to catch all the action."

"Right."

"How's the eye?"

"Same." I shifted into place. I was too anxious. Too ready for the ax to fall. Honestly. Waiting for a fight you knew was coming was the worst feeling ever.

"I'm going to go on up there. Make sure that I didn't just lie to you."

"See you."

I watched him go and told myself that everything was fine. It would be fine. Joey would be safe.

I just wasn't sure about the rest of us.

———

The world cracked when the barrier fell at exactly 12:01 in the afternoon. I know … because I heard it. Felt it when the ground shook so hard beneath me, I had to grab onto Apollo to remain upright. The warning signs had been coming at me all morning. The sky had turned black. The waves were so far away from the shore, I could have walked back to Venice.

Good. That would give me more room to move.

Apollo didn't look at me. He was too busy scanning the horizon. Zeus, Jonah, Achilles, and Poseidon? The same. My Eleventh family flanked us, every last one of them searching the sea for any sign of our opponent. The nine of us standing side by side on the shore. Waiting for all hell to break loose.

We didn't have to wait long.

The earth around us exploded within seconds of the last quake. This time, I was knocked flat on my back, but I didn't stay there. I rolled to my feet to see bodies crawling out of the earth. Men and women, entirely of bones, grasped my boots. I wanted to scream. I wanted to run.

I did neither. I swung my sword through two of them before I felt the air shift behind me. I ducked as a body flew over my head. It landed with a screech louder than the thunder that boomed overhead. I didn't give the man time to get back to his feet. I thrust my sword down. Right through his head.

Go in. Get the job done. Come home.

Jonah's words became my mantra as I fought. I ignored the skies when the clouds opened up to soak us in a sheet of rain so thick, it was blinding. The only light seemed to be the blue of Jonah's batons as he cut down the bastards around him.

That was good. That meant he was still upright. Still fighting.

I jerked my sword free just in time to see a woman in a nurse's uniform slam into me. She clawed at my eyes as her face shifted into the horrifying demons I had seen over the past few days. Her empty eye sockets seeping as she screamed within inches of my nose.

Oh, hell no. I slammed the hilt of my sword against the side of her head to knock her off me before she erupted in a ball of fire. I scrambled back to my feet to see my father standing a few feet away from me, his hands burning with the fire he controlled.

"You're too slow, daughter mine." He grinned at me. "Your old man is going to show you up."

"Behind you!"

Apollo whirled to palm another phantom. It shared the same fate as the first one. The two of us shared a grin as lightning cracked across the ground. The phantoms, the bone things, all screamed as Zeus pulled down his hands.

"Nice light show!" I yelled at him over the roar of the winds. "Would have been better twenty minutes ago, but whatever."

"Semantics," Zeus yelled back before the world shifted again.

We looked at each other when an ear-piercing shriek surrounded us.

I hissed, then grabbed my head as the shriek resounded against the waves. Against the rubble behind us.

"Move!" Achilles grabbed my waist, then slammed me down to the sand.

I started to roll away from him when I felt a ridiculous amount of heat envelop me. I buried my head in my arms as he held his shield between us and a wall of fire.

"The beast has conjured up reinforcements!"

"Thank you, Captain Obvious!" I yelled at him as the fire subsided. "Now, let me go!"

Achilles released me and shot back up.

I did as well and surveyed the battleground before me. Monsters, spirits, skeletons all rushed my people. They rushed me.

I twirled my sword then rushed into the melee. We weren't going down without a fight. Not today. Not ever.

SEVENTEEN

JONAH ROWE

JONAH LOOKED around after he'd taken down another monster.

Spader severed one's spine before glancing his way. "Dude, where the Hell is Typhon?" he demanded. "I thought *that* was who we came to help Eva fight!"

"Typhon is the father of monsters, Spader," Reena reminded him. "Surely you realized that monsters would precede his rise, right?"

Jonah braced himself and shook filth off his new batons as reptilian creatures crawled into the world. "Dracanae, I think," he said. "We need to get over there—"

"Let the gods handle them," Terrence blurted out suddenly, his eyes westward. "There are people down there!"

Jonah led his Eleventh friends down a decline as a smattering of people flailed this way and that at monsters. A man cried out as one of the dracanae tried to take a chunk out of his leg. Jonah gave it a hard shove before grabbing its arm and willing electrical ethereality through it. Its dampness didn't work in its favor; Jonah's current practically barbecued its ass in seconds. The monster collapsed, but Jonah didn't watch it fall. His attention was on the bleeding man.

"Sir, I've got you." Jonah moved in and helped the man to his feet. He was well aware that there was a strong chance the man wouldn't understand one word he was saying, but aid and assistance were a universal language. Even if his words were unintelligible, he hoped his actions would speak for themselves. "You may not understand m**e,** but that thing is gone. I'll try to move you away—"

The man lashed out and shoved Jonah away. He regarded him with scornful eyes and bared yellowing teeth before shouting in Japanese and raising his hands. To Jonah's shock, his palms gleamed red.

An Eleventh.

"Whoa, dude!" He darted to the side as a wave of ethereality swooped past him. "We're on the same side!"

The man bellowed, but Achilles descended like a hawk and took a quick, determined swipe; the Eleventh's head was nearly severed from its neck as he collapsed, the red glow fading from his hands.

"You fucking idiot!" Jonah cried, furious. "What the hell did you do that for?"

"T'was a lost cause, Rowe." Achilles glared at him. "His brains have been addled for too long by the effects of the essence. You said you two were on the same side? Unless you're on the side of insanity, that is an untruth."

"Yeah," Jonah shot back. "You'd be our in-house expert on crazy." He looked at his friends. "Guys! Some of these people are Elevenths! They're ... they're completely insane!"

"Who is that?" Eva asked suddenly, looking at an incline newly created by receding waters. "That man ... tied to rocks?"

Jonah looked, and frowned. Sure enough, a naked man was bound to a rock, from his throat to his ankles. The restraints were like the freshwater ones Delphin had used on Rhode.

It was Apollo who roared in rage. "Scamander!" he snarled. "You traitorous son of a bitch! I'll smite you!"

"No! Please!" the river god begged. "Don't hurt me! Typhon can't rise without me!"

"What?" Jonah cried, shoving away a skeletal beast.

"They betrayed me," the emaciated god rasped. "They said there would be glory for me with the Titans, but it was a trick! They needed a god's blood for the father of monsters to rise!"

The sun god's golden eyes blazed. "We need to keep the monsters from this turncoat!" he announced. "He is the linchpin of the enemy's plans!"

"What kind of ropes are those?" Eva yelled as the winds picked back up. "Why are they glowing?"

Jonah didn't have time to answer her as Reena and Spader took off towards the god tied to the rock. He started to rush after them as more creatures rose from the exposed sea floor.

Jonah grunted angrily as a bitch with two heads slammed into him. Her empty eye sockets were seeping something black as she ripped at his armor. He cracked her across the jaw, then impaled one of her heads before another one took her place.

Jonah kicked out before a skeleton could reach him. He followed it by bashing in its skull. He ducked seconds before one of the sea things flew over his head.

"Good move, brother!" Terrence laughed as he gave Jonah a fist bump. He whirled around when he heard Eva yell out.

"Jonah! Blue and gold!"

Jonah heard Eva call him as he shoved another wraith-looking thing away from him. He focused on the winds to clear his path to her, then grunted in surprise as Elevenths tackled him to the ground and began beating him.

"Jonah!" someone screamed.

He had no clue who it was. He lost all focus as he covered his head from the blows. If only he could conjure electricity, but with the rain, he ran the risk of hurting his family.

Then, blood spilled all over him. He yelped and hissed as another body fell. He looked up.

Achilles. He was an absolute murder machine as he cut down the afflicted ethereals.

Jonah watched him snap a middle-aged Eleventh's neck before he glanced Jonah's way. Jonah sneered. "Doesn't change anything," he grumbled. "Those were innocent people."

"Who were all about to beat you into the earth, boy. You should be thanking me on bended knee."

"I'll never get on my knees in front of you," Jonah snapped. "I ain't your sister. Now, if you'll excuse me, Eva needs me!"

Achilles scowled at him, "Once this is over, Rowe, we will see which man is still standing."

Jonah rose to his feet, then searched the battle just in time to see Eva going toe to toe with a bastard three times her size. He clapped Terrence on the shoulder before he rushed through an opening in the mob crowd.

Eva dropped to her knees as her opponent swung a large club at her head.

Jonah clocked the thing across the throat, then swung his other baton across its snarling mouth.

When it doubled over, Eva thrust her sword through it then shoved it away from them. "Thanks, handsome!" She popped up, kissed him quickly and offered a grin, then rushed towards the gods.

The rain was falling in sheets around them as Jonah dared to look over at the rock.

Reena and Spader were holding their own against various creatures, but there was no way they were going to last much longer on their own.

"Terrence! We gotta break ground!"

His brother heard him because he threw a ghastly looking woman over his hip, busted her face with determined knuckles, then yelled back, "Lead the way!"

Jonah ran full speed through the battles towards Scamander. If they could get him free, they stood a chance at disrupting this thing. They were less than half a football field away when another person literally blinked into existence. It was a hooded, hideous thing that looked around at the carnage as though it were a beautiful dream-worthy beach scene.

Hera. It was fucking Hera.

She pulled a dagger from her clothes and regarded Scamander, who was squawking like bitch and thrashing against his restraints.

Jonah growled and he felt his fingers sting with current. "Hera, you bitch hag!" he shouted. "Don't do it!"

"Jonah, the Cage!" Reena cried. "Do it! Shut her down!"

"Keep them off of me," Jonah yelled as he began to focus. He saw his ethereality erupt as he focused on the goddess who had become his enemy years before. One that had continued to work in the shadows.

She wasn't in the shadows now. Blue bars erupted around Hera, but she lunged forward before she was completely surrounded—to slam the dagger in her hand through the traitor's throat.

"God dammit!" Jonah roared in anger and terror, but it was too late.

The damage was done. Scamander wheezed one final time, and then went limp. His blood watered the ground within seconds.

The ugly shell of the once great goddess cackled with laughter. "Failed again, boy," she squealed gleefully. "There is no stopping it now! Those rumbles you hear now? They are the sound of your end—"

A lightning bolt slammed into the cage. Hera slammed against the side of the cage with a shout, then slid to the ground.

"Silence," Zeus growled.

But Jonah wasn't paying attention. "Reena! Spader! Move your asses!"

"What?" Reena brought her wrench across the neck of another empty-eyed bitch. "What did you say?"

"We gotta go!"

Jonah grabbed her arm and pulled her back towards the shore. Terrence and Spader were right beside him as they broke out into a run towards the gods and Eva.

"Eva, move!" Jonah caught her around the waist and the two of them slammed into the beach as he initiated his astral shielding.

The winds were screaming almost as loud as Scamander did before another wall of fire surrounded them.

"Jonah, what the—"

"Scamander is gone!" he yelled in her ear. "The sacrifice was done!"

Eva started to respond before she looked over his shoulder. He watched her eyes widen and her face go stark white while her lips parted.

Jonah followed her gaze and really wished he hadn't. Just offshore, a very large, very pissed off creature awaited. Jonah took in the thick torso of a man. The heads of snakes that extended out of its shoulders. Dragons that twisted around each other. Jonah took in the scales of his tail.

Yeah. Tail. Like a mermaid. Except Jonah was pretty sure the father of monsters wasn't going to be belting out show tunes.

Jonah clutched Eva as abject horror engulfed his entire being. In that moment, he understood why people pissed themselves.

"Holy fuck," he whispered, his throat raw. "In the name of God ..."

"That thing is even worse than the picture!" Spader cried.

"Do me a favor, Spader, and shut up," Jonah croaked. "Now is not the time!"

EIGHTEEN
EVA MCRAYNE

"WHAT THE F—" I started before the dragons screamed.

I got hit with such a force of wind, I jammed my sword into the beach to give me something to hold onto.

Jonah grabbed onto me and held on as the power behind nature's fury broke through his shield.

Good move on my part. For both our sakes. The waves that had receded now rushed forward. They crashed against us. Against the beach. And stole half my damn battlefield.

How the hell was I going to decapitate this thing? I doubled over when it shrieked again. The noise was maddening. Debilitating.

The truth was, I knew what I had to do. But dammit, I didn't want to. When another huge wave crashed over us, I shut myself down and released the knowledge I had taken from one of the most disturbed immortals I had ever known.

I opened my eyes and surveyed the battle raging in front of me. The gods were doing all they could to keep the thing away from the shore. Achilles had willed a bow to replace his shield and sword. Jonah had released me and was busy, getting rid of the last remaining demon things.

Reena, Terrence, and Spader were doing their damnedest to keep the creatures rising from the sands at bay. The Elevenths who had swarmed us. We were all being soaked by the rain. By the waves. Fighting an onslaught that was hellbent on taking us down.

We were doing it all wrong.

"Pappy Zeus!" I yelled across the sands. "Hit his heads with lightning! Achilles, aim for them, too! Daddy, blind him best you can with your fire! Poseidon, use the waves to get that bastard as close to us! Jonah, use the winds to help Poseidon! Spader, Reena, Terrence! Keep them off of me!"

"Are you insane?" Apollo yelled back at me. "He'll eat us all!"

"Not if he can't see us! Just do it!"

What choice did they have? We were getting nowhere fast. I made my way through the corpses as they went to work. Watching as this hellish beast was pulled forward. The snakes began to snap over my fellow fighters. The dragons shot fire anyway they could.

My heart plummeted when I watched every head that was destroyed grow back. It was crazy. And what I was about to do was certifiably insane. Hera might get her payment today, after all.

I embraced the adrenaline that coursed through my veins and took off like a shot.

"Eva McRayne!" Reena screamed when I dashed past her. "Get your skinny ass back here!"

"*Eva!*" Jonah yelled with her. "What in hell's name are you doing?"

Typhon was less than half a mile from the shore. His mermaid's tail slamming against the water to fight the pull Poseidon had on the sea. I rushed past the gods. I ignored the screams for me to get back as I launched myself onto the lowest head in the bunch.

I couldn't see out of either side as I stabbed my sword into the neck of the snake I was on. But neither could the creatures around me. When it swung around, I almost lost my grip.

Almost.

I used the beast's movements to launch myself onto the next one. Then the next. Each getting me closer to my goal. When I got to Typhon's neck, the noise was unimaginable.

I jerked my sword out of the dragon I had used, then threw

myself forward. My blade buried itself deep into the spine of the monster. I looked up just in time to see the largest of the dragon heads jerk upward. Its fire shot straight into the sky.

"Gotcha!" I pulled myself up onto Typhon's left shoulder as the heads began to disappear. All but one.

I jerked my weapon free one last time then swung its sharp edge against the thickest neck I'd ever seen. Then again. The result was a spray of blood that soaked me even more than the rain. Typhon began to jerk beneath me—so hard, I had to dig my free hand into the first patch of skin I could reach to stay on him.

I released a roar when I swung my beloved blade one last time. The beast stopped jerking. The noise ceased and I was sure I'd gone deaf as he stumbled backward. I tried to hold on, but he was too slick. I was too wet.

I slammed into the waves with a fleeting scream. The breath was knocked out of me as I was pulled down deeper. But I wasn't the only one to fall. I saw the water above me go black, so I forced myself downward, deeper into the sea that had started this whole mess to begin with.

Typhon's body crashed through the veil of water between us. I had to fight against the currents, but that was nothing compared to what I had just been through. I searched the darkness around me when my lungs began to burn. Every fiber in my being was aching for air.

I ignored the pain as I realized the body of the monster was shrinking. Down to a size no bigger than I was.

I grabbed the last remaining head when black spots began to dance in my vision. I looped my arm around the stump of a neck and shoved myself upward. I aimed towards the light. Or at least, the grayest waters.

I burst through the waves to see the gods and my fellow fighters searching the waves. I sucked in gulps of air as I swam towards the shore. When I was close enough to get my footing, I rose … dragging the head by the neck as the waves seemed to part for me.

Hell, maybe they did. Or maybe my rattled brain was imagining it.

I approached the four immortals and my Eleventh Percenter family who lined the shore. I tossed the dragon's head at Zeus' feet. He stared at it before he looked up at me. His silver eyes flashed as lightning danced through the clouds.

"Eva McRayne." His voice boomed louder than the thunder he controlled but I barely heard him thanks to the ringing in my ears. "Daughter of Apollo. Representative of Olympus. I now name you as my successor. Heiress of Olympus for time eternal. Should I ever fall, it will be you to lead our gods."

I moved past the gods and stumbled towards Jonah, who hit me with so much force, I would have fallen if he hadn't swept me off my feet in a hug.

My beloved Jonah lowered me down to crush me against him. I could see his mouth moving, but I couldn't hear what he was saying. I pointed to my ears and I saw a flash of understanding.

"Jonah?" I rasped. I thought I did. I couldn't hear myself either. "Just kiss me."

NINETEEN

JONAH ROWE

JONAH WAS SO relieved to see Eva more or less whole that his chest ached. But at Eva's request, he smiled. "You got it."

He tilted his head down and kissed her. He could taste the salt from the ocean on her, but he didn't mind. Especially when she wrapped her arms around his throat to deepen their embrace. Somewhere off to the side, he heard someone scoff.

"At a time like this, is that really necessary?" Achilles demanded.

"Shut up."

It was Spader. He finally got to say it to someone else.

Jonah heard them, but he didn't release Eva right away. When he did, he clasped her head between his palms and laughed. "You did it, Superstar. You did it."

She shook her head, then pointed to her ears again. When she spoke, she yelled. "Can't hear you! Ears shot!"

"I've got her, Jonah." Apollo appeared behind Eva and clasped her by the back of the neck. He pointed to the inside of the ruins and she nodded.

Eva hugged Reena, Terrence, then Spader, who grinned widely when she released him. For Achilles, she extended her hand.

He studied it before he accepted it.

Eva then turned and allowed her family and fellow Council members to lead her inside.

"Not to be a buzzkill, because we deserve to celebrate this victory." Reena jerked her thumb backward. "But what about them?"

Jonah looked past her to see a group of about thirty people. The crazed Elevenths who—now that they weren't being affected by Typhon's influence—milled around aimlessly on the beach.

"Dude/" Terrence looked at them sadly. "There has got to be something. Those people are completely insane. They don't deserve this."

Zeus had been following behind the others inside the ruins, but he stopped when he heard Terrence. The Olympian King snapped his fingers and they all turned towards him. "My son, Dionysus. Among other things, madness is his specialty. Perhaps he can assist these Ghostly Ones."

"Um, isn't Dionysus the god of wine?"

"And madness." Zeus wiped his brow as he beamed at them. "You shall all get titles. I will ensure it. But yes, we can assist your fellow brethren. 'Tis a shame that your people were so affected by our magicks."

"I mean, he does have a point." Spader laughed and held up his hands. "I know, I know. Shut up."

"What can we do to help?" Reena glanced back over at the group. "Will it take him long to get here?"

"No." Zeus shook his head. "We will take care of them. All that is required of you is to go inside and prepare to leave these accursed lands."

"Thank God for the Astralimes," Reena muttered as she fell in step with Jonah. When he raised an eyebrow at her, she frowned. "What?"

"Eva and Joey have a shit ton of equipment that has to be transported by the ferry."

"God dammit." She sighed. "I guess that means we can't cut and run, huh?"

"Nope." Jonah shook his head. His relief was still elevating him beyond the ground. "Not getting off that easy. Still got work to finish."

"Yeah, yeah." She threw her arm around him. "Rub it in, brother. Rub it in."

———

It took another three hours to completely disassemble the cameras Joey had put up around the island, then another two to get them packed up. Jonah, Reena, Spader, and Terrence stopped on the beach as they headed back to the ruins from the old graveyard.

Reena was the one who spoke first. "Can we not have any more monsters with snakeheads, please? I mean, I get that we love Evie, but damn."

"Dracanae should be extinct," Jonah said. "I just need them to stay gone. Hopefully, take Achilles with them."

"You think the Curaie is gonna want to know about his little murder spree?"

"Zeus has already presented them with information," Jonah said with glee. "The Japanese branch of the Curaie will be—oh, look."

"What the fuck?" Achilles' snarl alerted them all. He was in front of a dozen grim-faced Japanese S.P.G. practitioners. "What is the meaning of this?"

"Wells Cole, you're under arrest," an S.P.G. practitioner declared in English. "You're under investigation for over a dozen murders."

The last time Jonah had watched the SPG in action, he'd been pissed. Beyond livid. Now? He was thrilled.

Eva must have heard the commotion because she appeared in the doorway of the asylum. She went pale at the sight of the SPG uniforms.

"Turn around, Cole."

"You have no authority-"

"You are an Eleventh by blood. You have committed mass murder of Elevenths. So yes, we have authority. Turn around."

Achilles turned towards Eva, his voice like ice when he spoke. "You have used my own mind against me."

"I have no idea what you are talking about."

"You lying bitch!"

"Don't call Eva a bitch, motherfucker," Jonah spat at him. "She didn't use your mind against you. It wasn't your *mind* that slaughtered fourteen innocent Elevenths."

"You dared to tell them of my blood." Achilles ignored Jonah. "You said I was one of *them*!" Achilles willed his sword and shield in his hand, then charged.

Before Jonah could make it through the SPG agents that were standing between him and the fight, he heard a loud crashing noise. Metal on metal. He watched as Eva—who had willed a shield of her own—swung it as only an expert could. It cracked against the side of Achilles' head and he collapsed in a heap.

"There." She made the shield vanish, then spoke to the SPG agents. "Do what you have to do. He won't give you any trouble if he is knocked out."

The Practitioner in charge gave his people a signal, and they gathered up Achilles' unconscious form. He then walked toward Eva and shook her hand. "Thank you, Miss McRayne. Both the ethereal and the Tenth governments owe you a great debt."

"No problem," Eva said, relieved. "I just wish the one on American soil was as cordial as you."

"You may be surprised," the Practitioner said. "There's hope yet."

"Doubt it," Jonah muttered. "Those bastards are intractable."

"You haven't heard?" the Practitioner asked, surprised. "The old guard was deposed three nights ago."

Jonah's eyes widened. "What?"

"Yes." The Practitioner gave a small smile. "A Protector Guide by the name of Jonathan presented them with an ironclad case of no confidence and evidence that their time was done. He'd amassed such a groundswell of support that, despite their worst protests, they had no legs to stand on. A New Curaie of spirits and spiritesses is being established as we speak. What have you guys been doing? This has been huge news in our world!"

"Um, we've been stuck on this hell island?" Eva's shoulders

relaxed with relief. "But I'm glad that there are new Spirit Guides in charge."

"Evie, do you know what this means?" Jonah stepped over Achilles and grabbed her arms. "It means we can get the ban lifted. You can go home!"

"Let's talk to Jonathan first. I don't want to piss these new spirits off."

"If Jonathan vouches for them, then I'm not worried," Jonah said. "I can't believe he actually got those fools out! He was playing chess and they were playing ... whatever the hell they were playing. Either way, game over!"

"I'm not." Eva gave him a soft smile. "Jonathan can do anything."

"We will need statements from any who saw the carnage of the battle," an SPG agent said as he approached them. "Can you accompany us to Tokyo?"

"I didn't see anything." Eva shook her head. "I was too far away. Ya'll go. We'll take the ferry to Venice."

"I did," Jonah said, anger rising in him at the thought of it. "I even got blood on me as a result of Achilles' actions. I'll come with you to Tokyo, no problem."

"Us, too." Reena cut her eyes over to Eva. "You going to be ok with Joey?"

Eva looked down at Achilles as the SPG agents lifted him on a stretcher before she met Reena's gaze. "I think I can manage."

"How's he been since Apollo's magick broke?" Spader asked. "I haven't had any reason to be around him, so I don't know."

"Quiet," Eva shrugged. "He has. I thought he was still under the spell."

"You need me, you call." Jonah kissed her goodbye. "I'll call when we're done."

"Ok. Be careful."

Jonah turned to the SPG agent closest to him.

"Ready when you are, sir."

The man nodded and shook Jonah's hand. The second they touched, Poveglia Island became an office of glass and steel. Reena, Terrence, and Spader appeared next to him.

"Let's take that fucker down," Spader grinned brightly. "Then we can go home. Finally!"

"I want nothing more," Jonah told him. "He's been begging for it since the moment we met."

"From that moment, huh?"

"You have no idea, Terrence," Jonah clapped him on the shoulder. "No idea."

TWENTY

EVA MCRAYNE

I WATCHED Jonah and my friends vanish along with the SPG agents, who took Achilles with them. I was glad they were gone from this horrible place. It would be less than an hour before we were gone as well.

"Everything is packed and ready to go."

The sound of Joey's voice made me jump and I turned to look at him. He was pale. Shaking. I wasn't kidding when I told Spader that we hadn't spoken since before the battle. After what Joey had confessed under Apollo's power, I didn't want to talk to him now.

"Great. The boat will be here in half an hour."

"Joseph can handle the equipment, can't you?"

I jumped again when my father stepped out of the shadows.

He gave me a nod of greeting before he turned to Joey. "Leave us."

Joey said nothing as he went outside to the beach with his camera bag on his shoulder. I waited until he was out of earshot before I addressed my father.

"You aren't just here to take me home, are you?"

"No. Hera's execution is about to begin. You are being called to serve as a witness."

"Execution? How is that possible?"

"Anything is possible, daughter mine." Apollo extended his hand. "Come with me."

I hesitated before I took it. "I don't know if I want to see this."

"It will be good for you. Proof that your tormentor is no more."

"And having the fancy title has nothing to do with it?"

"It does. A little."

"Why? Why me? Why can't he name you his successor?"

"Because I am ancient. Too ancient." Apollo squeezed my hand. "Olympus needs to be modernized. Fools like the Traditionalists need to learn that their beliefs have no place in our world. Not anymore."

"And I'm the one to do that?"

"You already have. Are your friends still here?"

"No. They just left with the SPG and Achilles."

"Good. Perhaps, their new leaders will be better than the last."

"Jonathan helped to put them in place. I trust him."

"As do I, Evie."

Apollo said nothing else as he tapped my shoulder and my clothes became a white gown lined with gold. I could feel the laurel crown back on my head.

"Really?"

"Yes, really. If your upbringing had been a proper one during the Golden Age, this would have been your daily garb around Mount Olympus."

"Thank Olympus for modern day then."

Apollo laughed as he initiated shadow travel and the island became the dungeons under the Garden of the Gods. We were in a large white room I'd never seen before. I stayed next to my father as Zeus nodded in our direction. Hera was on her knees with her head bowed.

"I have said all I wish to say to you, Hera." Zeus seemed more dangerous now than he had on the battlefield. "Do you have any last words?"

Hera raised her head and her toxic green eyes latched onto mine. She began to whisper under her breath in a language that I didn't understand. Apparently, no one else did either. When she finished, the former goddess cackled.

"This may be the end of me, but one day, you will wish that you had done your part of our deal, half-breed. You will wish that on many, many days of your existence. But the peace of death will never come for you. You will survive, but you will suffer."

Zeus swung a large blade across the back of her neck and Hera's head slid from her body.

I saw the green blood that matched her eyes. I saw how her hatred still gleamed in them as it rolled away from us. I felt relief and nausea all at once when I realized she was gone.

"Eva, are you alright?"

"Yes," I managed. "I want to go home. Please."

"Which one?"

"Marseille," I whispered. "I need Marseille more than anything."

———

Ulysses insisted on staying at the house until Jonah could join me. I didn't protest his presence too much. Especially when he promised to stay downstairs while I attempted to scrub off the remaining bits of sand and bone from my skin.

I should have been happy. Ecstatic. I had been successful, despite my new disability. I had a new title and all the perks that came with it. Even Hera, the enemy who I had sold my life to for an antidote, was gone. The Curaie was under new guidance. And everyone was safe.

I was too tired to be happy. I was too exhausted to do anything except sit in the claw-foot tub and let the water beat down on me. I don't know how long I stayed in the water. I know I dozed in and out more than once.

I was dozing off again when I heard the bathroom door open. I recognized Jonah's footsteps as he crossed over to me.

"Hey," he whispered. "You awake?"

"Hmm." I forced myself to open my eyes. "Barely. How'd it go in Japan?"

"It went amazingly," he answered, savage pleasure in his tone. "Achilles is so self-loathing, he had zero contingencies in the ethereal world. He's on the hook for all those Elevenths he cut down just because he could. Some of the Elevenths that Dionysus cured of insanity even corroborated the murders. It's my understanding that he had the balls to appeal to Olympus for asylum. Zeus didn't even dignify the appeal with a response. I couldn't have asked for a better turn of events if I tried."

"I'm glad." I sat up and reached for the faucet. I turned the water off, then grabbed the towel on the bench. "It was kind of unnerving to see the SPG again. I had no idea what was going on, so at first, I thought they were coming to get me again."

"Not a chance, Evie," Jonah said, placing a hand on my shoulder for extra reassurance. "The Japanese Curaie is pretty solid. I researched them after they came for Achilles, and they're renowned for solid work and efficiency. So, arresting an innocent woman just to prove a point? Highly unlikely to happen."

"You work quick." I wrapped myself up. "When did you find time to research them between Poveglia and giving your statement?"

"Waiting room," he grinned. "They left me alone with my phone. Made some calls. Got some answers."

I chuckled and went to the vanity. I pulled out my hair dryer, then sat it on low. "Ever the professional, huh?"

"It's what I do."

I went to work on my hair and watched myself in the mirror.

Jonah came up behind me to place a kiss on my shoulder. "What'd you do after we left?"

"Apollo got me from the island and took me to the Garden." I watched Jonah through the mirror. "I had to serve as a witness to Hera's execution."

"So, you got vengeance, however indirectly. How did it make you feel?"

"Relieved because I know she is gone. Nauseous because it came to that point." I finished up my hair, then turned around to face him. "Her blood was green."

"Green?"

"Yeah. It was the weirdest thing. I don't know if that's because she was a goddess or what."

"How'd it all go down?"

"Zeus gave her a chance to say some last words. She told me I would suffer, then he cut her head off."

"The point is, she's gone. Achilles is now in the care of the ethereal police. The only one left is Lawson."

"I will call Apollo about him tomorrow. We left him to catch the ferry back to Venice with the equipment."

"Any word on Cyrus?"

I shook my head. "No. Ulysses said they are searching for him. Nothing yet."

"I saw Ulysses downstairs. He said he had to head out now that I'm home."

"Thank Olympus for you being home." I wrapped my arms around his waist. "We can get back to normal now."

"And you can be here in Marseille as Eva, not Lea." Jonah grinned at Eva. "More good news that Jonathan gave me permission to tell you. Your ban at the estate is now over. And your ethereal charge will be expunged. That is a bit of a process, but the ban is ended immediately. You are no longer an unmentionable."

"Really?"

"Yes, really." He ran his palms down my arms. "You can come back to Rome."

I felt such a sense of relief, tears formed in my eyes. I rested my head against Jonah's chest and he held me against him.

"Hey, it's ok, Evie—"

"I know. I'm happy. I just ... it feels like this massive weight has been lifted off of me."

"I know." Jonah hugged me tightly. "And a nice cherry on top? The handful of people who followed the Old Guard's hard line are now under investigation for conspiring to incite unrest. So, Marlon Hardy and that bitch who came to arrest you ... the one that wouldn't even let you have the deck of cards for Gotch Bible? Both suspended without pay. Meanwhile, Minako is coming out, smelling like roses."

"Oh?"

"Yeah," Jonah nodded. "My final peace offering was to save her from any undue trouble by telling the people in the Japanese branch of the Curaie that it was her investigation that led to Achilles being under suspicion. By killing those poor Elevenths, he practically gifted himself to Minako's case in a pretty little bow."

I smiled at that. "You're very gallant, you know that?"

"Nah, just helpful."

"I'm pretty sure 'helpful' isn't adequate enough to describe you."

Jonah grinned and took my hand. We headed into the bedroom. I grabbed my robe, slipped it on, and followed him out to the balcony. One breath of that salt air and every bit of stress that remained from the past few weeks vanished.

I sat in my chair and curled my legs beneath me. Jonah joined me then clasped my hand against the table. I grinned over at him.

"What?"

"We're like that little old couple from *Up*." I laughed out loud. "Sitting in our chairs, watching the world go by."

"The difference is, I'm not mourning your absence," Jonah said quietly. "You're right here, next to me."

"Always, handsome," I squeezed his hand. "Always."

END OF BOOK 4

Dear reader,

We hope you enjoyed reading *Gods & Monsters*. Please take a moment to leave a review, even if it's a short one. Your opinion is important to us.

Discover more books by Cynthia D. Witherspoon at https://www.nextchapter.pub/authors/cynthia-d-witherspoon

Discover more books by T.H. Morris at https://www.nextchapter.pub/authors/th-morris

Want to know when one of our books is free or discounted? Join the newsletter at http://eepurl.com/bqqB3H

Best regards,

Cynthia D. Witherspoon, T.H. Morris, and the Next Chapter Team

ABOUT THE AUTHORS

T.H. Morris has been writing in some way, shape, or form ever since he was strong enough to hold a pen or pencil, and was born and raised in Colerain, North Carolina, before relocating to Greensboro, North Carolina for twelve years. He is an avid reader, primarily in the genres of Science Fiction and Fantasy because he enjoys immersing himself in the worlds that have been created. He began writing *The 11th Percent* in 2011. He now resides in Colorado with his wife, Candace.

Cynthia D. Witherspoon is an award-winning writer of Southern Gothic, Paranormal Romance, and Urban Fantasy. She currently resides in South Carolina, but spent three years in Fayetteville, Arkansas. Always an avid reader, she began writing short stories in college. She graduated with a Bachelor's Degree in History from Converse College, and earned a Masters in Forensic Science at Oklahoma State University Center for Health Sciences.